PRAISE FOR ELI

"In this haunting novel, Topp delicately peels back the gilt layers of privilege to expose the true cost of living amid Manhattan's 1 percent, where the things that matter—ease, self-esteem, and love—are always tantalizingly out of reach . . . promised in the next purchase, the next investment, but never delivered. Topp dares to ask, If your child's admission to an elite school could be an entrée into this world, would you take it? Should you?"

—Nicola Kraus, coauthor of *The Nanny Diaries*

"Liz Topp brilliantly gets into the minds of five different women as they deal with the pride-swallowing process of applying to kindergarten in New York City. What could have been a predictable jaunt is made fresh and intriguing with a plot twist in the first chapter. You won't be able to put it down until the last."

—Laurie Gelman, author of *Class Mom*

"Sharp, unflinching, and dirty with secrets, *City People* speaks volumes about the isolation of motherhood, the shades of ambition, and the power of loss to push us together or pull us apart. In overlapping narratives that radiate from one cataclysmic event, Elizabeth Topp deftly explores the chasm between public persona and private reality, forcing us to question our own preoccupation with image versus truth."

—Nora Zelevansky, author of *Competitive Grieving*

"With echoes of *Big Little Lies*, *City People* offers a sharply observed portrait of Manhattan private school culture, disrupted by one mother's hidden pain and tragedy."

—Robin Kirman, author of *The End of Getting Lost*

CITY
PEOPLE

ALSO BY ELIZABETH TOPP

Perfectly Impossible

CITY PEOPLE

a novel

ELIZABETH TOPP

Little
a

Published by Little A, New York

www.apub.com

Amazon, the Amazon logo, and Little A are trademarks of Amazon.com, Inc., or its affiliates.

ISBN-13: 9781662507335 (hardcover)
ISBN-13: 9781662507311 (paperback)
ISBN-13: 9781662507328 (digital)

Cover design by Zoe Norvell
Cover photography by Jasper Léonard

Printed in the United States of America
First edition

For Anna,
my favorite city person

PROLOGUE

I f she could leave any message behind, it would be about how calm she felt at the very end. All set to simply stop. She would want everyone who had ever known her to somehow experience this sense of peace and resolve that came with complete surety. To comprehend that this was no impulse but rather a measured and reasonable response to her immutable circumstances.

The ledge lining her apartment building roof was encouragingly low—the last in the sequence of small signals that this was her destiny. There were so many reasons to leave and so few to stay. The memory of her daughter's face pierced her resolve, but only momentarily. Even that perfect little girl would be better off without her. She could hardly feel her hands pressed against the four-foot concrete edge of her world. There was so little tethering her to the cold city; even the slightest breeze could take her.

And would anyone truly be surprised? Anyone at all? She wondered this before remembering—*Oh, the release!*—that she no longer had to bother about other people. Or anything whatsoever. This was how her story was meant to end. It had been part of her life all along. For the first time in so long, she felt joy knowing that wherever it all went from here—whatever happened or failed to happen; whatever dreams were made, realized, or crushed—none of it would have anything to do with her any longer.

ONE

VIC

It's a matter of observable fact that there are certain kinds of people. City people, country people, and those in-between suburbanites. Public and private school kids. Fundamentally happy folks all the way down to the irretrievably depressed. The wealthy and those who aspire to be. Cheaters and the faithful. And everyone knows there are timely people and there are late people.

The strange thing—to Vic anyway—was that Vic was an on-time person! She was! She just . . . could not account for *why*, at 8:02 a.m. on this critical day, she was still two blocks short of her 8:00 a.m.–sharp destination. Vic's mind *tick tick ticked* through the list of explanations: traffic, detours, missteps, even the pending citywide transit strike, but none were viable excuses. Having traveled this exact route on foot about eight thousand times, she knew it took precisely fourteen minutes. From the moment she walked out of her apartment building, Vic was already tardy. And alone.

So even though she walked with purpose—a native's walk, long and fast strides—that new, loathsome feeling began creeping up Vic's back like ivy. The sudden panic that something was off—something was in fact missing and had been *missing* since she and Sean split. And it wasn't just his income! Which Vic had haughtily disdained having any part of after their cohabitation dissolved, the same way she had turned her nose up at marriage before that. Somehow, Sean's absence created a void that was larger than the space he had originally occupied in Vic's life. She told herself the stifling anxiety could not last more than a few months after he moved out, but, Vic shuddered to realize, it had been nearly a year and a half.

She could feel her phone spasming through the thick down of her coat with multiple texts from Bhavna, who had suggested meeting up all together outside, then insisted particularly that Vic be there. Though she couldn't remember how, Vic had apparently given her the impression that she would, in fact, go with the other six Woodmont moms whose children had made Nina's list. Only those families who received a recommendation from the executive director of their preschool could hope for admission to Kent, the best private school in New York, which, in Vic's estimation, made it the best private school in North America. Not all seven Woodmont children would be admitted, but as a Kent alumna, Vic felt she could approach the kindergarten admissions process—a famously harrowing endeavor among the city elite—with a certain composure and familiarity.

Which was why she was so annoyed with herself for being mysteriously late for this . . . What was it even? An information session? A tour? As if she needed one. Vic knew every inch of that building, had gone through many formative phases in various nooks and crannies. She could probably lead the damn tour! Vic pictured the other moms, surely now impatiently waiting for her out on the street. She raced west on Eighty-Eighth Street, glad she had opted for the suede sneakers as she jogged to make the light.

This, Vic had discovered, was the least appealing part of motherhood—at least in her corner of the city—having to play the parent version of yourself with the others, hiding the rough edges, amplifying the responsibility (and here she was, late!), and always, always being amiable. Because other parents are not your friends; they are your child's friend's associates, necessary channels to those essential early-childhood relationships. With almost no exceptions—really, just Susan—Vic never expected true intimacy and frankness from a "mommy friend." Sometimes she felt stifled at school cocktail parties, unable to locate a single perfectly anodyne thing to say.

With Susan, Vic never needed to filter out the juicy, inappropriate tidbits. The two friends tolerated one another's quirks. For example, Susan would no doubt grill whomever she could on the Kent tour about which ideology guided the school's nutritional policies, a war she had been losing for a year and a half at Woodmont. Vic was sympathetic if not completely aligned with Susan's thinking on these topics. White bread was known to be found in her household, and Vic had once given her daughter a Pop-Tart iced and coated in carcinogenic rainbow sprinkles. Vic understood Susan's obsession with corn syrup the way Susan understood Vic's occasional slips. Vic was a single mom! She should be forgiven for serving white flour to her child. And for being late! Susan would embrace her and help smooth out any awkwardness with the others.

Vic fought through the masses streaming toward the subway and dodged a dog lunging at a half-eaten bagel, sweat beading along her hairline, before finally, finally rounding the corner, a definite odor breaking through her all-natural deodorant. At least her hair had been recently highlighted, Vic thought, because as she took in the tableau of twenty-first-century New York City private school parents waiting for her on the curb in the cold, several realizations went off like firecrackers shot from the top of an adjacent apartment building.

First, no Susan. *Hmm.*

Then she saw parents. Not just moms. Nine faces strained in tension. Ugh, the creeping sensation of Sean not being there became a full-blown air horn sounding in her ear. Why had she gotten this so wrong? Vic was starting to think she might need to see a doctor; maybe she had a brain tumor. She made a little show of hustling toward them as quickly as she could while they all gaped at her like a tableau of wild animals caught in headlights.

There was Bhavna, makeup executive of some sort. Great hair. The thick knit of a Chanel suit poking from between the folds of camel hair, as she punched away at her phone. Bhavna's husband, a slender pillar at her elbow, her sentinel. She was short and soft where he was tall and stiff like a bone. He had some business going with Susan's husband, which was primarily how Vic knew them.

There were Penelope and Kara, the two stay-at-home moms (or SAHMs for short), heads close in conversation. Their oversize husbands stood behind them, absorbed in their phones. They were all from somewhere like Long Island or New Jersey or Westchester. The two women appeared to use the same stylists, trainers, dermatologists, perhaps even that very morning. The only traits that distinguished them from one another (to Vic) were that Penelope had some official role on the Parents' Association at Woodmont and enjoyed the services of more than one nanny. Meanwhile Kara projected extreme dedication to full-time motherhood. She was the sort of mom who appeared at every drop-off, pickup, and playdate with healthy homemade snacks and drinks for everyone. Meanwhile, Vic hardly ever carried even the basics, like water or tissues.

Today, Penelope and Kara both sported fresh shiny blowouts of their midlength brown hair and wore practically identical full-length Moncler coats, which led to Vic's third revelation as her eyes traveled down the twin pillars of Japanese nylon: every mom was wearing heels and a skirt.

In her "fancy" jeans (they were expensive!), not-so-new sneakers, and a couture blazer from many seasons ago when Vic could briefly afford such pieces, all tucked under an Amazon parka, Vic suddenly felt very alone and underdressed. Had she missed a memo? Were the parents being evaluated today? Sean was away at some architecture conference. It hadn't even occurred to Vic to ask him to come to this. Even though he did not understand private school and refused to pay for Kent tuition, Sean promised he would show up when needed, like to the parent interview. So she might have asked him if she knew all the other dads were coming. Everyone all paired up.

Except for Amy. Of course, Amy. Amy was always alone. An aloof executive in understated custom clothes and quietly exorbitant accessories, Amy was the only other single mom at their preschool. No one had yet ascertained the circumstances of her maternity, perhaps because she made it very clear that it was not anyone's business. Vic wanted so much to be friends! Or at least friend*ly*. But Amy radiated aloofness that stopped the words in Vic's throat.

Amy stood with Chandice and her incredibly hot husband, slightly off to the side in their trench coats, not talking. Of course, Amy would want to hang out with fabulous, serene Chandice, whose wide, calm eyes seemed to take in critical information lost on Vic. Her even skin practically shimmered, and today she had tied her long braids back from her face. Vic heard she was a corporate lawyer taking some time off while her son was little. Her apparent comfort in transitioning back and forth between full-time corporate attorney and stay-at-home mother impressed Vic, who viewed full-time motherhood suspiciously as an unbreakable trap.

"Let's go," Amy said as soon as Vic was within earshot. Bhavna was simultaneously texting and kissing Vic on both cheeks while moving her toward the front door.

"Sorry!" Vic said to no one and everyone.

"We're late!" Bhavna replied.

"Hi, hi!" Vic tossed back over her shoulder, catching a glimpse of grim expressions. Gosh, they all looked so nervous. Bhavna eyed Vic's dressy jeans. "Sorry!" Vic said again vaguely.

They passed through the iron gates and into a gothic twelve-story building on whose edifice were etched the words **KENT: THE WORLD IS YOURS**. Was it possible Vic had never noticed the inscription before, or was it new? She felt an unanticipated unbalanced lurch.

"Where's Susan?" Vic asked Bhavna, who practically dragged her inside by the bicep.

"Neither of them texted me back."

That was odd. Vic and Susan had joked many times about how eager she was to see the inside of Kent, even if Claude would never attend. Vic tried to make her understand that it wasn't so remarkable to look at—the Kent magic was all about the quality of the faculty and the networking opportunities.

But as she stepped into the school lobby of her youth after a long absence, Vic realized she had no idea what Kent was like these days. Where there was once a large seating area for students to relax (i.e., sitting on one another's laps while gently pawing each other just inside the main entrance of the building), there was now a security center with three guards manning computers, video screens, and terminals where students swiped their IDs. The visiting parents and applicant families were waved through by smiling administrators who handed them name tags and their own personal schedules. Other administrators hurried them into the theater. No longer the dingy make-out hideaway of Vic's youth, the auditorium was now bright, refreshed, charming, expanded to hold at least three hundred. And it was full.

As they took their seats, Vic scanned the room and found many familiar faces: both those she knew personally and those she recognized only by type. There were the alums, like her, generally the most underdressed people in the room, which communicated comfort and confidence. There were the incredibly wealthy, who attempted to project ownership of the space but, to the sharp eye, conveyed insecurity. These would be passed over in favor of bigger, smarter money, which did not need to jump up and down to be seen.

Other than skewing toward the rich, the room almost perfectly reflected the racial makeup of New York City. A third of the admitted students would receive financial aid, and half the kindergarten class would be kids of color.

Which sounded pretty good. Right? *Nothing to feel bad about!* Vic told herself again.

As the lights dimmed, Bhavna reached into her bag for her phone, vibrating with a call, and for a moment it looked like she might try and take it in the dark and quiet theater. Instead, she jotted off a quick text response. *So busy, that Bhavna,* Vic thought before turning her eyes forward.

The screen onstage filled with the cosmos, as seen from a satellite zooming through the stars with the production quality of a goddamn feature film. Weightless. Silent. Then the auditorium filled with a dense baritone voice. "This is Samuel Weller Bridges, Nobel Prize–winning physicist, bestselling author, and Newton Chair of Physics at Princeton University. But by far, my most cherished identity is that of a Kent parent. Why? Come with me on a little journey . . ."

The camera swooped down to planet Earth and over North America, growing closer to the Northeast, New York City, and then, seamlessly, all the way from outer space through the window of the new Kent science lab, where elaborate machines Vic could not identify clustered in a spotless, bright room lined with sinks and beakers. The dozen students inside wore lab coats with their names embroidered on one side and the Kent logo on the other as they worked in small groups. Although this bore no resemblance to the school of Vic's childhood, it was hard not to be impressed.

"It's not just science," Bridges continued like the voice of God. "Don't get me wrong, I love science. Science is what I'm all about. But my daughter . . ."

The camera looped over the heads of the students, then shot out the window and up, up, up to the art studio, where huge drafting tables soaked up the sun's rays streaming from the skylights overhead and creative teenagers made bold strokes of color on oversize sheets of thick paper.

". . . she's an artist." The camera hovered over the piece she was working on and blended into stop-motion through its completion, ultimately revealing a watercolor still life of a vibrant wildflower bouquet.

"And she's pretty good." The artist turned her face up to the camera—this must be Bridges's smiling daughter—and waved.

Then out the window again and down the street, two blocks and a right, to the gym facility, where Kent elementary students practiced yoga in a cozy, dimly lit studio while the high school basketball team practiced on another floor and middle schoolers took a spin class upstairs. The camera followed two students, two different shades of Brown, as they walked back to the main building, talking about what they liked best about Kent.

"I can be myself . . . no, not that exactly. It's more like, I'm *becoming* myself here."

"Yeah, exactly. Like there's a thing all Kent kids have in common."

"That we're . . . smart?"

"More than that. We're happy."

The camera left them outside and entered the building through a window in the cafeteria, filled with every skin color, all congenially mixed together. The director had made sure to include the food on offer: hot trays of what looked like lasagna and broccoli for the hungry. Crudités plates and individual French yogurts with nuts and berries. A burger stand and a frozen yogurt counter for the more conventional teen.

Vic checked the audience taking in this long Kent advertisement. Not one face revealed a hint of the question that whispered in the back of Vic's mind: Did Jetta need a chef making her an egg white omelet with extra cheese every single day of her life? Was that part of her education?

Then they traveled to the library, which looked like the sort of place that would convince even the most reticent reader to pick up a volume, clearly the pro bono work of a feng shui expert and Kent parent. There were couches, beanbags, easy chairs, little ergonomically correct nooks. There were tables for two, six, eight, and sixteen and a smattering of desks, all artfully arranged amid planters of bamboo under glorious three-level windows. Books lined the double-story walls as well as racks of newspapers in at least twenty different languages, a stack of iPads to be borrowed, and a few booths that advertised "total, complete silence."

The drone popped back out the window and started free-falling. It was almost frightening how quickly the camera plummeted down the side of the building, stopping only once to peer in on a middle school English class, the complete works of Shakespeare in every hand, and then down and through the front doors into the theater where they were all currently seated, and there was Samuel Weller Bridges, the world-famous physicist, on the screen in his characteristic blazer-and-sweater combination. His steady gaze and easy demeanor, coupled with his credentials, made him an unparalleled authority figure with this audience. He spoke with the sincerity of a public health official delivering lifesaving information. The camera inched closer.

"I chose Kent for my daughter because I knew she was bright and I knew she was talented. But I could never give her everything she needed to realize the promise of her unique gifts. There is only one institution that could offer that kind of extraordinary education. Simply put: there is no place on earth like the Kent School."

The lights came up, and the screen lifted to reveal the head of school, Glenn Goodyear, a lean, bald guy in his early sixties whose affability served as a constant reminder that his career in education had begun in the classroom. A beloved middle-grade English teacher at Kent, to be exact, where Vic had once wittily (if you asked her) mouthed off to him in an intellectual way (again, if you asked her) more than once. Word among the alumni was that his special gift was fundraising, to the tune of $200 million. He was the sort of approachable person with only two public faces: a "hey, this is great" smile and an "oh no, this is serious" frown. Today was for smiles.

He gave a little wave to the audience, many of whom clearly itched to applaud for him already. "Sorry I'm not quite as charismatic or as interesting as Samuel Weller Bridges. It's just me, Glenn. I want to welcome you all to the Kent School. We've already met your fabulous children, and today you'll get to tour our facilities, of which we're very proud. And you'll meet me or someone on my team. So you can save your questions for that time. But I wanted to share some thoughts with you as we embark on this admissions season."

Time for the serious expression.

"Another school director—I can't say from which school, but it's one we all know—said to me, 'In confidence, Glenn, how do you do it, year in, year out? How do you produce these bright, interesting, well-adjusted, funny, talented, brilliant young adults? What's your secret sauce?'"

Giddy laughter. This was what the crowd had come to hear. The parents sat up straighter in their seats. He didn't say it outright because he didn't need to: nearly half the seniors each year would go on to graduate from an Ivy League college.

"'Is it your world-class brand-new chemistry lab?' she asked me." From here it's a slow return to his beaming smile. "'Is it the international service trips? Is it the papermaking and ceramics studios? Is it your college-level physics program? Your national-champion chess team?'"

The theater grew warmer with the excitement of the parents. Vic thought about taking off her jacket, but then she would only have on an H&M cotton T-shirt. All around her, hedge-funders panted in their custom suits, gripped in the throes of desperately wanting something that could not be bought. Not for sure anyway.

"And I had to tell her: 'No, no, it's none of those things. It's the incredible community we have here: a demographic mirror of the city we live in, which is something very few schools in this town can claim.'"

It was true. When they'd had Jetta, Vic and Sean had dutifully visited all six public schools within walking distance, taking the tours and looking inside rooms that somehow felt . . . institutional. The better public schools had hardly any students of color. Maybe one or two in the whole building.

"We support this extraordinary community with a powerful anti-racism curriculum that is carefully interlaced into all our courses of instruction. So that we can be the best school we can be, all together . . ." He extended his arm out to the crowd, now smiling back at him, thrilled to be in the glow of his approval, even if it was theoretical. These were not all, Vic noted with a raised eyebrow, Kent families yet.

Perhaps that's why Susan had decided not to attend. Only Vic knew Susan's recent resolution to leave the city. It didn't make sense, she had explained to Vic. On Susan's and her husband's income, they could never pay for an apartment big enough for their two kids and two private school tuitions, even though Susan was a psychologist and her husband worked in finance. But there was finance and there was *finance*, Vic thought, looking down her row at the masters of the universe and their $100,000 watches, their success generally mapped to how unattractive and short they were compared to their modelesque wives.

"So what we do here . . ." Vic had tuned out for a while. Glenn was wrapping up his speech, which had reached its earnest phase. Vic supposed he had to pitch the school to this crowd, but it seemed so unnecessary. Weren't all these fancy, educated, thirsty parents ready to shank one another in the bathroom to get a spot for their child at Kent?

"We help your children become the best adults they can be," Glenn said. "Not with a mold. Not just"—he pressed his fist into his palm again and again, and Vic let her eyes drift over the crowd—"some sort of assembly line, but the nurturing free-form organic support in whatever direction your children in particular need to realize the happiest, most successful versions of themselves: the people they were meant to be."

Suddenly Vic realized she was staring at a former classmate: someone two years behind her. Had they played volleyball together? Vic gave a little wave, and the woman responded with a phony smile so half-hearted it looked more like an involuntary reflex she failed to completely suppress.

If Susan were here, they'd be silently gesturing at other parents and giggling at their seriousness, invisible in this darkened theater. Vic would miss Susan so much next year—almost as much as Vic's daughter, Jetta, would miss Susan's daughter, Claude. Claude and Jetta had been best friends since the age of two, and that had brought Vic and Susan together. But what made them friends was more than that. Susan was the only other mommy with whom Vic felt she could be herself. No doubt Susan felt the same way.

Could Vic get close like that with Bhavna or Chandice? Or Amy? She leaned over and peered at Amy, whose eyes never strayed from Glenn's presentation. That they were the only single moms seemed reason enough that they should be friends, but perhaps the similarities ended there. Amy always appeared effortlessly put together in expensive silk blouses with her shining, shoulder-length black hair. No makeup, just that perfect, opalescent skin. Then there was the $50,000 handbag, nestled in the crook of her lap.

Amy cut her eyes at Vic, her expression neutral but direct. Vic mouthed, "Nice shirt," but Amy only turned her gaze back toward the stage. All Amy's shirts were nice. The same perfect iteration of the ideal conservative silk blouse. Vic pictured a small factory on the outskirts of Taipei churning them out, each a slightly different shade of cream or light blue—some with bows, some with French cuffs—and, in the summer, silky tank tops cut to hang just so.

And then, the lights came on and everyone leaped to their feet, all the parents rushing to comply with instructions. Vic felt bad for them. She knew, as a New Yorker and Kent grad, that there was nothing less appealing to institutional gatekeepers than the appearance of trying too hard. They jockeyed their way out of the theater, rushing to be the first to find the administrator assigned to show them around. Bhavna studied her schedule along with Amy and Chandice.

"I think we're all going to the same spot," she said. The husbands hung back, and the Woodmont group fell into a neat line behind Bhavna, who soon located their guide, a bright-eyed junior admin just out of some solidly good college like Boston University or Michigan. She perkily took them on a tour of everything they had just seen in the video.

As they walked the many-times-over renovated halls and peered into classrooms bursting with supplies, technology, space, and light, Vic's initial impression standing outside under the freshly etched entablature was confirmed and reconfirmed again. Nothing would feel all that familiar. The cozy, pedestrian, vaguely gritty school of her youth had been washed away by oceans of money.

On one floor, which Vic was pretty sure had once been simple square classrooms and halls lined with lockers, there was a curving roadway through science labs kitted out with university-level equipment. "Is that an electron microscope?" Bhavna's husband asked while she typed out yet another text behind him. How tedious she was with her phone.

"Ha ha ha, yes!" the admin demurred.

"Is there really a retractable helicopter pad on the roof?" Kara's husband asked out of nowhere as they flowed down the undulating hallway and into the stairwell. Internally, Vic cringed on his behalf. Surely, he knew this sort of transparent materialism was not a good look at a liberal private school.

"Yes."

"Why wasn't it in the video?"

"It's not really that important—just a matter of convenience really."

"For who?" he asked, grinning at his own cheekiness.

"For those who travel by helicopter. In here, please . . ."

They were ushered into a wood-paneled conference room with a flawless, shining mahogany table and a fresh catered breakfast of fruit salad and bagels. A coffee cart stood alluringly in the corner, but the admin nonverbally ushered them toward the place cards at their seats, and not even Vic dared grab a cup. Leather-bound Kent yearbooks, scrapbooks, and other memorabilia lined the shelves alongside black-and-white photographs. Vic had, of course, been in this room before, but back then there had been an accessible, slightly worn quality to it. Or was that just her flawed memory filling in sympathetic details?

When Glenn, the head of school, entered the room all open palms and broad smiles, Bhavna practically leaped on him, shaking his hand as if her execution of this social ritual in particular was part of their family's assessment. Penelope and Kara inched up behind her for their chance while Vic held back, in no rush. But when Glenn looked up and saw her over their heads, his congenial smile grew into something wider, something that to all the world looked 100 percent sincere.

"Vic!" he said, reaching for her hand in between Penelope and Kara. He gave it the most professional squeeze.

"Hello, Mr. Goodyear."

"Call me Glenn. I knew I had to say hello to this group when I saw your name on the list. Welcome back!"

See, Vic thought to herself. *What had everyone been so nervous about?* "Thank you," she said warmly. All nine parents stared at Vic, and she willed the blood out of her cheeks. This was why Bhavna had wanted to be together.

"So . . . welcome. Welcome . . ." He gestured for everyone to sit and gave them a moment to compose themselves. Amy aligned her vertebrae and kept her expression neutral. Bhavna clasped her hands in front of herself, arranged her face in pleasant expectation, and looked for all the world like she was ready to be personally questioned, although parent interviews would not start until the following week. Chandice projected serenity as always. Vic wondered if it was too late to grab a coffee.

"You'll think I'm crazy, jumping way ahead," Glenn started, "but we don't have a lot of time here together, and I want to hear from all of you. So here's what I'd like you to think about." Vic was transported back over twenty years to discussions of *Moby-Dick*, beat poetry, Virginia Woolf. How she had disdained almost all of it, thinking she was so clever. But this wasn't about Vic; it was about Jetta.

Glenn continued, "In about fifteen years, you're going to be taking your kid to college. I know, I know, it seems like a long time from now. But when you do that—and yes, I promise, one day you will—do you know what sort of anxieties will be running through your mind? What concerns?" He looked from face to face.

Vic was used to this. She kept her expression placid. There was plenty of time to formulate her answers. Bhavna already had her hand in the air, but only for two seconds before it became apparent this was a rhetorical question. Kara's eyes bulged slightly while Penelope seemed to only be half paying attention. Chandice and Amy appeared to be the most ready and able for whatever came next.

"It won't be what they eat or if they brought enough shampoo or will remember to take their vitamins. It won't be clean underwear. It's going to be whether or not they're ready to face all the gray area decisions that are about to come their way in real time. I'm not talking about the black and white, but the area in which character is forged. What does it really mean to be a good student? A good friend? A good person." He let this sink in. Kara looked ready to hurl. Even Bhavna was getting a little shiny.

"So here's my question: What makes you think Kent is the right place for your kids to learn how to make those decisions?"

Bhavna's hand was again in the air. *Jesus Christ, Bhavna, have at it.* If she had been asked, Vic would have explained this sort of overeagerness was frowned upon in the Kent community. Very uncool. It was critical to impress others without any apparent effort.

"Bhavna." Glenn was game.

"I'm Bhavna, and my son is Harry. Everything my husband and I have seen about Kent . . . not just the facilities, but the faculty, the curriculum. It's all so thoughtful and extraordinary. I myself went to Roedean School in Brighton and know that it can be like a second family. That's what we want for our son, Harry."

Bhavna's husband patted her leg under the table, pleased with that answer. Glenn looked around the table expectantly. As the short silence lengthened, Vic knew it was just easier to speak than to wait as the nerves built up and other people potentially stole your lines. So she jumped in.

"I understand exactly what Bhavna means. I not only loved Kent, but I feel like it delivered on everything it promised. I don't know if you knew this about me, Mr. Goo . . . Glenn. But it was here, in Ms. Braver's second grade class, that I wrote my first story, a nine-page tale about a Korean prisoner of war who befriends a mouse, called 'Captured, But Not Alone.'"

Vic waited for this to be absorbed. She could have added that Kent had also taught her exactly this: how to show up completely unprepared for a critical group interview and speak comfortably, articulately. But she didn't need to say that.

"*Little Lions* and *XYZ*"—Vic dropped the names of the school's two literary magazines—"were critical in developing my passion into a career. There's a clear path from that early work to my first novel. I know Jetta would not only thrive here but eventually make real contributions to the Kent community."

Vic smiled congenially, ready to pass the mic. Kara's white face grew two bright-pink splotches on her forehead. Penelope looked like she was almost annoyed at having to answer any questions. Chandice, seeing her opening, waved a little at Glenn to get his attention.

"By all means, Chandice, please."

"I'm Chandice, and this is my husband, Joseph. We're both lawyers and have one son, Daniel. Like all of you, we've looked at a lot of schools. We are obviously interested in diversity efforts, and other places have really bent over backward with a whole dog and pony show to impress us with just how inclusive they are. A lot of it has been, frankly, hard to believe. I have found myself, at times, wondering how sincere— how deep—these efforts really run." Chandice looked around the table, again giving Vic the impression she could see and sense things that were lost on others. Weren't they, all of them there, committed to diversity? "But at other schools, we've felt tolerance. At Kent, we feel belonging."

Vic begrudgingly acknowledged the succinct articulateness and total untouchability of this response. If she could bet on their admission in some Park Avenue backroom gambling salon, she would.

Amy did not wait to be called on. "I'm Amy. I am in finance, so most of my work revolves around developing tools of assessment. When

I started thinking about my daughter's education, I was at a loss. I read every brochure, asked every parent I trusted, and toured every private school in Manhattan. But I don't need tools of assessment to know my daughter, Pearl, has the best chance of thriving here because her talents lie in so many quarters. Yes, she's good at math, but her drawings are special as well. I want to enable her to grow in any direction, and I know this is the place for her." It was more than Vic had ever heard Amy say at once. Glenn nodded sagely as he rose to his feet. Their five minutes with him were apparently coming to a close.

Before Glenn could escape, Bhavna clasped his hand in a final squeeze. As the door closed behind him, she turned to Vic. "So where were Susan and Michael? Did they decide not to apply?"

Taken aback, Vic could not even get out a quick "I don't know" before Bhavna continued, "Want to grab a quick coffee? I have"—she checked her watch—"fifteen before my next meeting."

"That sounds nice, but I"—Vic shouldered her bag, patted her pockets, looked around where she had been sitting—"I absolutely must get home. I'm on a *crushing* deadline."

"New novel?" Bhavna asked. Did Vic imagine the skepticism in her voice.

"That's what I do!"

Vic raced out behind Penelope and Kara, disdaining their midweek, midday SoulCycle. As soon as she was on the sidewalk, she called Susan, but it went straight to voice mail. She'd want a full report, but this was a workday after all. Susan had a busy practice, ambitious publication plans, and a role as one of two class parents; it was an overwhelming number of commitments. Though Susan said she couldn't afford private school, she had a full-time nanny for her two kids under five. When she wasn't posting about the critical importance of childhood nutrition, her IG feed flowed with aspirational images: Susan on wellness retreats and spa vacations, with friends and solo; Susan in flattering workout clothes at her Strengthen, Lengthen, Tone class; Susan at a fancy dinner downtown with Michael, their two flutes of champagne clinking (#celebrate). Her husband, while not a champion earner, was tall and handsome.

The only unenviable thing about Susan was that she was moving to Connecticut, where her brother-in-law lived. Lately she had even started to look forward to it after they found a house they could afford with a saltwater pool. Even Vic, a native New Yorker so entwined with the city she could never imagine living anywhere else, felt a pang of jealousy when she saw the landscaping, the smooth slate stones, the grouping of lounge chairs, the wide white umbrella. The front door was bright and shiny red, which Vic loved, but Susan would change it to chartreuse (against her husband's wishes, apparently). Inside: the newly renovated kitchen, gleaming appliances, two refrigerators, two dishwashers, a giant island, a TV room downstairs, so much space.

And Vic had to admit coveting the tiny room with built-in book-shelves, a little desk, and even a teensy window seat, where Susan would finish the last edits on her book, an academic work on teenage sui-cide. She had apparently written the whole thing over the summer, crammed in a walk-in closet with headphones on so she could not hear her children. She just sat down in a windowless space and banged out seventy-five thousand words that were now on their way to publication.

Good for Susan! Vic thought, mostly sincere. Maybe even now she was polishing up a few chapters in between seeing patients. With annoyance, Vic found she had been grinding her jaw. Her lower left molar ached. She rubbed the sides of her face as she rode the incredibly slow elevator to the eighth floor. It wasn't that Vic had anything to complain about, really. She lived in a large prewar apartment. One that hadn't been upgraded in any way in over four decades. It was beautiful but musty. A rent-stabilized classic six: a unicorn of New York City real estate, but still, someone's borrowed custom-made boot.

There was a particular smell to Vic's apartment that on sentimental days meant *home* and other times meant *unrenovated*. After the Kent tour, it was very much the latter. She would never be able to host the class cocktail party, as her parents had done in the very same apartment with inexpensive wine and a single cheese platter. Vic tossed her jacket on a table in the foyer on top of a pile of Jetta's strange clay sculptures that all resembled volcanoes at various stages of eruption.

At her desk in the guest bedroom, facing the grimy windows and the courtyard behind her apartment building, Vic turned on her computer. On her desktop, one icon stared her down: NEW NOVEL. She took a deep breath but did not open it. Got up, went to the kitchen, grabbed a glass of tap water. Returned. The icon, still there. Finally, Vic opened it to reveal . . .

A completely blank document.

Vic touched the keyboard tentatively, her fingers stroking the tops more than any decisive gesture that resembled typing. Always, in the past, Vic had sat down with just the germ of an idea and her fingers had practically guided themselves over the keys, the words coming quickly and consistently. When Jetta was a newborn, she had crammed in her last novel: a smart beach read sustained by the sexual tension between a thick, white American foreign aid worker and her physically perfect, emotionally stable Zambian fixer who shakes up all her preconceived notions about herself and her profession as they attempt to set up a community egg farm in the countryside of south-central Africa. It was charming enough. She had earned out her advance. Vic remembered writing it, Jetta tied to her with one of those fabric slings, the sound of the keys steadily clacking.

Since Jetta had started at Woodmont, Vic found herself back in possession of a nice advance as well as stretches of time when she was all alone. Yet somehow, since becoming a mother, something had switched inside her. Before, solitude had been essential to Vic's writing process. Now, the moment the door closed behind her in an empty apartment, she could practically feel the creative muscle in her shudder and die. The silence screamed in her ears. Sometimes, occasionally, ideas floated into Vic's mind and then back out of it before they became substantial enough to work with. This *Unnamed Future Novel* had been contractually promised so long ago, it seemed like nothing when she agreed to do it. Like no big deal when she cashed her publisher's check and proceeded to spend almost all of it without tapping out a single word.

At her desk, Vic gazed through the grime and into the courtyard behind her building where they hauled the trash and kept building materials. A tree struggled to grow in a sliver of sun. Vic gnawed intermittently on her cuticle, forced her eyes to the empty page. But all she could see was an endless string of one word: nothing, nothing, nothing, nothing . . .

When this first started happening, Sean had only been gone for a few months, and Vic had yet to experience much of the anxiety she now associated with his departure. Vic tried employing positive and affirming self-care talk with herself. *It is OK,* she told herself, *to take this time off. OK,* she said, *to wait for the muse to come. It will all be OK . . .* She thought about borrowing a friend's story about her mother, who was a Holocaust survivor, but that seemed to cross an ethical line. Vic had always looked down her nose at other writers—some of them quite famous—who stole other people's narratives and used them in their novels. Vic couldn't imagine having to face the people who knew she had stolen their stories. Her job was to make things up, after all.

But it just wasn't happening. The terrifying and extraordinary possibility of having to return her advance was followed closely by the realization that without income from this and future books, there was no way Vic could cover the insane Kent tuition. One of the reasons they had broken up was Sean's wholesale rejection of private school and his attendant refusal to pay a dime for it. Meanwhile, royalties from her previous novels dwindled along with the last advance. Money was tight.

Sometimes, Vic found, a cool glass of white wine helped get the creative juices flowing, so she poured herself one and sat back down. California chardonnay. Oaky. Delicious. Maybe she could write about a woman who ditched her corporate job in the big city to buy a dilapidated vineyard in Sardinia. But as soon as she reached for the keyboard, the idea turned to sand in her mind. What did she know about vine-yards, anyway?

And then, almost without realizing, she was on her phone scroll-ing to her favorite IG account: @lilikopelman. Vic herself was a zero on social media, much to her editor's chagrin. Initially, she even told herself that she was lurking on Lili's page for tips—and not to catch glimpses of her high school boyfriend—but it was immediately obvious that there was no way Vic could ever produce content like this. There was a new reel up about the landscaping at Lili's family's Sagaponack home: terrifically fertile plots for hydrangea, a field of wildflowers, rows of lavender. In boots and a darling blanket coat wrapped around her slim frame, she narrated the careful allotment of her vegetable garden, gushing over each selection. Her enthusiasm was in no way dimmed by the February chill, the months it would take for any of it to come to fruition: "Three different kinds of tomatoes! I just cannot get enough tomatoes! And eggplant! On the grill, in the summer!" *Who is filming her?* Vic wondered as she poured a little more wine. *Is it him?*

Lili, her incredibly lush, wavy chestnut hair (extensions, surely) just positively cascading off her shoulders, gamely narrated on. This was what Vic had felt like in high school on Scott's arm: attractive, appealing, deserving of attention. They had been Kent's "it" couple, sporty and fun, always down for a raucous game of quarters before sneaking off into some unsuspecting, out-of-town parents' bedroom. Vic refilled her wine.

The IG reel was finishing up, with Lili getting to the crux of her conundrum finally: strawberries or raspberries? There was a poll, the graphics inanely flashing and blinking at Vic, nudging her primal brain to push the button. But then, there he was, Scott, with the camera in hand aimed at a big mirror, framing the two of them. Him. Scott Hearst. And she's kissing him on the cheek, and his body language, well, it looks a little rigid. He's so tall and weekend chic in the light parka Lili surely picked out for him. He's grown a beard, which Vic had not seen on him in person. Not yet. She studied it. Not generally one for facial hair, she thought on him it looked . . . terribly sexy?

She screen capped it and zoomed in as close as she could get to confirm it: the beard was, indeed, awfully attractive. And his posture *was* stiff, his torso ever so slightly curving away from his new girlfriend. Her manicured long fingers curled around the inside of his wrist, but his own hand was stuffed in his pocket, and his expression was . . .

When the phone rang, Vic practically dropped it in a panic. The caller ID said WOODMONT SCHOOL. Becoming a mom turned any and all circumstances into worst-case scenarios. Being on her way to tipsy while stalking a high school ex when Jetta's preschool called in the middle of the day surely with some sort of emergency regarding her daughter was a pretty good setup for something terrible.

"Hello?" she choked out.

"Hi Vic, Jetta's fine, she's absolutely fine. This is Nina," said the head of the preschool, whose calls were unusual, to say the least. Had she heard some positive feedback from Glenn already after today's surprise interview?

"Vic, I have some bad news. Do you know Susan Harris?" Did Vic know Susan Harris?! What a silly question.

"Yes, of course. Susan and I are dear friends."

"I'm sorry, Vic, but"—Nina paused, giving Vic time to imagine an accident, a scandal, a bake sale? What?—"Susan's gone," Nina said. "She died this morning."

"Dead?" Vic blurted. Her voice sounded like someone else's coming out of her mouth. Instantly, denial rendered the word meaningless. Dead? DEAD? *Dead?* Surely not, like, *dead* dead. Suddenly, nothing— Vic's legs in front of her, her hand holding the phone, the windows of her childhood home—seemed real or familiar. "What happened?" Vic heard herself say. Reaching for the most outlandish explanation, Vic's mind flew to a decade-old story of a woman whose body was halved in a freak elevator malfunction. Had Susan lost her life similarly?

"We have no information at this time," Nina said in a monotone so featureless, it spoke louder than the words themselves. But Vic was too addled to understand. She pictured Susan in a likely death tableau: on the floor of her bathroom, a tiny blood clot lodged in exactly the wrong spot of her brain. Splayed in a crosswalk, a drunken cabdriver weeping in the back of a cop car.

"Oh my God," Vic realized she was speaking. "Was it . . ."

"We. Have. No. In. Formation," Nina said, clearly speaking in code. But after spending her entire life in this small part of the world, dealing with people like this, being in the know, living in the neighborhood, attending these schools, at this crisis point, Vic could not read the subtext. What happened to Susan?

TWO

BHAVNA

Striding from the conference room, Glenn's palm so recently pressed against her own, Bhavna allowed herself a small private moment of belonging at Kent. It felt like the beginning of a movie about her life—one she was finally dressed for. Bhavna ran a hand over the creamy bouclé of the Chanel suit no one knew she had purchased secondhand, ditto for the Cartier tank watch. But these were, inarguably and finally, authentic luxury goods. And with them on, Bhavna felt she had already become the successful New York executive, wife of same, and Kent mother she had always wanted to be.

As Bhavna had sat in that state-of-the-art auditorium and watched that jaw-dropping film (after stuffing her phone in her bag—Marie needed so much guidance!), it felt as if she were peering over the very last ridge and into nirvana. For those with the knowledge, connections, and resources, the city promised not the grind and struggle it shoved down everyone else's throat but rather the best of everything.

As she and Dev crossed the airy Kent lobby with its built-in window seat, two teenage girls glanced up disinterestedly from their shared tablet, and even this, with the light streaming in from the double-story window behind them and the lazy lift of their eyes, looked editorial: modern city schoolgirl. And here Bhavna was, a part of this scene.

Yet another perky twenty-something administrator waited for them by the door with a navy tote bag emblazoned with the mustard Kent *K*. As she handed it to Dev, she said, "Thank you for coming today," as if they might have skipped it for any reason other than hospitalization. Inside, a thick cotton hooded child's sweatshirt for her son to proudly wear.

If he got in. Which he would.

Out on the street, Bhavna resisted the urge to look at her phone immediately, turning instead to her husband. Stress had turned him thin and gray. Dev had been so run down with work lately, trying to close the "big deal." But so was Bhavna, and she still managed to look good. "What did you think?" she asked, pointing back at the school with her chin.

"I mean, come on. Incredible," he said, the answer self-evident.

"Right?"

"Harry has to go here." Bhavna winced a little thinking of their older child, whom Nina had not recommended to Kent and who now attended the public elementary school on Roosevelt Island. After the morning's events, everything about it seemed substandard, and Bhavna already hoped that Harry's admission would be the toehold they needed to get their daughter in as well.

"Right?"

"It's just perfect."

"I know! I wonder what happened to Michael and Susan," Bhavna mused. Michael led the deal team on the financing side of Dev's big project. Dev worked for a medium-size family-held real estate development firm in New York and had long wanted to take their business up a notch. He had finally secured the opportunity to bid on an enormous parcel on the Gowanus Canal in Brooklyn. But he needed to line up an additional $120 million in financing. Which was where Michael came in; he was Dev's counterpart at a much larger, more established firm. They would put up the extra money and partner with Dev on developing the land into premium apartments. Michael seemed like a reliable guy, or maybe it was just that Bhavna found him attractive.

Plus, Bhavna could not believe Susan would pass up the opportunity to inspect the Kent cafeteria after her total meltdown at the last Woodmont Parents' Association meeting. Susan had taken every opportunity to voice her displeasure that they offered snacks made with corn syrup, nutritionless white bread, and, worst of all, sugar-packed chocolate milk, but after gaining no ground with the administration, her frustration bubbled over into an unhinged rage. "You are giving our children poison!" she had screamed at Nina surrounded by the shocked faces of all the other parents. Penelope, the head of the Parents' Association and only other authority figure, had to step in to calm everything down, a role she clearly had little experience with. Meanwhile, in the village Bhavna's mother grew up in, preschool-age children died of malnutrition all the time, a fact she never mentioned to Susan, choosing instead to quietly sign her petition and bring in whole-grain bread when asked. Her suggestions for a double date had, so far, been rebuffed.

"We were supposed to have lunch last week, but Michael postponed to tomorrow. Accounting finishes its report this week, so maybe he's waiting on that."

"But Michael said it looked good, right?"

Dev smiled. The expression looked incongruous on his face, pale with sleeplessness. "I wouldn't be working this hard for nothing, right? How about you? Are you ready for today?"

"I've been ready for years!" Bhavna said, returning his smile. Here they were! On the cusp of greatness! Already, she was planning how they would celebrate their professional and personal successes: dinner at ABC Kitchen, couples massage at the Mandarin, maybe even a weekend in Paris. She spontaneously kissed Dev on the cheek and bounded off toward Park Avenue to grab one of the abundant cabs streaming downtown.

"Don't forget to get home before six tonight!" she called, remembering the deadline for negotiations to avoid a transit strike. The whole city would shut down that evening if the city failed to come to terms with its workers. Even the cabs like the one she was currently climbing into would become scarce as everyone scrambled to keep up their busy lives without the benefit of the subway or the bus.

It had killed Bhavna not to pick up Marie's earlier calls. Her new assistant was sweet but green. There were six texts from her, all explaining a problem: What floor is production on? They tell me the deck won't be ready until tomorrow! They only made four?? All were then quickly followed by: nvmd.

"Halo!" Marie answered on the third ring, and Bhavna mused that half the reason she had hired her was to have a delightful French accent in her ear.

"So, Marie, are we all set with everything for eleven?"

"Yes, we have eight presentations, the thumb drive, pastries, and coffee."

"And you confirmed with everyone?"

"Yes!"

"And—this is important, Marie—you did not show the deck to anyone."

"Yes! And!" Bhavna could hear Marie muffling the phone. "James was over here this morning trying to get a peek."

"You lock them in a drawer when you go to the bathroom, right?"

"Oh, yes . . ." She giggled delightfully, but Bhavna was stern.

"Seriously, Marie! You cannot leave them out. I don't want anyone to know what's coming."

"OK!" Marie said.

Bhavna had waited years to present a campaign at Bowery Beauty that was entirely her own. Sure, the whole Bowery marketing team had collaborated on the new tagline, "Go Global," but it had come out of Bhavna's mouth first as everyone struggled to impress the new chief marketing officer, some big agency head who came over for a nice chunk of Bowery equity. Bhavna had heard that the guy could be "brutal," but that was only secondhand from James, who probably just wanted to scare her. He had seemed nice enough when he turned to her and said, "Why don't you present the visuals next week? Go Global was your idea, after all."

In business school, Bhavna had learned that the key to any good presentation is narrative tension, which means the audience doesn't know exactly what's coming, but they are pleasantly surprised when it arrives. She couldn't have James, the other vice president of marketing and a constant thorn in Bhavna's side, making informed preparations to undermine her in front of the CMO and the rest of the team.

Always, always, Bhavna had to be so careful with every move and alliance. She had built a career in beauty marketing distinctive enough that if she pulled off the Go Global campaign, she herself would "go global" and leave to open up her own consultancy. One day, with an office in Paris. But first, she needed this bullet on her resumé: Conceived, designed, and executed Go Global campaign for Bowery Beauty. And obviously, she needed it to be a hit. This was the final brick in a wall she had spent years building.

For Bhavna, Kent's ultimate allure was that her Harry (and hopefully, his sister) would never have to hustle like she had. Rather, they would grow up alongside New York's most powerful families. How tantalizingly quiet the school itself remained on this topic, the institution's most extraordinary offering. Although that astounding video listed no credits, Bhavna had heard that Steven Spielberg's grandchildren went to Kent, so he had directed the film—effectively a five-minute advertisement—in exchange for a tax deduction. Glenn was absolutely right; it wasn't the science lab, rooftop greenhouse, retractable landing pad, pool, or anti-racism curriculum, whatever that was, but it was the connections that would truly expand their children's horizons.

The point was not to get to school in a helicopter but to become childhood friends with people who went to school in helicopters and then go through life with such cozy people as your classmates, then your professional network, and ultimately your fundraising pool. These were the people who wrote letters to co-op boards, colleges, hiring committees. Bhavna itched to put them all in her phone.

The only variable in the Kent equation was Harry himself, and Bhavna had done everything she could to make him a stronger applicant. Just that morning, they had woken up early for forty-five minutes with his tutor before preschool. Technically, it wasn't called "math" yet but numerical reasoning. As best Bhavna could tell, this consisted of the teacher arranging soft blocks on the floor so Harry could rearrange them for $275 per hour. Later that day, the "literacy specialist" would come and read to Harry in some special way that encouraged a love of books. She was a relative bargain at $150 per hour.

Before taking him to school, Bhavna had spooned soy yogurt into Harry's bowl as he squirmed on the barstool with a spoon at the ready. If Bhavna had learned anything from Susan's food crusade, it was the critical importance of resisting the dairy industry's marketing efforts. She cut up an apple and plated it with a dollop of almond butter, along with a sliced organic hard-boiled egg all made to look like a happy face with crazy fruit hair, as seen on Susan's IG.

It seemed like it was always time to trim his thick hair, which grew straight forward into his face. Always time for new pajamas. His *PAW Patrol* top that had once reached his wrists now gently squeezed the skin just below his elbows. And Harry didn't even like *PAW Patrol* anymore.

"It's a school day, my sweet." Instead of answering, he only nodded a vigorous yes, his big eyes on Bhavna. "Do you like school?" More nods, the egg paused in the air. "What do you like best about school?"

"My friends," Harry said emphatically. And Harry did cleave to a group of boys, all of whom would go on to public school. And Harry would grow, Bhavna saw, into the sort of boy who would behave like those around him. Put him with a group of studious, responsible, kind kids, and that's what he'd be. Stick him in a bigger pond with more varied kinds of fish, who knew what could happen? Bhavna did not want to find out. That's what she was willing to pay for: those who would sit in the seats next to Harry for the next thirteen years.

The lynchpin, Bhavna thought, in getting Harry in would be the letter Vic had promised to write on Harry's behalf. Bhavna knew Vic wasn't on the board of trustees or anything, but it could only help Bhavna to be seen as within the Kent orbit. Of their ilk. Bhavna had reminded Vic of this obligation as many times as she possibly could via texts, which went from breezy to ever so slightly firm. She had hoped to quadruple confirm over a quick coffee, but the deadline had passed anyway. Bhavna could only hope Vic had done as she said she would.

Optics, Bhavna knew, were everything: if perception is reality, then perception is also identity. Having kids in the same class at Woodmont could help get Harry into Kent, and later those Kent connections would only grease the wheels on deals like the one Dev was making with Michael. Ultimately, Harry himself would enjoy the same sort of advantages.

". . . miss . . . excuse me. Miss?" Bhavna realized, coming out of her reverie, that the cabdriver had been talking to her. "Where are you from?" he said in Hindi. He was about the same age as her own father. His brown eyes smiled warmly at her in the rearview mirror. This happened to Bhavna all the time.

"Sorry, I don't speak Hindi," Bhavna said, putting on her best British pronunciation and a smile. She looked decisively back at her phone.

In Midtown, she traveled down corridors of tall buildings to the glowing heart of the city. Traversing the massive and bright lobby, Bhavna greeted the security guards with a crisp "Good morning." On the elevator, crowded with shirt-and-tie types, Bhavna prepared herself for the gauntlet from the receptionist through the bullpen to her hard-earned and beloved office by applying lipstick: Bowery #37: Spitfire.

Through the glass doors, the Bowery offices were humming in preparation for the Go Global campaign. A collection of desks made four rows, with a central aisle down which Bhavna walked. The digital team huddled at one desk, all keen on some screen animation. The product people, facing into a circle of oversize monitors, were engrossed in chemistry, packaging, test results. Bhavna made a point of greeting the CMO's assistant with a "See you at eleven." Had she imagined, as she approached, the assistant quickly closing a window on her computer?

And there was Marie, on her feet, all the decks piled in her hands. She wore a jaunty scarf and heels, a step up for today's meeting, which Bhavna appreciated. "Good morning!" she said, following Bhavna into her office and immediately placing the printouts of the presentation on her desk. "I can't wait to get rid of these. They're like your baby." Bhavna reached out to turn one shiny bound deck to face her. All it said was #goglobalbowery, revealing nothing.

Half an hour later, Marie was distributing them around the large table in the Bowery conference room. Bhavna stood at the oval's long end. Three broad windows behind her framed Manhattan's Midtown, dense with gray and brown buildings. On the opposite wall, a screen with only #goglobalbowery. The CMO sat at the head of the table, with James to his right. A few junior executives and assistants filled out the room. As the last one took a presentation in their hands, Bhavna began.

"We all liked Go Global for the same reasons. It speaks to today's working woman as well as those of the leisure class. It's aspirational but attainable. And it provides us with a chance to do something really . . . colorful."

Marie dropped the blinds and dimmed the lights while Bhavna switched the slide: the outline of the six inhabited continents in white on black. Superimposed over each continent, the face of a model. As she clicked through, there was a notable range of skin colors. They had taken weeks casting an Aboriginal model from Australia who was not only gorgeous but also a transgender woman who used the pronouns they/them/their. They had chosen an ocher color palette to match the Australian setting sun and the earthy landscape, blurry in the background. The model looked like a younger, darker Emily Ratajkowski—unassailably gorgeous with that extra "interesting to look at" quality.

Bhavna cast her eye around the room. The CMO seemed bought in; he leaned toward the presentation ever so slightly, his eyes unwavering from the screen. One of the junior executives looked flat-out impressed already. Marie nodded her chin up and down like a bobblehead. All in all, aces so far. Bhavna pressed on, clicking through South America and Asia while talking generally about the possibilities for growing the campaign through various media from local to national.

For North America, they had cast broadly for a Native American and ended up with a young woman whose skin was the color of nutmeg. They chose a simple black dress, the jacket held over her shoulder on a finger. Her makeup was neutral, perfectly appropriate for the office, except for the addition of a bold red lip, which seemed to jibe with the slogan "Go Global." The graphic designer had inserted the text at just the right size and angle to gesture at the lipstick as if to remind the audience that all it took to meet your friends after work was a quick swipe of Bowery #7: Girls Night. In the background, the indiscernible neon sign of a swank bar in some unplaceable downtown at dusk. It was perfect.

She finished with Europe, a predictably blonde, predictably beautiful creature sitting at a train window with one eyebrow lifted suggestively, her eyes on the landscape ahead, just the vague suggestion of some sun-dappled, ancient stone seaside village in the background. She was alone, one delicate hand resting gently on her handbag (oh, the arguments Bhavna had had with the stylist about which purse said the right thing about this woman, that she was independent but responsible for herself, with nearly effortless instinctual style). Here she looked as if she was perhaps born perfect, with just a few dabs of Bowery Crushed Roses Balm #47. In fact, as Bhavna recalled, it had taken not only hours in glam but in postproduction as well to give the ad this overall nostalgia for "a moment that's never happened and could still yet happen" feeling.

"That's the first part of the presentation, but before we go on, I'd love to get some feedback." In case anyone had anything negative to say, Bhavna wanted to dispatch it before her big finale. But as Marie brought up the lights—slowly, as Bhavna had trained her—the CMO started applauding, and everyone joined in for a few short, blissful seconds. This was why she hadn't wanted anyone to see the presentation beforehand—so she could mark their genuine reactions. Which were overwhelmingly positive. Even James had to clap once or twice, begrudgingly.

"Really great work, Bhavna," the CMO said, smiling. Bhavna took a moment to collect herself by turning back to appreciatively appraise the holding slide of all the continents. As her back was turned, the CMO added, "Now let's tear it to shreds," and laughed. James laughed with him, and the two junior executives, unsure what to do, also tittered nervously. Bhavna slowly turned back around to face the room, willing herself to *breathe in, breathe out, breathe in, breathe out.* This was just a style thing, she told herself. Not personal. "The point is," the CMO continued, "even the best ideas have their flaws. So what are the flaws here?" he asked the room.

James looked like a starving lion presented with a hobbled antelope. He didn't know what to do with himself physically, his pale stubbly face contorting with the effort to stay silent. Strategically, he understood he could not be the first to speak. But while everyone else in the room also felt compelled to say something, Bhavna proudly noted, there wasn't much to say.

"It looks expensive to produce?" one of the junior executives offered, hoping to allay this course of conversation. The CMO nodded, his mouth turned down at the corners.

"OK," he conceded. "Anything else?"

James waited as long as he could. Bhavna imagined him counting to five in his mind. "Wellllll," he said, playing the part of a colleague pained to point out another's shortcomings in front of a superior, "the thing is, any campaign should mainly speak to the primary consumer."

"Not necessarily—" Bhavna tried to jump in.

But the CMO raised his hand. "Go on, James."

"As I was saying, Bowery's primary consumer is . . ." Here he made a show of shuffling some papers in front of himself, although Bhavna noted that the one he wanted was already flagged with a Post-it and highlighted extensively. He must have, like a goalie at a penalty shot, prepared for her to go in this direction. "Ah, here it is. Fifty-two percent of our sales last month were to white women in noncoastal midsize cities."

"Yes, that's why we need a campaign like this. To grow the business outside of those—" Bhavna tried again.

"It's interesting, though," the CMO cut Bhavna off. "What you're saying about market share. I had no idea we could get information that granular." It was as if the CMO and James were now in a private meeting from which Bhavna was excluded, as if a glass wall had come up, separating her from them.

"Sure, we have a whole department that can drill down . . ." James passed the CMO a sheet of paper. "Here, for example, is a breakdown of our most loyal customers by region." Now only James and the CMO had a copy of this information, and while the CMO reviewed it, James, with his mostly bald pate circled by a sickly scrape of short dark hair, dared to look up at Bhavna and give her a little smirk. And in that moment, Bhavna was reminded of something or someone enraging, but she couldn't quite place it.

James's twin sons had not gotten into Kent two years prior; they went to some equally expensive but less prestigious school downtown. She could not wait to rub Harry's Kent admission in his face. Bhavna let this thought soothe her before trying to regain control of her meeting. "Fascinating, James, and yes, we can look at all the sorts of customers we already have, but what I think we all agree is the primary objective of this and perhaps every outreach campaign is new customer acquisition." Before there could be any further discussion, Bhavna added, "Marie, let's go on."

Bhavna put up a slide that showed all the social networks, handles, and influencers they had in each category aligned to support their #goglobalbowery message. This had been the extra secret sauce that she prayed James had no argument against: How could he? "So, #goglobalbowery works as both the brand message and a vehicle with which to grow our social responsibility arm."

"Nice!" the CMO erupted, suddenly won over, as Bhavna knew he would be. He had made his name on the agency side by pushing social responsibility as a way to drive market share and had published several trade articles on this topic. Articles to which Bhavna would now subtly allude.

"Regional Bowery offices can take up different aims. We could even run some online polls to pick which causes and organizations we want to throw our weight behind. It would be nice to have some sort of makeup tie-in, of course. Like donating product to an organization that gets homeless women interview ready."

Bhavna clicked through the slide to show the pilot she had already run, which demonstrated the transformative impact of a little foundation and lipstick on the unemployed single mom preparing for her first waitressing interview. Of course, Bhavna had spared no expense for this particular shoot, hiring not just a makeup artist but a hair stylist and a photographer. The results were breathtaking, even to the bitter jerks she worked with.

"And she got the job!" Bhavna added, and one of the junior executives actually clapped with glee. James, his arms tightly crossed over his thin V-neck merino sweater, had turned from eggshell to dusty rose. Bhavna turned to the slide with the world and six main faces she had chosen for each continent. From the other side of the room, Marie gave her a little thumbs up before turning the lights on again.

"If there's anything people might like more than a makeover, it's a makeover with a tangible social benefit," Bhavna concluded as everyone paged through their decks.

"I tend to agree," the CMO mused. "What do you think, James?"

"I need to let it marinate," James said, giving the CMO a small smile that seemed to communicate between them the sort of understanding that had fueled James's career at Bowery so far, and, in a flash, Bhavna understood the connection in the back of her mind. James reminded her of Vic, who showed up at Kent in her jeans—jeans, for God's sake!—and late and was still greeted like the princess returning to the castle. In the moment it took for James's sentence to land, Bhavna allowed herself to feel a silent, split second of rage at the unfairness of it all that was gone with the blink of her cashmere lashes.

"Anyone else?" the CMO asked.

"I think it's pretty exciting," a junior executive squeaked.

"I love it," gushed Marie.

"Yeah, yeah, OK," the CMO said, as if blowing on hot tea.

Before he could get to his feet, signaling the end of the meeting, Bhavna added, "We all wanted a campaign that could grow organically in every direction, from print and TV ads to IG stories and viral TikToks. This approach drills down from the entire world and the most beautiful women in it all the way to local communities and then actual real people who live there as a natural way of showcasing Bowery and how our products can enhance every person's life."

While the CMO stayed seated and quiet for Bhavna's conclusion, he seemed to have already made a decision, nodding along absentmindedly. Then he was on his feet, and everyone followed. On his way out, the CMO extended his hand to Bhavna. "Great job," he said. "I'll look over the budget and let you know," and she took heart. Surely, he wouldn't say something like that if he wasn't going to green-light it. Maybe all that "rip her to shreds" stuff was just his way of challenging her?

"You were great!" Marie said back in Bhavna's office as she closed the door behind them. Bhavna took a seat at her desk, letting the meeting wash over herself. She breathed in the lavender from the diffuser on the windowsill, leaned back into the white leather of her desk chair, and ran a hand over the expansive glass desk, blank and ready for the next stage: casting, production, ad buys . . .

Marie was still standing there, waiting. For what? "Is something up?" Bhavna asked.

"I didn't want to show you this before the presentation," she said, handing over a slip of paper full of a colorful layout.

"What's this?" Bhavna asked reflexively.

"I found it on the office printer."

It was one sheet out of someone else's Go Global campaign presentation with a very different look and feel. In this iteration, the Bowery logo dominated the space, followed by a pretty but plain model floating in space with the Eiffel Tower in the background. Clearly this concept was more about Bowery's customers traveling to international destinations rather than being multicultural themselves—a stark contrast and clearly James's idea. All the stress from before the presentation rushed back into her neck and shoulders.

Marie nodded. "I think it's pretty lame."

"Does that matter, though? Life isn't a meritocracy." Was he waiting to present it until after he had shot enough holes in Bhavna's ideas? Or had he already showed the CMO? She thought back to his assistant quickly switching screens when she approached.

"What are you going to do now?" Marie asked, and Bhavna was surprised to see Marie literally wringing her hands with stress. She was taking this all so seriously, which heartened Bhavna. At least she could count on Marie.

"I'm not sure," Bhavna said, gazing at the alternate ad. It was so basic. On fire with indignation, she thought about storming over to James's desk. She'd crumple the ad up and throw it in his face. But as satisfying as this scene was to live in her mind, Bhavna could not imagine it generating a good outcome.

"I also wanted to talk about the strike," Marie said tentatively.

"OK?" Bhavna said. She hadn't really considered its impact beyond her immediate family.

"Since you live on Roosevelt Island, I figure we'll be working from home, right?"

It took longer than it should have for Bhavna to catch up. Marie was right. "I guess so. Let's hope it doesn't happen."

"Right!" Marie said with just the slightest bit of mirth, adding, as she backed out of Bhavna's office, "Let me know what you're going to do about, you know . . ." She gestured in the direction of James's office.

Bhavna tried to be productive with her time, but she kept finding herself pulling out James's stupid layout to hate-stare at it. Five o'clock arrived before she knew it, and she had to make it home before they shut the transit system. She was hardly alone in this thinking, and the crowds stretched down the stairs from the tram platform and around the corner onto Fifty-Ninth Street. Bhavna texted the nanny, suddenly disgusted with the indignity of living on Roosevelt Island, where their money went so much further but the distance from their would-be peers was greater than the water's width. *Why can't Dev's rich aunt just die already?* Bhavna thought, hating herself for it.

She finally boarded the gondola to cross the East River; on good days, Bhavna could appreciate the magical feeling of flying over the city—the "this is actually kind of nice" thoughts that she could occasionally allow. Here it was now, almost, that sense of everyday magic, of lifting up above the—

Her phone trilled the special triple ring she used to indicate a communication from Woodmont. The river, the city, the early evening light against the smudged glass, the barges piled with containers the size of buildings nudged along by tugboats, all of it underlining the industry and possibility just around the next corner, Lady Liberty herself beckoning the immigrant, giving assurances, and all of it lost on Bhavna, who read the email two times, still reading as she disembarked, allowing her body to be buffeted along and down the ramp to a place where she could pause, like a piece of flotsam on the shore.

Dear Parents,

With great sadness we are writing to share tragic news. Susan Harris, mother of Woodmont student Claude Harris, died unexpectedly this morning. The Harris family has asked for privacy. Although your concern is appreciated, they have requested no phone calls, no emails, and no gifts of any kind at this time.

41

Please do not discuss this tragic news in the school classrooms or hallways, or anywhere children might be able to overhear. Please remind your caregivers that this information should not be spoken of in front of the children.

Most sincerely,

Nina Durant
Executive Director
Woodmont School

Bhavna perched on a curve of concrete, only ten steps from the gondola exit, pausing to read the email again and think about whom to call. Dev texted her to meet by the river; obviously he had just gotten the news, too, and wanted to talk about it before going home. For some reason, Bhavna thought of all the soy milk yogurt with suspicion. Surely, all Susan's advice should be under review if not completely disregarded. Before Bhavna could read the email a third time, her phone rang: Vic.

Guess she can't call Susan about this one, Bhavna thought ruefully as she answered, "Vic, I'm so sorry!"

"Can you believe it?" Vic sounded flat, affectless, in shock.

Meanwhile, Bhavna thought not only of Susan's off the rails behavior at the last PA meeting but all the way back to last Halloween, when Woodmont had sponsored a trick or treat party. Susan tried to sell all the moms on letting the kids have only two pieces of candy but couldn't get any traction and then seemed distracted for the rest of the evening. Her eyes darted around the room, sizing everyone up. And didn't Susan study suicide or something alarming like that?

"Well . . . ," Bhavna said, hedging, testing to see if Vic had also noticed that something was off. But apparently, she hadn't.

"Do you know something?" Vic jumped on her hesitation.

"No. I just got the email from Nina."

"What do you think happened to her?" Vic asked in a rush.

Bhavna felt the answer was so obvious, it must be a trick question. "Don't you think she killed herself?" Bhavna blurted out. From the intake of air on the other end, the total vacuum of sound, it seemed that maybe it wasn't so clear to Vic. But then, Vic seemed like she perpetually had her head in the clouds. Woodmont's over-the-top "nothing to see here" messaging basically screamed suicide to Bhavna.

"You think?" Vic said.

"What else?" Bhavna said.

"A . . . stroke?" Vic suggested, already sounding unconvinced.

"And why wouldn't they say that? Why all this 'stay away' messaging?"

"Because . . . because . . . I just . . . you don't sound surprised." Something else was edging into Vic's tone, something other than shock and grief. Like she was annoyed with Bhavna for bringing her this news. Which made Bhavna second-guess her assumption.

But then it would not come as a great surprise to Bhavna to learn that Susan had been completely out of her mind and that Vic simply hadn't noticed. Sometimes she wondered about sending her kids to Kent when she considered Vic's cluelessness, but her bestselling novel was a testament to the sort of magic a Kent diploma could manifest.

"Of course, I'm surprised!" Bhavna protested. Which was true. She was surprised. She just wasn't *that* surprised.

"But, Bhavna, what do you really mean? Do you think she . . ." Bhavna had never before had Vic's attention like this. She let the seconds tick by; there was no reason to finish the sentence. It seemed implausible that a native New Yorker could be this naive.

"Well, of course, Vic, I don't know what happened," Bhavna said finally, though she would have bet $1,000 it was pills. "But the signs seem pretty clear. From a communications perspective."

"No!" Vic said, horrified, denial finally giving way to reality.

"I don't know," Bhavna said gently. There was no reason for Bhavna to insist. "Maybe I'm wrong!" Vic seemed much more distraught when they ended the call, but that was hardly Bhavna's fault.

Bhavna walked to her and Dev's usual meeting place, a bench on the water by their house. It wasn't like the city here—crowded and competitive, even just for a prime public seat on a beautiful evening. Dev was so smart to think of discussing such a traumatic topic before returning home to within earshot of the kids. He could no longer count on Michael, who would surely take a leave of absence. She wondered if Dev also wanted to say something about it to Harry. Harry wasn't that close with Claude, Susan's daughter, and the school explicitly said not to talk about it near the children, let alone with them. On the other hand, Bhavna didn't want him to hear something frightening and confusing from one of his mates.

Bhavna had no idea, though, how they would frame a classmate's mother's suicide for their five-year-old son. There was an emotion poking its way through the unavoidable shock. While Bhavna understood Susan must have been burdened by an excruciating and unavoidable illness, there was also part of her that struggled to comprehend her decision to the point of disdain. Susan had everything, and she threw it away because she felt sad? Bhavna felt down sometimes. Had even, after Harry's birth, been unable to get out of bed for a few days. She knew how heavy emotional weight could get, but in the end, you just forced yourself forward, and sooner or later things improved. For a brief moment, Bhavna wondered what might have become of her if she hadn't gotten herself together again. A fate like Susan's? But this seemed impossible. Bhavna was tenacious and patient. Susan, it seemed, simply could not wait, and a tiny voice inside of Bhavna insisted indignantly: *How dare she do this?*

Dev silently took a seat on the bench next to Bhavna, and for a moment they just held hands and looked at the glassine water streaming past. The East Side of Manhattan waved all the city's finery back at them. She and Dev had met at Cambridge and known right away that they wanted the same sort of life: secure, sophisticated, New York. These shared principles remained always in the front of Bhavna's mind, obscuring other thoughts, such as how she sometimes dreaded their forced date nights with their extended silences or how their sex life had never really heated up the way she had foolishly hoped it might over time.

But they were good at this: silent communion. And it felt right to take this moment in memory of another parent in their community. Bhavna could feel her husband processing the news, that in taking it in together, they would lessen its impact. This was intimacy too. As she turned her eyes from the river to his face, she found Dev rather more torn up than she expected. His tie was loosened, and in the light, now turning that beautiful golden color, she could see he had been crying.

"Oh, Dev! I didn't know you'd be so upset!" she said, squeezing his hand. Was there something she didn't know about Dev, or was there something wrong with her, she wondered? Why was she not moved to such sadness by this news? "When did you hear?" she asked.

"This morning."

"What? Did they call you?"

"No. Bhavna, they told me in person," he said, as if dismayed to have to explain it to her. She had never felt more disoriented in her life.

"Did you even know Susan Harris?" Bhavna asked.

Dev's face relaxed in momentary confusion. "Susan?" he said finally. *Wait a moment,* Bhavna thought, reeling as if she were on a Tilt-A-Whirl. If Dev didn't want to talk about Susan, why were they on the bench?

"What is it, Dev? Did they pass after all or what?" Bhavna's words came out as if she had been running. If Dev didn't get the financing for his big project, there was no way they'd be able to buy an apartment near Kent. No way they would be able to buy an apartment at all.

"Bhavna," Dev sighed, took her cool hand in his sweaty ones. "I don't know how to tell you this. I got laid off today."

Here was the true rush of shock and horror. Here the air compressed from her chest. The sound in her ears turned tinny and strange.

"What?" she heard someone say from the end of a tunnel.

And then Dev was speaking from the same faraway place. His words all jumbled around, but a few came at her in bold font. "Losses . . . no cash on hand . . . different visions . . ."

"Why didn't you tell me this was happening?"

"I didn't want you to worry."

"But I should have been worried. I'm seriously worried now."

"There's still a chance I can salvage the deal. With Michael. Maybe he and I can find a third partner, and I can manage the project as an LLC."

Bhavna's heart fell. "Dev," she said, truly devastated now by the news she had to share, "Susan Harris killed herself this morning."

Dev followed the line of thought back to himself. "That's terrible," he ultimately said.

The next domino tumbled in Bhavna's mind. No bonuses, indeed, no paychecks. Unemployed people didn't receive salaries. Spouses of unemployed people could not quit their jobs and start a new business. Kids with unemployed fathers didn't generally get to attend Kent or any private school. All the dreams that had, just that morning, been within reach receded once more.

But Bhavna wasn't going to sit back and let that happen.

THREE

KARA

Flashing lights dazzled Kara as she rounded the corner, immediately reminding her of that night years before, back home. Of course, there had only been one police car then, when now a phalanx of ambulances and cops crowded the broad avenue that separated Kara's and Susan's apartment buildings. There were more emergency vehicles before her than within a hundred miles of Kara's childhood home in a midwestern town whose name Kara had managed not to even whisper to herself in the ten years since she had moved to the city. Amazingly, no one ever inquired further about her place of birth after she told them it was in Missouri. People here were so caught up in their own business, it wasn't hard to get them to believe whatever they wanted about you.

The inevitable crowd of gawkers gathered on Kara's side of the street, and she paused with them. Kara texted Susan: Don't mean to alarm you but what is happening in your building? They weren't one-on-one texting friends, but Kara felt like this was clearly some sort of emergency. Then again, Susan had a career. Those working moms were always so hard to get a hold of and so haughty about it too. How she found time to argue with the school about Wonder Bread was beyond Kara, who couldn't care less what they were giving Oscar as long as it was one fewer meal for her to take care of. After Kara had declined signing Susan's petition, though, the woman's vague disdain had solidified into a full-on chill. Kara figured it would blow over, but after the whole corn syrup controversy (or "corntroversy," as she and Penelope joked) had ended with Nina categorically denying all Susan's requests, she became basically unreachable. Kara could not even remember the last time she had spoken to any grown-up in the Harris household other than the nanny.

There she was now—Susan's nanny, Isa, a warm Indonesian woman in her thirties, hustling down the block with both kids, which meant she had gotten Claude out of Woodmont early. It felt like the first piece clicking into place, a familiar sequence of events initiated. Isa clutched both the children against herself as she made her way through the crowd, which seemed to part ever so slightly for them. Her face was a streak of pain before it disappeared behind the ambulances and into the building.

Kara realized her third floor apartment would be a better vantage point, and anyway the sooner she got home the less she had to pay the babysitter, a neighbor's teenage daughter. As soon as the sitter was out the door, Kara removed her dress—a painstaking pattern that had taken hours to complete—and quickly steamed it before hanging it on the rack by her little sewing nook crammed in the corner. She wasn't about to get spit-up on that pricey silk she had special ordered. In leggings and a faded black T-shirt, Kara held the baby and perched on the radiator. She slid open the narrow, grimy window as far as it would go to watch the dozen or so cops across the street, scattered amid their cars and two ambulances.

When the baby fussed, she put him in the battery-operated swing from Goodwill, though she had previously limited use of the device to emergencies like making dinner and using the toilet. She had seen other mothers put their babies in those things for hours on end, their eyes opening into an unfocused glaze in between dozing. At once, Kara disdained and envied moms like that. She watched the baby anxiously, his marshmallowy fingers grasping a teething ring made of tiny plastic cars . . . What were those cars made of? Something toxic, surely? Where had that ring even come from? Isaac's mother on Staten Island? Kara snatched it out of the baby's hands, tossed it in the trash, and replaced it with that pricey French giraffe she had scoured eBay to find.

Kara returned her attention to the cops across the street. They stood in several small groups, interviewing the doormen and the porters, scratching notes on their department-issued notepads. She counted three female officers. Not that it meant anything, really, but it made her feel better. As if they might take greater care.

The ambulances pulled away without lighting their sirens—not a great sign. She had seen this, too, before. Kara searched Twitter and local news for word of what had happened. That was one thing about a small town. Back home, no one had to wait for bad news. But Kara's refurbished iPhone kept quietly to itself in its fake Louis Vuitton case.

When, an hour later, the baby was still in the swing, she had not moved from the window, and she had still received no response from Susan, a block of ice formed in Kara's gut. Her breathing was too fast and deep—the beginnings of an anxiety spiral. Kara sat on the love seat, legs apart and head between her knees. She recalled the soothing sounds of *Serenity, Maybe?* and the host's careful instructions for hot cocoa breaths. "Try to at least see the outline of what you don't know," the host had said, and Kara reminded herself that she did not really know anything yet. She just had a few observations.

But as the little bursts of light behind her eyes dimmed, Kara kept seeing Isa's face from earlier, marked with an anguish like one she had seen before, on her own mother when Kara's older sister had jumped to her death from a bridge. It felt like it was more than a coincidence that she, Kara, should be the one to bear witness to these things, that only she could connect these particular dots. Perhaps it was her responsibility, even, to look into Susan's death despite the fact that they were not close.

After the police cleared out, Kara strapped her six-month-old onto her back with a repurposed scarf and crossed the street. She still had an hour before she had to pick up Oscar at Woodmont and promised herself that she would work on her dress into the night to make up for this lost time. It felt important to get over there. Kara felt invigorated, having some meaningful business in the land of grown-ups when so rarely did she escape her two small children. But she was more than just a mother; Kara was like a journalist or detective, unwilling to turn a blind eye to the negative series of events unfolding.

Susan's building was massive and dense: a full block of bricks over forty stories high. More people lived within it than in all Kara's hometown. It had its own post office, gym, dry cleaner, and courtyard in the middle. One of three revolving glass doors deposited Kara in a brown marble lobby full of people. Residents conferred with doormen, porters, and handymen. The superintendent had at least a half dozen people semicircled around him. Kids ran around while mothers whispered among themselves. There had to be fifty people gathered there.

Strange that this should be the circumstance of Kara's first step inside Susan's building. Instantly, she second-guessed herself. It felt intrusive. She and Susan weren't *really* friends. What right had she to come sniffing around her lobby? All Kara had were assumptions. Which was why she'd come here, she reminded herself. To confirm her own abilities of deduction. Kara inched along the periphery of the room, watching for the groups that looked porous. Along the way, she picked up snippets.

"Police talked to everyone, but who's to say?"

". . . board liability?"

"Nah!"

". . . tragedy. Two kids . . ."

It had to be Susan, Kara concluded. She listened as strangers shared their stories, all of which sounded like they were about Susan. About how she appeared in the lobby—tidy, fit, crisp—and what people knew about her practice—esteemed, published, thriving. Someone said, "She always held the door for me." A porter said, "She shared Thanksgiving dinner with me once. Some weird tofu thing . . ."

Finally, Kara edged up on a U-shaped group of three with a uniformed and capped doorman in the middle. ". . . and the two little ones," the doorman said and shook his head. To his right, a woman with frizzy gray hair under a maroon beret wiped tears from her eyes with the heel of her hand.

Kara heard the tall man to the left sigh, and she murmured to him, "What happened?"

"Woman killed herself. A mother. Jumped."

"Susan Harris?" Kara said, locking eyes with the doorman, who cast his eyes down as he nodded yes. "Oh, God," Kara heard herself say. "I knew her," she added, her voice sounding like someone else talking. When she felt the tears coming, she studied the glittering rivulets in the brown stone beneath her feet. The tall man squeezed her shoulder. She had that familiar sensation of the oxygen in the room being cut off. The blossoms of light behind her eyes flickered on again.

Kara told herself to get a grip: she had the baby with her. What did the woman say on *Serenity, Maybe?* To "take hold of the mind through the body." The information triggered Kara; that was understandable. She thought of her sister, how at three years her junior, Kara thought she was the most gorgeous, stylish, cool girl who had ever lived. And what did Kara care, really, about Susan Harris? She found, in order to calm herself down, she was repeating over and over in her mind, *you didn't even know her, you didn't even know her, you didn't even know her.* Kara reminded herself that Susan had not wanted to be Kara's friend.

Even before the corntroversy, and even though Kara had lived across the street from Susan for years, and even though they had children roughly the same age who attended the same preschool, Kara could tell that Susan wanted to forestall any possible connection from the moment she had laid eyes on her. She referred Kara to Isa for playdates from the start, never deigning to give her the coveted weekend spot with actual mommy-to-mommy time. "Miss Harris is working on her book," Isa would dutifully report when she insisted each time that they meet outside, and Kara would feel oh so small even in the eyes of the nanny. Sure, she and the other SAHMs could gin up some self-righteousness about doing "the most important job" on earth, but everyone understood this was a job without salary, cachet, or coworkers, a job that basically tapered into nothing if you did it correctly.

"Are you all right?" the tall man was now asking Kara, his eyes boring into hers with concern, a hand up and ready to catch her.

"It's a shock," Kara said, and he nodded.

"How did you know her?" the beret asked, and instead of the whole corntroversy, Kara could only conjure instead Susan's IG grid, her life curated and thrown up for display. A life full of artfully arranged kids' meals, lush family beach vacations, yoga retreats. A life Kara would love to have herself. And Kara knew that she would never be satisfied with simply knowing that Susan Harris died or even that she killed herself. She wasn't concerned with the literal and macabre question of the manner in which she perished but the circumstances that led her to that place and the people who may or may not have been involved. Or even culpable. Kara was convinced, *in her grits*, as her grandmother would have said, that there was more to Susan's death than met the eye. It was a puzzle for her to put together.

She realized the three strangers were waiting for her to say something. "Our kids go to school together," she finally managed, and they all nodded sympathetically.

"It must be a terrible surprise," the woman said, her face drooping with concern. Before Kara could utter another sound, the doorman next to them let out a tiny gasp, and a hush fell over the lobby.

All eyes swiveled to Michael, Susan's husband, as he burst through the revolving doors and hesitated for a split second, taking in the unprecedented congregation of his building's staff and inhabitants. Back home, this would be the moment when someone in the crowd would rush to embrace him, and everyone, even relative strangers, would follow suit. But not here. The transient renters who came and went, the cynical staff who had seen all sorts of deaths, perhaps more tragic than this one, just gawked at Michael as he rushed past, eyes down, and went alone into a waiting elevator.

The silence sustained itself for three seconds before everyone turned back to their conversations with exclamations of empathy, shared behind the widower's back but not to his face. Kara was struck by the indifference of the city, how the anonymity bred such inhumanity. Could she herself survive it?

"How old is your other child?" the woman in the beret asked Kara.

"Actually, I have to go get him now!" Kara said with sudden emphasis, seized by a primal urge to touch him, hug him, squeeze him, make sure that nothing had happened to him. How had Susan chosen to never do that again? The woman nodded at her, as if she understood. The baby started to kick his little legs, and Kara headed for the doors.

But as she passed two women about her own age, heads close together, she slowed to catch their words. ". . . didn't seem that torn up, did he?"

"And it took him a while to get here. Where was he this morning, anyway?"

Michael. They were talking about Michael. Kara remembered a scene from years before. She had run out for cough medicine for Oscar late at night. He had one of those barking coughs that gave every mother heart palpitations. Kara had hustled head down, exhausted and sick herself, which is why she had almost run right into Susan and Michael, squared off, arguing.

It had felt as if she was trespassing on a private moment, even though they were on the sidewalk bathed in the fluorescent light of the Drugmart. In the city, people felt anonymous on the street; it was part of the great promise of New York, that you could reinvent yourself here meant that you could also be no one. At home, Kara knew from when she was a small child that anything she did in public would be reported back to her parents that same day.

But obviously Susan and Michael felt like they were all alone, and they never spotted nondescript Kara in her Target jacket slipping past them. Susan's hair fell in slightly disheveled glossy waves—the end of an evening. The light from the storefront illuminated her face, revealing worn-off lipstick and long lashes. Their words were not so loud, as Kara remembered, but their gestures were charged. The way she shook her head "no," the way he pointed in her face, and then—was her memory playing a trick on her?—the way Kara had seen him reach out and grab her arm above the elbow, hard, and pull her along.

Again, Kara felt, at this particular moment, that she alone was privy to a certain set of data and that it was no coincidence. What did the host say on *Serenity, Maybe?* "When you know something, don't disbelieve yourself." Kara had seen this film before. She knew how this went. When women die, an explanation is not always demanded, but one exists. Perhaps Susan did not *want* to commit to weekend playdates because in fact she *could* not meet on weekends. Kara saw Susan in her mind's eye, prone on a fluffy white couch in a bright two-bedroom apartment she owned with Michael, too deep in her own depression to go out and socialize. He, self-medicating with alcohol or pills or something. She, not getting the help she needed.

The unimaginable pain, Kara could understand. Her own sister hadn't been able to tolerate any more living.

Yet it all refused to add up to Kara, for whom melancholy and fakery were second nature. How hard was it, really, to just blend in when you basically had everything: the money, the real estate, the clothes, the career, the education, the network—and all you had to do was try a little extra hard to smile? No, it just didn't seem right. And as Kara's eyes traveled over the faces in the lobby, she saw disbelief there as well. She could not be alone in wondering: Could a mother of two children under the age of five really willingly end her own life?

Kara just couldn't accept it. And even if no one had literally pushed her out the window (although someone, like Michael, *could* have done that very thing) Kara understood that all along the way to a suicide, there are people who help or hinder the victim. Or was she the perpetrator? Kara shook her head to clear the fog she was in, rushing through the revolving doors to get Oscar from Woodmont.

As she went east on Eighty-Ninth Street, it occurred to Kara that a few people, Nina for one, would likely know about Susan's death, while others, like all the parents and staff, would not. Of course, as head of the Parents' Association, Penelope would have all the available information. But no one would know that Kara herself had figured this out, which sent a little thrill up her spine. People always thought she was such an empty-headed ninny.

Woodmont was in an old building that shared a leafy courtyard with a church. Kara practically ran into Vic, charging past like she was late. "Oh, sorry," she said absentmindedly, hurrying past Kara anyway. It didn't look like she'd been crying, exactly, and she was always a bit ruffled. Vic and Susan had been friendly, Kara recalled, and she made a note to herself to keep an eye on this one. Suicide, after all, was contagious. Her sister had been the second in a series of three.

As if remembering not to be so rude, Vic tossed over her shoulder, "How're you?" She slowed her step ever so slightly for Kara to catch up and deliver her answer.

"Oh, I'm all right," Kara said in a sing-songy way. She walked a step behind Vic up the stairs to their children's classroom. "How are you?" she asked.

Vic said, "Ummm." The answer seemed pretty clear: Vic was not well. Kara looked at her face, which appeared not only makeup-free but unwashed. Her stringy blonde hair pressed to her cheeks under her hat. Her eyes were cast down, so she didn't see Kara's brow furrow with concern. Vic hurried ahead, pulling open the door to the long corridor lined with one-way mirrors through which you could watch your children inside the classroom. Vic hustled to the nearest window and peered in. Kara looked over her shoulder, spotting Oscar with the blocks as always. There was Jetta, sitting by herself on the mat. Her back was to them, but it looked like she was cradling some sort of toy or stuffed animal. Vic's shoulders hunched. Maybe she knew. Maybe they both knew.

Kara's eyes searched the corridor for Penelope, whom she generally caught up with at pickup, but she wasn't there. She spotted Amy's assistant at the very front of the line. She wore a crepe pencil skirt and long-sleeved silk shirt with leather high heels. Whoever she was, she took less than zero interest in socializing with other caregivers, instead snapping pictures of Pearl through the glass with a special zoom lens affixed to her iPhone.

Chandice showed up behind Kara. "Hi," Kara said to her, resisting the urge to instantly divulge everything about Susan. She had been currying a friendship with Chandice for a while. As two SAHMs with boys the same age, it seemed like an obvious match to Kara. And she'd love for Oscar to have more diverse friends. Kara had to wait until she moved to New York to meet anyone all that different from herself. But Chandice proved elusive, putting off more playdates than she actually kept. "How are you, Chandice?" Kara asked.

"Great," Chandice said, and, unlike most of the moms who reflexively said "terrific" or "fine" or "busy!" and expected to hear exactly the same thing parroted back, Kara believed Chandice. She just seemed so genuine. "You?"

"Eh," Kara said, reaching for anything to talk about, lest she run the risk of just blurting out "Susan Harris is dead!" in the corridor. "What did you think of the tour today?"

Chandice blinked twice, taking in who else stood in their small corridor, and Kara realized it was gauche for her to be discussing Kent on Woodmont property. After all, only a handful of Woodmont students had made it onto Nina's short list. When Kara found out that Oscar had been recommended to Kent, it seemed like the confirmation she never expected that her small deceptions were substantially paying off. For Oscar to become a Kent graduate would mean that he could claim a genuine identity that Kara only pretended at. It was the previously unknown motivation behind all her efforts.

"It was impossible not to be impressed," Chandice said with quiet discretion.

"Yeah," Kara agreed. Chandice was waiting for Kara to say more than a single syllable. Which left only one topic. "Have you heard the latest episode of *Serenity, Maybe?*" This podcast had become the closest thing Kara had to a religion, perhaps because in dozens of episodes on all sorts of self-actualization and finding alternate routes to happiness and learning to tolerate and even mine negative emotions, she had never found anything the host said to be particularly incriminating of her own choices. Perhaps others had chosen to believe certain untruths about her that Kara did not go out of her way to disabuse them of. Perhaps she intentionally sewed herself and her children clothes meant to mimic expensive designers. But was this not still her manifesting her own authentic self? Should she be limited to creating clothes that more accurately reflected her solidly bland, culturally backward, middle-class socioeconomic status? Did she need to tell everyone that she hadn't graduated from high school?

"Not yet!" Chandice said with enthusiasm, and it took a beat for Kara to remember they were talking about *Serenity, Maybe?* She felt a rush of self-consciousness about recommending some sort of new age-y self-help podcast, but it was too late. "What's it about?" Chandice asked gamely.

"How you can know something but then unknow it, you know?" Kara winced at the ham-handedness of her own phrasing; she had clearly lost Chandice halfway through it. Kara's mind wandered back to her grubby window on Third Avenue. Had she missed an important sighting at Susan's? A chance to deepen her understanding of the situation?

When she snapped back into focus, Chandice had an eyebrow raised, and the classroom door was open for them to fetch their children. Vic rushed forward, and Kara was reminded of her own urgent need to see Oscar. She enfolded Oscar's small body fully against herself, and his little hands reached around to his brother on her back—a unit of three. She breathed in their unique scents and kissed Oscar's soft head, and by the time they got home, she was ready to return to the window to resume watch on what was left to learn about Susan Harris.

Throughout the late afternoon, Kara would periodically pull herself away to do some necessary task, then resume watch. In this way, she caught sight of Isa leaving for the night. She moved like an escapee, with rapidity and stealth, wide eyes darting in every direction. Horror and grief emanated from her, even from across the street. She seemed changed, older, stiffer as she scuttled away. Since she was on foot, she must live within walking distance. Kara hoped it was not too far; surely, no one in the Harris residence had bothered to ask how she would get home without the subway.

Afraid she might miss something, Kara fed and bathed both children with one eye on Susan's building, putting them down to sleep in the apartment's one small bedroom a full hour early. She prepared the dough for the next day's bread while running back and forth to the window, but decided to give up on fruit salad. She had washed two more loads of laundry but only got about a third of the way through folding before moving her sewing machine in front of the window to make her sons several pairs of spring-weight slacks and shirts, which she could do best while keeping an eye out. And she was exhausted, like always.

It was then that the phone rang. "Babe, I'm not gonna make it home," Isaac said. She had totally forgotten about him. She let the realization that Isaac was stuck across the river flood her body. "It's a two-hour wait and about three hundred bucks to Uber," he said. "Jason says I can crash on his couch for a while."

Kara's eyes were out the window and across the street. Michael rushed outside, his eyes straight ahead, arms held curved out from either side like padding.

"Oh, OK," Kara said. Michael walked, swinging his arms, establishing an impenetrable circumference around himself. His eyes scanned 180 degrees in front of himself, like he was on some sort of military operation. "I guess I'll let you get that squared away."

"Don't worry about me!" Isaac said sarcastically. Spotting a van parked in front of his building, Michael walked around it to the street side as if to get in. But instead, he stood on Third Avenue with the traffic rushing past him, his back pressed to the side of the vehicle. Kara was mesmerized. The bright streetlights made the avenue a stage. What was he going to do? Leap into traffic and orphan his children? Unconsciously, her right hand reached for the window as if to stop him.

"OK, bye!" Kara said and hung up. Michael felt around in his pocket. He pulled out a pack of Marlboro Reds, the same brand her sister's jerk boyfriend had smoked. Kara's body flooded with adrenaline. Michael lit one and got out his phone. He pressed it to his ear with one hand while with the other he steadily returned the cigarette to and from his mouth. Soon he was in tears, the smoking hand pressed to his forehead. He sobbed with grief, the sound eaten up by the mass of traffic, no one there to witness this breakdown except the person on the phone and Kara. He shook his head no, then yes. He smoked and smoked, the tears slowing, then ceasing altogether; then he tossed the butt into the street before storming back inside, phone still pressed to his head.

Though it was 10:30 p.m., the time she usually went to bed, Kara knew there was no way she could sleep. She just sat on the radiator cover, her body awash in terribly familiar feelings from when she was only fifteen and all the way back home. Michael came out two more times to smoke throughout the night. Kara knew because her eyes never left the front of his building. There he was, now just openly smoking, probably enjoying the anonymity of it being the middle of the night. Kara watched his face, trying to intuit: Was this guilty smoking? Sad smoking? Angry?

As the front doors closed behind him, guilt inundated Kara. She could hardly afford to lose all this time. Woodmont and Kent offered her a portal into the most beautiful parts of the city, but it was just so much work for her to fit through the gate. The dress she was making for Oscar's preschool graduation, for example, was based on a Celine piece she had seen Penelope try on at Bergdorfs but not buy, with a frilly back in muted tones and small crystals she herself would painstakingly sew along the seams and hem. She remembered how Penelope had run her hand along all that hard work and said, "I'm not sure about the bugle beads." Kara had switched them out in her rendition.

But now the garment in her hands felt like Everest. She dug her fingertips into the bowl of beads, hardly diminished since she started, and felt exhaustion reach up through her wrist and into her shoulder. She withdrew her empty hand.

Her mind traveled back, as it did more and more frequently, to the hair salon where she had made it to junior trainee with the head colorist. Sure, she reeked of chemicals and was on her feet twelve hours a day, but at least that workday came to an end. When Isaac was promoted to gym manager and Kara got pregnant, he insisted he could take care of all of them in the apartment he had rented from his uncle for over a decade. Looking back, Kara wondered if she would have quit her job without the mood-altering hormones coursing through her body. Everything had felt like a good idea then, including signing herself up for a 24/7 homemaker role on a limited budget in the most elitist place in North America.

First, she had to talk them into financial aid at Woodmont, a painstaking process that was helped along by the bulk of Isaac's income being cash. But then, at the very first parents' event, Penelope had mistaken her for someone else, someone of means, and Kara had not bothered to correct her, and since then it had not been that hard to evade her questions, shadow her style, and mimic her behaviors. By proximity, others had assumed Kara had money. How else could she not work?

While she had not exactly planned it from the outset, Kara leaned into this development. She had learned how to sidestep questions in such a way as to suggest wealth. Why couldn't Penelope come to Kara's place for a playdate? Not because it was a tiny one-bedroom with four human beings crammed inside along with a hodgepodge collection of furniture from Isaac's uncle in New Jersey. No, Kara didn't entertain, "because we're renting, and it just isn't up to my standards for entertaining. Let us have you over once we find our forever home." Why didn't Kara and Isaac attend the $1,000-per-plate Woodmont benefit dinner? "We have a terrible conflict with Isaac's family, but we will send a contribution." And so on. These were not lies but dressed-up truths that served a purpose in advancing their children's lives. They were practically second nature to Kara now; it had been hard to tell lately if and how the "authentic" Kara was different from the one she presented at private school events.

But now, who was this woman pulling an all-nighter at the window, keeping vigil? Was this the authentic Kara or someone new? She was startled when the baby started crying at 6:00 a.m. for his morning nursing session, and Kara railed at herself for staying up through the night. She raced inside but wasn't fast enough to prevent the crying from waking Oscar, who rolled over, his adorable little belly sticking out of his fire truck pajamas. Kara picked up the little one from the crib and lay down in the bed with Oscar, who snuggled up against her and went back to sleep. She was so warm, inside and out. How could Susan have chosen to leave this behind?

The baby finished nursing, and she burped him on her shoulder, forgetting to put a cloth down to catch the spit-up, which dribbled down her back instead. Kara set him down with blocks on the living room rug while she gave Oscar his breakfast. She thought about making coffee but didn't have enough time before taking him to school; she'd just rush there and back to collapse into bed if the baby would cooperate by going down too. Oscar carefully dipped his waffle in a small pool of real maple syrup and ate thoughtfully, his sleepy eyes on her. His brown curls ran wild on one side of his head, while on the other they were pressed flat.

"Mama," Oscar said. He reached out his perfect little pink hand across the table to grab Kara's thumb. "You OK?"

"Mama didn't sleep so well," Kara explained.

Oscar patted her hand gently. "Mama, you should take a nap while I'm at school today. You know what happens if you don't get enough sleep?" He was repeating her favorite lesson back to her. There was something so special about Oscar; he was an astonishingly good listener, but he didn't just regurgitate things at random. He understood them.

"You're not at your best," she said, and truer words had never been spoken. In the bathroom light, Kara looked half-dead. Instead of makeup, she went with oversize Dior-knockoff sunglasses she had purchased on the street and Penelope's hand-me-down Moncler, which Kara had volunteered to take to Goodwill and only slightly altered to avoid Penelope's noticing. At a glance, she looked like a Park Avenue mom. So she'd have to be quick about getting out of there. But as Oscar ran into the classroom, Kara heard, "Nice coat," from behind. Penelope kissed her son goodbye, completely and totally unruffled by recent events. Penelope would never have recognized her old coat anyway, sporting as she was a new fur-trimmed parka and professional blowout. "Are you coming?" Penelope asked. When Kara said nothing, slack jawed, Penelope added a little snootily, "The meeting with Nina about Susan?"

"Of course," she said reflexively, following Penelope to the family conference room. Dazed, Kara gratefully filled a paper cup with instant coffee from a cart in the hallway. She felt jittery with sleeplessness and stunned by the fluorescent lights. Thank goodness the baby was already in the midst of his morning nap so she could leave his stroller in the corner of the room. Nina, the unreadable head of Woodmont, sat on one side of the couch. Penelope took the seat on the other side. Vic had a chair, and Bhavna perched with a few other moms in the window area. Kara did not know what to do, but she couldn't stand. So she took the seat in between Penelope and Nina on the couch and settled back. She didn't want to miss a word of the information she was here to gain.

An expectant hush. Moms all looking at one another. Kara waited for Nina to start speaking. From Kara's vantage point on the couch, she studied the back of Nina's graying bob. Enough moments passed for everyone in the room to understand that there would be no sort of broadcast. Nothing new.

Finally, Nina cleared her throat. "The family asked me to share that the memorial will be Friday morning. 10:00 a.m. at St. Barts Cathedral." She looked around as if this answered every question.

"But Nina," Vic said, clearly distraught and frustrated. "What happened to Susan?"

"We have no information," Nina said, the slightest annoyance creeping into her tone.

"Did this have to do with the food thing?" Vic asked. Kara felt her stomach roll around. She hadn't thought of that connection. But could the corntroversy really have contributed to Susan's suicide?

"Oh, come on!" Penelope said, dismissing it.

"She took it pretty seriously," Vic said, tears springing to her eyes. Guilt rushed through Kara over the way she and Penelope had mocked Susan behind her back. She was glad they could not meet one another's eyes now.

"You were pretty harsh with her," Bhavna practically accused Nina, who didn't take the bait.

"Unfortunately, we still have no information," Nina repeated, almost with sympathy for the mothers, powerless under these circumstances.

Kara was surprised to hear herself speak and further shocked when she burst into tears midway. "People don't just disappear, Nina!" she said, a sob interrupting her. "Mothers don't just vanish without any information!"

Nina only sighed, handing Kara the box of tissues. "I'm sorry," she said.

"Nina, come on, throw us a bone here," Bhavna said.

"I've said all I can," Nina replied.

"Then why have this meeting?" Vic said.

"We're just trying to provide a space for grieving," Penelope interrupted, remembering her leadership role. With the use of the word "we," Penelope reminded Kara that she knew much more than she had shared, but when Kara suggested coffee after the meeting, Penelope declined without an excuse. Kara couldn't help but feel that Penelope sensed her interest in knowing more.

So Kara took it upon herself to learn as much as she could through observation. Kara always filled the time while Oscar was at Woodmont with chores and errands, but she couldn't tear herself away from the window. It had quickly become some sort of silent ritual, watching Michael sneak his smokes, clocking Isa coming and going on foot early in the morning and late at night. She took Susan's kids out once or twice, their small faces strangely normal looking. How many hours passed like this? Punctuated only by preschool drop-off and pickup? Without Isaac coming home at night to mark the passage of time, Kara was adrift. Oscar and the baby woke up, ate, played, and so on, but that was all in the background now, literally often going on behind her in the apartment while her gaze was on the street. It hardly mattered what time of day it was.

Isaac's key in the door startled Kara, who had been mostly glued to their open living room window for the better part of the roughly sixty hours since Susan died. From her new preferred perch on the radiator, Kara quickly saw the room the way Isaac would see it: the afternoon snacks half-eaten and still in plastic containers on the couch, the unfolded laundry piled high on the floor, the sink full of dishes, and Kara herself, in an uncharacteristically unflattering T-shirt she had gotten for free somewhere, hanging over stained sweatpants.

There was nowhere to hide. The "living room" also served as the family room, TV room, dining room, and Kara and Isaac's bedroom at night, when the threadbare love seat birthed a lumpy double bed. A small counter with two stools gave the postage-stamp kitchen the illusion of a window. The two kids had the small bedroom for sleep and play; the apartment's single small closet was for all their handmade clothes, secondhand toys, and the baby's changing table.

If only she had time to fix everything before Isaac walked in, a chance to cover the basic truth of the matter, which was that Kara had forgotten about everything but Susan since her death.

Because Kara uniquely understood how questions could go unanswered when a woman met an untimely end. So she had completely forgotten that Isaac had texted he'd be coming home to "grab some stuff." She hadn't seen him since the Kent tour. Normally, not only would the house be clean, but she would have some food for him to take with him. She'd be in a more flattering outfit. She'd—

"Hey, babe!" Isaac said, almost filling out the entire doorframe on his way inside. He tossed his one suit from days before over a chair and crossed the short distance to where Kara stood, motionless at the window.

The dough she had made the morning of the Kent tour sat, unbaked and crusted over with age, decomposing in a plastic bowl on the counter. The never-cut fruit sat next to it, two fruit flies buzzing about. Kara could see a dark rotten mark on one of the mangos from across the room. Laundry piled up on the floor by the couch, waiting to be folded.

Kara couldn't be sure if Isaac was tactfully ignoring the state of the apartment, or he sincerely didn't notice. He crossed the room toward her, and even this felt overwhelming. She had been mostly alone in the apartment with the children. "Hi," he said warmly. He dropped his gym bag on the floor and kissed her. "I heard about that other mom." Clearly, he credited this news with the apartment's disarray, which was, Kara realized, startled, the truth.

"Yeah," Kara said. "I didn't really know her," she added, leaving out her postmortem obsession.

"Are you going to the memorial?"

"Of course."

"I'm sorry, I don't know if I can make it," he said. "And Jason is outside waiting." Isaac reached out his hand and squeezed hers, which was still holding the graduation dress. She had, over the last few days, managed to sew on only about a dozen beads.

"Whatcha working on?" Isaac asked, and Kara was touched by his interest.

"A dress for the Woodmont graduation. I already made your shirt." Kara plucked the garment from the short rack behind her, made from a knockoff Etro fabric that looked rich. Since Oscar would be onstage, Kara could not leave Isaac out of it as she generally did. He simply could not blend in the way she might like, so she often simply told Nina or whoever asked that Isaac had to work and let them draw their own conclusions. What she wanted most was to avoid letting Isaac speak for himself—a dead giveaway of their backgrounds.

"What?" Isaac said, eyeing her back.

"Nothing," Kara said, returning the shirt to its rack and hanging up the dress. Isaac grabbed a small duffel from the hall closet and started to stuff his clothes inside. Kara returned to the window, watching Susan's building, now back to normal. The city was like that; it swallowed people. Who would even be speaking about Susan next week? Other than Kara.

"How are the kids?" Isaac asked as he pulled out several pairs of underwear from the drawer beneath their living room television.

"Good, fine, you know."

"Did you tell Oscar about Kent?" Just then, Michael charged out of the building, his phone pressed to his ear. Suddenly alert, like an animal, Kara took mental notes. The way he gripped the device between his chin and shoulder. The quick motion of his jaw as he spoke. The lack of emotion on his face. The only sign of duress the kneading of his hands.

"Why would I do that?" Kara said tonelessly.

"You're right. We could never afford it. Even if we could, it's insane!"

Kara quelled her growing disdain for Isaac. Could he not see the possibilities stretched out before their son? "Maybe they'd give us financial aid," she said.

"Please." Isaac scoffed. "It's ridiculous. To spend all that money for what? Lab coats and drone shoots?" He zipped up his bag and tossed it by the door. "Babe, I can't take another transit strike: it's just time to leave the city." He had said this sort of thing before, and always Kara fought him. "Let's just see what happens with the kids," she said, knowing instinctively that a place like Kent could really change Oscar's life in ways nowhere else could. But now she was focused on Michael, who looked up and down Third Avenue as if waiting for something.

"Whatcha doin', babe?" Isaac asked, all of a sudden right behind her. In their apartment—really, it was his apartment—the two of them were hardly ever more than an arm's length away from one another. Which was great for them, because there was one thing about Kara and Isaac that always gelled.

Isaac came to the window and tilted Kara forward, pulling just her leggings down but leaving on her black T-shirt. A black town car pulled up outside Susan's building. Michael reached out his hand for the woman inside, who unfolded herself stiffly to reveal a blonde helmet of hair. Kara held her breath as Isaac tweaked her nipples, watching as the woman—it couldn't be Michael's mother, she stood at such a distance from him—took stock of him. She kept a full foot between them at all times.

Isaac was so firm, so fit and hard, Kara could feel his physical confidence in the pads of his fingers. As he moved inside her, he slipped his hand around to stroke her. On the street outside, a man in a blazer joined the woman and extended a hand to Michael. A handshake. These must be Susan's parents, in town for the memorial the next day and seeing Michael for the first time after their daughter's death. If something had seemed off before, it was definitely coming to a point, the awkwardness across the street confirming Kara's suspicions that something was wrong in the Harris home, as Isaac's hands moved more and more insistently, making her come.

FOUR

CHANDICE

All she had to do was let it happen, Chandice reminded herself, settling back in her seat. For most of her life, it had been so important to work hard, harder, hardest. But there was no more she could contribute toward a "positive outcome" except to remain as calm and optimistic as she had always been. If only Chandice could figure out how to do that, exactly. Where was that robust woman? The unbothered one? What would a "positive outcome," as her doctor called it, even be at this point?

Chandice tried to shake these questions, which did not lead to "healing serenity" but rather its opposite. Conditions in the room were ideal for forgetting the purpose of her visit, and she tried to let the dim lights and formless Muzak lull her into a different state of consciousness. Meanwhile, the gentle nurse found the port in Chandice's chest, where she inserted the line that would deliver the most recently developed, extremely potent, experimental chemotherapy directly into Chandice's heart.

Chandice made every effort to relax. She adjusted the chair with the buttons on the side until she had it just right: feet elevated, knees bent. She navigated to the latest episode of *Queen Sugar* on her iPad. She pulled a blanket onto her lap and slid her bag onto the table by her right arm. She took in a "soothing breath" and then another one and was almost feeling the effects of the antianxiety medication they put in her IV when her mind doubled back on itself . . . Where had she learned that term? "Soothing breath." Or any of this nonsense language that had invaded her muddled mind like weeds? That annoying therapist? Or was it the stupid wellness podcast that Woodmont mom, Kara, recommended: *Serenity, Maybe?* She hated it and all it signified. Soothing breath? As in, you should be comforted by merely breathing?

She felt bad about Kara. That woman tried so hard! The problem was that while Chandice was technically no longer employed, she had, up until recently, been a lawyer. She had been in the world of suits and meetings and public argumentation. Her intellectual output had been valued at four digits per hour of work. It wasn't that she couldn't trade Impossible Meatball recipes with Kara; it was that she felt like she was somehow above it.

Chandice had never fit in with the other private school SAHMs, who made no bones about a lack of career in their past, present, or future. It wasn't just that Chandice had nothing to chat about with these women—after all, who really wants to talk about their jobs anyway?—but that they lacked real-life experience with grown-up situations and problems. Kara did not need to be in touch with the world in the way other adults had to be. Still, Chandice felt bad about blowing her off all the time. And feeling bad made her mad. Inanely, at Kara.

Maybe it was because Chandice was not, at the moment, an attorney nor did she feel truly motivated to return to work. It wasn't quite that Chandice did not like practicing law, but she had seen how her husband as well as her closest law school friend, Belinda, both took to their professional identities, whereas she struggled. Those two were born for their roles. They thrived on the billable hours and granular reasoning. Successful as she was, Chandice wondered nearly every day of her ten years as an attorney if anyone would ever find her exceptional at corporate law. There were times when she thought her aloof boss had his eye on her for bigger things at work—he spoke once of more interesting cases with bigger clients—but then her pregnancy began to show, and it seemed moot. Since then, their midsize firm had been acquired for some ridiculous amount of money, and he had probably forgotten every single thing about her. Chandice chided herself again for not being more diligent about maintaining her professional contacts.

This was Chandice's problem with trying to relax. She had been a pacifist all her life, but now, she wanted to fight hard, all the time. Usually with other people, occasionally with the world in general, and often with herself. It wasn't that she was angry. Chandice was hardly ever angry. Perhaps she was a little mad, which made sense. *It is OK to be angry!* That's what the woman said on *Serenity, Maybe?* All that woman ever did was say things were OK! It was all OK, as long as you knew how you felt. But after a life of unblemished optimism, Chandice found that she could no longer discern her own emotional landscape.

When Chandice was first diagnosed, she had so much wind in her sails. Her son, Daniel, was only two, and Joseph and Chandice had decided to expand their family and extend her break from work. While Chandice hadn't always loved being a lawyer—a corporate lawyer, anyway—Joseph seemed born to it. When he made partner at his firm, it seemed like a dream come true for Chandice. She could devote herself to becoming the mother of two (or three or four!) children that she had always wanted to be.

When her period was late, she went right to the doctor, breezing into her obstetrician's office all smiles. She didn't even have time to arrange childcare, bringing Daniel with her into the exam room, where she popped open a Pack 'N Play with the flick of a wrist. Chandice would never forget her feeling of mastery in that moment, that she had become the effortless mother she had long envisioned. Her skills came naturally, and her womb was fertile. As she lay on the table in her paper gown—her urine in a plastic cup on the counter, her son quietly banging two plastic toys together, her phone at the ready to call her loving husband with the good news, and a silly grin spread across her whole face—Chandice had a moment of prescient insight: *appreciate this.*

Chandice's doctor was thrilled to tell her she was pregnant, although it was too soon to hear the heartbeat. As she conducted a routine breast exam, Chandice upright with one arm over her head, a microexpression of concern flashed across her face. A law school friend had suggested they take a class on how to watch for these incredibly telling moments, when people nakedly reveal their most true and inner thoughts but only for a split second before covering it over. It was, in all Chandice's education, the most valuable life skill she had learned in a classroom setting.

"Are you still nursing?" the doctor asked, pointedly.

"Nope," Chandice said, trying to tell herself this must all be some sort of hormonal development in her breast tissue.

"*Hmm,*" her doctor said. "I think we have to check this out, Chandice, and I think we should go straight to a biopsy."

"Biopsy? For what?" Chandice said, denial seizing hold right away.

Her doctor reached out and gripped Chandice's shoulder, lest she faint and fall right off the table. "Cancer, Chandice." And the way the doctor said it, Chandice knew that she was already pretty much certain. A week after the biopsy, she had her first surgery, followed by her first round of chemo and, a week after that, her first miscarriage. It was enough to take down the most dyed-in-the-wool optimist.

Eight months of semiconsciousness punctuated by treatments and illness were all worth it, though, in the end. All the doctors said that they had caught it early enough! They were practically congratulating each other when she responded right away to treatment. The tumors were gone. Chandice felt great!

And for two glorious years, Chandice enjoyed remission. She succumbed to the constant monitoring—the scans and prodding doctors—but gave up the anxiety as each visit yielded the same good news: no cancer. She and Joseph had started, tentatively, to speak again of another child.

Until two months ago, when a marker came up in her blood, and the tumor presented itself on a scan. In her brain. Her oncologist at Sloan Kettering had pulled all the strings to enroll her in a promising treatment just starting clinical trials. So here Chandice was, the object of an experiment.

The medicine didn't really feel like much. A little pressure. Maybe she imagined a slight chill. That led to a shiver and the nurse pulling the blanket up for her before ducking out. Chandice pulled her tablet closer, enlarged the screen on Ralph Angel's gorgeous face, and pressed play.

Which was when the email came in from Woodmont.

Subject: Harris Memorial

Chandice knew, instinctively, she shouldn't look at it when she was supposed to be "letting the healing happen." She knew that the email would not help her get better. Susan Harris's death had meant nothing but negative, toxic feelings. She had known, right away—*how could you not have known?*—just by the tone of Nina's email how Susan had died. Chandice had then purposefully not attended the meeting that morning. To do what? More *not* talking about Susan's suicide? But here it was, in her face, and, of course, Chandice could not stop herself from reading this email right away.

> . . . memorial service Friday . . . respect the family's privacy . . . no phone calls, no emails, and no gifts . . .

She chose this, Chandice thought, as she allowed a new chemical compound to *drip drip drip* directly into the left atrium of her heart in order to sustain her life for as long as possible. Meanwhile, Susan had taken her life and her perfectly good body and thrown them away.

Huh.

Mindlessly, Chandice called Joseph, always her first instinct when she felt rudderless, but he did not answer. She had asked his assistant to mark out all the times she was in chemotherapy in case she wanted to talk to someone. It seemed fair as she couldn't expect him to be the sole breadwinner and sit with her for three hours in the middle of the work week. But still . . .

Oh, well.

Chandice lived by an adage her godmother had taught her back in Barbuda as a small girl, and that was, "Don't dwell on the shit."

She couldn't really call anyone else because no one, not her college pals or family or even Daniel, knew yet that she was sick again. Very few of them even knew that Chandice had breast cancer in the first place. She remembered how she had broken it to her brother and sister, in the parlor at her Harlem town house. They knew something was up—Why would Chandice want to meet with just them? Her sister thought it was about setting up guardianship for Daniel, which it was, but when she told them the impetus was a stage-three breast cancer diagnosis, her brother collapsed into tears, and her sister just kept squeezing various parts of her until she escaped. In an instant, she had transformed from Chandice, their lawyer supermom sister with an enviable life, to dead woman walking.

She couldn't go through that again until it was unavoidable.

Realities like this, though, can't stay all bottled up inside one person, and it had to come out all at once, like a purge—everything from the lost second pregnancy to her grim prognosis. Chandice knew she could only share it with someone distant, someone she felt some kinship with but who was far from actual kin. Someone who would never accidentally spill the beans to anyone close to Chandice.

At the class outing to the Metropolitan Museum back in January, Chandice had been surprised to find Amy chaperoning as well. Amy, who was always so intensely focused on some distant and complex problem, so wealthy and preternaturally composed. Chandice just knew Amy was the sort of person with many more important things to do than gossip and therefore was the perfect vessel to receive this load of bad news and never speak a word of it.

As they walked past mummies and sarcophagi, the children and teachers a safe distance ahead, Chandice felt herself comprehensively answering Amy's innocuous, "How are you?" As Chandice talked, Amy's eyes widened, and she reached out for her. This is what everyone did when Chandice told them she was sick—just started reflexively touching her. But Amy's was such a gentle, almost formal gesture; her cool hand rested lightly on Chandice's forearm as they gazed into a two-thousand-year-old tomb.

"Oh, Chandice," Amy said. "How terrible."

And that was comfort enough. Chandice wasn't about to call Amy to commiserate about Susan's death. Or should she? Chandice read the email again. What did she remember about Susan? Not much. Of course, everyone knew about how she freaked out at the PA meeting. But personally, Chandice had only ever felt a slight antipathy from Susan. Sometimes it felt like she was watching Chandice, although they had never exchanged more than a pleasant hello in the hallway at pickup. Joseph only talked with her once at a school event. She thought of Susan's daughter and her smaller son, whom she had seen with their nanny, Isa, at drop-off and pickup. Susan left behind two children under the age of five. Their faces loomed in Chandice's mind. A damn shame.

Then the nurse was back, removing the line, giving her a glass of water, and helping her back on her feet. It always felt a little weird to leave the hushed cocoon of treatment, where everyone knew her only as "cancer patient," and reenter the land of the living. Chandice's medication cocktail included powerful steroids that made her want to take the subway, but then she remembered the strike. She had to admire the flower shop and the grocery store, with their colorful goods spilling onto the street, from the window of the town car Joseph's assistant had arranged. The city itself was alive and well despite all odds.

Chandice stirred the beans in the Crockpot, paid the babysitter, and peeked in on her son. Daniel sat on the rug in his room, a sky blue oval with puffs of white meant to look like clouds, and carefully affixed a Lego to the wing of the Millennium Falcon. She went inside and sat on the floor with him, watching him quietly as he thoughtfully studied the piece in his hand. She did not want to interrupt his concentration. This kit was intended for a much older kid, but Daniel was up to the task. Chandice had always known he had an unusual capacity for staying focused and learning. He pored over the instructions, finally returning the piece in his hand to the pile and finding the right one, which he affixed to the body of the craft.

"Can I have a kiss now?" Chandice asked, pulling him into her lap and squeezing him. The smell of her child was the most intoxicating, magical scent in the world. Her most painful and persistent nightmare was that Daniel would have to grow up without her. How could Susan have given this up?

"Were you pulling on my invisible string today?" Chandice asked. They had recently read this book about the unbreakable connection between mother and child. She worried about her son—of course, she did. She would do whatever she could to make his future more secure, with or without her. Was a place like Kent really the answer? She wasn't certain.

Daniel nodded. "I missed you at lunchtime," he admitted.

"I knew it," Chandice said, touching her nose to his. "We'll always be connected even when we're not together." Daniel wrapped his arms around her neck, and she did not allow herself to cry, even for a second, even over his shoulder. She watched him continue his project a little longer, then went to freshen up for Joseph.

In the bathroom, she splashed some water on her face and toweled off, leaning into the mirror to inspect the bare truth. The dark circles under her eyes and hyperpigmentation were only getting worse. Her beauty concerns commenced with chemotherapy, but unlike the disease, these were issues she could actively tackle rather than glumly accept. The patient saleswoman at Sephora had shown her how to use a color corrector—a garish coral that she would never have chosen herself—underneath her foundation. Every day, she sponged the coral on, carefully blending in the skin shade on top, and found that if she took this time, she could achieve a result that was almost what she looked like getting out of bed four years prior. A little blush and mascara, and she was her old self. Maybe even with a little extra glow.

Chandice changed into something lower cut that showed off her new, bouncy synthetic breasts, but still concealed the port in her chest, and assessed the result in the mirror. She took down her braids and let them loose. They told her that she'd lose them soon, but tonight, she was looking pretty good. For a dying woman.

When Joseph breezed in, his tie loose and his suit in need of refreshing, Chandice greeted him at the door with a kiss. He wrapped his arm around her. "The city's a mess. Thank God Jen booked all our cars weeks ago . . ." Joseph looked into Chandice's eyes. He could easily read her strained expression; clearly, she had something to say. "Sorry I missed your call," he said cautiously. "How was it?"

"Eh. Did you hear about Susan's memorial?"

"Susan who?" he asked.

"You didn't see Nina's email yesterday?"

"About?"

Chandice gestured for Joseph to follow her into the kitchen, where she pulled a chilled shaker out of the fridge and poured them both a daiquiri.

"So it's gonna be that kind of evening," Joseph said, playfully pulling Chandice toward him, but her expression remained grave.

"One of Daniel's classmate's mothers . . ."

"At Kent?"

She slapped his arm. "We didn't get into Kent yet."

"Oh, right," Joseph said, winking. "Not yet."

"Joseph!"

"That place was really something," Joseph said. "Daniel's life will be so different than ours."

"Maybe *too* different." Chandice had a hard time believing in this bespoke educational environment, where each precious snowflake got all the nurturing and support they needed to become their best self. It sounded . . . suspect, somehow, to her. Was what they were offering even possible?

"Don't say that about our son's school!" Joseph joked, but Chandice just glared at him. "Look, Daniel's a great kid. He deserves this. And *you* nailed the interview today."

"Thanks. That line always goes over so well," she added, recalling the heartened expressions on the headmasters of every private school in Manhattan, all of whom touted their Diversity, Equity, and Inclusion efforts in ways that ranged from well meaning but still uncomfortable to embarrassingly ham-handed. "Can I finish what I was saying?" Chandice said. "One of the Woodmont moms committed suicide this morning."

"No kidding," Joseph said. "How'd she do it?" he asked.

"I'd guess pills," Chandice said. "Right?"

"Probably," Joseph agreed. He reached for his drink and lifted it. "To . . . what was her name?"

"Susan," Chandice said.

Joseph blanched. "Susan Harris?"

"Yeah! Did you know her?"

"She's, um, got a daughter, right?" Joseph downed half his drink. "What was wrong with her?" he said, obviously more concerned now that he had a face to put with the name. Two faces, if you included Claude. Poor thing.

"I guess we'll never know," Chandice said. "But I think basically nothing. I mean—"

"Nothing like what's wrong with you," Joseph finished, reaching out for her hand.

Since her diagnosis, Joseph had been a steady ship in a turbulent sea. Perhaps because his own mother had died of pancreatic cancer, he always seemed to know just what to say. When they were dating, Chandice's sister said Joseph was too good to be true. But then, he turned out to be true.

"When's dinner?" he asked, smiling. "Those beans smell amazing."

That night, Chandice sat up in bed, pillows propped up behind her, a novel in her hands. Her eyes traveled from word to word, then paragraph to paragraph, but at the end of the page, she had absorbed nothing from the text. She turned on the television instead. The news was always bad, but again, the words just washed over her, the light from the TV making jerky, bright designs on their bed.

Joseph came out of the bathroom in his boxers, and even though they had been married twelve years and together far longer than that, she still appreciated how attractive he was. When they couldn't have another child, it was as if he had channeled all that extra time, energy, and money into the gym. He hadn't been in shape like this since they met in college. Maybe not even then.

But Chandice's body was another story. A total betrayal, in fact. And even though she still looked fine enough on the outside, inside she knew she was rotting and felt it keenly on chemo days. Joseph slid into bed next to her and ran his hand up her flank. He snaked his arm around and pulled her close. It was nice to be like this, two spoons, snuggled up. Then his hands started traveling down.

"Joseph, sweetheart, today's not a good day. I just don't . . ."

Between the chemo racing through her heart, destroying all the rapidly reproducing cells, and the steroids pumping synthetic energy into her muscles, she felt like an electric eel. He knew this about chemo days from the last round, but maybe he forgot?

"I just can't keep my hands off of you," Joseph murmured, rolling back onto his pillow. His snoring started three minutes later. Maybe she should have had sex with him, Chandice thought absentmindedly, listening to the sawlike quality of her husband's breathing as she lay wide awake hours later, still feeling the effects of the steroids.

Finally, Chandice got up and padded downstairs to her favorite place in their home. They had renovated half the first floor into the kitchen of her New York dreams. Pots and pans dangled over a beautifully lit island. A huge window onto the garden hung dark over the oversize kitchen sink. The open cabinet shelves displayed the tidy piles of simple white dishware that had been their wedding china. She opened the doors into the large pantry, retrieved a label maker from her desk drawer, and, without thinking too much about it, turned on the latest episode of that stupid wellness podcast *Serenity, Maybe?* Much as she might disdain almost everything about it, something kept her coming back.

The show's opening music played, some sort of panpipe melody, as Chandice arrayed bins of foodstuffs on the butcher-block island, already feeling just a bit lighter. Not that she would ever admit this, but when the host welcomed her audience, it felt like she was speaking directly to Chandice somehow. The timbre of this woman's voice communicated acceptance to Chandice—that her feelings, whatever they were, would inevitably be OK. That she, in turn, would inevitably be OK. Even if the words were explicitly about something else. Sometimes it felt like the content didn't even matter that much.

"Tonight's show is about knowing what we know." Chandice reached for a bag of chia seeds in the back of the cabinet as a grimace crossed her face. Sounded like a stupid topic already. "Now, I can imagine what you all are thinking!" The host laughed. "*Know* what we *know?* Could it get any more basic?"

Chandice had all the plastic containers out on the island, individual plastic bins for each category of food—condiments, baking, nuts and seeds—and she proceeded to pull each hand-labeled jar and package out of each larger container, her hands busy, the episode continuing. She let the host's voice resonate in her eardrums.

"Here's the problem." The cadence of the host's voice slowed way down. "There are things that we know, but we do not wish to know. We wish so hard that they were different, our mind makes the wish true."

Chandice's hands stopped moving. "We wish for all sorts of things with our subconscious mind! We can't face regret. We tell ourselves that people will change in the way we want them to. We reject bad qualities in ourselves or our loved ones."

Yes! Exactly! Chandice thought. Isn't this one of the keys to happiness? Seeing the good instead of the bad? Isn't this, in fact, optimism? As the host went on, Chandice proceeded to examine each package for damage, expiration, proper labeling. She married containers, pouring all-purpose flour into a tall plastic cube, scooping walnuts from one jar into another with her hands.

"So when we are faced with something we wish so fervently were different, what do we do?" Chandice rolled her eyes in her kitchen. She knew a lot about wishing very hard indeed that things were different. But she also had to think good thoughts, come to terms with uncertainty, not let anxiety seize control of her entire life. "When we are faced with something we cannot accept, we *un*know it." Again, Chandice paused and lifted her head to listen. "Stay with me here. We like to believe, for example, that when you divorce someone, they turn into a nonresponsive and emotionally unstable grifter. But the truth is that the root of this behavior was there all along."

Chandice suddenly thought of Susan again. The strange way she caught her staring, would actually feel eyes on her back as she buttoned Daniel's coat and, turning quickly, catch that microexpression flash across her face clear as day: envy. Susan Harris felt envious. Envy means dissatisfaction. Perhaps part of a suicidal impulse. That, even Chandice had noticed.

"And as you look at your own life, know that there are things even now that you are unseeing. Things your mind both knows and wants desperately not to know. Our work as humans is to come to terms with the division between the autobiography we have in our own minds and the reality of how we have acted and felt on this planet. Understand that not only are other people largely projections, but you yourself are as well both projector and projection."

As fresh labels rolled off the device in her hand, Chandice wondered about Susan's husband . . . Michael? What had he *un*known? How much had he projected of Susan versus the real lived experience? Chandice snipped the edges of her fresh labels and affixed them to various jars and bins, and, in this way, with every label and font and appropriately sized container, Chandice felt in control of her life. And it seemed somehow OK that if she, Chandice, could sit here in the middle of the night in her gorgeously restored Harlem townhome and devote this time to meticulously organizing her pantry, then she didn't need to even think about Susan's death, because Chandice was still living. Thus Susan's suicide was not some perverse inversion of every existential belief Chandice held dear. The world could still be a navigable place if only the slivered almonds went into a labeled mason jar of the exact right size.

By the time the sky began to lighten, Chandice had not only cleaned out any aging or undesired groceries and snacks from her shelves, she had reconceived their organization and alphabetized the bins, which she now lifted back onto their shelves. If Chandice participated in any social media, like Susan had, she would take pictures to post them. In her case, the only people she cared about seeing her handiwork were her son and husband, who would most likely not even notice.

But that wasn't the point. The point was to make all her home projects, like baking breads and muffins, cooking stocks and reductions, and pickling vegetables more pleasant. Lately, she had barely had time to do any of these things between the private school tours and interviews. It was a part-time job Chandice could not wait to be done with so she could turn her attention back to her home.

The next day, her hands were covered in chopped peppers, the makings of a goat curry spread out on her kitchen island. She had to get the meat browned and in the slow cooker before pickup so it could get nice and tender, but when her phone rang and the screen said Kent School, she jumped. Parent interviews were not until the following week, so this call was a mystery. Had she forgotten some form? Her finger deposited a tiny rectangle of pepper on the screen of her phone as she hit Speaker.

"Hi, Chandice, it's Glenn," said the voice.

"Goodyear?" she asked, wiping her hands on a dish towel.

"Yes, of course, *ha ha*. From Kent. I'm so sorry, how rude of me. How are you?" Chandice raised an eyebrow at her unseeing phone.

"Fine, thank you. How are you?"

"I'm great! I just wanted to reach out personally and say not just what a pleasure it was to meet you and Joseph but how impressed my staff is with Daniel."

While she knew Glenn was flattering her family, she couldn't stop herself from smiling. "Thank you," she said.

"In particular, he showed acuity in numerical reasoning that was just off the charts. Kent offers a special lab starting in kindergarten to support young mathematicians like Daniel in a peer group of other advanced thinkers."

Chandice thought of her son—his extensive periods of concentration through elaborate Lego projects, his precise negotiation tactics, and his intuitive grasp of fractions ("How about 2¾ chocolates?"). But even as his mother, would she consider his thinking in these areas "off the charts"? She felt again that sense that they were being singled out. Even in a complimentary way, it left her cold.

"OK, sounds good," Chandice said noncommittally, waiting for him to fill in the blank where the reason for his call was supposed to go.

"I just wanted to see if I could answer any questions for you or address any concerns whatsoever before acceptance letters go out."

Chandice took a moment to consider his question. An elite group of privileged people composed Kent, and they, for possibly dubious reasons, wished to expand their school community beyond the bounds of the uppermost echelon of New York City. That was OK with Chandice even if their motivation lacked ethical purity. But what rubbed her wrong was that the institution would simultaneously bill itself as somehow inclusive while actively excluding the vast majority of their applicants who were, as a group, a self-selected collection of the particularly moneyed and educationally motivated.

In other words, it seemed that there was some confusion over what words like *diversity*, *equity*, and *inclusion* even meant. The school was, by definition, exclusive. The question remained only on what basis it was acceptable to exclude the majority of applicants. There would never be equity in terms of the impact of the school's sizable tuition on Kent families, and financial aid just barely alleviated the potential for bankruptcy. When it came to diversity, it was one thing to create rainbow classrooms and another to actively dismantle institutional racism.

Lastly, and most pressingly, she wondered if Glenn was personally calling all potential Kent families or just the ones of color. There was just so much unfairness and hypocrisy built into the model, but Chandice could not argue with the outcomes. Kent kids went all the right places in life. She would not forego this opportunity for Daniel just to prove some larger point. Would she?

She could feel Glenn smiling on the other end of the phone, waiting for her response.

"As I said at our meeting, we are truly impressed and downright comfortable at Kent. I can only hope we have the opportunity to deepen our relationship." As she heard the phrase come out of her mouth, she winced. Who spoke like this? Oh God, that damn wellness podcast again! Even when she thought the host's voice was just washing over her brain, she was being trained to cough up these trite empty phrases. What did it mean to "deepen their relationship" other than for Kent to accept Daniel and educate him until college?

But Glenn was clearly more of an aficionado of wellness podcasts than she knew. "Wonderful, Chandice!" He sounded truly heartened. "I will truly look forward to that."

While the phone was still in her hand, the text came that her car was outside. They were coming earlier and earlier since the transit strike had snarled traffic throughout the city. Annoyed, Chandice surveyed her half-done curry with distaste. In fact, the smell nauseated her. She stuffed the goat meat in the fridge unwrapped, grabbed her bag, and practically ran out her front door and down the steps. Her hands in her lap filled the car with the smell of onions.

But they got there much sooner than they had planned, and instead of sitting in the car, impulsively Chandice ducked inside an Italian lingerie store on the corner by Woodmont. Before today, it had always seemed preposterous. But if not now, when? Because of her silicone breasts, Chandice would actually feel more comfortable than she ever had in some of these ridiculously impractical getups. The salesgirl helped her navigate a few options for "sexy evening with husband," and she left with a very brief slip of silk and lace that cost almost as much as she would normally spend on a new outfit.

For a few moments on the sidewalk, Chandice carried the shopping bag proudly, announcing to the world that, yes, she was a woman who wore sexy nighttime things. A woman to be admired and desired. But she stuffed the telltale tote into her purse before she was within twenty feet of the Woodmont entrance. She didn't need all the other SAHMs seeing that side of her, especially at pickup, where some moms loved to chitchat. This was where Kara had mentioned *Serenity, Maybe?* Mostly, though, there were nannies, so Chandice was surprised to see Amy (and not Ming) step out from under a tree in the Woodmont courtyard, clearly eager to engage her.

Chandice had no idea what Amy did professionally. She wasn't the sort of person to always be on her phone or tied to a desk. Yet she transmitted a steady intensity, whether the topic was the rain date for the class picnic or Chandice's cancer recurrence. Now she stood awkwardly, hands together in front of her pleated silk skirt.

"Chandice," she said at just above a whisper and reached again with her soft, cool hand to lightly touch her arm. "How are you? I've been thinking about you!"

That Amy would make this connection herself and recognize how Susan's death would land on Chandice made her feel so unexpectedly and completely seen that Chandice almost burst into tears on the spot.

The fact was that Susan's suicide was hitting her in a certain kind of way, which was, well, not good.

"I can't imagine how this is making you feel," Amy said.

The strange thing was, neither could Chandice! She *wasn't* angry. What was there to be angry about? It's not as if Chandice could have lived in Susan's body. Like Susan tossed out a perfectly serviceable EpiPen that might have saved her from a fatal allergic reaction. Susan's body was Susan's to decide about, Chandice thought rationally, as the tears started running down her face.

"Oh, no!" Amy said, struggling momentarily to pop open the silly metal contraption on her stiff handbag and reach in for a pressed handkerchief. Chandice hesitated only the briefest of moments before accepting.

"It's just the chemo," Chandice whispered, casting two quick glances behind them to make sure no other moms or caregivers were rounding the corner.

"You must be angry," Amy said. "I would be."

"Why?"

"She threw her life away!" Amy said, a little too loudly, as a nanny came storming their way with an empty stroller, parked it, and waited for the doors to open. "Are you going to the memorial tomorrow?" Amy asked more quietly as Chandice carefully dabbed underneath her eyes, trying not to disrupt her makeup. "Do you want to go together? I can pick you up."

"Oh, that's nice. But I think I'll probably go with my husband."

"I can pick you both up," Amy said, and Chandice felt encouraged by her generosity.

"Hey, did you get any calls from Kent this week?" Chandice asked without thinking too much about it.

"No, did you?" Amy's eyes narrowed. It felt like a dangerous topic. Why had Chandice said anything? Oh God, she forgot that chemo could confuse your thoughts like this.

And although she was an honest person, Chandice found herself saying, "No."

That night, after she put Daniel to bed, Chandice and Joseph sat sipping a red burgundy on the sectional couch in their cozy wood-paneled living room. Joseph talked about his day: he had a big case coming up that was going to require a lot of travel.

"Should I turn it down?" he asked. "Normally I would just pass on this, but it's for kids with cancer."

"Of course, take it! Do it. I don't ever want to hold you back," Chandice said earnestly. Joseph leaned over and gave her a warm kiss on the lips and sat back in his seat, smiling at her.

"How was your day?" he asked.

Chandice told Joseph about Glenn's call. Of course, he saw nothing but good in it. "Sounds like a lock to me, what did I tell you?" he said. "Why don't you seem happy? Kent is the golden ticket." It was true. Chandice's moms' group, which was her font of information for most things relating to Daniel, held Kent in the highest esteem. Not only were they arguably academically the strongest, their institutional commitment to a diverse community seemed the most genuine.

"I *am* happy about that. It's just . . ."

"What?"

"It's . . . about this suicide."

"Susan Harris?" Joseph said. He was so good with names, Chandice thought.

"There's a memorial," Chandice said cautiously.

"And?"

"I'm not sure I want to go," she admitted.

"So don't go."

There was something about the way he said this that flipped her like a switch. It was like he couldn't care less. Even Amy, a woman Chandice hardly knew, had understood that a peer's suicide at this point in her life would be striking, to say the least.

"Why are you acting like that?" Chandice asked.

"Like what?"

"Like you don't care."

"About what?" he said. For the first time in nearly two decades, Chandice felt like they had fallen out of step.

"Never mind. I'm going to go," Chandice said. "Will you come with me?"

"Depends on when it is. I have meetings lined up for this new case. It's gonna be like that for a while. Why don't you check with Jen in the morning?"

Shortly after that, he said he was going to bed.

"OK, I'll meet you there," Chandice said. Joseph turned to look at her, and she gave him a suggestive brow lift. He smiled back at her—so handsome. In the kitchen, Chandice put the last few dishes in the dishwasher and started it. Then she texted Amy: I'd love to go to the memorial with you. Thank you.

It would be much better anyway to be with someone who understood her unique view on the day's tragic subject. Joseph had been such a caring, reliable husband to her over the last few years, it was understandable if he had finally gotten back into work and could not be expected to be as attentive to Chandice's emotional needs. *He has to live his life too!* Chandice thought to herself. He didn't need any part of this Susan tragedy. And Chandice, too, had bigger things to think about: not just beating cancer but giving her husband an evening to remember after turning him down all week.

Chandice retrieved the shopping bag from the hall closet. She quickly slipped out of her clothes and into the lavender-and-black slip that hugged and dipped in all the right places. But although Chandice got to the bedroom only five minutes behind him, Joseph was already snoring.

FIVE

VIC

Vic clung to the metal rail up the cement steps to a Midtown office building as professionals in trench coats flowed past her on either side like she was a rock in their river. She wished it wasn't raining so she could sit down to swap out her sneakers for heels. In fact, Vic fervently wished for many impossible things. First, that she had the money for an Uber. Second, that Susan had not died. And she wished Sean, or even inanely that Scott, her high school boyfriend, could be with her, if only to hold the umbrella she balanced uneasily on her shoulder as she pulled off a damp sock. She felt so alone and exposed, her bare foot splattered by rain before she could cram it into an uncomfortable formal shoe. Without mass transit, she had to walk. Vic stuffed her sneakers into her bag as if they were shameful contraband.

No one would know by the sight of her shoes, she reminded herself, that she hadn't been able to write a word in months. No one could see, in her footwear, how she had liquidated her IRA the previous week to pay the rent. How she had laboriously combed through her bills and eliminated everything she could—cable television, the gym around the corner—and even considered canceling her life insurance policy. She had quietly inquired about teaching jobs, to no response. Soon, she'd have to consider asking her ex for help, which not only made Vic tremble with distaste, but had led to her first-ever real bout of insomnia.

Vic tottered around the corner, already uncomfortable in these seldom-worn shoes. Hordes of grievers mobbed the shining wet steps of the cathedral. Though it had only been four days, news of Susan's death had resounded through every corridor of her life. Clustered tightly together at the top of the steps, the Woodmont parents waited for Vic once more, and she craved the comfort of this sympathetic group. Surely, these moms understood that, for Vic, Susan wasn't just another parent. They were real friends. Weren't they?

The moms looked serious and uncertain, clustered together under umbrellas. As Vic crested the last step, Penelope squeezed her tightly. It was such a comfort, as the rain fell on their faces, to be so immediately enfolded. As they parted, Penelope nodded knowingly at Vic. Would she learn the whole story of Susan's death today?

Bhavna was grim but clearly resigned; she gave Vic's upper arm three quick rubs after their hug. And then Vic was surprised to find herself in Chandice's arms. She smelled like sandalwood and eucalyptus. Vic felt the scratch of Chandice's braids on her ear. Once more, the rain on her face before Amy gave her a sort of distant shoulder squeeze. As she was embraced by these virtual strangers, Vic kept waiting for the focus to sharpen on her reality, as if someone were going to whisper the truth in her ear. But not yet, not yet.

There was just so much that Vic had taken for granted that suddenly seemed completely unknown. She had been dreading Susan's memorial, but it had also become the only opportunity Vic could imagine to gain some insight into this dead friend of hers, who had never once mentioned a single medication or health issue—emotional, physical, or otherwise.

Incredibly, other than Bhavna's naked conjectures, there had indeed been not a shred of further information about Susan's death. Nina's meeting had elucidated nothing. Meanwhile, just down the corridor, Susan's daughter, Claude, had played with Jetta. It seemed impossible that there would be no further guidance on this topic from their well-regarded, extremely expensive institution of early learning other than "We have no information" and "Please don't speak about this."

Vic hung back after the meeting. "I need to say something to Jetta," she said to Nina.

"Yes, I think that's right," Nina said, waving her back to the administrative office as if she had been expecting this. As Nina handed over a few children's books on death, a discordant rendition of "You Are My Sunshine" drifting out of the three-year-old classroom next door, Vic asked, "But Nina, what do I say? When she asks me how Claude's mama died?"

"Just say her body stopped working."

"And what about when she asks me if I'm going to die."

"Say you will, but a long, long, long, long time from now."

Which had made Vic wonder: How does Nina know? Vic had always rejected the easy lies parents told their kids to shorten difficult conversations. In this case, though, she could only imagine what Susan's daughter, Claude, was even at that moment reporting to Jetta, who had always been the sort of child to quietly connect the dots. She would swiftly deduce that if Claude's mom could be present and fine one day only to be dead and gone the next, the same thing could happen to Vic. She wondered how much Claude understood about Susan's demise when all the adults knew so little.

At Jetta's bedtime, Vic dutifully opened one of the children's books Nina had given her, the fictionalized true story of two Central Park Zoo polar bears who were best friends. One of them got sick, and they both knew she was going to die. The bears lay together on the rocks outside her cave and saw a plane crossing the sky. The healthy bear remarked to his sick pal, "Look at that plane! We don't know where it's going, just like we don't know where you're going!" But Vic couldn't get the last few words out because she was crying so hard.

This alarmed Jetta more than anything else that had happened. She gawked at her mother, crying for the first time in front of her. "Mama, what's wrong?" she asked, her eyes wide like an anime character. Jetta, with her darling bangs and her wide-open enthusiasm for life, who before now had enjoyed a blissfully tragedy-free existence.

"You heard about Claude's mama?" Vic asked.

"Yes. She died." Even Jetta, her little five-year-old, seemed to somehow have wrapped her mind around this reality in a way that Vic could not. Vic lifted her chin up and down, tears practically spurting out of her eyes. Jetta wrapped her soft arms around her mother and said soothingly, "If she was a real friend, you will always have her in your heart." Vic had quieted her crying to steady tears and fallen asleep in Jetta's arms, exhausted.

There was a crush of people inside the church. There was no way the ceremony would start even close to on time. Hundreds and hundreds of people inched past two arrays of framed photographs. Susan at her college graduation, gorgeous, tan, proud. Susan and her handsome husband, holding hands on the beach in their wedding garb, gazing adoringly into one another's eyes. Susan, with newborn Claude on her chest, serene, maternal. Susan and her two kids at Claude's first day at Woodmont. Susan proudly proffering a supersize crudités platter. The family of four on vacation in Nantucket and Miami. Christmas in the country, a fire roaring in a stone hearth.

Could a healthy and beautiful wife and mother with such a gorgeous life really have killed herself? Suddenly, Bhavna's suppositions seemed silly. *What did she know anyway?* Vic eyed her, two people ahead, holding her husband's elbow. Bhavna wasn't even looking at the pictures. Her eyes scanned the faces in the enormous room ahead. For whom? A networking opportunity? Bhavna's husband at least seemed moved by what was happening; his shadowed and stunned eyes stared blankly at the pictures in front of him.

Amy and Chandice hung together, grim and quiet. Where was Chandice's handsome husband? Penelope and Kara held seats for the rest of the Woodmont crowd, as it appeared possible that not everyone would find a spot.

Vic had never seen a cathedral this full: colleagues, classmates, school friends, camp friends, family. Maybe a thousand people, slowly filling up the pews, and all around, Vic looked for clues. Behind the altar, on an elevated platform, an enormous coffin loomed but offered no further information. To Vic it looked unreal, like a prop meant to indicate what sort of ceremony they were here for rather than an actual vessel within which lay the remains of Susan Harris.

The Harris family sat in the first row. Michael, Susan's husband, mostly kept his back to the room, but when he did turn his head, Vic found herself thinking that he looked less terrible than she had expected. But then, what had she been looking for? Sackcloth and wrenching public sobbing? There he was, alive, a little pink in his pale cheeks, jacket and tie in place, light eyes on the matter before them. Susan's kids had to be at home with their longtime nanny. Her parents looked solemn but relaxed, sitting in quiet contemplation of their daughter's coffin. They were both cartoonishly stout and excessively preppy. Pearl earrings next to a navy blazer.

A man in his midthirties stood next to them, facing the room. He thrust his hands into the pockets of dark suit pants and almost immediately pulled them out again. The tan suggested to Vic that this was Susan's brother from somewhere in the South. He wore his clothes uncomfortably, accustomed to the breathable fabrics worn in warmer climates. His pinky ring flashed as he scratched his ear. He looked unappealing, but it was hard to believe this was the wayward brother whom Susan had run down to Vic a few times.

Because there he stood, awkwardly avoiding his parents, no evidence of his alcoholism or mail-order Russian wife. He was alive and in the flesh, while Susan herself was in the coffin. Whatever she had said about him and his self-destruction was, in retrospect, projection, as she herself, the psychologist, might have pointed out.

Then again, maybe Susan had a stroke? Vic thought. *Maybe Bhavna was wrong?*

The minister approached the pulpit and began the service, but her words offered no insights. "Susan Harris will be loved . . . Susan will be missed . . . Susan will be alive in our hearts . . ." Vic suspected Susan had never met this person. Perhaps she had never even been to this church before. Still, there was a comfort in the vague quality of this opening. It made Vic think there was hope for normalcy here—that somehow if the minister delivered the usual funeral sermon, perhaps Susan had experienced a natural death.

Vic studied the program. The first speaker was described as "a college friend." Which friend was this? The one from California with the bad marriage? The single doctor from Philadelphia? There were two more after her: another friend and a cousin. It seemed impossible that there could be a whole slate of contributors and no one would hint as to the cause of her death.

The poor woman chosen to commence the personal tributes was compressed with grief and duty, her shoulders hunched and her gait heavy on the steps. Vic felt for her, here to do the impossible. Her pale face hung and quivered like thin drapes in a breeze. She placed her speech in front of her. Vic hungered for any hint that might help her understand.

She leaned in, her lips millimeters from the metal crosshairs of the microphone. She wanted her audience to hear every one of her first words. Vic felt her body instinctively drawn forward, like a magnet. "Susan. Was. Bold," the friend said, then repeated the last word. *"Bold."*

What the fuck did that mean? Vic wondered. The speaker left those three words hanging like a smoke signal before continuing.

"When I met Susan, in the bathroom of our freshman dorm, she was coloring her gorgeous light hair cobalt blue in the bathroom sink. I couldn't believe it. I could not understand why she would change something so perfect. She said it was just time to try something new, something she would never have gotten away with at home."

Clues, clues, clues, Vic mused. Where were the clues? Kara started crying. Amy passed her a handkerchief. Chandice remained stone faced, and Penelope, too, looked calm now, here in her official capacity. The friend went on to paint a loving but shallow picture of the woman Vic recognized: irreverent, reliable, fun.

The next speaker—described as a "lifelong friend"—was a raven-haired man who brought no notes with him to the podium. Susan had never mentioned anyone who fit this description. His hooded eyes took in the crowded cathedral. He nodded, as if to himself, and said, emphatically, "Susan would have loved this."

Vic quietly gasped, and Amy jerked her head at her. It sounded a discordant note in Vic's mind. Susan would have loved her own funeral? Susan was a popularity seeker? It didn't make sense. Most of what he went on to say didn't connect to Vic's memories of Susan either. He described how they lived first across the street from each other as children and ultimately together as adults in New Orleans. Susan lived in New Orleans? And had never mentioned it? Nothing was adding up.

"When it came time for me to get married, there was no one else who I wanted to sanctify my union other than Susan. She studied up on different marital customs, she interviewed our parents about us, and she flew down to talk to me about it. She took the job so seriously. Told me she was losing sleep and was all worked up about it. Then when the time came last year, the truth is that what mattered most to me—to Steven and me—was how moved she was. How thrilled she was to see us together." Last year? Vic had known Susan "last year," when she was supposedly studying up for this seminal event. Had Vic forgotten? Rather than clues to piece together, Vic felt like the truth was disassembling itself piece by piece. "As with any friendship, there were dark moments over the decades: late-night visits, midnight calls, tears and doubts and pain. But that's life! That's what we would say to each other after each bad episode: That's life! We are here! Oh, Susan, I wish you were here!" He burst into sobs and left the podium weeping into his cuff.

Vic started turning over the phrase "each bad episode" in her mind like a pebble. It seemed irrefutable, yet still, could it have been drugs? A chronic illness? Vic, a creative writer who made up stories for a living, had been in full-time narrative mode trying to come up with some alternate explanation for Susan's death, but she was reaching the bottom of the barrel in terms of new ideas, which meant the end of denial and the start of . . . acceptance? Anger?

Vic almost didn't want to hear from the cousin, a youthful redhead with light eyes that anxiously pierced the first row. Her dress, polyester navy with cap sleeves, said she did not come from an urban center. She pulled out a crumpled piece of legal paper with some notes.

"Growing up, we always knew that Susan was going to do something extraordinary. She got the idea of being a psychologist from Lucy in *Peanuts*, and she actually set up a booth at our grandma's house one summer and made me pay to talk to her about the neighbor I had a crush on." A ripple of laughter in the crowd broke the tension for one blessed second. Vic prayed for her to continue on like this, just happy memories.

"Susan always had plans. Not just plans, but plans that came to fruition. To beautiful fruition. Susan had the life we kept our eyes on, talked about, sent pictures to one another of. Susan's big-city life . . ." She was drifting into tears now. Everyone in the room seemed to stop breathing. Her tone was incredulous and a little angry. The sound of her own tears hitting the podium, amplified by the microphone, jarred her back into focus. She cleared her throat. "Susan did it. She got the life she wanted. A beautiful life."

The service was over. Had it been five minutes? Five hours? While it seemed, on the one hand, quite clear Susan had killed herself, everything else around that fact had become more confused. Everyone and everything deflated. Even the room was smaller as they waited to file out, and back, to their loved ones and lives. They would all run home to their children and embrace them longer, closer. It felt newly shocking that Susan would choose not to.

The reality settled onto Vic like a weighted mantle. She kept her head down and drifted outside with the Woodmont crowd, past the pictures, which now seemed like suspicious, staged interludes between something ugly. Bhavna skirted the tables, passing down an empty pew with her husband in tow as they made their way toward Susan's husband, Michael. Vic wondered if she, too, should go give her condolences—it was so confusing!—when she saw Bhavna throw her arms around Michael, who awkwardly put his hands on either side of her very upper back, almost moving her away. *Bhavna could be so pushy!* Vic thought. She yapped at him for a second, and he nodded before continuing down the aisle.

As Vic inched toward the door, she saw Susan's mother only a few feet away in the midst of a small crowd, like a celebrity. She turned to greet someone—a man about Susan's age the size of a linebacker. For a moment, Susan's mother's flushed face shone as if in a spotlight. She smiled up at him, no trace of melancholy, just happy to see this man and eager to make him comfortable in her presence. She reached for him as he bent for a hug. Over his shoulder, Vic looked closely at Susan's mother's smiling face for evidence of tears, saw none, and shivered.

This wasn't like one of Vic's novels, where all the pieces fit neatly together. Her creative mind could not keep spinning out explanations for what her eyes and ears were observing. She stumbled out of the church without any new insight into how Susan Harris's heart stopped beating four days prior, just the eerie emotional confirmation of Bhavna's hypothesis. All the dads went to work, and all the moms agreed to find the nearest bar that was open at 11:00 a.m. on a weekday.

The memorial achieved the opposite of its intended purpose. Rather than providing a sense of closure, the service had instilled in everyone an even deeper unease. The imbalance between what they all seemed to now understand—Susan Harris had ended her own life—coupled with the void surrounding her actual cause of death, morbid as that may sound, left them all shocked afresh. Even Bhavna wore a new dazed expression as they silently focused on finding a nearby hotel. It was an unusual moment when this discordant group was, for once, all in harmony. It was the sort of thing one couldn't put a finger on—why was Susan's death so newly unsettling?—but they all felt jarred.

The bartender, in a white shirt and black vest, drying a cognac glass with a dish towel, did not look as surprised as Vic expected he might when their solemn mommy group descended on him midmorning.

"What'll it be?" he said congenially. "Marys or mimosas?"

There was a beat of hesitation. This was so outside normal official mommy behavior, where one might look askance at someone for hitting the hard liquor before lunch.

"Marys," Penelope said. "It's not a celebration."

He made up a pitcher while the moms, for the most part, stared at the middle distance. Conversations started in fits. "It was weird, right?" Vic suddenly ejected. "Amirite that it was kind of strange?" Lots of nodding.

"Those speeches," Bhavna said. More nodding.

"I just don't know how we're supposed to feel now," Kara remarked, and while later Vic might dissect this sort of statement, in the moment, it seemed exactly right.

"Right," Chandice said. "Of course, it's a tragedy, and we're all sad. But, that service was—"

"Definitely weird," Amy said, and everyone's heads swiveled to look at her, speaking up. She stirred her Bloody Mary. "So American," she said, and everyone looked to Bhavna to respond.

"So creepy, really. Were her parents off, or was it just me?" Bhavna asked.

"She wasn't that close with her parents, right?" Vic volunteered, looking to Penelope for confirmation.

"No," Penelope confirmed.

"But they seemed . . . ," Vic prodded. The group hung on their words.

"Fine," Penelope said, in between sips on her cocktail straw. "That was actually the weirdest part to me was that they seemed fine."

They broke up into small groups, moving organically in and out of the same conversations. It didn't hurt that they were all downing Bloody Marys like Gatorade after a soccer game. Vic saw Amy slip the bartender a one-hundred-dollar bill and lean over to explain the loose facts of their gathering. After that, he refilled their glasses without being asked. It started to feel like Vic's mouth was running itself while her mind wandered in and out of the words coming out of Kara's face; she distantly remembered they were talking about the future.

"We were thinking of sending Oscar to camp, but the bus . . ." Ah yes, the bus. This represented some of the most fruitful writing time for Vic, waving as Jetta pulled away for a day of fun outside with her friends. The thought of writing—and how she used to type away in a rush to get all her ideas out—made Vic's stomach lurch, and she pushed the thought away. Susan's death had put work even further from Vic's mind, and she had started contemplating giving her editor a few chapters from a book she had begun years ago and scrapped. But she couldn't even bring herself to read the pages yet.

"I love the bus," Vic's mouth said inanely, but it was enough of a prompt for Kara to continue talking. This was by far the longest they had ever spent in conversation, and Vic hoped they would never surpass it. Her eyes wandered over to a corner where Amy and Penelope stood together, intent on conversation. This was an unlikely pairing. Vic wasn't sure she had ever seen the two of them speak before. She realized that Kara had stopped talking and was looking at her for a response. Vic just nodded vigorously.

"That's what I thought," Kara said, nodding knowingly. Vic would never know what she had emphatically confirmed and soon drifted away and forgot about it entirely. All that was really on Vic's mind was Susan and, moreover, Claude. Still, incomprehensible.

"I can't believe you knew right away," Vic said to Bhavna, midway through the conversation in her mind.

"It's all about presentation, not content," Bhavna replied. This gave Vic the chills. Surely, it was somewhat about the content? She felt suddenly like Bhavna had dropped one mask only to reveal another mask, and behind that there might only be another mask. And maybe it wasn't just Bhavna. Vic put her drink on the bar and asked for water. Bhavna joined Penelope in consoling Kara, who wept again. Something was wrong with her, Vic thought; it's not like she and Susan were that close. Kara suddenly seemed very annoying.

"Does anyone ever call you Penny?" Bhavna asked Penelope over Kara's bowed head. They each had a hand on the stricken woman's back.

"No," she deadpanned, which made Vic chuckle.

Feeling confident, Vic spun around in her bar stool and swooped in on Chandice and Amy. Chandice kindly reached out for Vic to put a steadying hand on her shoulder. She was so serene and responsible, Vic thought, she practically glowed. "How are you doing?" Chandice asked, sounding as if she wasn't just asking about her emotional state but also, perhaps, her physical one. Vic willed herself to sober up a little.

"'Susan was bold.' What did that mean?" Vic found herself asking them.

"Some people think suicide is a brave choice," Chandice said, clearly distancing herself from that notion.

"What do you think?" Vic asked.

"I think it's selfish," Amy interjected sharply. "There are people fighting for their lives." Before Vic could respond to this surprisingly charged statement from Amy, Chandice smoothed it over by saying, "I couldn't agree more." Did Vic imagine her giving Amy a bit of a glare?

Amy insisted, "There is no honor in suicide."

Vic peeled off to find the bathroom, a long walk through the hotel lobby. What a strange comfort it was to be with these other women. She had never really much cared for the company of other mothers before: it was too constricting having to behave responsibly—keep everything PG and appropriate and nice. But Susan's death made it possible for them to transcend all that.

As she sat on the toilet, Vic fiddled with her phone and navigated to IG for a fix. Lili in the garden (swipe), Lili rearranging her fridge (swipe), Lili and her perfectly clean fridge (swipe, yawn!), and then, there he was, grinning, at the kitchen island, a spread of appetizers before him. Scott. Vic zoomed in close; she could see Lili in her floral maxi dress reflected in his glass. Tiny crinkles were starting around his eyes from his smile, which seemed, to her, to be just a touch fake. Just a smidge inauthentic. She gave it the fire emoji anyway. Her phone clattered to the marble floor next to the toilet as she tried to stuff it in her pocket.

There was definitely evidence of alcohol in Vic's appearance and movements. Her makeup-free face was lax with booze. She had to concentrate to walk properly in her shoes: leather pumps with three-inch stacked heels. She should probably switch back to her sneakers. Vic splashed water on her face and pressed flyaways to her head, tightening up the clip in her loose, messy chignon. This would do.

Penelope waited just outside the restroom door. Vic hadn't gotten a good look at her before, but her navy sleeveless crepe dress with a shiny slim belt fit her perfectly. Women like this, always so physically spot-on, impressed Vic in the way she was moved by Olympic athletes. It was nothing she aspired to, but good for Penelope. Vic was about to compliment her when she said, "Vic, can we talk for a sec?"

Usually, Vic would have immediately begun to hypothesize the reason for this meeting, but her neurons had trouble sputtering to life. Perhaps Penelope wanted to organize some sort of fund in Susan's memory? Figure out how to help the family? They found a cozy perch in the back corner of the hotel lobby, knee to knee on a plush plum banquette. Up close, Penelope really was so put together: perfect no-makeup makeup (which does generally look better than actually not wearing makeup), her chin-length hair undulating in all the right ways, just the right amount of shine. Vic wondered if Penelope was as drunk as she was. It certainly did not appear so.

"I think you should know what happened," Penelope said, and for a moment, Vic thought she meant back at the bar while she was in the bathroom. She must have looked pretty blank because Penelope added, "With Susan. Vic, I want to tell you what happened to Susan."

Everything around them—the flowery carpet beneath their shoes, the dramatic floral bouquet in a recessed nook across from them, the small scar on Penelope's cheek by her left ear—everything finally ratcheted into focus. Vic realized that as the head of the Parents' Association at Woodmont, Penelope had known the full story all along. It was like in a movie when you realize the answer has been in front of your face the whole time! Gratitude rushed through Vic. She would finally have all the pieces to the puzzle. "But you have to decide if you want to know," Penelope added.

"Why wouldn't I want to know?" Vic asked automatically.

"It's . . . traumatic."

The choice momentarily interested Vic. Could she decide to stay ignorant? After wanting the knowledge so badly? Was the truth in fact worse than she had envisioned? Fueled by a bottomless Bloody Mary, Vic philosophically mused to herself that ignorance was always bliss. Penelope was offering her the chance to save herself. But that was never a real option. Vic had to know the whole truth.

"Pills?" Vic heard herself say.

"No . . ."

"Wrists?" Vic said. She couldn't seem to stop herself from guessing.

"No."

"Murder?"

"Vic, no. Susan jumped from the top of her building."

An imaginary old-time film projector sputtered to life in Vic's mind, the machine-gun shutter hammering away. Susan's building had to have thirty, maybe forty, stories. There Vic stood at the bottom, craning her neck all the way up, up, up. Acidic nightshade, pulp and seeds, gurgled in the back of Vic's throat.

The film kept rolling, like the Kent video; only this time, they zoomed up to the roof, to where Susan stood. The air was whipping her gorgeous hair, so much wind at that height. There were, of course, safety mechanisms: metal fencing meant to prevent just this sort of thing. Susan scaled and outwitted these devices, which had taken time, and all the while she held to herself the decisiveness of knowing, from that height, that there would be no resuscitation. This was no cry for help. She committed completely to her decision to say a final farewell to her children and everything else she held dear and travel the eight or nine seconds past the point of no return to the destruction of her own body.

Vic ran back to the bathroom to vomit convulsively, her phone slipping out of her pocket and into the toilet midhurl.

SIX

AMY

The world-famous architect had given Amy exactly what she requested: a clean, sensible design to suit an enormous space within which she could quietly conduct global financial business while raising a future Yale graduate. The office took up one end of the great room, marked by wood-and-copper library ladders and two enormous desks whose screens sank into them when not in use. A circular table ten feet in diameter made from salvaged teak served as a place for board meetings, a buffet for events, and a workspace for Pearl's science experiments. The clean slate mantle dominated the pristine stiff sectional in the living room. At the bar made of stone, hand-carved wooden stools sat halfway under the ledge, all tilted at exactly forty-five degrees. Chef had to keep the open kitchen as neat as the rest of the living room because it was all one piece—from office to stove top, one city block of uninterrupted lines. And every day it looked exactly as it had on the morning of the *Architectural Digest* shoot, save the rotating seasonal floral arrangements throughout.

Amy loved the feeling of open space around herself while she worked. It meant that she rarely felt the need to leave her apartment, which was where she conducted business with her longtime assistant, Ming. They could sit at their desks, which faced each other at an off-center angle, quietly working for hours on end. Rather than inter-rupt one another, they each kept a list of things to discuss at lunch, generally sushi or salad but occasionally ramen or stew if Pearl was home, served by Chef at the bar. In the afternoon, Ming would whisk Amy's favorite green tea. But otherwise, it was quiet when Pearl was out of the house. So Amy's phone, which sounded like a bomb exploding, echoed through the entire apartment. This was the ringtone Ming had set for Amy's father.

"Uh-oh," Ming said as Amy's expression darkened. The two of them always spoke Mandarin in private.

Amy held her phone up to show her: You were late??? is all it said in Mandarin, from BABA.

"I can't believe it took this long," Ming said. Had the meeting been with a closer partner to her father's business, he would have known that very afternoon. As it happened, word had to travel through rarefied public and private East Asian multinational channels before getting to him a week later. Amy wondered who had finally told her father, the austere and much-respected chief of the Taiwanese branch of the third largest bank in China. No one relished bringing him bad news, which meant information changed hands and was simplified and distanced many times before it reached him. He was more and more isolated in his Taipei office. Amy would worry about him if he wasn't one of the most powerful men in Taiwan.

And now, this. She stared at his text. Her father had warned her that this particular contact was not so picky about the provenance of his funding, but he did have a screw loose about time. A purist. Which was not a problem since Amy was not a timely person; she was an early person. Even so, Ming insisted they leave twenty minutes before they usually would, giving them over half an hour of extra time.

Amy had a long rope at her job running a small private equity fund because of her skill at placing her father's and his friends' money. In her vintage year, she lucked into a Series C round with a Yale friend right before they were acquired. They went public the next year, and she started kicking out healthy distributions, which had been her hallmark and her protection.

Because even as she made her clients more money than most other fund managers, she knew it would never be enough to prevent people from trying to unseat her, a woman. Worse, a single mother whose child was of unknown genetic origin. On her business trips, at client dinners, over elaborate feasts in the private rooms of exclusive clubs in Taipei's gated enclaves, these men would laugh, their faces red, their bellies full of exotic creatures. She had made these men millions and millions of dollars, and they happily toasted Amy to her face.

At one such dinner, Ming had returned to the banquet room to tip the staff while everyone else waited for their cars. There, she found Amy's father with two of his friends, each of whom clutched one of Amy's father's hands.

"What does she need such a big job for?" one of his friends said. He had been receiving a 19 percent average return over the previous four years investing with Amy, but he had more pressing concerns.

"His son is graduating from Harvard!" the other one said. "He needs an income!"

Ming had held her breath, waiting for what Amy's father would say. She knew all too well what his approval meant to her. To grant love in private was hard enough for him. To back his daughter to two crusty business associates might be a bridge too far.

Amy's father laughed. "What? She doesn't make you enough money? You want twenty percent next year! Ha!" he clapped one on the back and strode toward the door. Ming shrank into the bathroom alcove. As he passed, she heard him say, "Assholes," under his breath.

Finding investments in the States that paid solid, reliable returns while also remaining a safe enough place to park, say, a few billion dollars was easy for Amy, as long as the economy was good, introductions kept flowing, and financial growth was a given. After all, she was the one with the money and the potent Andover and Yale networks. But the better the target investment, the pickier the management team could be about their investor. So this meeting had mattered.

Worse, one deal had already fallen through, after Amy had made the capital call. This meant she had her clients' cash on hand, earning a crappy 5 percent. She only had five days until monthly statements went out and the phones started ringing.

And there she was, suddenly glued in place on Second Avenue. "Does this have to do with the transit strike?" Amy asked the driver in English.

"No, that's not till tonight," he said. "Looks like there was some sort of bad accident."

Amy peered through the window but could see nothing but cars. "The traffic in New York is getting almost as bad as Shanghai," Amy said to Ming in Mandarin as she poked uselessly at her iPhone, searching for an alternate route. Ambulances and fire trucks blocked the street ahead in a big, disorganized clump. Their car was stuck in the middle lane, stranded in a sea of vehicles, literally nothing to be done about it for twenty-seven agonizing minutes.

Amy and Ming arrived only ten minutes late for the meeting, but in the end he said he'd have to think about it. On the maddeningly smooth ride back to Central Park South, Amy received his email declining without even making a counteroffer, which was unusual. Amy's deal terms were better than industry standard.

Amy now understood it had been Susan Harris and whatever mess she left behind that had caused the delay. Of course, it had taken a while to connect the dots. It wasn't until that afternoon, with Nina's email, that Amy would learn of Susan's death and Ming would confirm her address on the Woodmont class list. Everyone knew Susan because of all that food nonsense. Amy could never understand why she would get so worked up over five meals per week, the maximum their preschool was responsible for. It accounted for slightly less than a quarter of the kids' overall food intake—simply not worth the cost in social capital with the school bureaucracy.

But the fact that Susan was irrational wasn't the real reason Amy disliked her. Just before winter break, Susan, as class parent, had sent an email to all the moms looking for chaperones for the January field trip to the Metropolitan Museum. Only Amy never received it because she wasn't included. The only reason she knew about the email was because of Chandice, who asked if she was going.

When Amy confronted Susan about being left off the email, just before pickup in the courtyard outside school, Amy thought she looked jittery and evasive. Her hair was unwashed, maybe even unbrushed, and held up in an excessively messy bun. The neck of Susan's T-shirt gaped dramatically; the exposed swath of her chest was pinkened by the winter chill.

"I just thought," Susan said, practically stammering. "I don't know. You're so . . . busy?" she finished. Had Amy been included on the initial outreach looking for parents to attend the field trip, she would not have given a single thought to attending. But the fact that she would be excluded from the ranks of mothers out of hand rubbed Amy the wrong way.

"I'd like to attend."

"But there's no . . ." Susan thought about it. "Of course. Take my spot."

"Thank you," Amy said.

But what had at first appeared malicious—somehow motivated by negative judgment of Amy as a single parent, perhaps—now seemed much less sinister.

That Susan had apparently ended her own life confirmed Amy's lack of interest in her and her silly friend Vic. Especially given what Chandice was going through, Susan throwing her life away disgusted Amy. There was something so dishonorable about suicide, with its ripples of unintended consequences. Around the time Amy's mother died, a neighbor's mother killed herself. As a child, Amy could not fathom a woman choosing for her own family what had quite traumatically happened to Amy's. As an adult, she understood even less how a parent could do such a thing to their loved ones.

Amy and Ming had gone into high gear after blowing that meeting, shaking the trees on three continents, but it was one of those times when there was more cash than premium investment opportunities. They had some ideas but nothing solid. And the investor statement was going out in forty-eight hours.

Amy called her father without even checking the time difference: if he was texting, he was up. But he didn't answer. Even now that she was thirty-seven, he could make her feel like a little girl being sent to her room. Amy left him an all-business message reporting that she had alternatives and not to worry.

For years, Amy had been eager to expand her portfolio outside technology and finance, the two industries her father knew best, and bring him something new. An idea all her own that he could be proud of. But so far, they hadn't come up with anything that was both the right size deal and at the right time.

Now her shoulders slumped as she stared at the home screen on her phone: a picture of her father and Pearl together in Capri the previous summer. He had taken a whole three days off to join them at the Quisisana, an incredible gift of his time. There could be no surer sign of his approval. Of course, her earnings then were at their peak. Neither Amy nor Pearl had seen him face to face since her fund's trajectory started to flatten, an inevitability for any business. Amy hated that her father could still so easily make her hate herself.

After reading his simple but scathing text, Ming said, "It'll be OK. We'll figure it out." They locked eyes. Amy gave Ming the slightest nod: *thank you.* "You're all set for today?"

"I think so," Amy said.

"I know this is premature, but take a look."

Ming placed a slender portfolio in front of Amy on her desk: KENT PROSPECTS it said on the cover. Amy turned the pages. On each one, a headshot of each parent, followed by a bulleted list of information: name, age, educational background, positions, net worth, relevant industries, etc.

"This is really very nicely put together," Amy said, sparing a glance at Ming.

"Thank you." Ming flipped to Penelope's page. Her picture was taken at a formal event: she wore a black ball gown and long black gloves, a simple strand of diamonds around her neck and at each ear. She stood at the top of a red carpeted stairway. She looked perfectly boring.

Amy's eye drifted down the page. Penelope sat on the board of her family office. Ming pointed one clear-polished fingernail at Penelope's net worth, an impressive sum even to Amy. And then, her relevant industries, which were many. Ming's delicate finger moved down: finance, real estate, pharmaceuticals, ultimately landing on infrastructure. Specifically, rail-travel manufacturing.

"I got you a banquette at Bar Italia."

"OK," Amy said, distracted. "You don't think it's a waste of time?"

Ming knew very well that Amy loathed cultivating relationships among the American mothers at her daughter's school and had basically not bothered at Woodmont because Pearl would only be there for three years. Amy found Americans intrusive. They always wanted to ask a million personal questions straightaway and fill the air with talking. It was as if no one in the States had ever heard the phrase "comfortable silence."

Kent, of course, would be a different kettle of fish, as evidenced by Ming's prospect list. This was a critical channel for Amy to cultivate and grow her contacts, and a key reason for her and no one else to be running the business in North America. Beyond this, Amy cared only about Pearl's eventual college placement. Kent was like a cannon Amy was pointing at Yale, which made Pearl the cannonball.

That Kent would provide the best possible education was of tertiary importance, apparently to everyone—including that goon who asked about the helicopters. He obviously didn't want to get in. Even Amy had her qualms. She hoped, for example, they were putting as much work into developing and implementing their academic curriculum as they were into producing incredibly fancy and expensive looking promotional videos. Is that what they were doing with the contributions she'd been shelling out since Pearl was a fetus? she wondered. Contracting drone photography? And what was all that about an anti-racism curriculum? Was that really necessary for nonwhite students?

The main driver of Amy's frustrations with Kent, of course, had only one focus: after hundreds of thousands of dollars in gifts to the school's endowment in Pearl's name, they had not been granted a single assurance about her future there. Amy had been told many times by the city's top kindergarten-placement consultant that there simply were no guarantees. They hoped that being an immigrant and "person of color" (a phrase Amy detested) would help Pearl stand out in a competition where being different was an advantage. But after that tour she wasn't so sure. To her carefully tuned ear and eye, there seemed to be many nonwhite immigrants in the room. The consultant said Pearl had a 65 percent chance of getting into Kent without the contributions. The money probably nudged it closer to 90 percent. Still Amy found her sleep disturbed by nightmares full of rejection letters.

Lately, Amy wondered if bringing Pearl to the States had been such a great idea after all. An American education was, anyone could tell you, the most coveted prize in all East Asia, and the earlier you started, the more likely you were to end up with one of those invaluable universal perpetual passports: an Ivy League diploma. Amy herself knew the freedom such a credential could buy.

But still, these people were nuts.

Could Susan Harris's service have been more awkward? Amy pondered it all week. A public gathering for a shameful event like a suicide made her cringe. Because then you have no choice but to resort to strange statements like "Susan was bold." Why not just say Susan jumped off the top of a building? Why not say that Susan was the sort of fundamentally irresponsible person who would handicap her own children rather than figure out how to live? No one had it easy, Susan.

Except for maybe Susan's friend Vic, who was equally odious in Amy's mind. Their conversations were always so inane, it made Amy question the quality and rigor of the Kent curriculum. Vic always asked what Amy "did," and when Amy told her "private equity," it was as if she could not even sustain interest through all five syllables. Vic always wanted to connect as two single moms, but Amy identified as a working mother. Her relationship status was irrelevant.

Chandice was the only one Amy genuinely liked, and it helped that she was not in a position to be useful to Amy's business. Between them, it could stay 100 percent personal.

The only reason Amy had gone to the bar after the memorial was to finally get her chance to speak to that Penelope woman. According to Ming's numbers, Penelope's family business would require a few billion for capital improvement if they wanted in on the pending Railroad Revivification Act in Congress. The very expensive political consultant assured them it was a solid investment. To Amy it signified something more—an idea all her own (well, Ming's, too, of course) to present to her father.

While the Woodmont moms downed Bloody Marys, Amy slipped the bartender one hundred dollars to refill only her glass with tomato juice, lemon, and ice. She had been using this tactic since college, and it always worked to her advantage as first friends, then dates, and finally business associates would let slip the disguises they wore. Amy remained cool as a cucumber, hamming it up at times, through their teary confessions and secrets revealed.

She hadn't felt the need to correct everyone when they assumed Susan overdosed. Had, in fact, instinctively taken the opportunity to misdirect everyone, suggesting it was a "cry for help" when, of course, she knew personally it was no such thing. Then Vic jumped in with the asinine suggestion that an otherwise healthy woman would attempt to kill herself rather than move to Connecticut.

Amy let a few rounds sink in, and, as Penelope finished up a text in the corner, she sidled over. "We've never really had a chance to talk before," Amy said, smiling congenially. She sipped her drink and allowed Penelope to assess her: the custom shirt from her tailor in Hong Kong, the limited-edition black snakeskin Hermès Kelly with the platinum hardware, her black Chanel ceramic watch with the diamond face, the neat waves of her bob blown out during an early-morning stylist visit arranged by Ming.

"We haven't!" Penelope finally said, an approximation of warmth sneaking into her voice.

"How about that Kent tour?" Amy said.

Penelope's small smile was inscrutable. Did she know something about Kent or her child's application status? American corruption was so opaque. In Taiwan, the same rules for graft applied to everyone; if you had the money, you could bribe the right person. But in the States, there were rules and then there were people for whom the rules didn't apply. Was Penelope one of those people? Perhaps Kent had already let her know, on the side, unofficially, that her son had been accepted.

Amy suppressed any fruitless anger that these thoughts might lead to. On the contrary, if she could work the system, good for her. "Pretty impressive," Penelope finally said, blandly. "My brother went there," she added, sighing. "Loved it."

"Are you applying anywhere else?" Amy asked.

"Yeardly. You?" Penelope's kid definitely had a seat at Kent, Amy concluded from the lassitude with which she delivered these responses, like it was all so moot.

"Same," Amy said, without mentioning that in fact she had the private school consultant take care of Pearl's application to the top dozen private schools in Manhattan. Her eyes wandered to Kara, talking rapid fire at Vic, who was obviously too drunk to be absorbing anything.

"Looks like we just might be together forever," Penelope said neutrally.

"With luck," Amy concurred, and Penelope clinked her glass.

"What do you make of this?" Penelope swirled her drink in the air to indicate the general vicinity.

"Susan, you mean?" Amy asked, not at all clear what Penelope meant by "this," but Amy decided to just let Penelope go on.

Penelope nodded, as if Amy had said something insightful. Finally, she said, "She wasn't well. I knew that. I just . . . had no idea how unwell."

"I'm sorry, this must be so difficult for you. I hardly knew Susan."

"She thought you had the best style."

"I'm sorry?"

"She just obsessed about that bag," Penelope nodded at the Kelly as if it were another person. She was definitely not sober, but none of them were. Except Amy, of course.

"Let me take you to lunch!" Amy had offered, sensing that this was not the time for any conversation Penelope might hope to remember.

Ming had only had a few days between then and now for research, concluding, "There's no way to really know how much power Penelope has in her family business. There are only three siblings who sit on the board with their mother." As far as Amy could tell, Penelope had a stranglehold on all sorts of parental posts at Woodmont, steadily rising from class mom to journal chair to president of the Parents' Association. There were those rare women who worked and volunteered, like Susan. Was Penelope one of them too? "So be prepared for anything. But not too much business right away." Instead of a suit, Amy wore a green dress to just below the knee. No briefcase. "Just two moms chatting over a meal," Ming said as she handed her a nylon Prada cross-body bag, packed with all the right cards, lipsticks, hand sanitizer, and lotion. "Have fun," Ming said.

"Yeah, right," Amy said, feeling like an actress in an ill-suited role. Of all the hats she had to wear—dutiful daughter, hard-nosed businesswoman, wise mother—"mommy friend" was Amy's least favorite, and Penelope was in many ways like a supermommy. How much else could she have on her plate beyond planning the fundraising auction and sending out emails on behalf of the school? Around women like her, Amy vowed to pick Pearl up more, go to more events. And she would have to at Kent. Amy's stomach churned in dread, but then she thought of her father and how much it would mean to him for her to land a piece of a century-old white-owned American infrastructure business.

Amy arrived her usual five minutes early, nodded at the maître d's *buon giorno*, and was taken aback to find Penelope already seated at the banquette, typing away on her phone. She almost didn't look at Amy when she arrived at the table, finally tossing her phone aside and slipping to her feet. Amy allowed Penelope to kiss each cheek to hers, still back on her heels. Then they were seated, and Amy realized she had not had a chance to arrange for her faux alcoholic beverages with the waiter. Penelope held her hand on the table and earnestly looked in her eyes.

"How are you? Can you have a glass of wine with me?" she asked.

"Of course," Amy said automatically.

"Actually," Penelope said to the waiter, "let's make it champagne. All right by you?" Amy nodded. "And I'll have the shrimp salad."

"I'll have the same," Amy said and smiled at Penelope. She tried to turn the conversation to more congenial topics while fleshing out the actualities of Penelope's professional life, if any, without asking the dreaded "So what do you do?" question. "It's so nice to get out for lunch. Do you eat out every day?"

"Not every day," Penelope said.

"Do you have somewhere to be later?"

"Not for a while," Penelope said.

Amy gave up. "Do you work?" she asked bluntly.

Penelope blinked a few times before answering. She was inscrutable! Was she offended by Amy's question or just slow to answer? "I sit on my family board, which lately has been a huge amount of work." Something about the way she said this made Amy question if Penelope knew anything about hard work. "I'm also on the board of the natural history museum and the public library. How about you?"

"I place money for a living. My fund is based in Taiwan, where my family is. I'm also on the board of my father's bank." Amy had crafted this thumbnail bio to mirror Penelope's. In most other circumstances, she would have left out the words *family* and *my father*. But that worked like a charm.

"We lost my father last year," Penelope said, and Amy caught herself before asking where they had misplaced him.

"Were you close?" Amy asked.

"Not really. Are you close with your dad?"

"Not really," Amy agreed. "Fathers can be so . . ." She waited for Penelope to finish the sentence.

"Horrible," Penelope said.

"Difficult," Amy agreed.

The waiter dropped their lunch plates, but there was hardly any real food on them: lettuce leaves and eight small shrimp. Amy slowly consumed the entire breadbasket except for one slice she left out of politeness for Penelope, who would surely never touch it, favoring carbohydrates in wine form. Amy sipped hers as slowly as possible, but still, a warmth had started to creep up her shoulder blades. When she noticed forty-five minutes had already passed, Amy suddenly blurted, "I have heard your family is involved in rail transport. Is that true?"

Penelope was taken aback but not as much as one might think considering Amy had interrupted her midsentence about the Kent chess team and their national championship in Rio the previous year. "Yes," she said. "We manufacture railway rolling stock. Well, it's one of our businesses. Why?"

"Is there someone you could put me in touch with who handles that business? Maybe at your office?" Penelope blinked at Amy, like she didn't understand the request. "I'd like to fund a major capital improvement," Amy added.

Penelope chewed a tiny shrimp for a solid twenty seconds. Her lashes seemed drawn onto her cheeks, her eyes were so low and still. She dabbed her mouth with her napkin. It was all very dramatic, and it took every ounce of willpower she had for Amy not to repeat the question more loudly.

"Can I tell you something, Amy?" Penelope said, lifting her eyes slowly to meet hers. "About me?" A little smile turned the corners of Penelope's lips up, creasing her otherwise seamless face.

"Of course, Penelope," Amy said. In all her dealings with men from all over the world, she had never before been as unsure of what was about to be said.

Penelope's smile grew wider, into something bright and real. "It's my birthday today," she said, raising her champagne flute.

Amy met it with hers. "Happy birthday!" she said, feeling that familiar uncertainty. Was Penelope off, or was Amy misreading the situation? Was she going to ignore her previous question? In her time running a private equity fund, hardly anyone let it drop when Amy brought up investing in their business. "Do you have anything special . . ."

"The thing is, Amy," Penelope interrupted, "it's me. I'm able to vet investors now." This sudden change in tone—was it defiance?—plus the vocabulary made Amy sit up in her seat.

"OK," she said. "So do you need financing?"

Penelope looked to her upper left, as if referencing the part of her brain where this information was stored. Her big brown eyes darted a millimeter this way and that, as if looking at a spreadsheet in her mind. *Was she secretly brilliant?* Amy wondered. Had she underestimated this mommy friend? Amy eyed her own glass of wine, now slightly less than half full. She took a big gulp of ice water.

"Yes, I suppose we could always use cash," Penelope finally admitted. "How much do you have on hand?"

"Now? Five hundred million dollars." Penelope looked underwhelmed. "But I can get more. I have just under five billion committed." Penelope nodded but remained quiet. "What's the process?" Amy asked cautiously. Ming's voice in her head warned her: if it seems too good to be true, it probably is.

"You make an offer and I accept, decline, or counter," Penelope said evenly, smiling. Amy couldn't tell if she had done this a hundred times or never.

Ming had made sure that Amy was prepared for anything. "I'm going to offer you five hundred million dollars for five percent of the rail-manufacturing business." By Ming's calculations, if the rail legislation went through, they'd start earning in under three years.

"I'll have to present it to the board," Penelope said, finishing her champagne. "But I think, for my birthday, they'll give it special consideration." She extended her perfectly manicured hand, her enormous emerald cut diamond glinting and sharp. Amy carefully avoided it with her own unadorned fingers. Was this the Kent magic already at work? It seemed inconceivably easy to do business this way.

On the way home, Amy engaged in the fantasies of how her conversation with her father would go. How she would put his mind at ease. How proud of her he would be. This was, as ever, her only real wish. After her mother had died, there was only him and his faraway love. The things he really spent his time on—money, status, power—were not things a child could provide. But as Amy grew, her value to him had grown in step with her ability to enhance his prestige.

Amy didn't want to be too celebratory with Ming, whose nature it was to scrutinize everything. Especially things that came too easily. She tossed her coat on the back of her chair as Ming turned to eye her skeptically.

"I don't think it could have gone any better," Amy said, hands on her hips, bracing for some blowback.

"Have you been drinking?" Ming asked, puzzled.

"It was unavoidable," Amy said, sitting on the squarish leather chaise in the office. "She says she's the one who vets investors."

Ming snorted.

"You think she's lying?"

"I think at best she is exaggerating."

"I called her bluff then."

"I wouldn't count the chickens yet."

Amy understood perfectly well that Ming was advising her not to report on the day's meeting to her father or mention it in their investor memo. That it was unwise to take a verbal contract to the bank. But Ming was the product of two present and doting parents. She never worried about their approval or what they thought of her life in New York. Amy felt like every day she ran a marathon to justify her existence. And telling her father about the meeting with Penelope would make today's race that much easier.

She waited until 7:00 a.m. Taipei time to FaceTime him. She knew he was an early riser.

"Baba." He was already at his desk in the heart of downtown, the Taipei 101 building (briefly the world's tallest) just over his left shoulder. "You're at work already?" He laughed ruefully, though he looked haggard. A shadow darkened his jowls, which hung loosely. He was losing weight. "What, you never left the office last night? What will Chia-Jung say?" Amy teased, trying to keep the mood light.

"You'll have to call her to find out." His tone was flippant, but the content was not. He had an infuriating way of attempting to conceal bad news with an insincere smile. Whenever he took a long business trip when she was little, he would always say, "I'll be back in five minutes," as he stepped out the door. She would ask her grandparents every minute, "When will Baba be back?" for hours.

"Ba, what are you talking about?" Amy asked.

"She left."

Amy swallowed. Chia-Jung had been with her father for so long, they often introduced each other as husband and wife, though they weren't married. And now, they weren't anything.

"When? Why?"

"She was sick of my working. She could never understand. This is where the money comes from."

"But Baba, you have more money than you could spend in one hundred lifetimes. Why not retire?"

"So I can do what? Die?"

"Baba, there's more to life than work."

"Is that why you were late to the meeting?"

"Actually, another mom at Pearl's school jumped off the top of her building."

Amy was surprised to hear her father gasp. "She jumped?" he said. She couldn't tell if he was horrified or intrigued.

"Forty stories."

He shook his head in disbelief. Were those tears in his eyes? "A friend of yours?"

"No, but the traffic . . ." Amy couldn't finish her sentence because of the sudden stone in the back of her throat. For some reason, Amy thought of her mother, dead for almost three decades.

"Ba, I found a new acquisition. A share in a railway manufacturer." Ba only huffed his usual grunt of approval. "I've been eyeing this sector for months. Our government consultant says it's solid."

"OK, Amy," her father said. He suddenly looked so old, his skin like gray crepe. "Can you put it in the investor memo?"

Don't do it! Ming's voice shouted at her in her mind. But Ming didn't understand! For Amy, her father's love was as irresistible as it was fickle. Everything was better—she was a better mother, a better investor, a better employer—when she felt she was in her father's good graces. It was, in a way, a drug.

"Yes, Baba. I'll add a paragraph about it."

"Good, good. I can't have anything else turn out poorly for me right now."

SEVEN

PENELOPE

The last touches of her toilette felt like the final steps of chore-ography in a long sequence that would at last, tonight, deliver Penelope to her rightful place. The controlled flicks of her wrist, the cobalt along her lash line, the seamless curve of her derriere on the white leather and Lucite bench at her vanity, the run of her palm over the tailored Gucci cocktail dress: all this had been destined years before. The lights, installed just about within the floor-to-ceiling mirrors, were flattering, but all her hard work at SoulCycle and with her dermatologist, aesthetician, hair colorist, etc. had paid off. At forty, she had never looked better. Flush with confidence, she felt almost completely ready to take her seat at the table.

Penelope had bought a black Gucci evening bag to go with her dress at the urging of her stylist. In general, she bought a lot of small handbags, so she always had a tidy spot for the Klonopin, which was more like a security object than a medication, Penelope told herself. It just comforted her to know it was *right there*, but tonight she left it on the upholstered chaise lounge by the king-size bed after breaking a pill and taking only a restrained half.

She thought once more of poor Susan and the time Penelope had offered her a Klonopin after she complained about being overwhelmed, a classic New York state of mind. It was at lunch, someplace by Susan's job. Over coffee, Penelope had offered the pill in a little basket she made of her manicured fingers. "Here. For emergencies," she said, and Susan had held up her palm, refusing it as if Penelope were handing over a vial of crack. At the time, Penelope had barely noticed, slipping it back in her Judith Leiber pillbox. Maybe Susan had some sort of substance problem, Penelope had reasoned at the time. But since her death, she kept replaying that moment, Susan's face strained, with fear? But why? Surely, she could have used some relief. The scene repeated in Penelope's mind, along with a voice-over of Penelope saying over and over, "Just take the Klon, Susan."

Penelope did not wonder what sort of abyss might open beneath her if she stopped self-medicating, and she had, in fact, been overindulging since Nina had called her that awful morning. People were strange. People had secrets. And both were doubly true of city people. Maybe Susan really didn't want to move to Larchmont or wherever she was going, a sentiment Penelope very well understood. It couldn't have to do with the corntroversy, Penelope told herself, shunting off any possibility of feeling bad for having made fun of a dead woman who clearly had mental problems. They'd never know the whole story. She certainly wasn't going to develop some wacko obsession like Kara or remain wide eyed and befuddled like Vic. Penelope hadn't planned to tell her the whole story in the hotel lobby, but something made her want to shock Vic. What was she so incredulous about? Hadn't Susan been a cutter in high school? Or was that just a mommy rumor? Even Graham, who rarely commented on other moms, said, when he heard the news, "I can see that."

That was about the level of interest Graham showed in most things these days. Penelope's family and their lawyers would arrive in fifteen minutes, but her husband was not yet home. She shook off memories of Susan and turned her attention to finding Graham. He answered on the second ring. "Are you coming?" Penelope asked. She could hear him trying to muffle the sounds of a sports bar, his favorite escape only two blocks away.

"Babe, come on . . ." Penelope heard him swing open one of those heavy doors onto the street. She could picture him in her mind's eye, standing outside on Sixtieth Street amid the smokers, eyeing them with envy as he gently blew her off. ". . . you know I hate these things." While Graham lived in luxury off Penelope's family wealth, he did not like to be reminded of that by having to spend an excruciating hour in the salon with the ladies while the men conducted business in the other room.

"But this one's different. I just wanted you to, you know, be here to support me."

"From the other room? With your mom and sisters-in-law? Give me a break, Penelope."

Now that Penelope herself would be voting, her husband felt more emasculated, even as it elevated their nuclear family. "It's a big deal," she said quietly.

Instead of answering, Graham only cleared his throat, and Penelope could hear her therapist saying, *Do you want to be right, or do you want to be happy?* Sometimes, she felt like demanding so much more from Graham, starting with his respect. It was clear that he had never had a reason to give her much credit for the fortune her grandfather had built, her father had grown, and her brothers had sustained for a decade. In fact, no one recognized her as having any part in it.

But now, if she could demonstrate some acumen—if she could, in other words, do business for the family—they would all start to see her differently. It's not as if they needed any more money, but for Penelope, the way to some sort of greater identity included her initials next to big numbers on a spreadsheet. She needed to get some points on the scoreboard. Not just to stick it to Andrew, but to prove to her husband that she was more than a Parents' Association president. Maybe she also had something to prove to herself. "I'll be there for dinner," he finally said.

Penelope had to get going. The only enjoyable part of the evening would be before anyone in her family arrived. Except Boris. Despite her mother's overbearingness and Andrew's disdain, Boris and she had managed to eke out a tentative side partnership. Her youngest brother was the only one of them who didn't give her crippling anxiety that demanded multiple avenues of chemical intervention, both medically and self-prescribed.

For now, though, Penelope was every molecule the Upper East Side hostess, preparing her prewar Park Avenue co-op for a party, as so many ladies had done before her. She dipped into each of her children's rooms, kissed them good night, gave final instructions to the two nannies, and spent a few minutes tucking in her firstborn, Felix. He sat up in his crisp cotton pajamas covered in navy stars, his damp hair combed in a neat side part. He had the book out that he wanted to read: *Eloise*. He loved *Eloise*! So Penelope dutifully read it to him, again.

"Mama, can we go there for tea again?" Felix asked. "Just you and me?"

"All right, but this time you can't spend all your time in the bathroom." The last time they'd gone, Penelope had had to sneak into the men's room, where she found Felix transfixed by the incredibly tacky faux-gold fixtures set in marble. He just stood there turning the water on and off.

"Mama, can I have these?" he asked her, and when she said, "No," he added, "Please?!" Though she would never admit it to anyone, Penelope had thought of her son, *Thank God he's rich*.

As she left, Penelope dimmed the lights in the residential hall. No reason for guests to come this way when there were two bathrooms off the living room and one behind the dining room. The last thing she needed was her mother stumbling into the baby's room to use the toilet on her way out at midnight.

Penelope floated into the living room, checking her own reflection in the windowpanes. The candles and lamplight were very flattering. Then she turned her attention to her first order of business: the bar.

Some of Penelope's favorite creatures were the cater waiters that staffed Manhattan's cocktail parties. Anywhere else in America, these generally tall, usually gorgeous aspiring actors or models would be remarkable, but in the city, they were everywhere: interchangeable, affable, unlikely to succeed. This one, about six foot two with a thick swath of straight brown hair that practically demanded to be tousled, was like all the others. He smiled at her, the boss, the tipper, the arbiter of his success this evening.

"Hi there, I'm Penelope."

"I know," he said, smiling. Maybe this one wasn't gay.

"What I'd like is a Bombay martini up with a twist. And lots of ice splinters."

"You got it." His hands, oversize on the silver shaker, were a blur. He poured the drink, cloudy with ice, into one of her grandmother's crystal martini glasses. She sipped it. Perfection.

"So now," Penelope said, speaking slowly so the particulars of her request could be absorbed and understood, "would you please get one of these to me about every forty minutes for the night with a glass of lemon ice water in between."

"You got it," he said.

Penelope sighed, comforted, as she drifted around needlessly fluffing pillows, rearranging flowers, and nudging candles a few inches this way or that while sipping her drink. The anxious catering staff presented various trays of canapés for her to sample, the only thing she would be sure of eating all night as the martinis flowed. In the dining room, peonies—her favorite—spilled over low silver bowls. She walked around the table, checking her seating arrangement. Penelope tended to put couples together, but tonight, that wouldn't do. They were only seven. They had always been eight before: Penelope and Graham. Her two brothers and their wives. And their parents.

Penelope's father had only been dead a year. When Penelope thought of him, it was with a vaguely metallic taste in the back of her throat. Like a minerally white wine, he was pale and chilly. Rigid, with

Elizabeth Topp

antiquated principles. He didn't ever seem to expect anything from Penelope: not a pithy comment at the dinner table or a career. Not even a basic job. When she thought of her father, he was always with Andrew, his favorite, the two of them begrudgingly, occasionally, including Boris but never her.

Her father had gone to Kent and pulled every string for Andrew to attend as well, but when it came time for Penelope to apply, he moved the family to Greenwich instead, and she attended public school after not getting into Andover or Choate. Boris claimed not to care, but Penelope always felt robbed of her birthright.

Kent had made Andrew half the things he had become, one domino leading to the next. When he finally had his growth spurt in the eleventh grade, brooding, unathletic, geeky Andrew became a debate star and rebranded himself a future litigator, drawing the attention of their father's longtime personal lawyer, who wrote Andrew's glowing recommendation to Yale Law School. At the right moment, her father and his lawyer provided the seed funding for his new firm. The bulk of his first clients had been Kent alumni (and their father, of course). Now his was among the top five firms in the United States. And all because of Kent.

As she moved Andrew's place card even farther away from her own, reshuffling some of the others, Penelope seethed as if the wounds were fresh. Everything had been prepared and arranged for him. What sort of connections was she to have made at a Connecticut public school? At least her own three children would all attend and benefit from Kent. Felix was smart enough, given that she had been dutifully making her $10,000 annual fund contributions to Kent since the year of his birth.

Penelope went across the living room, through the foyer, and into the library. This was her first opportunity to host a meeting of the family board, and she reassured herself that the room, with its Park Avenue views, built-in bookshelves, and oval mahogany table, was up to the austere task at hand. Subconsciously, she had designed the space (in collaboration with their interior decorator and architect) for this very

128

event. She smiled to herself. It was all coming together as Penelope envisioned. For once.

Penelope's mother did not bother to ring the doorbell, bursting into the foyer like the lady of the house. No matter where they were in the world—the family's Aspen ski chalet, the Four Seasons hotel, or a stranger's house—Penelope's mother, Evelyn, entered the space like she owned it. In this way, she made it easy for everyone to decide right away if they liked her or not. Now that her husband was dead, her children were grown, and she had more money than she could possibly spend, Penelope's mother had arrived at some preternatural state of doubtlessness that made her more unbearable than ever.

Tonight, Evelyn wore a wool cape over a simple suit that must have been made for her in Italy out of some hyperluxurious cream-colored rare alpaca. Her hair, somewhere between blonde and platinum, curled in perfect rounds. Penelope knew that Evelyn was actually seventy-two, but she looked somewhat closer to fifty. It occurred to Penelope for the first time, as she watched her mother twirl around once to show off her outfit before approaching her daughter for a cheek-to-cheek air-kiss, that Evelyn would find a boyfriend soon. As she stepped back, all flushed and freshened up after a small face-lift while in mourning, it looked like maybe she had already taken a lover.

It must be the Klonopin, Penelope thought, opening up all these avenues of thought. She found herself not shrinking away, as she usually would, from her critical mother and her passive nastiness. By way of greeting, Evelyn took a step back for "the inspection," as Penelope and her therapist called it. Evelyn reached out a diamond-encrusted hand to brush some hair back from Penelope's face, making a show of eyeing her daughter's nearly empty martini glass.

"It's my birthday," Penelope said, finding that she was in such a perfect place vis-à-vis the medication and the alcohol that she did not even care that her mother had to be reminded.

"Happy birthday, Penny," her mother said, smiling from a foot away.

"Hey, Mom," Penelope started, already disliking the immature way she sounded. Something about her mother's presence reduced her to a stammering preteen, struggling to ask for a ride to a friend's house and endure the inevitable intrusive interview that request entailed. "Please don't call me that." Evelyn's lips curved up in acknowledgment.

Penelope cleared her throat and puffed out her chest; this was the start of getting taken seriously. Right now. She met and held her mother's violet-eyed gaze, attempting once more to invoke her mother's empathy. Penelope spoke up. "I'd really love it if you sat in on this meeting." Evelyn's eyes skittered away, and Penelope couldn't find them again. "Just because, well, it is my birthday." The family frequently coupled these gatherings with birthday celebrations to cut down on the hassle of scheduling. When this got no reply, Penelope continued. "I could really use your support in there. You know how Andrew—"

"No, darling," her mother said firmly. It was such a familiar tone and word pairing that it punctured the fog. Penelope felt the cut of her mother's rejection. Again. That the men of the family clumped together should have meant that Penelope and Evelyn were close, currying confidences and shaping an alliance. But Evelyn had never taken much interest in Penelope or her preferences.

Worse, from Penelope's point of view, she had also remained firmly apart from the business of the family office, despite being entitled all along to a voting seat. Her mother had abdicated long ago, allowing her lawyer to represent her interests. It drove Penelope crazy that her mother chose to disenfranchise herself. Her mother, who had gone to Vassar for God's sake! Didn't she want more from life than white linen luncheons, shopping excursions, cocktail parties, and international travel?

"I'll hold down the fort with the wives, Penny," Evelyn said. "Penelope, I mean. Oh, and Graham, of course." There was no reason to tell her mother that her husband, a veteran of these board meetings, would not materialize until minutes before they sat down to eat.

Penelope practically pounced on her lawyer the moment she arrived. They left Evelyn to greet people in the foyer, Penelope ushering her attorney down the service hallway, through the kitchen bustling with activity, and into the butler's pantry, where she shut the door behind them. They stood in a rose marble rectangle with twelve-foot-high glass cabinets, undercabinet lighting, a tiny sink. There was just enough room for the two of them to stand with six inches between themselves.

Penelope's lawyer, a powder keg of a woman, hoisted her briefcase onto the counter and pulled out an iPad. Amy's black-and-white corporate portrait filled the screen: arms crossed, black shirt, white backdrop, face dead serious. The caption read FOUNDER & PRESIDENT, Taipei Partners LLC. Penelope filled with envy. "This is your mommy friend?" her attorney asked. Penelope nodded. "Well, she's definitely legitimate. Looks like her dad has some ties to China, but their money flows through Taiwan. Which is good. What's she like?"

Penelope thought back to their lunch. In truth, most of it was kind of fuzzy. She had taken half a Klon beforehand. While she'd like to think of herself as a working mom, board memberships didn't really count. And moms with careers could be so snooty to the SAHMs. Penelope recalled the vague sense of being interrogated. "Don't you work?" Amy had asked, in a pretty judgy way. And then, out of nowhere, the rail thing. Like Amy wanted her to be off balance.

"She seemed"—Penelope's eyes narrowed—"prepared."

"Yeah, I bet she was."

"And she definitely caught me off guard." Penelope remembered how her mind had grasped at straws; the chord change from domineering fathers to a major capital-improvement investment had been so abrupt and unexpected, it had triggered Penelope. Andrew used the same sort of surprise tactics on her, and it often left her gasping like a fish on the shore. Her therapist suggested, in moments when she found herself confused or overwhelmed like this, that instead of just charging ahead impulsively, she should take three deep breaths before doing anything at all.

"Of course, there's another level of scrutiny Taipei Partners will have to go through, but at first glance"—the lawyer shrugged—"she checks out."

Penelope smiled, her eyes flashing, eager now to kick the meeting off. People were always trying to play her for a fool, but not this time. She reached for the door, practically licking her lips, but the lawyer's hand on Penelope's arm stopped her. "But Penelope, I wouldn't do this tonight."

She turned back around, her face drooping in disappointment like a child's. "What? Why not?"

"This is your first real meeting—your first chance to cast a vote. My advice is to sit back, let me do the talking, and vote the way I tell you." Penelope flinched, and the lawyer offered consolingly, "We can flesh out this investment deal for the next meeting." Penelope nodded noncommittally. It had been drummed into her practically since birth to listen to the lawyers, but they always wanted to dull any possibility of excitement.

When Penelope entered the library, five men—all in bespoke suits, all white, all between forty and sixty—rose to their feet. Only Boris deviated from the dress code, having added a light wool scarf to his suit instead of a tie, which looked rather French. He wore his usual hesitant smile, his head lolling like a puppy's at the end of his neck. Boris charged forward to give Penelope a bear hug.

"Happy birthday, sis!" he said in her ear. His scarf was soft against her chin, and he smelled like pine, and it brought a tear to her eye. Boris was a bit of a ski bum who had made good on his hobby by launching a line of high-end equipment that despite being popular in Aspen, would never make money. Still, it was something to put on a business card, and she did not begrudge Boris his professional identity.

Andrew, in pomade and pinstripes, stood broodingly across the table at its head. Father made him chairman of the board even before his death, a role Andrew had been groomed for. He looked more and more like Father all the time, the hair on the top of his head thinning as his body thickened. There was something unfinished about his face, his features undersize and his complexion like a cold ham. He smirked at Penelope as much as smiled at her. There had always been something between them, a natural resentment when she came along that endured, mutated, and metastasized into a contempt so thorough and palpable, Penelope's therapist insisted it stood in for something else. What that was, neither she nor Penelope could say.

Even now, on her birthday, Penelope could feel the waves of animosity rolling off him toward her. Rather than make a show of climbing around the table, she used the excuse of distance to exchange an awkward wave rather than an actual hug. "Hello, Andrew," she said, disliking that an adversarial note had already crept into her tone. It was lost on no one.

"Penny," Andrew said, nodding at her formally. Though she tried to suppress it, she knew her cheeks were aflame with rage. Penelope hated herself for still wishing her mother had chosen to attend, rather than hiding out with the other women in the salon. They all took their seats, and Penelope sipped her ice water.

Andrew called the meeting to order. Sitting there, in their father's rightful chair, ramrod straight and full of himself. Penelope understood the fullness of her plan, which was not just to vote in the evening's meeting, but to slowly, over time, accrue influence not just with Boris but with Evelyn's lawyer as well. It could take years for her to carefully build her cabal, whose sole purpose, unbeknownst to them, would be to unseat Andrew and ultimately replace him. Penelope saw herself at the head of the table, Boris smiling proudly, as she took them through the board protocols and motions to make it all official.

Finally, Andrew got to the part Penelope had been waiting for. "As you all know, the rail-manufacturing business needs some financing." Penelope shifted in her chair. "The Railroad Revivification Act could mean all sorts of opportunities for us, but only if we can bring our machinery up to date, which could take an investment of hundreds of millions," Andrew said, letting the magnitude of this number sink in. "Or, we could just sell the business." He seemed to be slowing the meeting down, each step coming out painstakingly slowly. "I move for a vote on whether we want to seek investment or sell."

"Obviously, seek investment," Penelope's lawyer whispered to her as all the lawyers except Evelyn's shared instructions with their clients.

"All those in favor of seeking investment . . . ," Andrew said.

Boris and Penelope raised their hands. Andrew looked from one to the other, a slow smile creeping onto his face like a spider. "I'm sorry, I think there's been some misunderstanding," he said slowly. "You still don't get to vote, Penelope."

Was this a nightmare? Penelope wondered, not for the first time since the whole family-board situation blew up. Before she turned eighteen, Andrew and her father had rewritten the bylaws to exclude Penelope from voting until she turned forty. They never made this change for Boris, who had been participating since he turned eighteen. No one had seemed to care that Penelope had been treated so unfairly, and even her own lawyer had been powerless to stop it. Thousands of days she had waited, and now this. "What are you talking about, Andrew?" her lawyer barked.

"Explain it," Andrew instructed his lawyer.

"Your father felt that it was important each of you bring something to the table," the lawyer dutifully explained, handing over a document to Penelope and her attorney, who scanned the two pages, her face getting increasingly inflamed. Penelope didn't even touch the papers, leaving them in front of herself.

"This isn't like all your charities where you throw events and spend the profit. We need to make money with money," Andrew interjected. Penelope tried not to get angry. The martini and Klon helped. She knew she would say something rash and possibly destructive if she allowed herself to become enraged. She tried to remember to breathe deeply.

"Your father," Andrew's lawyer continued, "added a clause that to start voting, you, Penelope, need to raise or make two hundred and fifty million dollars."

"Before I can vote?"

"Before you can vote," Penelope's lawyer confirmed. Andrew practically glowed in his triumph. Boris's eyes were cast down into his lap.

"You two were meeting on the side?" Penelope said, pointing from Boris to Andrew and back again. It seemed she would be excluded well past her father's death.

"It's perfectly legal," Boris's lawyer chimed in. And all of a sudden, she could see it. Boris, happy to go along with his big brother, who had never given him much notice before. "Sure, Andrew, whatever you say, Andrew . . ." Boris was always the Labrador in a family of high-strung terriers. She'd have to get him back in line later. For now, Penelope's rage was for Andrew and Andrew alone.

"So as I was saying . . . ," Andrew continued, and Penelope felt hatred burning her up internally. Like there were flames licking the inside of her eyeballs, making it hard for her to see. ". . . do we want to seek investment or sale? All those for sale . . ." Andrew raised his hand, his disdain so galling, it felt like Penelope would have in that moment done anything to wipe the smirk from his face.

"Wait," Penelope said quietly, her eyes on the table in front of her.

"Penelope, don't," her lawyer whispered, but this was only fanning the fire.

"Wait," Penelope said louder. "I'm allowed to talk, aren't I?" She met Andrew's cockiness with her own.

"Of course," Boris said, putting his hand down and making a show of sitting up to listen. Not that Penelope would forgive him, but she appreciated this small effort. "What is it, Penelope?"

"I have an investor."

"Well, you just . . . ," Andrew interrupted, but Penelope cut him off.

"Cash. Hundreds of millions. Maybe billions." She could feel the energy in the room change. "A Kent family," she said, knowing it would mean enough to at least make Andrew hesitate.

"And what does that mean, exactly?" Andrew's lawyer said, projecting skepticism.

"She wants in on the rail business. Five percent for five hundred million dollars."

The lawyers all scribbled this sum down.

"And how do we know this is real, sis?" Andrew said, sighing. "How do we know this isn't another one of your half-brained film production companies or candle boutiques?"

"It's real," Penelope's lawyer said. "Taipei Partners LLC." More scribbling.

"Sounds good to me," Boris said gamely.

"Well, sorry, Penny, I'm not buying," Andrew said, as if this put an end to the matter.

"I'd like to hear more." Evelyn's lawyer, the elder statesman of the group, rarely spoke, and when he did, it carried some weight. Evelyn's voting power was twice that of each child. Perhaps it was good she hadn't come to the meeting, Penelope suddenly realized, smiling. Just then, there was a knock at the door, and two waiters entered to refill water glasses. The handsome bartender deposited a fresh martini before Penelope. She lifted her drink and proposed a toast. "To staying in the rail business!"

"Hear! Hear!" said Boris. Penelope eyed him testily over the table before clinking her glass to his.

Dinner after meetings such as this could be more than a little tense, and almost every time each family member silently wondered if they should do away with this scheduling convenience and decouple business and pleasure, church and state. Wouldn't that make more sense? But they shared an amnesia about it, brought on by drinking too much, and it was only as they all went through from the living room into the dining room that each of them felt a pang of dread.

Penelope, on her third martini and second half Klon, retrieved in a premeal bathroom break, was the only one that night who remained blissfully numb. She hardly even cared when Graham showed up tardy and smelling of beer. She didn't mind that Andrew said not a single word, glaring at the peonies with hatred, as his wife, a South American beauty queen, flitted about conversationally to cover for the black hole her husband left across the table. All Penelope could think about was how, still, tonight she had been disenfranchised. This time, in her own home. She held Amy's picture in her mind. Amy, so accomplished, so much to offer. *I could be like that,* she thought to herself. She had everything it took.

As the servers cleared the salad plates, Evelyn made her characteristic pre–public speaking gestures of touching up her lipstick and straightening her hair in the reflection on the back of her spoon. Penelope, her mind elsewhere, didn't feel the usual trepidation she might at the thought of her mother delivering a birthday speech. Generally, Evelyn used public speaking opportunities to take jabs at whoever was the object of the event. Often she made jokes about how Penelope spent too much and did too little. Tonight was supposed to be the beginning of the end of all that, Penelope told herself as Evelyn stood, wineglass in hand.

"Happy birthday to my beautiful daughter. You're radiant. Gorgeous. You look, only maybe thirty-seven . . . *ha ha.* Anyway, I was thinking about *you* and what I could possibly get or do for *you*"—the way she emphasized the "you" made it seem like she had hardly ever thought of Penelope before—"a woman who, much like myself, has everything." Graham chortled, and Evelyn smiled at him indulgently. "And I thought of the kids. All your kids. Even the ones you don't have yet." Here Evelyn looked meaningfully at Andrew, who, despite being the oldest, had yet to produce any offspring, much to his mother's chagrin. Boris, meanwhile, and his wife, a quiet little blonde pet from Aspen, had happily generated four blondes in the five years before he turned thirty-five.

"And I thought, what better gift is there than education? So I called up the Kent School . . ."

"Mother!" Andrew said for some reason.

". . . and I made an appointment with their development director. And we sketched out a ten-year, ten-million-dollar pledge from our family to the school."

Penelope found herself at once relieved and pissed off. Her measly $10,000 seemed like pocket change now. Did Felix really need $10 million of help to get into his uncle's and grandfather's alma mater? Fine, he wasn't lighting the world on fire with his crackerjack intellect, but he wasn't some mouth-breathing moron. Worst of all, Penelope felt a creeping sense of strange envy for her own children. Why hadn't Penelope herself gotten to attend Kent if it was this important?

Andrew was inscrutable, never one to be particularly happy about anything. Boris's wife looked like she might cry with joy. "Oh, that's wonderful," she kept saying. But Evelyn's eyes were on the birthday girl, who had forgotten she was not alone.

"Penny, darling, you don't seem happy," Evelyn said nudgingly.

Penelope blinked back the tears; the peonies, candles, and plates all smeared into a glowing pink streak. As counterintuitive as it might seem, there was just something so depressing about being handed everything like this. Didn't Evelyn see how she and Father had handicapped her? How hard it was for Penelope in any way to chart her own course.

Penelope promised herself to lock that railroad deal down. She knew Amy was exactly what she claimed to be and that this one thing would come through, and like Kent for Andrew, the dominoes would fall in the right direction for Penelope as well. To her credit, Penelope understood that no one would ever feel bad for her. Nor did she feel deserving, really, of anyone's sympathy, least of all from the family gathered at her dining room table, who were all, to some degree—even now at her own birthday party—looking at her askance, as if she had completely forgotten what was being said.

"Of course, I'm happy, Mother," Penelope said without slurring a single bit.

EIGHT

VIC

When her editor suggested lunch at Xaviers, Vic just knew it meant good news. She had only sent over the new chapters a few days prior and just ahead of her deadline. Right away, *boom*. For those in publishing, Xaviers was the most exciting restaurant in which to have lunch, and Vic only got to eat there once each novel. Her editor must really love those pages. It was thrilling just to tweet Going to eat @Xaviers with my editor! Almost instantly, three people liked it.

The lunch meant that Vic had finally slept again, an unimaginable relief after five endless nights staring at the ceiling, heart racing, mind uncovering every dark or unpleasant thought and then turning it over again and again. After she had exhausted all the possible ways she could and probably would experience bankruptcy, she would obsess about Susan for a while before inevitably arriving at one of her favorite regrets to torture herself about: Scott Hearst. When they were together at Kent, everything had seemed possible. And not in some pie-in-the-sky way, like anything and everything could happen to them by just being together. She had thought, at the time, that life was full of sexy men who would want to be with her. Then a seventeen-year-old arrogant Vic had decided he just wasn't smart enough, but twenty years later, Vic wondered, *Smart enough for what?* Loathe to start college with some long-term boyfriend baggage, she had dumped him. But in the middle of the night, with the radiator banging and a big empty space in her bed, she thought about the mistake she had made breaking up with Scott much more than anything to do with Jetta's father, Sean.

After she had gone down that rabbit hole, Vic would think about herself and all the ways that all her mistakes revealed her to be nothing like the person she had intended to be. Vic obsessed about how she had not seen the obvious signs that her friend was suicidal and what it said about her powers of perception. The call with Bhavna haunted Vic—how quickly she had been able to grasp real meaning from what was *not* said in that robotic email. As a novelist, Vic was known for her thoughtful construction of multidimensional, complicated characters. She had always assumed this sprang from a real-life acuity with others and prided herself on her relationships. But when she thought back to the time she had spent with Susan, how attentive had Vic been to the details? How deeply had she delved beneath the absolute uppermost layer?

Since the Xaviers lunch invitation had materialized only two days ago, Vic no longer needed to worry. Once more, she could lay her head down on the pillow and pick it up again eight hours later. She stopped thinking about financial ruin, Susan, and Scott all the time. She would have money for rent, tuition, and an Uber to her lunch. She ordered the car with plenty of time to spare. She felt like herself again—effortlessly punctual. As she got on the elevator, the app updated her car arrival time from two minutes to six minutes—still plenty of time. But as she waited on the curb under the awning, staring at her phone in her white-knuckled hand, the arrival time advanced again, this time to nine minutes. She'd never make it!

Once the car arrived, Vic texted her editor that she'd be ten minutes late. This seemed like a good estimate until they pulled onto Broadway and traffic slowed to five miles per hour. Vic studied her watch, the flashing taillights ahead, her clog boots with their plastic platform soles. There were no real options. Vic had to run to collect her prize.

A sheen of sweat covered Vic's made-up face as she came through the glass revolving doors of Xaviers. The hostess eyed her up and down and said, "Would you like to check your coat?" Vic wanted nothing more than to ditch the knee-length, double-breasted Alexander McQueen she had found at a pricey consignment store, but as she slipped off a wool sleeve, she found her armpits were wet through underneath.

"Never mind," Vic said, trying to smile at the disgusted hostess, who promptly led her to a table in the back room, which was less bustling than the main dining room and quieter, with walls of windows like a greenhouse. Vic's editor was a very tall, very serious woman somewhere between ten and twenty years Vic's senior who had been kind enough to publish all Vic's four previous novels. She sat at a table far from everyone—*intimate!* Vic thought—ice water in front of her, thumbs flying over her phone, brow deeply creased.

"Sorry I'm late!" Vic said, still standing. She was nearly fifteen minutes late in the end.

"No problem," her editor said evenly, rising to embrace her. "Transit strike, right?" she said over her shoulder. Today she was swathed in camel-color wools and fringe. She had done a little work on her face and sported a fresh manicure.

"Love your glasses," Vic said, feeling lucky to have such a chic editor to publish her work. Once they ordered lunch, the waiter removed both their menus and any reason to forestall more serious conversation. Vic smiled broadly, anticipating the words that would come next. Something like, "Tell me more about . . . ," or "When can you have this finished?"

"The thing is, Vic," her editor said, "this just is not something I think our readers are going to be drawn to."

Had Vic missed something? Were they still talking about the menu or . . . ? "What?" she choked out. She wanted to add, *But we're at Xaviers!*

"The whole, you know, feminist dystopia. It's just not really . . ." She actually cleared her throat. "We have no idea how to market that sort of thing."

After another agonizing "writing" day spent not writing, then drinking, then cyberstalking Scott via Lili, Vic had faced reality and scoured all the old files on her computer for the most substantial discarded scraps in the trash heap. There were bits of a story about a veterinarian who wants to start her own practice or a solitary woman who becomes obsessed with her apartment renovation after inheriting a fortune from the nasty aunt she actually murdered . . . but they were only scraps.

So now, after almost a decade of building up a readership who had remained faithful through four stories about plucky, unique heroines navigating the travails and hijinks of their professional lives, Vic had turned in two rough chapters of a feminist dystopian novel about a future in which every woman has lethal power over every man. It was violent, edgy, sexy, and had nothing at all to do with anything she had ever written before. Also, it was quite possibly terrible.

Vic longed to take off her jacket; it felt illogically like the lapels were trying to strangle her. Sweat ran down her spine and into her underwear. "OK, well I have other ideas," Vic started, swallowing hard to sound less croaky. "You know, what about a single woman who—"

"Look." Her editor, always so nice before, had her palm up. "Vic, I don't want you to pitch me right now." Vic felt a wave of relief. Thank goodness, because she didn't have anything. "I want you to go home, think about it, and really come up with a next book that's like all your other books, but *better*."

Vic found herself grinning like an idiot even as she continued to sweat. Only moments before, Vic was a capable professional. She felt reduced to gawking at her editor as her mind ran away from the table screaming. All the anxieties that had been dormant for the previous forty-eight hours sprang back to full-blooded life and worse. Would she have to pay back her advance? Visions of her future traipsed across Vic's mind. She'd have to get a job—any sort of paid work! What would she do? Spray perfume on shoppers at Bloomingdale's? Become a secretary? Work at a tollbooth? At Kent alumni events when people said, "What are you up to?" Vic would have to say . . .

"Your last book didn't do quite as well as the others, so you really need to bring something . . . *extra*. You know?" Her editor sipped her water.

Vic closed her mouth and nodded, buying some time while trying to find an intelligent response to this. She took a minute to pat her shiny face with her napkin; there was no point in hiding her perspiration any longer.

"Look, I . . . ," Vic said.

"I know you have it in you," her editor interrupted.

But Vic understood already that neither of them was sure anymore.

Stumbling toward Central Park in a daze after lunch, Vic racked her empty brain for the grain of an idea, but her mind had become a useless anxiety cloud. Oh God, she felt sick. It suddenly felt like everyone else had gainful employment. Bhavna and Amy. Chandice was on leave from being a doctor. Or something. Vic wasn't certain. Susan had like a whole career and a half. Had Vic ever even had what one could call a "real job"? It was time to enact her plan B and start reaching out in earnest for teaching jobs. But the thought was overwhelming. Did she even have the experience to land those jobs anymore? She took big gulping breaths, trying not to puke, forearms on her thighs.

When her phone buzzed, she had the completely fantastical thought that it was her editor changing her mind. Vic looked at her phone with hope. But it wasn't good news. It was just an IG notification: @lilikopelman was going live.

All right, sure, why not. *Could be a nice distraction,* Vic thought.

And there she was, midsentence, outside in the glorious spring sun that Vic had not even noticed until she saw it glinting off Lili's pricey highlights. She wore slim pants, thigh-high leather boots that were made for her, and a long belted cape that seemed to be swaying along with her incredibly bouncy hair, so plentiful it couldn't possibly all be hers. The setting was golden and familiar, green stands and root vegetables, cashmere-scarved shoppers: the Union Square farmers market in early spring.

". . . being such a doll for cooking," Lili said. Scott stood next to her with his back to the camera, just a big hulking mass of gray wool. He tried to get away with an over-the-shoulder wave, but Lili coaxed him into turning around, revealing a sexy black ski sweater and a parsnip in one hand. "He's such a dear to do the cooking tonight for my sister, Violet." And then his scene was over. Violet stepped onscreen with her sister. They were both model types, Lili with wavy beachy blonde hair and an all-American vibe, while her sister sported dark, choppy bangs and sharp cheekbones. They looked like they had been bred in an IG lab to do live broadcasts.

"Congrats, V!" Lili enthused. Violet removed her glove to flash a knuckle-to-knuckle emerald cut diamond. The comments flooded with thousands and thousands of flame emoji, hearts, and high fives. Lili and her sister smiled and tilted their heads this way and that. "Maybe it'll be my turn next!" Lili enthused, smiling and batting her eyes at Scott's turned back. Violet gave her a high five with one hand while crossing the fingers of her other. "Must get freshened up for the partay!" Lili said after they had suitably vamped for a good twenty seconds.

"We'll leave you to it then." Lili backed up again to Scott, who had occupied himself with the produce table. She put her hand on his bicep and smiled up at him adoringly. Then she gave him a little nod, and, as if remembering, he leaned in and kissed her. She wrapped her hand around his head to hold him there a moment, and then she released him. "Love you," she said.

"Love you," he responded, his back to the camera. The stream ended.

When Vic saw someone hopping out of a livery car, as rare as a bald eagle during the transit strike, her city feet were swift on the pavement. "Can you take me to Union Square for twenty bucks?" she barked at the driver, who nodded and waved her inside. She was thrilled to be caught up in something that wasn't impending bankruptcy, her friend's grisly suicide, or the potential end of her career. This was something else entirely. Miraculously, the midday traffic had cleared, and she was stepping out at Union Square in a New York minute.

The scene was just as it had been on Lili's feed. Manhattan's biggest farmers market, sprawled over a large parking lot on the north and west sides of Union Square, crawling with all sorts of hip and gorgeous people happy to spend the extra money for produce that not only tasted better but made them feel virtuous. The transit strike did not appear to be denting the swift commerce. And no wonder Lili had chosen to shoot here; the afternoon light was perfect.

"You knew it was live!" Before even recognizing Lili's voice, Vic knew enough to duck behind the post of a vegetable stand, stick her chin into her chest, and pretend to examine some squash. "Don't say you didn't know!" she said. God, Lili's voice was annoying!

Vic lifted her eyes, disbelieving her good fortune. Scott stood there, Lili jutting a perfect oval lavender fingernail at his chest. Everyone around gave them a wide berth, so Vic had no trouble seeing what was unfolding before her in real life, which was so, so much better than any social media, movie, or TV show. Her high school boyfriend was having a very public argument with his influencer girlfriend, in almost exactly the same spot where, not ten minutes before, they were broadcasting kisses and "I love yous."

Violet, who in person reminded Vic of a praying mantis in a lovely dress, loomed ten feet in the background smoking sullenly. When the black T-shirted Brooklyn lackey who shot the video tried to take a few pictures of Violet smoking with all the cabbages in the background, she waved him off, annoyed. Instead, they, too, watched Lili and Scott's argument from a distance, both glaring impatiently.

"Lili, look, can you take a break from influencing for a goddamn minute and just live your life?" Scott said. The pile of parsnips and leeks he had picked out sat on a table to their left. He was all heated, his neck bright red around the high neck of his sweater. Vic was always surprised by how tall he was, and it looked like he had decided to start a skin-care regimen. Surely Lili's handiwork.

In person, Lili was every bit as beautiful as she was on IG, if not more so. But when she talked, the fictional qualities of social media were laid bare. She could auto-tune out her shrill and grating tone online, but in real life Lili's voice was like a chainsaw on a chalkboard. "I'm about to get my first paid sponsorship!" she shrieked. The sounds coming out of her mouth made several people turn around to stare.

"I know! What do you think I'm doing all this work for?" Scott said, tilting his head and flashing his palm at all the produce ready for him to purchase and prepare. This reminder did not seem to have the intended effect. Instead of mollifying him, Lili took two aggressive steps forward and fixed on him her most pitying expression.

"Sco-ott." She made his name into two syllables somehow with a rising inflection. Vic hated Lili. "You didn't really think we were counting on you to make this party happen, did you?"

Scott looked down at her, not understanding for a minute, and Vic's heart went out to him. She remembered once, when they were just teenagers, he had made her a spaghetti dinner with chocolate chip cookies for dessert. Apparently, judging by the leeks, his cooking had come a long way since then, and Lili had caught him off guard. "Please, Scott. Get serious. The caterers are coming at six."

Vic held her breath as Scott's face went from bright red to a pale, pale white, like the hottest part of the flame. "Lili, I took off work for this," he said through gritted teeth. Each word came out like a tiny bullet. "You said it was important to you that I cook for your launch party, and I . . ."

"Later," she said, cutting him off and looking at her watch. "We have to make this appointment," Lili said, gesturing at Violet and the camera guy and shrugging at the same time. In real life, she was a collection of physical tics and verbal manipulations. Scott could only glare back. He had never been the sharpest tack in the drawer. "Look, it's a load off, right? You don't have to worry or do anything!" Lili continued, trying a different argument. "Except don't forget to play ball on camera, OK?" Her attitude had gone through so many key changes, Vic was having trouble keeping up. Maybe Lili had a personality disorder? She stepped closer to him, and, fingering the zipper at the neck of his mock turtleneck, she cooed, "Let's not ruin Violet's special day or my sponsorship, OK?"

"K."

There was an awkward moment that Vic absolutely loved where they couldn't decide how they were going to part ways. Lili reached for Scott, and he bent down awkwardly and then . . .

"Vic!" She practically jumped into the post she was hiding behind, Bhavna so startled her. Standing right behind Vic, container of food in one hand with a napkin and plastic fork and that big eager smile. "Hey! What are you doing here?" Bhavna said. Vic cast a final glance over her shoulder to see Scott looking their way. Had he heard Bhavna? She felt a sudden rage.

"Bhavna! Hello. I'm . . ." She realized how strange she must look standing there, staring. How long had Bhavna observed her before coming over? ". . . just left a meeting with my editor, and I guess I'm just absorbing it still."

"I get it! I had a big meeting myself and thought I'd grab some lunch!" Bhavna lifted her food aloft like a prop.

"Good for you," Vic said vaguely. She checked again. Lili and her crew had cleared out, and Scott was nowhere to be found. How could she break free from Bhavna?

"How's Susan's family doing?" Bhavna asked, and it occurred to Vic that she had no idea. The school had been pretty clear about not interacting with them. "How's Michael?" Bhavna added, her eyes flying from Vic's face to somewhere over her shoulder. Vic's mouth hung open, but when only air went in and out, Bhavna continued. "So I wanted to ask you . . . about that letter." Vic could only continue to stare at her quizzically. "The letter you said you'd—"

"Vic?" There he was. Scott. All six feet and four inches of him. He was becoming more attractive as he got older, Vic realized, a twist in her gut. She was most certainly not. His big charcoal woolen peacoat screamed masculinity. Had an unusual amount of time passed since they'd been this physically close to one another?

"Scott!" Vic said, hoping she sounded surprised. "Hi!" As she looked to introduce her, Vic was surprised to see a huge smile had spread across Bhavna's face, as if Scott were some famous actor. I mean, Vic knew he was handsome, but Bhavna just looked so . . . thirsty. "This is Bhavna," Vic said.

"So nice to meet you!" Bhavna said, extending her hand and beaming at him.

"Her son is applying to Kent now with my daughter."

"Yes, we love the school. His name is Harry! Harry Shah," Bhavna added eagerly. Vic gave her a very gentle stink eye. Why would Scott care?

"Wow, that's crazy," Scott said charitably, shaking his head.

"Scott and I went to Kent together," Vic said.

"Is that all we did?" he said cheekily. He grinned at her. Vic felt like she was right back at a high school party, flirting with this Adonis two years her senior. Captain of the basketball team. Bit of a lothario. Wealthy family. Vineyard house right on the beach. The whole nine.

"Yes, how wonderful. I hope my son, Harry, gets to make those same kinds of friends. I mean," she blushed, "not the same kind of friends . . . anyway, I should go," Bhavna said, backing away. No one was going to stop her. Vic turned her eyes to Scott, and he smiled at her. "See you soon, Vic," Bhavna said from what felt like ten miles away.

Vic forced herself to look in her direction and say, "Yes, see you later!" Then Scott and Vic were alone in Union Square Greenmarket gawping at each other. Vic wished she had freshened up her makeup or combed her hair or anything before this encounter. Body odor wafted out of her wool jacket.

But Scott didn't seem to notice. He smiled down at her. "It's good to see you, Vic."

They strolled down the central lane of the farmers market, taking no interest in much of anything but feeling the presence of the other person, right there, next to each other, and the weird familiarity of that. They had dated for two formative years, but it felt like millennia ago. Small talk seemed impossible.

"Are you doing anything right now?" Scott asked abruptly.

"Not really," Vic admitted.

"Drink?" Scott looked down at her. The sun was behind his head, and in half silhouette he almost looked like he was seventeen again. Which made Vic fifteen.

"Sure!"

They went to a tiny place that was mostly a window onto East Sixteenth Street. The oversize antique mirror behind the bar listed the wines by the glass in white grease pen. It was empty because it was only about 3:00 p.m. The affable bartender in shirtsleeves nodded at Scott.

"Jameson and soda. Make it a double."

"Me too," Vic smiled gamely at Scott. They took their drinks to a small table by the window and held them aloft.

"Here's to running into old friends on bad days," Scott said.

"What's going on?" Vic asked, but Scott only sighed. "That bad?" He took a gulp of his drink. They were quiet, Vic remembering what it had been like to be with this strong, handsome man who seemed to be content just to watch her. Closely.

"You really look good," he said, finally coming to a complete assessment.

"You do too," Vic responded, and he actually blushed, which made her feel all warm inside her rib cage.

"So, seriously," he cleared his throat. "Tell me more about what's really going on with you?"

"My mommy friend killed herself last week," Vic blurted without thought, extinguishing any sexual tension that might have been creeping up on them.

"Oh, no, that's terrible!" Scott resettled his body, giving Vic his full-faced attention. Vic told him about Susan, sketched her out for him, but resisted the urge to get out pictures or make it too maudlin. He listened, shaking his head. "Tragic," he finally said. "Did you have any idea?"

Vic had been mulling over this very question every few minutes for ten days, and she kept returning to a lunch they'd had at a seasonal restaurant on a boat docked off the West Side of Manhattan. Blazingly hot and without much shade on deck, they were two mommies let loose for one of the first times since having kids. Susan wore a tight, stretchy, long-sleeved high-neck shirt, although it was steaming. As they downed vodka-cranberry iced teas, she let out a little false laugh and said, "You probably think I'm crazy in these long sleeves today."

And Vic, who was on her third drink and seeking only to comfort her friend, said, "No, I hadn't really noticed." She had thought that this would be the best way to put her buddy at ease; her first instinct was to at least try to make other people feel comfortable. But what bothered Vic now was her own lack of curiosity to look beneath the surface.

"In retrospect," Vic explained to Scott, "I wonder if it was, you know, a cry for help, because she was a cutter or something, and she was trying to tell me, and I couldn't even be bothered to notice."

Scott seemed to be thinking about this. He was quiet for a minute. "You know, Vic, you've always been too hard on yourself." He paused and eyed her meaningfully, sipping his almost empty cocktail. Was he right? *Maybe,* Vic realized. "And I think this is no exception. This was your daughter's friend's mom. She wasn't your responsibility."

Vic appreciated Scott trying to make her feel better, even ineffectually, but she was more grateful when Scott changed the subject. "Who's your"—he searched for the right words—"daughter's father?" Vic filled him in on Sean, a nice enough guy. Their breakup was as drama-free as the rest of their relationship, which was probably part of the problem. Sean was the steady, nice guy Vic could not quite convince herself to be satisfied with.

"I could do with less drama," Scott admitted.

Vic nodded sagely. "Do you want to have kids?" she asked.

"With Lili?" he asked, as if the thought had never occurred to him. "I mean, I guess I'd have to eventually." This made them both laugh. "Do you like being a mom?"

Vic thought this over, uncovering nothing particularly new or insightful to say. Being a mother is all the extremes: exciting, boring, rewarding, thankless, satisfying, empty, honorable, common. Becoming a mother meant, on occasion, being gripped by sudden, throat-crushing fear. You had to do it to understand. Instead, she said, "I can't believe my daughter is applying to Kent now. It seems like it wasn't so long ago we were students there."

Scott's eyebrow went up a millimeter. Vic had been so distracted by her own illicit ideas and behavior, she had lost sight of the most important data point. Scott was on the board of trustees at Kent! No doubt he could at the very least put in a good word with the headmaster, Glenn. Knowing Kent, she realized there was probably some sort of list he quietly kept of "friends of trustees"—a list Jetta should be on. "Maybe you could . . . ," Vic said.

"Consider it done," Scott said, lifting his glass to toast their agreement.

NINE

BHAVNA

Bhavna wandered the Union Square Greenmarket like an apparition, drifting with the flow of chic urbanites amid unmanicured produce: cabbage heads bigger than basketballs, garlic with the stalks still on, fava beans in their oversize shells. Who were these people, with time to trim and wash and shuck in the evenings and shop during a weekday afternoon in the middle of a transit strike? She was here to get away from her work situation.

And, come to think of it, her home situation, from which she had finally escaped after nine long days. While it had seemed tremendously unnecessary for Bhavna to spend the hundreds of dollars and several hours' time commuting each day, she had not come close to achieving the successful alchemy of working from the same apartment where her two small children and spouse also resided. The interruptions! The noise! The nightmarish melting of every relentless moment into the next.

The transit strike stranded Bhavna on Roosevelt Island and kept all their childcare stuck across the water. This setup had not helped with the Kent interview, which she and Dev had conducted while their children watched cartoons in the living room and, they prayed, did not find a way to suffocate or electrocute themselves. Bhavna did everything she could to make it successful, firing up the ring light and styling Dev's hair. But when they clicked the link for their exactly twenty minutes, they did not find the Buddha-like face of one of New York's most famed backroom private school power brokers, but some junior-level admissions administrator. This itself was a bad sign. Bhavna had gleaned that the most favored applicants would be interviewed by none other than the famed Libby Langsford, head of admissions for the entire Kent School. From what Bhavna understood, that was practically a sure sign of acceptance. The woman who "interviewed" them appeared to be just out of college—not the kingmaker by a long shot. And doing the whole thing virtually—with the inevitable connectivity lags and fear of her children somehow escaping their pillowy television prison in the other room—did not help.

It was even worse at work. From the beginning, the CMO begrudged her staying home, frowning and grumbling over every disruption. She moved all of her and Dev's clothes onto racks in the hallway, put up a folding table, and was relieved to just barely have enough space to shut the closet door behind herself. From there, she tried to regain the momentum from her presentation, but she could sense her new boss withdrawing from her, almost literally receding with each meeting further and further into the background of his Zoom square.

Maddeningly, Marie returned to the office almost immediately after the strike started, despite their face-to-face conversation about doing the opposite. Between that and the sheet Marie had found on the printer, Bhavna was not surprised when the CMO announced James would also present his Go Global campaign. She quickly made plans to commute via car, although she had to pay a premium for service on Roosevelt Island. The driver still arrived late and charged her over a hundred dollars just to get to her office, which usually took forty minutes and that day took nearly an hour and a half with all the extra cars on the road to replace the loss of mass transit. She was glad she'd only have to do it once.

But the bad feelings did not dissipate the moment she physically arrived at the office. The chill wasn't just from the air-conditioning. Bhavna was surprised to see everyone present. Then she realized there were no other mothers in the office. No other residents of waterlocked Roosevelt Island. These youngsters lived in tiny boxes in the East Village, converted factories in Williamsburg. They were childless and fancy-free, able to embark on a ninety-minute walk each way and call it fitness. They all wore chunky sneakers and comfortable clothes. Even her own assistant, Marie, popped up and around her desk in a vintage tracksuit.

"Oh, hi," she said, sounding a little more surprised than was appropriate. "Good to see you," she added to smooth it over. Bhavna only nodded wordlessly and continued straight to her desk. God, she loved her office. This was a room of her own. With a window. Bhavna sighed, her hands on the glass desk, blissfully clear of all fingerprints and debris. No oddly shaped plastic snack jars. No sudden interruptions or unexpected demands. Bhavna sat back in her chair, closed her eyes, and breathed in the professional environment.

"Ahem." The CMO nearly eclipsed the open door of Bhavna's office with his blocklike body. "Oh, good," he said. "You're here." Bhavna tried not to bristle at his passive-aggressive remark; she had been working every bit as hard from her closet, probably even harder. She put on what she hoped was a convincingly expectant smile. "Look, about today," he said, sounding almost conciliatory. "I'm new here, and I just want to hear all ideas. Maybe it's time to shake things up a little," he said in a neutral tone that told Bhavna nothing about what he might actually mean. Was she vying for a promotion with James? "I want you to know, I really loved your presentation," he said. Much as she wanted to simply believe him, she knew there was more to the story.

When her nemesis delivered a straight-up influencer campaign for Go Global, Bhavna felt secure that her more sophisticated, brand-forward ideas would trump what James outlined, which, he assured everyone, would include a viral makeover video competition.

As if one could guarantee the success of such a thing. Bhavna started to believe that if there was a promotion to be had, it was hers.

When the lights in the room came up, Bhavna was shocked to see the CMO's face alight with enthusiasm for this half-baked idea. "Amazing," mused the CMO. "You cut out the whole production budget."

"That's right!" James beamed back at him. "And since we saved so much money, we take the winning video, edit it, and air it at the Super Bowl!" He practically shouted the last few words. "And that's what will make it go viral," he said with some satisfaction. "Everyone wants a shot at America's biggest audience."

"The Super Bowl?" Bhavna blurted out incredulously. "Bowery makeup enthusiasts care about the Super Bowl?" She scanned the room with her wide eyes, lined perfectly with Bowery navy liqui-pencil, but no one appeared to share her outrage. There was nothing creative or artistic about James's idea. It could be applied to any product.

"You have heard of the Super Bowl?" snickered James. "A few people watch it."

"I just watch it for the commercials," Marie said dreamily. Bhavna shot daggers at her with her eyes.

"It's pretty amazing visibility. A milestone for any brand," the CMO mused, seeing a Super Bowl commercial as a feather in his own cap. Was he going to look for the flaws in James's plan as he had with Bhavna's?

"But . . ." She was grasping at straws. Her eyes panned the room for a hint of support, but even Marie only blinked bovinely. "What about social responsibility?" *Aha!* Bhavna locked eyes with the CMO, and he nodded as if, yes, he understood the words she had just uttered, but they were meaningless to him in this context.

"Of course, social responsibility is a part of our corporate mission, but every campaign can't have that explicitly at its core." The CMO fielded Bhavna's question the way a professor might address an uppity student.

"I'm sure we can work it in somewhere," James said, practically winking at their new boss. It seemed hopeless. Usually, she was management's favorite, especially in cosmetics. How had she lost out to this pale, balding middle-aged gay guy who didn't even wear makeup? This had consumed Bhavna's thoughts as she fled the office after the meeting. Automatically, she walked to the farmers market, which had always soothed her before with its photogenic produce and quality food trucks. And it was an objectively gorgeous early spring day that already felt like spring.

But instead of relaxing, sitting down somewhere, and eating, she found herself wandering around aimlessly with a carton of takeout in her hand as her mind went from one worry to the next. There was Dev, at home, jobless. Most of their professional network was in London. It had been harder than she expected to establish ties in New York; Kent would change that. If Harry got in. Which he would . . .

A small crowd had clumped discreetly around the periphery of something that at first sounded like the squawks of a dying bird. Maybe they were slaughtering a turkey? Bhavna peeked over the shoulder of the stout, flannel-clad man in front of her who pretended to examine some onions and saw that the object of everyone's attention was a very attractive couple in a lovers' spat. The woman involved—a perfectly presented but unremarkable blonde—had a screeching voice impossible for even the most seasoned New Yorker to stroll past unbothered. And then there was the man, who looked familiar. Tall with a sexy salt-and-pepper beard, slightly weathered but in a preppy, manicured way with just the right . . .

Scott Hearst, Kent trustee, chair of the admissions committee, heir to his father's real estate empire. Bhavna recognized him from the Kent information packet she had spent her commutes studying. Weirdly, of all the people on earth, he was someone she most wanted to meet, someone who could put his finger on the lever for Harry. And there he was, right in front of her. Too bad he was arguing with his girlfriend in public. She could hardly march up to him, hand outstretched, right at that moment.

Bhavna turned as nonchalantly as possible against the flow of shoppers and picked her way onto a patch of grass. She ducked behind a tree, her Stuart Weitzman suede boots sinking into the grass until she placed them decisively on a root. And there she perched and thought about how she would approach Scott in order to just say her son's name once or twice in his presence. Bhavna winced as his girlfriend squawked at him.

It was only then from her slightly elevated perch on the grass that Bhavna spotted Vic standing under a yellowed tent trying, like Bhavna, to remain unseen. But there was no mistaking Vic's characteristic straight dark-blonde hair and her trademark outfit, fitted jacket and jeans. It looked like she had blown her hair out for a change, Bhavna noted. Was this a planned "bump into a Kent trustee" meeting? Vic acted like she was all laid back, but here she was, staking out the admissions committee guy just like Bhavna, who felt heartened by this revelation. Even for an alumna like Vic, Scott Hearst could take a candidate from reject to Kent student with a single email.

Bhavna would have to latch on to Vic before Scott finished his argument. Plus, she wanted to ask about Michael Harris, Susan's husband. Maybe Vic could confirm those rumors about him leaving his job, which would be an extraordinary opportunity for Dev. Michael's position was essentially the same as Dev's old role, just for a much bigger, richer real estate company. Dev could carry on developing that parcel on the Gowanus if Michael recommended him on the way out. If he was, in fact, on his way out. Maybe Vic would know?

Vic was so focused on Scott that she did not hear Bhavna's unconcealed approach. "Hi!" Bhavna said, but it did not penetrate Vic's concentration. "Vic," Bhavna said more loudly from one foot behind her elbow. Still no response. Bhavna reached out and touched Vic's arm, and she nearly jumped out of her skin. Vic gave a little yelp and leaped backward, almost knocking the table over.

"You scared me!" she said, hand pressed to her chest dramatically. *Geez, high strung much?*

But it became immediately clear why she was so cagey as soon as Scott came over to say hello: Vic was selfish. She did not want to share this encounter with Bhavna and wanted to only talk about Jetta. Which was why she basically dismissed Bhavna, practically waving her away. The nerve. Bhavna wondered if Vic had even written the letter of recommendation for Harry as she had promised she would.

As she wended her way back toward the office, Bhavna pulled out her phone to call Dev and fill him in on the Scott run-in, because she had managed to get Harry's name into the conversation more than once, after all. This was as good a pretext as any for grilling him on his job search. But before she could even unlock her phone, she looked up and saw none other than the CMO refilling James's glass with sake in the window of their neighborhood sushi restaurant—the nice one where they took investors and editors, not the take-out place. It looked a lot more like a date than a business meeting. The CMO laughed at something James said, and James smiled back in satisfaction. Gross.

Bhavna felt her desire to work drain completely from her body. If these two were canoodling in the window of Yama for all the world to see, the writing was on the wall. Bowery Beauty was not a good fit anymore. But Bhavna's problems went beyond the office, beyond James and his new boyfriend—their boss—beyond the beauty world and its narrow standards. Because she could leave that all behind. If her husband had a job. A good job.

The days since Dev had become unemployed had been unsettling ones for Bhavna. Her primary concern was Kent tuition, a sum roughly equivalent to the down payment on a small apartment. If Dev remained unemployed, they would simply have to inform Kent when Harry was accepted and apply for financial aid. Although Kent said late requests such as theirs would be impossible to honor, Bhavna could think of no other course of action to secure Harry his life-changing seat there. After today's meeting, she felt she could even use Vic's name to call upon Scott Hearst. Why shouldn't her family be entitled to some special help too?

But all that was Bhavna's plan B. Her husband needed work. And while Bhavna had been sending out emails and chasing down coffee dates with friends in finance, nothing had come of her efforts yet. There was only one lead she had not yet had the courage to pursue. She looked down at her uneaten lunch, lamb biryani with a side of dal, and reconsidered its role in her life. Would this work as a ruse? Why not? But how would she get there?

Bhavna looked across Union Square at the banks of pedicab drivers. She had taken rickshaws in India with her grandparents in their neighborhood as a girl—Dev's New Delhi family was far too fancy for such conveyances. And now, they were the only way to get around New York, just like Varanasi.

"I hate to leave this down here. It really should be refrigerated! I made it myself," Bhavna gushed, giving the old Irish doorman her best British accent. She fanned herself with her hand for no reason, seeking to distract him from what he had just told her, that Susan's family had asked that all gifts be left downstairs. Bhavna leaned in a few inches over the counter and brought her voice way down, as if imparting a confidence. "We're all a little worried about him," she said vaguely.

"Oh, all right," the doorman said. "Go on."

Bhavna waited anxiously at the bank of elevators, irrationally fearing that he would, at any second, change his mind and rush after her, white glove outstretched. She rushed onto the lift when it finally arrived. Susan's apartment building was as big as Bhavna's Midtown office and hideously impersonal. But it was also so close to school. How easy it must have been to drop Claude at Woodmont. Didn't make much of a difference to Susan, though, Bhavna concluded.

On the ride up to seventeen, Bhavna hastened to straighten up her appearance in the elevator mirror. She smoothed her flyaways and added a quick swipe of Bowery #37. Four different corridors splayed out from the elevator. It took Bhavna a moment to find the right one and then finally Susan's door, and there the wind left her sails. Bhavna stood just outside the Harris residence, listening for clues of who might be inside. She did not want to face Susan's emotionless mother or the traumatized nanny with Susan's young son on her hip. But there was only silence within.

Bhavna looked down the fifteen feet to the end of the hallway, where a window cut a square out of the sky. They were so high up! *Wasn't this floor good enough?* Bhavna mused to herself. *Susan had to go up to the roof?*

Michael had disappeared after Susan's memorial, not showing his face at school, birthday parties, or playdates. Of course, you could understand not wanting to deal with the judgment and assumptions, knowing always that people were especially watching and talking about you. Even when he wasn't present, he was on everyone's mind and lips. Bhavna herself had only met Michael a few times at Woodmont parent events. She really didn't know him at all, Bhavna reminded herself. The poor man was probably a wreck in there, eking out a few minutes to sob in the bathroom after ten sleepless nights comforting his two motherless children.

But then Bhavna replayed her awkward but useful conversation with Kara after the memorial. They had, like everyone, been drinking and somehow ended up in a twosome at the end of the bar. There was something about Kara that Bhavna found hard to place. She seemed to have the money for expensive clothes and upkeep, but her accessories were minimal. Plus, she had a touch of crazy eye when she spoke to Bhavna, which was rarely. Bhavna thought of her as Penelope's sidekick, and she was valuable for that reason alone. As head of the Parents' Association, Penelope had access to privileged information.

Which was why it was a little off putting the way Kara squeezed Bhavna's bicep to draw closer to her and, eye to crazy eye, said, "How are *you* doing, Bhavna?" Without meaning to, she felt herself physically withdraw from this intrusive and patronizing gesture. Surely, she was referencing Dev being out of work. Bhavna wasn't sure how she had found out—it had only been a few days—but why else the overblown concern? What did Kara know about work anyway?

"I'm smashing," Bhavna said in her poshest accent. "How 'bout yourself?"

"Well . . . I . . . I'm OK I guess?" she said, a naked invitation to inquire further, which Bhavna ignored.

"Good, good," Bhavna said crisply, then leaned into Kara and said in a low voice, "What have you heard about Michael Harris?"

Kara's head snapped back quickly toward Bhavna's and then away, like a nervous bird. "He's pretty tortured. I don't think he can go on like this," she said vaguely. Had this come from Penelope's mouth?

"I knew they were leaving the city, but . . . ," Bhavna said leadingly.

"I wouldn't be surprised," Kara said, an urgency now underlining her words, "at all if he wanted a clean break." She made the motion of breaking something, like a twig, in the air between them. She had said this as if Bhavna would understand the negative connotations of this eventuality. But Bhavna felt differently. Who could fault Michael for wanting to turn the page on this chapter of his life? And Dev could slide right into the job and save Michael's employer the hassle of searching for a candidate. Though it was another project manager job, it would really be more like a promotion. Bhavna knew all too well what would become possible if Dev's income went up 20 or 30 percent; in her mind's eye, she saw Harry ensconced at Kent and herself flush with entrepreneurial opportunities.

That's why she was at his door now, as a wife and mother.

Bhavna steeled herself for whoever might answer. She raised one hand, take-out container held chest high with the other. It felt like anyone could be on the other side. She took a deep breath and finally knocked twice. Crisply. Then, on second thought, she punched the doorbell once. Inside she heard a hollow *ding-dong*. Then nothing.

Bhavna waited, shifting her weight from one boot to the other. Out the window at the end of the hallway, the clouds separated and merged, making new formations. As Bhavna's eyes were on them, she thought of herself floating away, out of the rat race she had always run. She, too, could be light as a cloud and drift away to Chappaqua or Larchmont or Greenwich or . . .

The door scraped against the floor as Michael swung it open. He was not the hollow-eyed, baseball-shirt-wearing specter she had anticipated. Rather his peach button-down showed nary a wrinkle, and his khakis appeared freshly creased. Bhavna remembered distantly how she used to find him handsome. Behind him, she spied packing boxes and a quiet apartment. What was she expecting? A collection of sobbing family members? Rooms full of refuse?

"Michael, hi," Bhavna said, meekly tilting her head to one side. His expression remained completely neutral. "I brought you some food," she said, displaying the cardboard box as if it were in fact homemade and enough to feed a family of three when it was neither. Michael's eyes traveled briefly to the brown paper box in her hand, but he made no move to take it.

"Thank you," Michael said, remaining as still as a statue.

"Bhavna. Dev's wife," she said, placing her fingertips on her sternum. He only nodded. Would he leave her standing in the hallway? The silence stretched on. Bhavna thought she could hear the electricity buzzing in the light bulb over her head.

"Come in," Michael finally said.

He was definitely packing. The apartment itself was one of those white interchangeable cubes that never warmed up no matter how long you lived there. The spare architecture, semiemptiness, and, of course, the tragedy that loomed over the Harris home cast everything in a dusty gloom. Large pieces of furniture remained, but everything else—all pictures, knickknacks, throw pillows, signs of this family or Susan—had either never been there or were already within the open boxes dotting the living room. A Goyard tote with an orange monogram hung ominously from the back of a dinner table chair, surely just as Susan had left it. Bhavna wondered if perhaps when Michael departed, he would leave the chair and the bag just as they were, a symbol of his wish to simply walk away.

Their window looked down on Third Avenue, currently clogged with cars. Without intending to, Bhavna studied the casing. There was no way to open it, which explained the roof. She pressed her forehead against the glass and looked down seventeen stories. It was a long, long way. A lump appeared out of nowhere in Bhavna's throat, which she quickly swallowed.

Michael sighed as he tossed the food in the fridge and poured Bhavna a glass of water from a chilled pitcher. He handed it to her over the kitchen counter in a murky glass that seemed like the saddest thing in the world and drank his own icy carbonated beverage. For a minute, they sipped in silence while Bhavna searched for an opening line.

"The kids are at the park with the nanny," Michael said, apropos of nothing. "We told them today she's not coming to Westport with us."

"Oh," Bhavna said, taken aback. "That's sad." The two kids had been with the same caregiver their whole lives and had just lost their mother. Michael only nodded grimly. Bhavna judged this to be another sign his job could be available shortly. Bhavna replayed Kara's words: "A clean break." Bhavna didn't want to mess this up.

"Sit," Michael said, ignoring her comment and moving to stand before the couch. He gestured for Bhavna to sit next to him. She figured this was her invitation to be empathetic. To be a friend.

"Michael, I . . ." She started, but he raised his hand.

"I know," he said, "why you're here." Of course, he did! Relief flooded Bhavna. She wouldn't have to do the whole awkward conversational meandering back to Dev and his job and the position her family was in. The groveling.

Without much thought, Bhavna reached out a hand and squeezed his forearm. "Oh, Michael, that's such a relief."

Michael glanced at her hand on his arm and took a big drink. "I know there are questions"—Michael eyed her, his eyes a bit pink at the rims—"about Susan." Bhavna didn't particularly have any questions. No, not about Susan. Bhavna gently removed her hand from his forearm, but he inched closer to her on the couch. Only then did Bhavna smell the gin. She glanced at his pint-size glass, half-empty, the ice cubes, on closer inspection, mostly melted. "People want to know, was she on drugs."

Quickly Bhavna calculated the dearth of routes from where the conversation had gone to where she wanted it to be. Bhavna could not care less about Susan's drug use. Susan had cashed in her chips and was no longer playing the game of life, but Bhavna was! Bhavna was not there to discuss a dead woman.

"That's not why—" Bhavna said, but Michael cut her off.

"The truth is," Michael said, jostling his ice around in the glass and finally meeting Bhavna's eyes again, "she was."

"I . . . ," Bhavna said, thinking of Dev. Thinking of Kent. She wanted no part in this Harris family drama. ". . . had no idea. I . . ."

"She had tried the benzos, you know, for the anxiety. And they just . . . it was like . . ." Michael turned his eyes on her, and she could see then the unwellness. Something was not right. She should not have come. She was in alien territory. No, Bhavna was the alien. And now, never mind about Dev's job, all Bhavna wanted was to get out. "They didn't help," Michael said.

He took her hand, his eyes full of tears. Bhavna couldn't just drop it and leave now! She squeezed his palm. "I know, I know," she cooed, almost soothingly.

"She was on them when she died, I just know it," Michael said, growling with emotion. Their heads were bowed. She looked at her brown, delicate hand in his oversize white one. She tried to feel good about what she was doing. She hadn't come here for the right reasons, but nevertheless Bhavna was present, in the right place, giving comfort to this member of her community. Even if Bhavna's intentions had been selfish and all she had thought of were Harry and Kent and Dev and a job and money and herself. Here she was, providing real solace to a grieving widower in his time of need when no one else had the courage to walk through the bullshit and show up at his door and insist . . .

OhmyGod his hand was on her boob. His right hand had come up from the glass on the coffee table, and, for a second, Bhavna thought he was going to scratch his face or brush his hair back, but that giant white hand had reached out and cupped her left breast in such an unexpected and casual way. Plus, his palm covered the padding of her bra, such that she could hardly feel it. She had to actually look down to believe that the very slight upward pressure she felt was indeed Michael's hand on her left breast. And in all that time it took so long—too long!—to respond. He was already leaning over, like this was all some nightmare teenage setup at an older boy's house that only Bhavna was not privy to, and here he was swooping in. And for a second, she was paralyzed.

But just for a second.

Bhavna swatted at Michael's hand on her breast like it was a bee and leaped to her feet. Through her alarm, she dimly remembered to grab her bag off the couch as she ran. She burst through the heavy front door, but before she heard it click behind herself, she heard the ghostly sound as it reverberated through the hallway of Michael yelling a garbled, pained, "Sorry," like he was a wounded animal and couldn't be faulted for his behavior. Bhavna felt her stomach bubbling up into her throat. She could still see more than feel his hand—how weird that sensation! Like it had all been something she had read about and not her actual life.

She ran down the long corridor, a featureless city block with that looming window. God, this building was right out of a Stanley Kubrick film. In her mind's eye, the rectangle of blue at the end of the hallway slowly started spinning. Bhavna could see why Susan wanted the hell out of here. She punched the elevator button a dozen times, panting.

Bhavna couldn't tell if it was simply the relief of getting home after another two-hour ordeal with Uber or her extrasensory perception that something good had finally happened, but Bhavna felt better as soon as she walked into her apartment. She had always loathed being across the river from the rest of Manhattan, more so since the transit strike, but now she beheld her spacious apartment with changed eyes. A wall of windows spanned their living and dining area onto a narrow private garden. Their table expanded to seat up to ten. They had two full bedrooms and three bathrooms. They wouldn't be able to afford that in Manhattan, which was why they were on this little island so far from Midtown, and now Bhavna discovered she didn't much care anymore. *So what? So we're not in Manhattan! Ha! Manhattan is full of assholes.* It felt liberating just to think that.

Dev sat on the carpet with the two kids, jazz playing lightly in the background. When she walked in, he looked up with a huge smile that made Bhavna feel all the worse for the news she was about to impart. "Mama's home!" Dev said with glee. While he got to his feet, Bhavna kissed her children. She loved them so much. How would they ever be able to afford to send Harry to Kent now, she wondered every single time she breathed.

But Dev looked happier than he had in some time. He grabbed her by the waist and kissed her, which made her immediately feel guilty. *It's not your fault Michael groped you,* her mind screamed as her body recoiled in shame from her husband. "Come with me," Dev said, walking to the kitchen.

Bhavna watched curiously as Dev carefully placed the two crystal champagne flutes they had used at their wedding on the counter. She rushed to join him there. "Oh Dev," Bhavna gushed. "Did you get a job?"

"Not yet, love." He crinkled his nose at her as he pulled out a bottle of Veuve Clicquot.

"Then what?"

"Aunt Meera died." Dev popped the cork.

"No!"

Dev's mother's eldest sister had never married or had children, choosing instead to become a titan of a medium-size textile business. Her will had been a matter of much discussion over the years, as her hobby was to revise it and publicly announce the alterations. As she got older, these announcements bore less and less resemblance to legal reality. But where and when the truth had stopped, no one knew. All seven nieces and nephews had been in and out of favor over the years. When they were still young and childless, Dev had tried to cobble together an agreement that they split everything seven ways no matter what, but no one had wanted to sign on, preferring instead to roll the dice. After all, sometimes Aunt Meera had said she was going to leave all of it to just one person.

"I got one-third," Dev said. It was more than they'd ever dreamed of.

"Oh, Dev! This means that Harry—"

"Harry can go to Kent from now until college. Both of them can."

"Oh, God!" Bhavna kissed Dev. They clinked glasses. Bhavna felt like Dev's windfall reduced the day's problems to meaningless bits of lint on her sleeve. The path before her son was smooth; there would be no unseemly disruptions as he embarked on his fortunate life. Dev and Bhavna watched Harry color with his sister. He was as smart as any of those other kids, and he deserved every advantage. Looking at her five-year-old son, Bhavna felt like she had already accomplished the hardest part in raising him and stood ready to give him gifts other families could not conceive of.

In one stroke, their family's good fortune would erase Michael's groping in Bhavna's mind. She could not bring that indignity and discomfort into their beautiful future, staining this day forever in their minds. No—she could put it away, so far down that even she would forget it was there soon enough.

TEN

VIC

Vic burst into the Kent lobby a maddening two minutes late for her parent interview. Sean examined the chess-trophy case as he waited for her, his posture relaxed, hands in his pockets. He looked good, it pained Vic to notice, all buffed up and cool in a new gray suit, white shirt, no tie. Vic had told him this was the uniform of the urban professional, and here he was, embodying it. His skin had a new glow that suggested regular intentional cardiovascular exercise.

Meanwhile, Vic's only workout lately was sweating at inopportune times. Here she was once more, several degrees warmer than she might like and in the same jacket she had worn to the tour, this time with silk pants and ill-fitting heels, which she blamed for her mild tardiness. Her feet already throbbed in protest. At least she had nixed the jeans. Vic didn't want Libby to think she was taking anything for granted. She walked a very thin line between not appearing to try too hard and not appearing to be trying at all.

"Hi," Sean said awkwardly from a distance. Surely, he could tell at a glance that she was a little frazzled.

"Hey," Vic said, willing herself to relax, for Jetta. Sean was doing this at Vic's insistence. It was up to her to make the meeting go smoothly. After all, it was nice of him to come, kind of him to make this effort despite not understanding why Vic would ever want to spend so much money on something she could get for free. She felt a rush of warmth for him, remembering that this was why she had liked him so much in the first place, because he could always be counted on. A steady boat in turbulent waters. It was not sexy or exciting, but maybe Vic didn't need sexy and exciting. The slightest "what if" nudged its way into her consciousness. What if she had not said to him, "Let's face the fact that this isn't working"? What if she hadn't said to him, "I don't need any money, just go"? What if . . .

"So you're sure about this?" he said, smiling, just as he had the day he left her apartment for the last time. After all the things she had once thought to say in favor of Kent, now Vic could only shrug. The truth was, she wasn't sure about anything anymore.

The purpose of their meeting with the head of admissions at Kent, a misleadingly diminutive no-nonsense woman with short brown hair in an impeccable sweater set who now led them down a corridor, was unclear. Vic deduced that she and Sean were meant to demonstrate that they were not totally insane or terribly annoying or some other quality that might put off other members of the Kent community. Libby ensured all parents made suitable guests at the inevitable deluge of cocktail parties. Why else interview the parents?

She ushered them into a tiny, windowed room with a small love seat for the parents and an easy chair for herself. Libby launched into her spiel about community, pedagogy, anti-racism, blah, blah, the words ran together. Hadn't their application signaled an enthusiasm for the Kent way of doing things? Vic was surprised to see how interested Sean appeared in Libby's words. She herself was having trouble displaying the level of engagement Libby clearly expected. Vic suddenly felt very, very tired. After her last bout of good sleep just before lunch with her editor, Vic had been gripped by the worst insomnia of her life. Every morning, she thought it could not go on like this. Every day, her manuscript went unwritten and her emails seeking work unanswered. And every night, she lay awake as if her eyelids were pinned open.

"Tell me about Jetta," Libby asked, her pen poised on her legal pad, carefully tilted away from Sean's and Vic's views. A simple enough question. In her mind's eye, Vic held up an image of Jetta at the playground, running toward Claude, who was trailed by a smiling Susan.

"Jetta loves her friends," Vic said. How long ago was that gorgeous day in the park when everything was still OK? Could it only have been last year? She had been finishing up the revisions on her last novel, playing hooky to meet Susan at the park. They had laughed conspiratorially, muting their phones and pouring rosé from a paper bag into plastic cups. Was the sickness in her then? Was it in both of them?

Libby waited patiently for Vic to say more, but just as was happening at her computer every goddamn day, the words stopped. All she had was a long stream of jettajettajettajettajetta. Did she not even know her own daughter in any meaningful way? Vic now understood exactly where the expression *to choke* had come from. Suddenly rendered speechless, Vic could only turn her eyes to Sean, tacitly passing the ball to the guy who didn't even want Jetta to go to Kent. Sean cleared his throat. "Yeah, that's the thing, Jetta just loves working and learning collaboratively. There was this slightly younger kid in her classroom last year, and Jetta spent all her free time with him practicing his shapes, which actually helped her get a head start in geometry, if you know what I mean?" Sean said hesitantly, but Libby nodded along, encouraging him to continue, which he thankfully did.

It was probably better that Vic not say anything. She was frightened that if she opened her mouth, the truth might come out. What was the point of even being there if it was completely out of reach financially? Vic's stomach twisted into a knot, not about the interview she was currently enduring, but the conversation afterward. The one where she would ask Sean for a loan. His architecture firm was doing really well. He had bought a place a few months back and had enough to renovate it. Surely, he could help the mother of his child get by.

Because, the sad truth was, Vic needed money. Pretty desperately. After that dreadful lunch at Xaviers and the subsequent lack of inspiration, Vic faced the hard truth that it was time to implement plan B. After all, she was no idiot. She knew all along that at any point her career could implode, and she'd need something to fall back on, which was teaching, of course. After all, she had an Ivy League master's degree and four novels under her belt. She glibly jotted off email after email to old professors in whose classrooms she had not distinguished herself, classmates who had gone on to be successful in academia, heads of departments. She was professional, confident, friendly, and absolutely positive that a handful of the twenty-four people to whom she had reached out would respond to her.

She got two quick notes back right away: sorry, I can't help you. And then, nothing. Silence. Days passed. Vic combed her contact list and called her alumni offices, who explained that not only was it extremely difficult to find full-time university-level teaching posts in creative writing, but it was also the wrong time of year. Several people suggested she try again in the fall, but Vic had to figure out how she would pay the rent between now and then.

She stopped sleeping and started liquidating anything she had of value—her grandmother's gold necklace she had never really liked, her mother's old alligator bag, her uncle's Rolex—in order to keep the lights on. Vic's father had left her mother with just enough to live on when he died—nothing to spare. Vic made lists of other jobs she might be able to secure: librarian, waitress, high school teacher, assistant. They all seemed bleak but preferable to homelessness. How to begin, though? How to make every effort to become something she never wanted to be?

Worst of all, if somehow, through a miracle, Jetta did get to attend Kent, Vic would have to return to that community where she was once a star student and homecoming queen. And everyone who once looked up to her would reconsider. There would be nasty talk. Because they all expected more from Vic than to be starting out as a waitress on the cusp of forty.

"We're just looking for normal families. That's my job," Libby was saying, now speaking almost exclusively to Sean. "Just regular people," she said again, which was the oddest way to describe those wealthy enough to pay college tuition every year starting when their children turned five. Still, Vic found herself smiling along as if, of course, this made perfect sense and weren't she and Sean emblematic of exactly the sort of normal but also extraordinary family Libby was describing. Still, words did not form on Vic's tongue until the very last second as Libby artfully ushered them to the door.

"Thank you!" Vic suddenly gushed, as the fist that had been clenching her larynx released. "Thank you so much," she said, hoping that with just the sincerity of her expression and the warmth with which she clasped both Libby's hands, she would overcome her strange silence in the actual meeting.

Out on the street, Vic felt as if she could breathe again.

"You didn't say much in there," Sean said, eyeing her. He absolutely knew something was wrong and clearly did not want to deal with it. Which was fair. Vic was no longer his problem.

"I know, I was distracted. I need to talk to you about something."

"Me too!" Sean said, congenially, as if this were a happy coincidence. Obviously, his was good news.

"You first," Vic insisted, hoping he had a huge new project that would bring in tons of money.

"I met someone. I mean, I met her a while ago now but . . ." The pause dragged on, and dread built in Vic's body. "She's pregnant!" he finally said. "I know it's going to stretch me thin financially, what with having just bought the apartment, but I'm excited about it." He said this with the self-satisfied glee and utter disregard characteristic of men. Vic's head fell to one side as her plan C blew up in her face. Was she just really bad at making plans? Or were circumstances unusually set against her? "At least she's OK with public schools, so . . ." Sean drifted into happy silence.

"Huh," was all she could come up with.

"What's your news?"

"Never mind."

"How's the book, anyway?" he asked.

"Fine."

"And you?"

"I'm fine," Vic said ruefully and without any effort to conceal the obvious lie.

But, of course, Vic was anything but, and all she could do to save a scrap of her dignity was to get away from Sean as quickly as possible. Thank goodness she had spared herself the shame of him turning her down for a loan. She left him standing in front of Kent and hustled off to her new reality—living on credit by day, not sleeping at night.

Over the next few days, Vic grew less and less present in the goings-on of her life. Sure, she got up with Jetta, gave her the overnight oats with almond milk and a soft-boiled egg from the farmers market. She took her to preschool and kissed her goodbye. But everything happened through a thick haze of constant anxiety. Vic found herself in previously unexplored dark corners of her mind, wondering, "What happened to me?"

What Susan had done at first had seemed so far from Vic's comprehension and beyond the range of where she herself would be able to go emotionally. But no longer. Vic had come to understand that some black holes were internal. She could now imagine doing anything to stop the dreadful dark sucking feeling that opened up in her if she stopped moving for too long.

At home one afternoon while Jetta was at school, Vic found herself digging through her filing cabinet for her life insurance policy. She read the whole thing—nothing better to do!—and found that there were no exclusions. The one million dollars would go to Jetta when she died, no matter how she died. As long as the premiums were all paid up.

Vic's phone hardly ever rang, and every alert triggered her omnipresent hierarchy of fears. First, always, was Jetta: any call could mean that something terrible had happened to her daughter. But her secondary fear would quickly gobble up the first, that too much time had elapsed, and her editor or agent was ringing to tell her she had just as well not bother submitting anything and she should immediately return the advance.

Sometimes, Vic hoped it would be Scott. Their drunken afternoon had ended as platonically as it had begun. Mention of Susan's death had dampened the sexual tension, and then Jetta's Kent application doused it completely. Vic was both comforted and disappointed by the lack of any impropriety given that Scott was in a relationship. In the time since they parted with a friendly hug, Scott had sent one "Nice to see you" text, which she had "hearted" just to confirm they were in touch. And somehow, with that tiny stupid icon, it had felt like a timer had begun. Something set into motion that would now have to be derailed or consummated.

And yet there was no further progress. Not a single call or text or anything. Vic absorbed all Lili's IG content like a sponge, watching Violet's engagement-party stories multiple times and screen capping shots of the trays of food, supposedly cooked by Scott, Lili kissing Scott on the cheek, Violet and Lili together in complementary jewel-toned chiffon dresses. Vic studied Scott's mannerisms and movements for signs of the half liter of whiskey he drank beforehand and found none. He played his part perfectly, allowing Lili to toast him and his "amazing cooking" with a smile and a kiss.

Vic returned the insurance policy to the cabinet and sat at her desk staring at the same blank document that had gotten the better of her for months. She had a half hour before she had to pick up Jetta. Her phone chimed with none other than an @lilikopelman live video, which felt like perfect timing.

Lili—in a snug woolen sweater and jeans, hair pulled back in a ponytail, cotton apron on—announced her intention to prepare some ultrahealthy dish. Arrayed in front of her, piles of potatoes, onions, garlic, and expensive-looking implements to prepare them with. #soup-week! appeared in a pink bubble over her head.

"There is nowhere I like to cook more than my boyfriend's family's Martha's Vineyard home."

Duh, thought Vic. Who wouldn't want to cook there? Lili stood at a dark marble island countertop in a spacious kitchen. Ancient wooden rafters soared overhead, and three broad windows with huge panes five across provided the perfect backdrop. A velvety window seat stretched across the length of them; a fire crackled in the corner where they roasted meats and baked pizzas. It was hard to begrudge Lili her social media ambitions when she had settings like this to work with.

A 212 number rang on Vic's phone in her hand, interrupting Lili just as she was about to demonstrate the proper way to cut up a head of garlic. Vic jolted to attention as her anxieties ran one by one through her mind like gazelles dashing across a field. It wasn't Woodmont, so it wasn't about Jetta. It wasn't her agent or her editor. She tried to feel hopeful. Maybe it was . . . someone calling about a teaching post? A waitressing job? Or it could be . . . Scott?

"Hello?" she said breathily.

"Is this Vic?" said a man's voice on the other end. All business and definitely not Scott.

"Yes, who's this?" Vic's mind seized on possibilities. The doctor at the hospital where they had admitted Jetta? Her agent's new assistant?

"It's Glenn Goodyear!"

Vic racked her mind first for something genteel or lighthearted or even simply appropriate, but she wasn't quite sure why Kent's head of school was calling. She had not expected to hear from Kent for at least another week or two, but then again, her grasp of the school-admissions season was flimsy at best. She had, in fact, been dreading this moment, knowing it was as out of reach for her as an oceangoing yacht. "Oh, wow," Vic said inanely. "Glenn, how nice to hear from you."

"I know," Glenn said, acknowledging that it was very special for him to be on the phone. "I only make a handful of these calls each year. But I just wanted to reach out to you, as a valued member of the Kent community, to let you know we are going to take Jetta next year." This was said with authority and benevolence, as if she were being knighted.

Was Vic a valued member of the community? Was that code for having made it onto Scott Hearst's list?

Vic realized she had not yet said anything in response to this incredible news. "Oh, wow!" Vic said again and winced. What was wrong with her? "Thank you so much," she added, thinking only of the looming tuition bill.

Glenn's voice turned stern, and in her mind's eye she could see him switching from his cheery to solemn face. "But I have to ask you not to talk about this with anyone yet. We're only calling special friends of the school and those who were wait-listed so they can feel out their options."

He waited for Vic to respond. "Yes, of course, understood."

Not talking about it would be no problem. Vic was terrified. She had called in a favor for something she couldn't afford. Vic now understood why she hadn't heard anything from Scott; he knew Vic would have to get in touch to thank him.

"All right, then . . . ," Glenn said leadingly.

"Thank you so much, Glenn. I'm overwhelmed. I wasn't expecting an early call. Thank you again," Vic gushed, finally finding her footing enough to show the appreciation that was warranted—and that Glenn clearly expected. Vic tried to feel the happiness she had projected, but everything was happening too quickly. She would soon have to put down some enormous deposit. Her bluff would get called within weeks.

At pickup that afternoon, Vic tried to shake off the tension that she felt radiating through her thin coat. That nut Kara stood at the end of the line of caregivers in the corridor waiting to pick up their preschoolers. As soon as Vic joined the line, Kara turned her intense eyes on her and took a step closer. The way she got right in her face was off putting.

"How are you, Vic?" Kara said with misplaced intensity, her tone meant to convey that she was *really* asking. If Vic was going to confide in someone, it wasn't going to be this ditz. Kara struck Vic as one of those upper-middle-class housewives who simply did not have enough to do other than chase the affections of a wealthier housewife. She wore one of those overpriced Moncler parkas and clearly spent a lot of money on her highlights, but she'd never catch up to Penelope.

"I'm fine! How are you, Kara?" This came out only slightly more condescending than Vic would have liked.

"Well, I'm worried, actually," Kara said.

"About?"

"Michael Harris . . ."

Just then, Amy came through the door. She wore a custom-made full-length camel coat and carried a leather briefcase in her gloved hand that Vic suspected was Hermès. There was always an air about her as if she were entering the room for a board meeting. They barely had time to greet her before she asked, "Have either of you heard anything from Kent?" She said this to both of them, but her eyes stayed only on Vic.

Before she could overthink it, Vic said, "No, have you?"

"No," Amy said immediately.

They both thought to turn their attention to Kara. "Me neither," she said. But the fact that Amy asked on the very same day that Glenn had in fact called seemed like an unlikely coincidence. More likely, Amy had achieved "friend of the community" status through a healthy cash donation. She would never have to worry about tuition. Vic felt an unusual pang of envy. This was yet another thing that had changed. Vic didn't fit in at Kent anymore, with people who could shell out tens of thousands of dollars without thinking about it. These perfectly appointed women of the world bore little resemblance to the doctors and lawyers who had made up Kent's pool of parents in Vic's day.

It was Sean's weekend with Jetta. She went down to his Murray Hill apartment, the one that he owned and now planned to redo. Something that would never have been possible in Vic's oversize rent-stabilized space. Vic had come to understand the renovation in a new light; Sean was adding a bedroom for the baby.

"I'm so excited to be a big sister," Jetta gushed to Vic. As she squeezed her daughter's hand and smiled down at her, Vic's heart broke just a little. This would be such an important part of Jetta's life that Vic would have no part of. It was selfish. They stood outside the door waiting for Sean to open it, and then it was open, but it wasn't Sean. His girlfriend was not only round and resplendent in her fertility but easily a decade younger than Vic. Jetta ran to her and put her cheek on her belly.

"Hi, baby," she yelled into the belly and ran off to her room, leaving the two women alone.

"You must be Vic," she said, extending her soft, delicate hand. She introduced herself, but no way was Vic committing her name to memory.

"Congratulations," Vic found herself saying, before backing away down the corridor and practically vanishing.

Alone in her apartment, Vic wandered from her bedroom to Jetta's, to the living room and the guest room through the dining room. She had lived here her whole life. Had sex for the first time in here, the guest room, with Scott. She sat on the double bed and faced the dingy window out into the courtyard. This room had felt so sexy then, so clandestine. Now, after nights of sleeplessness, days devoid of work and inspiration, it felt like the perfect metaphor for her life. A tiny space poorly laid out, full of cast-off furniture from Vic's parents. This, too, had at first felt temporary but had at some point ossified into permanence.

Vic made herself a drink: whiskey soda, to remind herself of Scott as an adult. She sat on the couch in the living room, where she never sat, with a book open on her lap, but there was no way she could absorb any of it. This was just a way to pass the moments until she had enough alcohol in herself to make this important call. He answered on the second ring.

"I've been wondering when I would hear from you," Scott said.

"God, you sound like my Jewish grandmother," Vic said. "I'm calling you now to say thank you."

"And?" Scott said. She could hear him smiling.

"And," Vic said, smiling back in spite of herself, "I *really* appreciate it."

"Annnnnd . . . ," he said again. Silence. "I think you at least owe me dinner."

Vic hesitated for a moment. She knew this was probably a big step in the wrong direction, but maybe she just needed to have some fun? It wasn't like Scott was married. Maybe they weren't even exclusive? It was just dinner at a public place. "How about tonight?"

Scott picked the restaurant where they had their first real date over two decades prior. It was hidden on a tiny side street in the West Village that had taken Vic almost an hour to find as a teenager. Because of the transit strike, he sent a car for her, so she was right on time. Which just made logistic sense, Vic told herself, and was not part of an elaborate courting ritual.

The place was even more charming than she remembered. They sat at the very same tiny bistro table, tucked in a nook with lots of candles dripping along the molding, illuminating peeling celadon paint. Big stained mirrors hung from every wall. They drank martinis and ordered a large steak to share, Vic straining to both enjoy how much this felt like a date while reminding herself that it was almost definitely not a date.

It was just that Scott looked more handsome than he ever had before, in his white shirt, his beard neatly manicured. Vic had to dig through her underwear drawer for the bra that gave her the best cleavage and then searched half the closet for the snug Missoni top that showed it all off. They both looked polished up, like they had taken extra care to look effortlessly appealing.

The energy between them crackled with sexual tension that made it hard to settle on a topic of conversation. Probably because what they really wanted to know about each other would be terribly awkward to just blurt out. Halfway through the bottle of red wine, as their meal was served, Scott finally spoke of Lili. "It's just . . . social media is not my thing."

"Me neither!" Vic admitted. "Much to my editor's chagrin," she added, thrilled to be able to include this little misleading but technically true statement.

"But she lives by it, and that means that I have to live it too," he said, slicing his meat with enthusiasm. "This is the first hot food I've gotten to eat in months." He lifted his eyes from his plate and caught Vic's confused expression. "Because she has to take a thousand pictures of everything before we can touch it."

"Sounds tedious."

"You have no idea." He chewed his meat with such gusto. Vic was too amped up to eat, preferring instead to just nibble her bread and stare at Scott. "But Vic, tell me about your life now. Are you still in that same old apartment?"

Vic winced a little. "Yup." But it wasn't all bad. She told him about Jetta, their day-to-day, how thrilling and tedious it was being a mom. Vic had forgotten what a great listener Scott was. At least when she was talking.

"So, what's your major problem?" he asked over profiteroles and brandy. Vic knew she couldn't be completely frank. First of all, it was terribly unattractive to be a broke failure. If she told Scott the truth, it would not only ruin their evening, but worse, it might jeopardize everything for Jetta. She wasn't ready to let go of that dream yet.

"What?" Scott nudged. "I shared!"

"Promise you won't laugh."

"I promise."

"I have writer's block, Scott."

"That doesn't sound too terrible."

"If I don't figure out what to write, I'm not sure I can afford Kent," she admitted, substantially sugarcoating the truth.

"Why don't you just write about your crazy friend who killed herself?" Scott said, his mouth half-full of profiterole cream.

"Susan?" Vic said, as if her name would clarify anything for him. It seemed somehow wrong to write about her. She had felt guilty about not being a true or insightful enough friend to Susan and now to cast her as a character? Yet as soon as Scott suggested it, Vic knew he was onto something. "I don't think I knew her well enough to write about her," she said, more and more open to it.

"Aren't you a novelist?" Scott asked. Vic thought back to what Kara had said earlier that day, that she was worried about Michael. Kara had practically suggested Vic call him. Maybe she would organize a playdate for Jetta and Claude before she moved away. Maybe Isa, Susan's nanny, would be able to fill in some of the blanks. Help flesh out the story.

"You know," Vic said, recognizing for the first time in forever that initial spark of invention. "That's not a half-bad idea."

"That's two solids I've done you, today alone," Scott said, smiling in a big sincere way that made Vic tingle. They had effectively cheated reality and arrived in some alternate version of the present, where they had been together all this time. Or, even more magically, they were both once again teenagers, king and queen of the homecoming dance. "Plus, you owe me for not holding a grudge about the way you dumped me."

Vic's mouth fell open in surprise. "I'm not sure . . ."

But Scott never was one to let an opening pass. He had her by the elbow and was over their tiny round table in a second, his lips as firm and confident as she remembered. God, the way he kissed her, it was like everything she had hoped kissing could be at fifteen and more. Now it was like a transporting, overwhelming, full-body experience.

"Come home with me," Scott said, his mouth still against hers.

"What about Lili?" Vic asked, wanting to hear that she was out of the picture.

"She's on the Vineyard."

"Ohhhh," Vic moaned into his mouth. She had known that all along. It wasn't ideal, but it was good enough, so, of course, she went. Because didn't Vic, too, deserve just the smallest measure of joy?

ELEVEN

KARA

Kara would have to keep an eye on Vic. She just didn't look right. Not at all. She had been Kara's pick all along to succumb to sadness after Susan's death. Kara knew too well the contagion of suicidal ideation, the way one can lead to another and another. This was why she hadn't told anyone the method of Susan's suicide—because she knew that details like that could trigger those around the victim, like Vic. It was for the best that she didn't know the whole story.

As the host said on *Serenity, Maybe?*, "Sometimes, it is enough just to move forward." Kara took this to mean that she should always keep busy and have a purpose in life, even if that purpose had been reduced to simply tracking the movements of the family across the street. For days on end, she could throw herself into watching the Harris family's comings and goings. Occasionally, she even went on little "excursions," as she called them in her mind. No harm done. Just, you know, research.

Because there was obviously, *obviously*, something else going on there. What the hell was Bhavna doing there? The kids had gone out with the nanny, and then, twelve minutes later, there's Bhavna, charging inside as if on a mission and, fourteen minutes after that, fleeing as if she'd seen something horrible. Obviously, Michael had called her. But why?

Would an objective third party call Kara's behavior "obsessional"? Quite possibly. There were few guardrails in her life now that Isaac had been reduced to an occasional visitor in their home as the transit strike finished an unbelievable third week. He had only been back twice, and each time Kara had managed to tidy up enough to obscure the strange adjustments in the apartment to suit her new lifestyle.

Indeed, she had reoriented her existence toward the window, so she could always keep one eye out. Kara swapped a side table for her desk, moving it down so that she could sit at her sewing machine or computer and keep her view on the front door across the street. It was at the window that she prepared meals, played with and changed the baby, folded laundry, sewed and mended the family's clothing, and completed all the administrative work that went along with being an adult in New York. As the days went on, she spent more and more time in quiet contemplation, or really more like an unbreakable negative thought spiral, her body going still as her mind ran through a series of linked negative thoughts: *Susan jumped right there, just right there, from all the way up there, she jumped she jumped just like my sister who jumped why why why am I alive? Shouldn't I also be dead? But I could never jump like Susan. Susan jumped just right there.*

Something pierced the cyclone of Kara's thoughts, a sensation . . . a noise! An incredibly loud sound. Baby crying! The baby was crying! Kara rushed into the bedroom to find her younger son, red faced, furious, his diaper leaking, and piss all over his crib. The fan was off, and the room was stifling. It felt like he'd been poached in his own urine. Kara hated herself. How long had he been like this?

The drying rack stood extended and heavy with everyone's long-dry clothes, preventing Kara from giving the baby a quick proper bath. So she took him to the kitchen sink, which was full of dishes. In the end, Kara ended up back at the window, with the baby on her makeshift desk and a brick of wipes. She stripped off his clothes with her eyes on the Harris front door. There they were! Isa was pushing a stroller with Claude holding the handle, her little face set grumpily against the world. Kara's heart broke just wondering what she had seen that morning.

They turned the corner, and Michael ran from the building like a shot. He wore a cap that obscured his face and had the collar of his jacket inanely up, chin tucked in as if this made him look any less conspicuous. But soon he, too, was gone. No more Harrises to observe. Kara realized her hand was still in midair with the third wipe, the baby wriggling underneath her palm on the table. She finished swabbing him, put him in a fresh onesie, and gave him some rice puffs.

It was the first time since Susan's death that the whole family was all out at the same time. It felt like she could finally take a break. She sat on the couch for the first time in a long while and looked at her phone, awash in notifications and alerts. Right at the top, KENT PARENT INTERVIEW: TOMORROW.

Panic. First of all, what would they wear? Second of all, how would Isaac get there? Or was this a blessing in disguise? After all, he was so unpolished. So likely to say something off color. So when she called him, she was ready to play the part of selfless mother.

"No, no, don't worry. How could we have known there would be a transit strike?" she said, almost cooing.

"Let me see if I can borrow Jose's car. He already offered a few times."

"OK, but . . ." Kara searched for another compelling reason why he could skip it. "You really don't have to," she said lamely.

"I know it's important to you," Isaac said.

The next twenty-four hours were a forced return to normalcy, with Kara throwing herself back into the work required to get the apartment and herself presentable. She moved the furniture back and vacuumed. She folded the laundry rather than leaving it in a pile on the floor. She took care of all the things that took her away from her post at the window: she did her highlights and tweezed the errant hairs on her face. She had to adjust her dress—her body was also sort of rearranging itself, too, into an unfortunate pear—and press all her and Isaac's clothes. Polish their shoes.

It was grueling and unappreciated, and sometimes Kara wondered if they wouldn't be better off moving out of the city. Isaac could commute, the kids could go to public school, and she could make simple clothes rather than these haute couture imitations. By the time Kara and Isaac were walking arm in arm through Kent's doors, she had spent hours and hours making garments just for this one day.

And there, across the lobby, Penelope and her husband were bidding goodbye to Libby, the famed admissions director everyone was so scared of. She actually reached for Penelope's shoulder and drew her in for a kiss on each cheek. With her endless designer clothes and handbags, Penelope was like an entirely different creature—not another city mom trying to get by but a swan, glorious and graceful, swooping and gliding along, occasionally dropping from her polished talons a no-longer-wanted pair of Gucci heels or a Moncler coat. For her, her children, and maybe even their children, life would be easy. Every gate in town stood open before them, every gatekeeper ready to plant kisses on all their cheeks. But for people like Kara—outsiders with shallow pockets—trying to inhabit this private school–SAHM identity utterly sucked the life out of you.

"Hi!" Penelope beamed at Kara and Isaac as they passed, giving Kara a quick embrace as they breezed out. Things had been off between them in the three days since Kara had divulged seeing Bhavna fleeing the Harris building. "She was in tears!" Kara had practically hissed at Penelope. They sat over ten-dollar bowls of café au lait. It was a Saturday morning, so the kids were with Penelope's two nannies at the park. The bustling café was full of people who knew people they knew, and Kara leaned over the white marble two-top so as to not be overheard. "And she was only up there fourteen minutes."

This new information penetrated the thick veneer of indifference Penelope had developed toward all details having to do with Susan. Which had been difficult for their friendship because Kara hardly had anything to talk about other than what had recently happened at the Harris building. It was also surprising to Kara, who thought Penelope had been out to lunch with Susan once or twice; they seemed to have more than a passing relationship. But Penelope had been useless, going on and on about some family business that clearly operated quite smoothly without her having to worry the tiniest bit about it.

"Could it have been going on all this time?" Penelope mused, her eyes narrowing in reflection. Obviously, this very question consumed Kara. Had Bhavna been having an affair with Michael? Had Susan uncovered it, contributing to her death? Did Michael break it off after the suicide? Kara felt like she was finally gaining some traction with her friend, and they could sleuth it out together.

"But did they know each other in any other way? I feel like I hardly ever saw them together until Susan's memorial," Kara said, continuing her line of thinking.

"Didn't Michael work with Bhavna's husband or something?" They both mused on this a little, and in Kara's mind another light went on—another data point that only she knew to connect.

"Well, actually, they are first degree connections on LinkedIn," Kara said, expecting her friend to, if not congratulate her on her research, at least admit this was a salient fact.

"Who?"

"Michael Harris and Bhavna's husband."

Penelope's body sort of jerked back six inches, and her head tilted to a forty-five-degree angle, where it stayed, as if she wanted to examine Kara from a new perspective. This was not exactly the reaction Kara had hoped for. She could feel Penelope's judgment. "Kara, let's be serious. It's not like Susan killed herself because Michael was having an affair," Penelope concluded, somewhat dismissively. "It's as silly as the idea that she offed herself because of the corntroversy." She waited for Kara to acknowledge this and move on, but Kara was working to trace the steps backward. It wasn't that Susan had killed herself because of Michael's affair, but rather that this was an indicator of something more. Didn't Penelope understand?

Kara's sister had jumped off a bridge, as her mother told it, over some stupid boy. But Kara had always known that the whole "stupid boy" thing was only a sign of deeper problems and not the issue itself. Kara tried to work out how to make this critical point to Penelope, but as always happened with New Yorkers, you could never take more than a split second to formulate your thoughts or the conversation moved on. Penelope was already trying to change the subject. "I wanted to—"

"Wait, wait a sec," Kara interrupted, unwilling to let her theory die. "You don't think it could have been a contributing factor?" she said. She had to speak loudly now that Penelope was leaning away from her, and it sounded more aggressive than she intended. An older Park Avenue type at a nearby table turned her snooty face on them to quiet Kara down.

"Look, Kara," Penelope clucked and sighed as if resigned to imparting this next bit of wisdom. "Susan was just way, way more fucked up than anyone knew. There's nothing more to it than that." Kara couldn't help but look stricken. Penelope's words shocked her with their brazen lack of empathy for both Kara and Susan. Penelope's tight face told Kara she really had no wish to talk about this further, a reality Kara struggled to accept. "You seem, like, really stressed about this, though. Can I offer you a Klonopin?"

"Is that like Valium?" Kara asked, taken aback. She had never thought her friend was medicated. Kara had only had Valium at the hospital the night her sister died. The kind doctor had given her a few to take home, and she expected she would never again get to experience the kind of guaranteed emotional relief that came out of a bottle.

"Oh, honey, Klon's way better than Valium," Penelope said, digging into her Dior bag. She pulled out a quarter-full bottle and handed the whole thing to Kara. "Just take a half when you're feeling"—Penelope had examined Kara's face, finding all the shortcomings in her daily ablutions: the puffiness under her eyes, the patches of dry skin, the unstyled hair—"overwhelmed."

So, of course, Kara had taken half a Klonopin that very morning and didn't feel flustered at all to see Libby waiting for them as she said a quick hi to Penelope. Penelope had been rather chilly to her since that day, but it didn't matter much now. Everything was just fine.

Because if there was one thing Kara could still talk about, it was Oscar. Truth be told, Kara wasn't sure where Oscar had come from. He had started beating milestones from the first week—holding up his head, pulling himself up, walking, talking—doing all of it months if not years ahead of schedule. It was the day care manager who had suggested Kara take him to Woodmont, and Nina who had plucked him out of the group for Kent because he was frequently obviously ahead of his peers. Kara had even prepared a little anecdote about how Oscar could do basic arithmetic, when Libby started by asking, "Tell me about you guys."

"Us?" Kara said, taken aback. "Well, I'm a homemaker from the Midwest, and Isaac is a physical fitness trainer."

"Uh-huh," Libby said encouragingly, as if to say, "Surely, there's more to it than that." But what? Not only were Kara's responsibilities never ending, they were also monotonous. Hence moving everything to the window, where she could multitask. She often spent the entire day in the company only of the baby, who slept and ate and smiled and did tummy time and all those things babies do. But who would not turn to Kara and say, "Hey, you over there at the window? You might be obsessing just a bit!"

"I think the thing I'd like to talk about," Kara said, "is Oscar. You know, we're not the exceptional ones." She placed a hand on Isaac's knee. "Oscar is."

"I agree," Libby said, surprising them. "He appears, according to his interviewer, to be able to read quite a bit," Libby said. "I take it neither of you taught him?"

"He taught himself," Isaac said. Libby looked to Kara, who nodded in agreement. Libby's pen swirled around on her legal pad. "OK, tell me more," she said. This was the last test, their final chance to make the case for this life-changing opportunity. Thanks to the Klonopin, Kara could tell story after story of how intelligent and insightful her son was without her mind wandering back to the Harris building and whatever critical occurrences might transpire there in her absence.

TWELVE

AMY

B ut when you say *wait-listed*, Glenn, what does that mean exactly?"
Amy said into the phone, mostly for Ming's benefit. They all knew
exactly what it meant. Amy, for one, just couldn't believe that Pearl's
admission to Kent was in question. Ming leaped to her feet and stood
behind Amy, as if jumping to attention. To do what, Amy wasn't sure,
but her springing into action gave Amy heart. Surely together they
would figure out how to remedy this situation.

"We just had so many qualified applicants this year, Amy . . ."
Glenn sounded like a recording of himself. The nerve of this man to
call her like this with a maybe when in every other conversation—most
of which were about the size of her contributions and what they would
buy for the institution—he had been so definitive.

"Glenn, I thought my gifts were substantial." Ming grabbed a
nearby tablet off her desk and called up the numbers on a spreadsheet
of all the private schools and Amy's cash gifts. Kent stood at the top:
$500,000.

"About five hundred thousand dollars," Glenn said, sounding not
as pained as Amy would have hoped at the idea of losing her as a donor.

"That's right . . . half a million dollars, and I'm not even entitled
to some feedback?"

Amy couldn't help but wonder if she had overplayed her hand at the parent interview. Ming had attended as Amy's interpreter, which was wholly unnecessary, but her presence always made Amy more comfortable. Ming had mostly remained silent, but when Libby started to describe their curriculum, Amy couldn't stop herself.

"Excuse me, Libby, I'm not sure I know this word 'anti-racism.'" Then she turned to Ming and in Mandarin said, "Someone like her is going to teach Pearl about racism?"

"Stop being such a smart-ass," Ming had responded.

Is it possible Libby spoke Mandarin? It was the only potential bad mark against them in the whole application process. When Glenn remained silent, Amy continued to prod him. "You can't even tell me precisely why Pearl is on the wait-list?"

"I'm afraid not, Amy."

"How about odds, Glenn? Can you tell me what number she is? How many spots still available?" Amy had built her life on careful calculations. She knew he could probably give her the information if he really wanted to. Which infuriated her all the way through the heat of rage to the point where she felt as if this conversation had turned her into a block of carved ice.

"All I can tell you is that you'll hear if Pearl gets a spot."

"When?"

"On a rolling basis."

"Thanks so much," Amy said.

Glenn had interrupted Ming and Amy's afternoon, the quiet of their work generally only disturbed by the sound of green tea being poured into mugs. The two of them could get completely focused and silent when they were on a specific project—in this case, assembling corollary railway investments. Amy envisioned a portfolio with Penelope as the key first deal. Ming cast a wide net, seeking out small to midsize companies in North American rail, then passing her picks to Amy. Most of these had ended up in the pewter trash can tucked discreetly under Amy's desk, but some she had passed back to Ming for further research.

Glenn's call would surely ruin their afternoon of work. Amy sighed as she hung up. Hardly ever had she failed to hit the mark. Ming placed a reassuring hand on her shoulder, and Amy looked up at her. Ming's pointed face, eyes tight and focused behind her tortoiseshell glasses, hair held tidily back by a black satin headband broad enough to resemble the visor of a small helmet—all signaling determination and readiness. She looked fierce, whereas Amy felt defeated already. "I don't know how to work this system," she said, frustrated.

"We'll figure it out," said Ming, returning to her desk. First, she demanded the consultant they hired to navigate the private school–admissions process appear, given they had paid her tens of thousands of dollars. While they waited, Ming made sure Nina would be at Woodmont to discuss the Kent situation. What was Nina's recommendation worth anyway?

Ming and Amy met the consultant in the foyer, both of them waiting with crossed arms after the doorman announced her arrival in the lobby. It had taken her less than an hour to arrive, as polished and unbothered as ever even when Ming demanded the moment she stepped over the threshold, "What happened at Kent?"

Everything about her was the highest-quality ready-to-wear and very expensive but also devoid of style. She was a beige box of a person. Even her hair seemed to consist of ivory rectangles. A former admissions director at a second-tier school, her résumé had been examined from every angle by Ming, who had called seven of her references, including well-known billionaires, royalty, and major celebrities. This had been a miscalculation in that even to the consultant, Amy was a small player, a disadvantage Amy wished she had foreseen.

But Amy, the benevolent employer said, "Why don't you come in and have some tea?" They sat in the office, gave her a cup. Chef brought over an assortment of sweet steamed buns on an oversize Song dynasty plate. Amy could see the consultant eyeing them and said, "Please," while handing her a napkin. The consultant grabbed a bun and tossed the whole thing in her mouth. Amy gave Ming a little nod of encouragement.

"What do we do now?" Ming pressed.

The consultant nodded, chewing through what Amy knew was a pliant doughy pocket of delicious red bean paste. Amy held her hands on her lap and waited patiently.

"Do you know anyone on the board?" the consultant finally asked, chasing her bun with a sip of tea. "Ooh, this is delicious tea," she said, slurping some more. Ming had flagged all the members of the Kent Board months ago, highlighting in particular those members of the admissions committee in her phone book of research. But they had been over this all already.

"Not really," Ming said. "As I recall, you said half a million would be enough."

"And I also recall saying there are absolutely no guarantees for anyone," the consultant said, dabbing her mouth with the napkin and rearranging herself on the low ottoman she had chosen as a seat.

"Listen, we'd just like to understand why they didn't take Pearl," Amy said, once more the voice of reason.

She shrugged. "More likely, there was another child too much like her who had a little bit more of a tie to the school—an older sibling perhaps or a legacy. It's not that there's something wrong with Pearl. There was just something more right about another applicant. Maybe they'll decide to go somewhere else, and you'll get their spot."

Amy's brow furrowed. She hated the idea of pinning her happiness on a stranger's preferences. Ming knew exactly what Amy was thinking. "We're very disappointed," she said. Just then, Amy's phone emitted a loud bomb sound, and the consultant flinched.

She waited for them to ask more questions, but Amy and Ming only exchanged a concerned glance. First the Kent call, and now Amy's father sent a rare text. The consultant grabbed another bun while reminding them, "I still think Pearl will have options. Be a little bit patient?" she said, rising to her feet with a bun encased in a napkin in her hand. Amy's phone *kaboomed* again. "That's some ring," the consultant remarked. "I actually have a few more families in the same boat I have to go talk to," she said, making her exit without the apologies and groveling Amy had expected.

This frustrated Amy to no end. She had found the best fixer, paid her fees, done everything as instructed, and now, this regretless lack of results. This sort of outcome would definitely have cost Amy a client. That's why she was unhappy to read the text message from her father: The investors here are most excited about your railway investment. From her father, this was tremendous praise. Then the second text (there was *always* a second text): When can we confirm?

This was the holdup—Amy wasn't quite sure. Ming had watched from the wings, arms crossed over her body, as Penelope proceeded to put off Amy's increasingly insistent inquiries as to the status of the deal to which she had so readily committed. To Amy's carefully worded three-paragraph emails with two attachments, Penelope would respond, Working on it! Amy could no longer tolerate her delays.

When Ming came back in her coat to go pick up Pearl at Woodmont, Amy said, "I should go," and Ming nodded. There was much to be uncovered among the mothers, and while Amy hated chatting with them, she would do it for her father and for Pearl. As she pulled on her favorite cashmere camel coat, Ming slipped Amy's briefcase into her gloved hands.

"But what do I—"

"Sends a message," Ming said. And Amy slipped it under her arm like a weapon.

As if from an important meeting, Amy arrived with only a minute to spare. Vic, who had surely heard something from Kent, was chatting with that nitwit Kara. Ming's research revealed she had an impossibly low household income and no prospects to speak of. She had never understood why Kara was so frequently in Penelope's company. But where was Penelope today?

195

The doors of the classroom would open any second, so Amy blurted at Vic, "Have you heard from Kent?" hoping the surprise of the sudden question would leave the truth on her face, if only for a quick second. And it did. Clearly, she had gotten a call, which meant that Jetta was also wait-listed. But Vic denied it. She was lazy and ineffective even in her dishonesty.

After grabbing Pearl and her coat from the classroom, Amy loitered in the hallway outside Nina's office while her daughter played with the toys in the nearby waiting area. Conveniently, Penelope was still inside, so there was no subterfuge about this run-in. When Penelope did open the door into the hall, she had a huge smile on her face that shifted only a millimeter when she saw Amy waiting for her outside Nina's office.

"I'm so glad you're here," Penelope gushed, taking Amy aback for a second.

"You are?" Amy couldn't keep herself from asking.

"Yes, it's often hard for me to communicate," she said vaguely. "But I can tell you now that we're face to face." She stepped closer to Amy as if about to impart a secret. Over Penelope's shoulder, Nina appeared in the doorway of her office, waving Amy inside. In a hushed tone, Penelope said, "I'll have confirmation at next week's board meeting."

"Penelope, I need to be able to count on this," Amy said.

"Me too," she said, which gave Amy no comfort at all. But what more was there to say? Maybe Ming had read Penelope correctly, that she actually had no power at all, and the deal would never happen. Ming had been right more than once. Amy watched Penelope walk away, already texting someone.

Nina's office was incredibly small and cramped, to Amy's eye, for such a prestigious and powerful position. Amy could never understand it. Nina, at her desk up against the wall, swiveled around and gestured for Amy to take someone else's ratty chair from the second desk by the printer. But the shoddy space was of no consequence. Nina herself possessed the same self-assurance of all these city gatekeepers. Perhaps her role as preschool admissions and, more importantly, exmissions director meant nothing 95 percent of the time, but for some people, Nina held all the keys.

"I'm sure you're disappointed."

"I just don't understand what happened," Amy said.

"Nothing 'happened,'" Nina said. "On a different day or in another year, Pearl would have been accepted right away."

"Pearl had your highest recommendation, isn't that right?"

Nina's eyebrows went up at that slight. "Of course, it is. But when it comes to schools like Kent, nothing is certain."

Amy tried to switch gears. She couldn't leave empty handed. "I just thought that Woodmont prepared Pearl perfectly for Kent, and then once we made your list . . ." Amy went silent and waited expectantly, a trick Ming had taught her to get people talking.

Nina regarded Amy for a moment, as if deciding whether or not to throw her a bone. "Look, I can tell you, confidentially, a lot of people were unsatisfied with Kent's admission practices this season." Amy tucked this piece of information away.

"And how does that help Pearl, exactly?"

"It doesn't. I'm just letting you know you're not alone." Ha! As if Amy minded flying solo. In fact, she preferred it. "A class by herself" was where she would happily reside.

In the car, Amy realized she hadn't seen Chandice at pickup or in some time. It was a good reminder that Amy had little to complain about. Chandice put on a brave front, but her odds were not good. Amy would call her to check in on her health, and also . . . perhaps *she* had heard from Kent? The call went to voice mail.

Amy turned her attention to Pearl in the car, a rare private moment between the two of them. Pearl had no expectation that Amy would talk to her; her attention was quietly on the street outside. How Amy had wanted this child! The lengths to which she had gone to secure all the necessary parts and people, the way she went into hiding for six months to avoid the inevitable questions, which she would not answer. When Pearl was born, it was like Amy had enacted a small miracle in this world, but lately all this had fallen from Amy's mind. She undid her seat belt and slid over the seat, looping her arm over Pearl's small shoulders and giving them a squeeze.

"Mama, put on your seat belt, please," Pearl said, sounding exactly like Ming. Amy put on the middle belt.

"You take good care of me, my little Pearl," Amy said, kissing her hair and experiencing the powerful, intoxicating effect of her daughter's scent. She squeezed her again around the shoulders, and Pearl took her mother's other hand in hers. All Amy's efforts were in service of this precious gem: the city, Woodmont, Kent, and some day Yale would ensure that Pearl would have whatever kind of life she wanted. "Are you excited to speak to Baba when we get home?" Amy prodded, but Pearl only shrugged.

Though they saw each other in person at least twice a year and video chatted like this once a week, she couldn't quite get the embers of a relationship to ignite between granddaughter and grandfather past vague pleasantries. It was as if her father had never really spoken to a child, and he asked her open-ended questions that all could be answered in a word or two. Back at the desk in Pearl's room, Amy watched her father on the screen over her daughter's shoulder. He looked like he was shrinking in relation to his office desk, where he always seemed to be.

Amy flushed with guilt. This was the trouble in working with family: when there was a professional problem, it could often become a personal one. She had been avoiding her father's calls until she had a timeline from Penelope, so at least there was something to say. Even if it wasn't progress, they at least knew when progress might be expected. When the nanny collected Pearl for study time, Amy reported, "Penelope says we'll know next month for sure." But her father seemed to barely be listening. His eyes drifted off the screen and back again. "Baba, how are you? Have you heard from Chia-Jung?"

Her father only snorted in reply. "You know who I've been thinking about?" Amy waited. "Mama. I've been going to the temple." Amy's father rarely talked about her mother, the love of his life killed in a car accident at age thirty-nine. Only two years older than Amy was now. It did not get any easier to believe, even as the years and milestones passed without her, but her father hardly ever said her name after Chia-Jung was on the scene. "I miss her very much."

Amy, who for many of the years after her mother died had wanted nothing more than to speak to her father in this way—to commiserate and share their feelings—felt that this door was now firmly closed. She had never developed the vocabulary to describe the terrible loneliness she carried with her all the time. She looked at the framed black-and-white photograph on the wall over Pearl's desk of her mother posing with Amy in front of her prestigious Taipei kindergarten. In her smart suit, hair up in a tidy bun, she looked every inch the banker's wife and wholesome mother.

"I'm worried about this Kent school, Baba. It was my first choice and . . ." He waited for her to finish, clearly not understanding how money could not readily solve any problem except death. "I'm not sure I'm going to be able to figure this out," Amy said.

"Can't Ming help you?" This was her father's solution to everything; he thought the world of Ming, which made Amy proud.

"We've already done everything we can think of." As she said the words, the exhaustion seeped in. She had lived in cities on several continents, but none taxed Amy like New York. Nowhere was it so outright competitive; whether it was for a table at the hottest $400-a-person omakase spot, a midday Midtown taxi, or a place at the Kent School, you couldn't just buy your way in.

Amy's father nodded. He understood, of course. "Are you sure you've tried everything?" he said at last.

Amy thought about that question for a long time after the call ended. All through dinner with Ming and Pearl, during bath time and bedtime, even as she turned the pages of Pearl's picture book and read the words mindlessly, she knew she had not tried or even thought of everything. She lay awake in her own bed for hours, blinking in the dark. Surely, he was right.

Giving up on sleep, Amy went to her desk. She studied Ming's book of Kent contacts: who was on the board, their interests and investments, who might be able to help. But there was nothing new there, nothing they had missed before. She went to the windows overlooking Central Park and stood there, thinking.

At some point close to 2:00 a.m., Ming appeared. She always sensed when Amy couldn't sleep. Maybe even knew before Amy did which nights she might struggle. Ming wore that black silk robe they'd had made in Shanghai. It fit her perfectly, the shoulders tucked and tidy, the waist nipped, and the V of skin at its center extended to only a few inches above her belly button. Her shoulder-length hair, always so neat and controlled, was tousled by sleep.

"You work too hard," Ming said.

She pressed her body into Amy from behind, reaching her hands up and around to the front of her shoulders. "Come to bed," she whispered in her ear. They had agreed years ago that this would be possible, to work by day and love at night. They were committed to it, really. As far as they knew, no one but household staff guessed at the second nature of their relationship.

Amy twisted only her head toward Ming, leaving no gaps between them. They kissed like this, delicately, mouths open, until Amy finally turned her whole body around, a single column of silk for just a minute.

THIRTEEN
CHANDICE

*T*his *isn't going to work,* Chandice thought. *None of it.* She opened her eyes in the dark room, its broad paned windows blacked out by the curtains. Her oversize bed was like a raft in the nighttime ocean, an island of safety she could cling to indefinitely. Still so early in the morning, and yet Chandice felt hollowed out. She was half-glad that Joseph was away on business, traveling to see the families of sick kids he was representing in that class action suit. Chandice couldn't remember where he was. If she felt better, she would call him.

She thought, with a start, of Daniel: Where was he? The panic stirred Chandice, and she lurched for her phone. The reminder on it flooded her with relief. Their sitter had taken him to school and would be with him all afternoon.

Chandice knew when treatment started again that some days would be like this, and there she was, flattened in her bed, trying only to cultivate the sort of energy she would need to banter with her old pal, Belinda. This required much more nuance than a job interview. As Belinda chatted, Chandice would discreetly and casually explore the edges of what might be possible for herself professionally in the medium-term future. That had been her plan, along with a morning stuffed full of errands before lunch with her old school and work colleague near their former office.

But now she could only watch the edge of the dark curtain brighten with the sun, leaving every other thought and movement purposely aside. Her cheek on the pillow, her hand on the sheet, even her eyes blinking as slowly as possible. Soon she would have to get up, shower, put herself back together as good as new. But not yet.

Chandice chided herself for not predicting that the day she chose to return to her professional life was the same day chemo would lay her low. Even her doctors didn't seem to understand all the side effects of her experimental regimen. The day before, she had felt almost good. Hopeful even. This outing for lunch with Belinda was a relatively low-stakes way of exploring her options. To see if corporate law was something Chandice might want to return to after all. Maybe she had been too hasty in dismissing the career she had spent years and hours and so much money qualifying herself for.

But more than that, it felt important to think about the future in a constructive way. As a place with possibilities beyond merely staying alive. A place where she would exist and grow and change.

"If you are just surviving, you will never get on with the business of living." That's what the woman said on *Serenity, Maybe?* Every episode, Chandice found herself listening with one skeptical ear to the vague but always positive nonsensical things streaming at her. And then, the host would say something powerful that stopped her in her tracks.

When she had heard that thing the previous week—about surviving versus living—Chandice had been chopping fresh herbs to add to a big pot of beans on the stove. She stopped what she was doing, wiped her hands on her apron, and gazed out the large kitchen window into the backyard. She listened to the host go on about the richness of the soup of life, a coincidental metaphor that interlaced so neatly with the fabric of Chandice's life. She knew you needed that umami to make it worthwhile. It couldn't be all vegetables and water.

It always annoyed Chandice when she found real solace in a podcast that silly woman Kara had recommended. Something wasn't right with her. She talked right over Chandice every time she saw her. But that's what had started the wheels turning. What was Chandice going to do? Make beans for the rest of her life? Hang out with moms like Kara? There was only one place to go: back to work.

When her phone rang at the same moment she began contemplating a return to the office, Chandice irrationally thought maybe it was Belinda. Could it be that somehow, she had reached her old friend through the ether, and here she was, spontaneously contacting Chandice, as if it were all meant to be?

"Hi, Chandice?" When it was a man's voice, her fantasy extended to Chandice's old, inscrutable boss, whom both she and Belinda had revered. It was hard to believe he would even remember Chandice's name, yet here she was fantasizing that he had called to offer her a job.

"Yes," she said a little breathlessly, as if she were being awarded a prize.

"It's Glenn *Goodyear!*" He said this like a punchline, which he alone proceeded to laugh at. "From Kent!"

Chandice was confused. They weren't supposed to hear from private schools for another two weeks. Chandice's moms' group had done a whole online seminar with a consultant who was very clear about the rules governing private school–application timelines.

"Hello, Glenn," she said noncommittally.

"Chandice, I just wanted to call you a little early and personally let you know how thrilled we would be to welcome Daniel to our kindergarten class."

"Wow, Glenn, I don't know what to say." It seemed weird. She knew the school was expressly forbidden from notifying families early.

"Say, 'You'll see Daniel in the fall!'" he said congenially, yet Chandice sensed the slight nudge of a salesman. He wanted her commitment. In her mind, it felt like he was pushing a contract across the table and putting a pen in her face.

"I can't wait to tell Joseph," Chandice said, stalling. "And thank you so much for calling," she added, sensing he was searching for an opening.

"Chandice, I'm sensing some hesitation. Is there something I can say to allay your concerns?"

Chandice squared her shoulders and looked out at her small square of earth only weeks away from its first planting. Kent was Joseph's clear first choice. It had been hers too. She should be elated, but something held Chandice back. Breathing in deeply, she said, "Well, Glenn, I'm just taken aback. I didn't expect to hear from any independent schools until next week."

"That's true, which is why I have to ask you to keep this call confidential. We are only reaching out to the applicants we are most excited about." This was precisely why the timeline had been established to begin with—to avoid schools notifying earlier and earlier to attract the "top" talent. Chandice refused to be flattered by him.

"I have to discuss this with Joseph," she said. But after the call ended, she thought not of her husband and letting him know the good news about their son, but instead her mind turned to a job for herself. After Glenn's phone call, it seemed somehow important not for the cash—they had the money on Joseph's growing salary alone—but for her idea of herself. Her phone was already in her hands, and she did not want to lose this momentum.

"Belinda Bouvier's office," a very self-impressed voice answered.

Belinda and Chandice had graduated from NYU law school together and were recruited to different departments in the same firm. When Belinda had her kids, she was back at work six weeks later. Before Chandice herself became a mother, six weeks seemed like ample time. And even though Belinda had three kids, they hadn't dented her career. Chandice had hardly been in touch since Daniel was born, which she knew was not great. But Belinda was less intimidating than trying to get time with their old boss, who had traded in running his own midsize shop to managing the North American business of the second-largest law firm in the world. Belinda herself had some huge job now, but Belinda and Chandice were real friends! Or at least they had been. Hadn't they?

"Hello," she said, trying not to be surprised Belinda had her own snooty assistant now. And office. "This is Chandice Hutson," she said, using her maiden name. "I worked with Belinda for about ten years. Is she in?"

They had picked a risky date in relation to chemotherapy for their lunch, but Belinda traveled so much, it was the only time she had available in the next three months. And now, the fateful day had arrived, and Chandice felt like a crumpled-up rag. She watched the time pass, giving herself until 10:00 a.m., then padded to the kitchen for a big mug of tea, trying to psych herself up for the meeting.

In school, Chandice had been the star. Confident at both studying and retention. Great argumentation both oral and written. But in the corporate world, Belinda had a knack for the politics Chandice simply couldn't master. Belinda put people at ease because she was a chameleon, able to communicate in the way that worked best for her audience. As a colleague, you always felt like she would probably throw you under the bus the moment your back was turned, and as a friend, you were never quite sure where you stood. Even so, people wanted to work with her, whereas the feedback Chandice had received included words like *harsh* and *intimidating*.

Since she had the babysitter and the car that Joseph had so brilliantly reserved for her weeks ahead of time, Chandice had planned on filling the morning with grocery shopping and food preparation. But now the only thing she still hoped to accomplish was picking up something special for Daniel, whose birthday was just two months away. One of the best children's art-supply stores in town was right by Chandice's old office. It had seemed like a fantastic idea to support a local business conveniently across the street from where she was going, and they had the exact art set Daniel had said he wanted.

But what she hadn't counted on when she placed the order was how incredibly large it was. The set itself had everything, all nestled in a great wooden box, that itself went inside another protective cardboard box and then into an oversize shopping bag with the store's bright balloon-letter logo emblazoned on the side. Thank goodness she had asked the car to wait so she could put it inside before the lunch, but as she came outside onto the street, her driver was nowhere to be found. He couldn't have gone far; he had only just dropped her off, and the street was crammed with slowly moving cars.

"Sir, could you please come back to where you dropped me off?" she said when he answered on the first ring. She had only a few minutes to spare.

"Of course! A cop made me move. Five minutes," he said. But she didn't have five minutes. She'd be late if she waited one more second. The thought of chucking the whole shopping bag in the metal trash bin on the corner flew through Chandice's mind. Ridiculous bag still in hand, she rode the elevator she used to take every day to the floor above the one she last worked on. She cursed herself for ordering the stupid art set. It must have weighed thirty pounds.

Stepping off the elevator into the foyer, Chandice was surprised to find the human receptionist replaced by a glass wall and a video intercom. When Belinda's assistant, an officious millennial evidently feeling very proud of herself in her first suit, came to greet her, Chandice asked about the receptionist.

"They let her go right before I started," she said, guiding Chandice down a series of windowless corridors that reminded her visually of how the job felt. A jolt of trepidation. They went through a door into a small anteroom where the assistant's desk sat in a small rectangular space that felt strangely familiar for something so nondescript. Then she was in Belinda's office, which, of course, Chandice recognized right away: the huge triangular window, vast space, window seat.

"You have Steve's old office!"

She had made it her own with red-and-gold wisteria wallpaper and a Carrara marble desk where a traditional boxy wooden one had once squatted. As far back as their first year at the firm, they had both had their eye on this space with its private bathroom and cozy window seat for important client tête-à-têtes. They had—at one drunken point, Chandice was pained to remember—agreed to race each other for this office. "May the best woman win!" they had said, clinking their third Manhattans at Bemelmans. *Guess Belinda won,* Chandice thought ruefully. She had likely relished this victory many, many times already.

Belinda stood behind her desk, fingers regally entwined, surely enjoying watching Chandice take it all in for the first time. Remembering the art set, Chandice placed it on the floor by the door. "I forgot I ordered this ages ago," she said lamely. Belinda eyed the bright-pink bag for a moment. She had straightened her hair and wore a killer bloodred pantsuit that made Chandice wish she had found something a little more tailored than this stretchy plum long-sleeved dress that only seemed corporate at a parents' cocktail party. More than the suit, though, was the toned body underneath it. The ivory manicure.

"Chandice! It's good to see you!" Belinda said, interrupting Chandice's inspection by coming around the desk, her heels making a muffled thump as she crossed the carpeted floor with purpose to give her a real hug that felt like a confirmation of their friendship. Chandice tried to remember to be gracious.

"This is amazing!" Chandice enthused. "Let me take a quick look around before we go to lunch." She examined the framed photographs on the wall. Belinda with her husband and three children at their Hamptons beach house. Belinda with the mayor. Belinda with the CFO of General Electric, a client. *Is this the road not taken?* Chandice marveled. Had five years really made all this difference? She'd have to fight to keep in mind that they were peers.

Chandice arranged a big smile on her face and breathed in deeply, setting aside the waves of fatigue and the omnipresent nausea. *It's just lunch,* Chandice told herself. *You can handle this.* Then she turned to her colleague, all warmth and positive energy. "Belinda! You made it!" Chandice finally exclaimed.

Belinda returned the smile. "It feels good," she admitted.

Around the corner in some overpriced pan-Asian spot designed for the droves of suited professionals eating there, Chandice struggled to wrest the conversation away from Belinda's occupational achievements. She didn't want to begrudge her, and yet her law school friend had acquired a new high-handedness. It was boring, which made it hard to keep the weariness at bay. Chandice found her mind drifting to her bed, her pillows, how soon she could get back there.

When Belinda finally took a break to chew her lobster fried rice, Chandice interjected, "How difficult was it coming back to work after the kids?"

"Which part?" Belinda said, glancing up from her dish, the meal itself contained in half a grilled pineapple, which bobbled on the plate as she poked at it.

"Was it hard? Professionally? Emotionally?" Chandice said leadingly.

"Um . . . professionally, not so much. I mean, for the first six months you just have to kill yourself proving to everyone that it didn't change you. Prepare for that."

Belinda said this in an off-handed way, as if it were like saying there was a staff meeting at 9:00 a.m. every Monday. "You mean, like, getting new business?" Chandice asked.

"No, no, like volunteering for all the worst garbage, following up relentlessly, getting everything done early, which you know never happens generally." At work, Chandice had felt like she was always having to exceed every expectation and standard just to stay competitive. What Belinda described seemed impossible. Could it even be true?

"And emotionally?" Chandice prodded.

"Who can remember?" Belinda said as she practically tossed her black American Express card at the waiter, making sure to pass it right in front of Chandice's nose. For a moment, Chandice remembered that she was supposed to treat for lunch, but then, why? "Are you thinking about it?" Belinda asked.

"Yeah . . . I . . ." Chandice could not find any of her corporate patter. She just didn't have it in her to pitch herself to Belinda. She had missed the chance to emphatically and instantly answer in the affirmative. Belinda would sense her hesitation, but Chandice tried anyway. "I know that I need to get back to work, Belinda, and this seems like the best fit."

"Well, let me talk to you-know-who," Belinda said, rolling her eyes and referencing their boss. Chandice nodded despite not being 100 percent convinced it was in her best interest to allow Belinda to represent her. "I'm going to run to the loo," Belinda said, grabbing her bag.

Chandice checked her phone as the waiters cleared the table. There was a text from Joseph: Miss you! Hope you feel OK! *What a love,* Chandice thought but wished that he had called her instead. There was a text from one of her mommy group friends. Hey I know you're not on social media, so thought you'd want to see this. It was a link to a letter to the editor published in the *New York Times* that had only posted a few hours before.

To the Editor:

Re: "City's Private Schools Take Aim at White Privilege, But Who Is in the Crosshairs?"

Unfortunately, the students will suffer most as schools like Kent force themselves to adhere to some untested "anti-racist" set of principles, setting these ahead of educational excellence. Kent in particular seems to have confused progressive education with progressive politics, as was made crystal clear to prospective parents on a recent tour. There, the administration proclaimed the entire curriculum upon which they have built their reputation will be quickly and completely revamped to address systemic inequities in every classroom, from art to Spanish to math. In their haste to do the right thing, Kent has reduced human beings—our children, no less!—to nothing more than skin color.

Worst of all is how these "woke" practices play out in admissions practices, which adhere to a perfect rainbow. No classroom should be too dark or too light. And no one can complain too loudly for fear of being labeled racist.

People who look like me feel unwelcome at schools like Kent these days, and the Board of Trustees is unable or unwilling to act on behalf of genuine equity and inclusion.

To be clear, I'm no racist. But I do want what's fair for my child.

Signed,
Parent of a Current Applicant to the Kent School

In reading this letter, it was as if something Chandice had only subliminally suspected became true. Or perhaps, as they said on *Serenity, Maybe?*, she was coming to know something she had willed herself to unknow. Something was not what it seemed at the Kent School. She read the whole letter twice; the words "I'm no racist" made her gag with their irony. Glenn's shady phone call, and the whole vaguely pressurized way he spoke to her, took on a new meaning she still could not yet completely discern.

When Joseph had gotten home the night Glenn had called, Chandice couldn't characterize it in a way that justified her discomfort. It came out sounding just the way Glenn had wanted: like he was enthusiastic about their son and welcoming of their family. But there was an undercurrent that Chandice had not been able to put into words.

"So, did you tell him how excited we are at least? I mean, I get that you didn't want to commit, I guess . . . ," her husband had said. But obviously he didn't understand. For him, Kent was a home run. Why *wouldn't* she want to commit? Here was the reason.

The weird thing was how familiar the letter sounded. Something about the wording or the tone rang close by. It wasn't the grievances or the phrasing exactly, but the actual words sounded like someone she knew. Could it have been Vic? She read it again—*where was Belinda anyway? Probably writing work emails in the bathroom*—and then the penny dropped. It sounded like . . . Kara. Kara wrote this, Chandice was suddenly certain. Goodness, she hated that woman. Such entitlement.

"You look like you've seen a ghost." Belinda stood at the side of their table, clearly not going to sit down again. She grabbed her coat from the banquette. "So good to see you." She was already making her way toward the door. Chandice had to hustle to keep up with her, overcoming a wave of light-headedness as she stood up. "So, I'll be in touch," Belinda said outside the office building. "It would be great to have you back." A hint of genuineness crept into her voice, but just a hint. They embraced once more, quickly this time, and Belinda disappeared inside.

Chandice felt like she had run into an unmovable object. Returning to work seemed not only distasteful but hopelessly impossible. She had tried to put the effects of the chemotherapy entirely out of her mind. It was certainly the last thing she wanted to mention to Belinda, who would only perceive it as another weakness and possible company expense. But now lethargy overwhelmed her. Chandice reeled on the corner, trying to reorient herself. Where was the car? She fished around in her bag for her cell phone before remembering Daniel's coveted art set, upstairs in Belinda's office.

Chandice thought for a good thirty seconds about just abandoning it, but that seemed too sad. Would Belinda just give it to her own children? Throw it away? Chandice steeled herself and went back inside. Upstairs, someone held the door for her, so she didn't have to buzz Belinda's assistant. She found her way back, her feet tracing familiar steps. Both the assistant's door and Belinda's stood open, so Chandice stepped inside. Hearing the murmur of voices, she stopped herself just outside Belinda's door to catch her remark, ". . . sad really. She used to be so sharp. Now she's just a mom, I guess." Chandice felt the slap of cruelty.

"She had that mommy glazed-over look, you know?" the assistant added.

Chandice heard in her head the voice of *Serenity, Maybe?* saying, "It's OK to be angry, Chandice," as if the host were speaking directly to her in that moment. And suddenly she was, in fact, full of fury. And it was a powerful, wonderful chemo-conquering feeling, this rage. She strolled slowly into the room to let them know that she had heard what they said. For the first time in months, she felt in control of the situation. Both women, jaws slack, turned their shocked faces on Chandice.

"Guess I can't count on your recommendation after all," she said, her eyes steady on Belinda's. "Despite what you just said to my face two minutes ago."

"Chandice . . . I . . ."

"Belinda, please, save it," Chandice said, picking up her bag, which announced to the world *this woman is a mother* with its bright colors and balloon letters. "Even in law school everyone knew you were full of shit."

FOURTEEN

VIC

What in the actual fuck? Vic thought, her eyes traveling over the *New York Times* letter that about thirty people had texted her. She was outraged. It felt like a personal affront she couldn't quite believe. Kent was *her* school. Now Jetta's school. Well, at least until the unpayable deposit came due. Vic squirmed coming into contact with that suppressed thought. But still. Who would do this? The subtext of the letter was clearly in someone's self-interest, but whose?

Her first thought was Penelope. That phrase "People who look like me" just screamed Penelope, with all her entitlement and superficial obsessions. No way it was Kara; she seemed too lost in space to write something that succinct. Could it be Bhavna? But then, did Brown families really not feel welcome at Kent? The truth was that Vic had no idea.

Vic studied the Upper East Side Moms page, which quickly devolved into borderline uncivil discourse on either side of the "woke" issue. On one side, the rational voices, to Vic's ear, the ones insisting that incorporating the concept of race into the curriculum would enhance, not denigrate, it.

We love our rainbow classrooms!
Diversity is education.
Go somewhere else if you don't feel welcome.

Here and there, though, the vague dissents started popping up from parents who knew enough to shield their identities behind an organization, Parents Against Racism. Their posts innocuously dotted the liberal landscape:

Schools should unite us, not divide us.
We care about diversity—and we are not all white.
Everyone is afraid to speak honestly and publicly about these matters.

The last one sent a little chill down Vic's spine. It made her take a look at everyone around her through a slightly different lens; surely, she was not alone in feeling suspicious of her fellow parents. This letter wasn't the work of just one bad apple.

Vic realized, with a start, that she had been scrolling for who knows how long and that she would soon be late. Actually, she was already late, the snacks still midpreparation on the counter, Jetta playing on the floor in her underwear, Vic in her ratty fuzzy robe. She had invited them over, but Susan's nanny, Isa, had explained that "Mr. Harris does not want the kids in anyone else's house." Plus, Kara had weirdly said something about Claude needing to get outside more. Vic put her half-empty mug down and hustled to get Jetta ready for the park, but her mind was elsewhere.

As she put Jetta's shirt on inside out, she fumed about Kent. The thing that Vic could not understand was how Kent was coming under attack for the very thing that made it different—and better!—than other schools. Kent had always been at the forefront of liberal thinking, whether it was on sex education or diversity issues. Racial and ethnic variety were, in Vic's view, the leading differentiator between

Kent and "comparable" institutions. Were outsiders surprised that the student body would reflect the ethnic makeup of the city? Wasn't that ideal? In Vic's view it was patently obvious that Kent's ultimate luxury was the sort of diversity you simply could not find in the city's racially segregated public school system.

Your thoughts, Vic texted Scott with a link to the letter. The Board is pissed, he texted back right away. Kent trustees loathed nothing more than press, and bad press was basically unheard of. Someone would have to answer for this. I'll tell you more when I see you. Vic's heart gave a little stutter step. *When he sees me?* she thought to herself. *That's promising!* Being with him was intoxicating, which was exactly what her situation called for. Leaving town for a while. A while? What the hell was that? Days? Weeks? Months? Vic hated that they had already fallen back into some sort of restrained dating communication. She couldn't demand anything from him: information, dates, his presence. Not yet. Miss you, he added. Vic smiled, pleased.

She was back on a teenage emotional roller coaster, which was better than existing in her actual day-to-day life. After having to jump through months of administrative hoops, Vic had been able to liquidate her final asset, some Exxon stock her grandmother had left Vic in her will. This gave her enough to last a few months, tops. Vic had given herself, with this money, two weeks to work on the new novel before trying in earnest to get a high school–teaching or waitressing job, the prospect of which made her gag. She had neither natural talent nor work experience with either.

Since Scott had suggested it, Vic had been haunted by the question of whether or not she could really be "inspired" by her mommy friend's suicide. It seemed ironic to imagine that she could recreate a character on the page made from strands of a woman she had obviously hardly known. But—and this was a crucial *but*—she didn't have any other ideas.

Vic texted Isa for a playdate after only the slightest hesitation about having, at best, dual purposes in mind. Surely, Isa had endured interrogations by law enforcement and the Harris family. She'd be tired of talking about that terrible morning. How would Vic get her to open up? She had been contemplating this very question when the Kent email came out, but Vic was a novelist, not a journalist. She didn't have the discipline or pushiness to extract information.

Vic still felt distracted when she practically dragged Jetta through the gates of the playground, only eleven minutes late. Isa, in a beige knit poncho and hat, stood by the gates rolling a stroller back and forth. Claude let go of Isa's other hand and ran to Jetta, her little blonde curls bouncing out from behind her headband. It jolted Vic with the most profound déjà vu, but when she looked up, Isa's somber face took the place of Susan's smile.

The two girls ran off to the play structure. Isa, having successfully gotten the toddler to sleep, rolled the stroller over to a few benches where she and Vic could commence what became an awkward silence. They sat a few feet apart. Vic turned to face Isa, who gently pushed the stroller back and forth between them. The bronze freckles dotting the middle of Isa's face made her look much younger than the early thirties Vic knew her to be. She couldn't remember ever being alone with Susan's nanny before, although they had met several times. Had Susan said something about a fiancé? Future plans for children?

"How are you?" Vic asked.

Isa jutted out her trembling chin and sniffled a little. "I'm OK."

Vic nodded encouragingly. She wanted to do much more listening than talking. Also, she had no idea what to say.

The silence broken, Isa now seemed to be studying Vic, who tried to project a trustworthy openness. "You and her, you two were real friends, right?" Isa asked. A lot of other questions nestled inside that one, and Vic did not have the answers to any of them.

"I thought we were," Vic said, her mouth twisted up in consternation.

This seemed to satisfy Isa, who said simply, "I worry about the children." They both turned their eyes to Claude, who was at the top of the slide with Jetta. The two girls paused to talk avidly about something before going down one after the other. It was a pretty scene, but of course, Claude would never be the same.

"What do you mean?" Vic said, as it seemed Isa wanted to share something more.

"I heard him say to Claude, 'Don't worry, I'll get you a new mother.'"

This struck Vic like a sudden slap in the face. For some reason, her anticipation of this conversation had not included anything still going on. Everything she had hoped to learn from Isa was supposed to be in the past. But, of course, the damage was ongoing. It was like Michael taking a tiny hammer to his child's delicate psyche, Claude's already thin memory of her mother tattering even further with such denigration. Surely, he was angry, but . . .

"That morning," Isa went on and paused to see if Vic wanted to hear more. She nodded. Of course, she did. Isa went on. "She said, 'Don't tell him.'"

"What?" Vic said, not following.

"She was home when I got there, still in her pajamas. She said she was sick but not to tell Mr. Harris." Vic pictured Susan in cotton pajamas with buttons down the front and a collar, her hair braided, her face distraught. "When I walked in, she had a screwdriver in the living room window, like she was fixing something, but I think she was trying to open it." Vic remembered the big picture window, surely impossible to open. Yet there she was, going at the metal frame and attempting to dislodge it while her children watched.

"She tried to take off the guards in her room, too, but she couldn't." Isa's eyes were back there, watching Susan with the tool, going from room to room, frustrated and all worked up. Sweating and weeping, the terrified eyes of the children following her around the apartment instead of looking at the television in front of them, but she doesn't notice.

"When she realized she could not, she went into the bathroom and locked the door." Vic could not believe the way the story was pouring out of Isa. Clearly, she was traumatized, and in the shuffle between the widower and the children, no one had thought to even ask her maybe anything at all, let alone how she was doing. It was as if Vic had pressed the play button on a recording; the story was going to pour out without a single prompt. Vic had the urge to take Isa's hand, but that seemed like too much. Instead, she'd go home and write everything down before she forgot it.

"She shouted at me through the door to take the kids to the park, but Mrs. Harris was so upset. She upset Claude." Isa's eyes remained distant and dry, wide and terrorized. Vic herself felt sick to her stomach. A sudden lurch as she saw in her mind's eye her friend, doubled over and crying in the bathroom, screaming for her children to leave so that she could proceed with what she knew would come next.

"Claude wanted a hug. Before we left."

Tears flowed down Vic's cheeks. Poor Claude, standing outside the bathroom door in her little pink parka, saying, "Mommy, mommy." As if she had known this was her last and only chance to save her mother's life. And Susan resisting, knowing that if she hugged her daughter, smelled her unique child scent, that it might trigger just enough of those maternal love hormones to dissuade her from her plan.

"Claude refused to leave, and finally, Mrs. Harris came out and gave her a quick"—Isa lifted her arms as if suddenly reanimated and gave the air a brief squeeze—"nothing hug, like this. And went right back in the bathroom." Isa continued to stare at the middle distance, her face now all weighed down with sadness, but still no tears. Vic wondered if she was too traumatized still to cry, whereas she herself shuddered with a little sob. A nearby duo of moms with babies threw her a suspicious glance. Only children cried at the playground.

"When we came back from the park, the ambulance was there. I saw her pajamas sticking out. I tried to shield them, but . . . I don't know." Vic's eyes flew to Isa's. "I don't know if they saw." Vic tried to hide the horror of this revelation, but surely it meant that Claude had comprehended in some way the self-inflicted death of her own mother, had on some level registered the misshapen flatness of the gurney they wheeled her out on. How had Susan done that to her children?

"I'm worried about Claude," Isa said. *No shit,* Vic thought. "She is afraid of the bathroom now."

Vic looked into Claude's future, to her first good therapist, who would surely wonder aloud with her the role that the bathroom had played in her mother jumping off the roof of their building. And here was the only person who knew the answer. And Isa surely would never be able to tell Claude. It felt like an impossible mystery to let someone live with. All the details of that morning would redound within Claude for the rest of her life, despite being completely inaccessible to her conscious mind. Vic felt like screaming.

"And what about you, Isa? When they move to Connecticut?"

"I offered to come. I said, just a few months to help out." This was such a relief. At least the kids would have some continuity. "But he said, 'No. it's better this way. To make it a clean break.'"

This seemed pretty heartless to Vic.

"Is there anything you could do to help? Talk to him, maybe?" *Oh, no,* Vic thought with a sudden shudder. It felt like the bill had come for Isa's story. How could Vic not talk to Michael if she had been Susan's real friend?

But then Vic thought about her nonexistent relationship with Michael, who would always be "Susan's Husband" in her mind. She could in no way envision how she might suggest that Michael retain their nanny for a few months. She didn't want to judge him for it, but he clearly wanted to turn the page. "I'll try, Isa," she said noncommittally, with no clear plan to make any effort, and this was plainly visible to them both. Isa's face, so open a moment before, closed up. Isa stood to stretch, and Vic could see for the first time the outline of a pregnancy.

"How many months?"

"Seven." She rubbed her belly reflexively.

"You'll know how to do everything," Vic said, jutting her chin at Claude, who was dangling from the monkey bars with Jetta. Vic herself had practically no experience with children before becoming a mother herself. They watched Claude safely land on her feet and run around to get back on the rings.

"I guess so," Isa said doubtfully.

As soon as they got home, Vic switched on never-ending cartoons for Jetta and went to her computer for the first time in weeks. Did it only seem dusty in her imagination? Her intention was to not overthink it—just write down everything Isa had said so she wouldn't forget it. Not that she wanted to exploit Isa's experience or Susan's suicide, but Vic had to start somewhere. And this was good material.

She knew because of the way it flowed out of her. Vic had forgotten the feeling she could occasionally achieve when she was really in the zone and her fingers flying on the keyboard were like those of a concert pianist, changing rhythms and places and creating something. It was thrilling. Better even than it used to be because she had known life without this ability. She wrote, embellishing the things Isa had said, altering the details of their meeting, adding and deleting with a flourish. In ninety minutes, she had 2,371 words and could have cried with joy.

Vic poured herself a cocktail in the kitchen. Like the bathrooms, it was in serious need of renovation, from the grotty metal sinks to the chipped linoleum floor, but it was large, with a butler's pantry. Vic stood there, sipping her whiskey, listening to the childhood tones of the *My Little Pony* theme song from the other room. She herself had watched the same show in the same apartment more than thirty years before. She threw dinner—a tray of frozen lasagna from Whole Foods—in the oven. Vic counted the spinach pasta as a vegetable. Susan would have disapproved.

Wednesday at the Mercer? Scott texted. She'd have to talk to him about his girlfriend. There was no way she could watch Lili's TikToks of them dancing and kissing on the Vineyard at sunset and pretend like everything was normal. She'd address it head-on and refuse to be someone's secret.

OK, she wrote back. The Mercer was one of their old haunts.

Bar @ 9 is all he wrote. Jetta would be with Sean and his budding family while Vic time-traveled back to fifteen again, on a clandestine rendezvous with the captain of the basketball team. She couldn't wait to talk to him about that anonymous letter. It was just so odious. It created an air of suspicion all around. She wondered if Penelope really had it in her to hatch this plot. Furthermore, what motive did she have?

Vic realized she had hardly said a word over dinner, which was unusual. Jetta's big brown eyes on her seemed concerned. Could she have been picking up on Vic's intense anxieties and insomnia? Obviously.

"Someone wrote a not nice letter to the newspaper about Mommy's old school today," Vic explained.

"And?" Jetta's eyes widened, imagining what bad might flow from there.

"The funny thing about this letter is that the person who wrote it didn't sign it. So they don't want people to know who they are." Jetta attended to Vic's words. She found herself making this into a teachable moment. "That's when you know you're doing something wrong—when you have to hide."

The following week at drop-off, Bhavna breezed past Vic with a quick open-palmed, "Hi." This was how Vic realized that the transit strike must have ended, and Vic expected an earful about how inconvenient it had been for her. Bhavna had generally been all over Vic for a coffee or a playdate, so this cold greeting felt intentionally rude. *Could she somehow know about Scott?* Vic wondered, recalling their Union Square run-in. But then, on her way out of the building, Chandice also put her head down when she saw Vic, averting her gaze and only mumbling a hello. And that's when Vic put one and one together: Did they think *she* wrote the letter? No one would ever suspect Vic. Would they?

FIFTEEN

KARA

Since Kara was down to one emergency Klon, her obsession with Susan had picked back up again. The good news, as far as Kara was concerned, was that Vic was also still clearly stuck on her friend's suicide, so Kara was relieved to see her on the end of the pickup line. Since Vic was the only other mom still reeling from Susan's death, Kara hoped she could make that a point of connection between them. Just not in a creepy way.

"Hi, Vic!" Kara said cheerfully. Vic drew away from her in the close hallway, where there was hardly any space to breathe as it was. "How was the playdate? With Claude?"

Vic looked taken aback. "How did you know . . . about the playdate?"

"Well, I suggested it, didn't I?" Kara said.

For a minute, it looked like Vic might actually pretend not to know what Kara was talking about. But Kara already *knew* about Vic's playdate just the day before with Isa and the kids because Kara had, in a very casual fashion (she had to go out anyway, so it wasn't really stalking) followed Isa when she left the Harris building with both children late in the afternoon. Kara sat on a bench just outside the playground and watched Isa and Vic's conversation unfold. The baby gnawed on a rice cake. Oscar watched her phone on a bench with his back to the play-ground because if he had seen Claude and Jetta, he would have wanted to run screaming at them, as boys do.

Kara watched Isa talk, wishing she could hear the words. All that information must be so . . . helpful! So instructive. She watched Vic listening and hardly speaking; then she was crying quietly, the tears falling one after the other, then small sobs. Kara watched agog as this scene unfolded, practically shoving rice-cake bits into the baby's fists and mouth. What was Isa saying? That Michael and Susan had fought? That she struggled with depression? What?

The whole time, Kara felt terrible. So guilty. She wasn't supposed to be following Susan Harris's kids and their nanny around. On some level, Kara knew that her behavior wasn't good for herself or her family. She had been doing so well! Lately, when she picked Oscar up from Woodmont with the baby, they all went for a long walk and played in the park with other kids and had a healthy snack of sliced fruit and nuts. The apartment was neat as a pin. She'd stayed up into the night to finish her dress for the Woodmont graduation and had only the sleeves and hem to finish. As she stitched the neckline, peaceful resignation settled in on her. Maybe Oscar would simply not get into Kent, and, as disappointing as that might be, this would be the last painstakingly difficult knockoff sundress she would have to make.

And all the while, Kara had kept her promise to herself that she wouldn't think about Susan Harris any longer. Which had been easy as long as she'd had the Klonopin. Just a half pill in the morning, half in the afternoon, and everything came so easily to her. No distractions or emergencies. Time had passed quickly, whole hours rushing by without a thought of the suicide. Now here she was, nosing around at pickup for some more clues about Susan.

As if just remembering the playdate had even happened, Vic said uncertainly, "Oh! Oh, right, it was OK."

"Did you . . . learn anything?" Kara said vaguely.

"Not really," Vic said.

Kara knew from having observed them together that this, in fact, was not the case. And she resented Vic for withholding it from her. This was the nature of the city, dense with experiences and possibilities. Only more and more, Kara felt their unattainability, as if she herself were pressed against glass, coveting unattainable things.

The next afternoon, Kara planned to ask Penelope for more Klonopin at their weekly coffee date, which Penelope had blown off several times. But almost immediately she had launched into a monologue about her brother and how he had it in for her, but she was going to show him—blah, blah, blah. It remained unclear what exactly her brother had ever done to her or what was so wrong with him. Kara could only discern that there was an important meeting that evening. Something about a board, like for their family? It seemed impossibly pompous and equally unimportant.

They sat at their usual tiny marble two-top. Fronds of a nearby hanging plant kept poking the back of Kara's head. When Penelope finally stopped talking, Kara found herself eager to share a confidence also. She was grasping at straws to reestablish intimacy. Besides, if Penelope wanted to go on about her family, couldn't Kara talk about hers? Were they friends or not?

"You know, I think I understand why Susan's death hit me so hard," Kara said when Penelope finally ceased speaking for more than two seconds. Penelope sighed, swirling her spoon around the foam at the bottom of her bowl of cappuccino. "I mean, I don't know if you know this, but my sister committed suicide," Kara said. She waited for this to have its inevitable impact on the unsuspecting audience, but Penelope's face remained placid.

"That's terrible," she said when it was clear Kara expected some sort of response. "No wonder."

"She was the second of a cluster in my small town—"

"Midwest somewhere?" Penelope interjected.

"Right."

Penelope pressed her lips together as if this was enough reason to stop talking about it, but Kara would not be deterred. It felt suddenly like she just had to keep going, that unfortunately, Penelope was the only adult around to listen, and Kara desperately needed someone to hear her—really hear her out on this. Penelope looked like she was trying not to reach for her phone, like she just wanted to leave.

"That makes sense, but still," Penelope said, "enough is enough."

Kara blanched. It felt for a moment like she might gag on her own tongue. Tears reflexively sprang to her eyes. It seemed to Kara like she was asking so little of Penelope. Forget real friendship, whatever that was, how about just performative sympathy? Kara suddenly hated Penelope and all the other New Yorkers like her who had no interest in getting caught up in anyone else's misfortune. Kara gulped.

"Kara, did the Klonopin help?" Penelope finally asked coolly.

Kara came alive with hopefulness. She hadn't had to even bring it up herself. Penelope probably had cartloads of pills, plenty to share. Kara wanted to formulate her words carefully. "Yes, I . . ." But she never got out her hopeless plea.

"You need to see a doctor," Penelope said, and it was time to go. They walked the two blustery blocks to pickup in ominous silence. Kara had mistaken this fake friendship—a relationship built on essentially misleading one another—for something else. The whole reason she was able to convince Penelope that she had money was that she was not paying any attention. Penelope didn't want to know Kara. She thought of Susan and how, with friends like Penelope and Vic, she could easily have been clinically depressed without anyone noticing. She watched Penelope pulling open Woodmont's heavy wooden front door, her eyes ahead but her mind clearly elsewhere. It felt like Penelope might not even notice if they never spoke again.

Back at home, Kara felt her resolve weakening. She kept getting out her emergency Klon, looking at it in the palm of her hand, then returning it to its bottle in the cabinet. It was raining, and the kids were anesthetized by the television. Which meant it was time to consume all Susan's brother's social media accounts one by one. In fairness, there wasn't much to see. He was a real estate agent somewhere near Miami with a big stucco house, where he lived with his Russian wife and their small daughter. The wife preferred less clothing and more hair, both for herself and her four-year-old. He looked proud of his family, stable in his work, physically healthy. A normal individual.

She nibbled a cuticle, a new habit, while curled over her phone, one knee tucked up next to her face, her socked heel perched on the seat, scrolling IG while Oscar and the baby watched cartoons behind her. There was not much personal content—definitely not adequate for her purposes. Kara zoomed in on Susan's brother's face. There was a similar hesitancy in the eyes, perhaps a shared understanding between siblings.

Kara just knew that he could help put her mind at ease, even if she wasn't sure how. It was like the early text-based computer games from her childhood, where the point was simply to have an adventure. The object remained obscure as the player followed the dry creek bed to explore a vast and cavernous cave complex full of dangers, trusting that there had to be some *there* there, some point to it all. And this was as good a metaphor for life as Kara could find. You just had to keep the faith that there was a purpose that could only be uncovered if you kept going. So here she was, clicking through Susan Harris's brother's IG stories, video after video of condominiums in Sunny Isles Beach, Florida.

Surely, it would be all right for her to send him a note, she reasoned. Something bland. See if he responded. Sorry for bothering you. I just wanted to reach out with condolences for your sister. My son goes to school with your niece. She read it over twenty times. Was it too short? Too emotionless? Too . . . Isaac's key in the lock so surprised her, Kara hit the send button before shutting her phone off. She didn't know he was coming home!

"Transit strike's over!" he announced, coming through the door.

There was just a beat of hesitation before Kara threw up her arms. "Daddy's home!" she gushed. The kids leaped off the couch—the only thing that could get them to turn away from the television was their father—and ran shrieking to embrace him. Isaac kissed Kara and picked each of the kids up so they could all have one big family hug, and, for a second, Kara felt perfect serenity. It was moments like this that made the rest bearable.

Kara threw on an apron as if that had been her intention all along, although it was already pretty late for the kids to have dinner. Still, she tucked her hair up in a messy bun and tried to approximate the capable homemaker she used to be. It felt like acting. All she had to do was make rice and heat up the beef stew she had prepared days earlier. But her mind was going in all different directions. What were the implications of Isaac's surprise return?

"I see you rearranged the furniture," he said, eyeing the desk by the window. Thankfully, the apartment was still neat from her stint on Penelope's medication.

"I wanted to get more light on my sewing," Kara found herself saying, the lie coming conveniently into her mouth. She had to look up the ratio of water to rice on her phone, she felt so rattled. Her hands were shaking as she measured the grains over the sink, tiny white pellets spilling from the cup and raining down the drain. It felt like she didn't know how to do anything anymore.

"Have you seen this? It's about that crazy Kent School." Isaac held the paper out over the bar area in the light. The headline blared "Anti-Racism Tug-of-War at Elite Private School." Kara felt more and more distant from that place and life, as if she had already passed the juncture and was on the road taking her elsewhere. Some other kind of journey.

"I haven't seen it," she said without reading it.

"It says someone wrote an anonymous letter to the *New York Times*. A parent of someone who's applying."

"And?"

"You wouldn't . . . ," Isaac said, throwing a glance behind himself at their kids on the couch to make sure they weren't listening to this exchange. "You didn't write the letter, did you?"

Kara could only gape at him. She hadn't even read the thing. What was he even talking about? "Do I seem like a 'letter to the editor' kind of person to you?" she asked Isaac, mystified to be fielding this particular accusation. But still, he watched her, assessing. He knew something was off, but he wasn't sure what. "I didn't write the letter," Kara said clearly, happy he had accused her of something she could sincerely and vehemently deny.

The anger gave her thoughts and actions clarity. Rethinking dinner, she steamed edamame, which she knew Oscar would eat. She had homemade almond milk and mango chutney, too: a meal even Susan would have applauded. And Isaac dared to come home from nearly three weeks in Brooklyn and accuse her of anything? As she spooned food into bowls, Kara kept one eye on him, watching cartoons with his son, holding the baby with a toy. She put dinner on the table. She got it all done. She watched Isaac eating his meat and potatoes—nice and bland, just like he liked it. What was Isaac's problem? She suddenly hated him.

"Why don't you do bedtime?" she said curtly as she cleared the table.

As soon as the bedroom door closed, her phone pinged. She couldn't believe it was a response from Susan's brother so quickly. **Dear Kara, Thank you for writing. Best regards.** He was obviously open to talking, Kara thought, and had responded quickly to keep the dialogue going. She typed out a response, then erased it. Tried again. Couldn't quite get the tone right. She started gnawing on a fingernail.

I'm so glad to know my sentiments were helpful to you. I can't help but have questions . . .

She erased it and started again. **Thanks for responding . . .** No, not quite right either. She had ripped off the top fifth of a fingernail. Blood pooled in the cuticle.

"Kara?" Isaac said quietly from the bedroom door, where he had been observing her for who knew how long. She practically threw her phone in the air, he gave her such a fright. She had been so deep in thought she had forgotten he was even home. Reluctantly, she set the phone aside. "What's going on?" he said.

"Nothing, really," Kara said. She tried smiling at him, but her cheeks were stiff and her eyes unconvincing.

"I'm worried about you," Isaac said. "You just don't seem like yourself."

When he said that, Kara wondered whom he was talking about. The Kara he had met in the Brighton Beach Russian nightclub eight years ago? That Kara had been gone for a long time. Did he mean private school Kara in the pretend fancy clothes? Or the stay-at-home mother with string cheese in her hair? Or the newly self-appointed private detective, sleuthing out the root causes of a neighborhood suicide?

None of the identities seemed to suit her. Maybe that was what Isaac was getting at, but Kara was in no mood for a downer discussion.

"I'm just tired, OK?"

This disappointing exchange unsettled Kara, making her feel even more anxious than she had before the Klonopin. When she got home with the kids the next day, she stayed away from Susan's brother and all social media. She avoided the window. But she still wasn't quite herself. The next day was some random holiday, so both kids would be home, and it was raining.

She would take them to the natural history museum, Kara decided, now that the transit strike was over. On her most capable day, this would be an epic journey requiring collapsing the stroller to take it on not just a bus but also the subway while ensuring neither of her two small children were maimed in the process. Plus, she would have to make it fun. She listlessly prepared the bag of things she would need to take with her: diapers, wipes, changing mat, extra clothes, snacks, a bottle, a pacifier, water, the stroller. Before she turned her attention to the two actual children, watching *Sesame Street* on her iPad together adorably on the couch, she would take a moment to sit down at her desk.

Only, the moment she stopped moving, an inertia settled over her. As if magnetized, her pupils found their way to the Harris front door.

Of course, there would be nothing to see. It was already late morning. But still, the kids had a day off. They were still upstairs with Isa. They could walk out at any moment. She'd just sit and wait for two minutes. Five minutes. Twelve minutes . . . And as she watched and waited, Kara's mind returned to the unimaginable fact that *Susan jumped right there, just right over there from up up up there. My God it was* right there *that she jumped she jumped just like my sister why did she why why why am I alive? Shouldn't I also be dead? I could never jump. Susan did it just right there.*

When she heard Isaac's key in the door, Kara jumped to turn off the cartoons Oscar had been watching for the better part of the day, which made him burst into angry tears. Kara snatched the baby out of the motorized swing. She spun around as Isaac entered with a bag of take-out food and ran to him, baby in her arms, to distract from Oscar's meltdown on the couch.

Before he could take his coat off, she gave him a swift kiss on the lips and launched into her tales from the day, ignoring Oscar's red-faced screams behind her. "So Isa only took the kids out once today, for like twenty minutes. Isn't that weird? That they're just stuck inside all day. Should I call for a playdate?"

Isaac left his coat on the back of the armchair at the dining table and went to Oscar on the couch, who crawled into his arms and calmed to a low blubber.

"Wasn't there school?" he asked as he stroked his son's head. Kara felt her hackles go up. She blamed Susan's death for the awkward and unpleasant state of her marriage, but Kara also knew her reaction to the tragedy and almost everything since—like Isaac's innocuous question—were a bit oversize. And yet someone had died. It made sense to be upset.

"No, it's some weird holiday," she said shortly. Oscar had calmed down and was now climbing all over Isaac.

"Did our kids get outside today?" Isaac asked, poking his head around a now-giggling Oscar to cast his eyes around the cluttered apartment, with empty kids' plastic bowls on the coffee table, a half-finished art project strewn across the floor, the kitchen sink full of sticky sippy cups.

"Of course!" Kara said, realizing that they hadn't. She felt only indignance. Didn't Isaac understand that what Kara was doing was important? Who was going to keep an eye on how angry or sad Michael was on his curbside calls? Or who came to see them and when?

She switched Oscar's cartoons back on so she could have 100 percent of Isaac's attention. She had waited all day for the company of another adult. As Oscar reglued himself to the iPad, Isaac turned his eyes to Kara, who continued on as if there had been no interruption.

"What I'm saying is, I didn't see Michael at all today. Like coming or going."

Isaac nodded at her, as if to say, yes, he understood why she was telling him these things and how naturally she had come to know them. But instead of responding, he said gently, "Uh, honey, it's a mess in here." Kara looked listlessly around the apartment, most of which she had kept behind her back all day.

"Oh, I . . ." He was right. Things that she could not accomplish while looking out the window had fallen away from her perception. "I guess I better clean it up right away!" she said, jumping into action and drawing both her children's eyes. She hadn't moved this quickly or briskly in weeks, and she could feel the new jiggle at her waist from all her sedentary observations in place of her online workout classes. Kara started gathering stray toys and clothes from around the living room, piling them on one arm to go into the laundry.

As she moved around, hunched over, gathering other people's items, Kara caught a reflection of herself in the mirror, her usually shiny hair reduced to a frizzy dollop on top of her head, her skin pale with patches of dry pink. A quick glance at her hands confirmed frayed cuticles and chipped polish from before their Kent interview. Dinner sat in cardboard containers within a plastic bag on the counter. The kids had spent the late afternoon eating the last of the defrosted kale puffs, followed by ice cream. They already wore their pajamas, unbathed, but it wasn't like they were playing in the park or anything. They had never made it, she realized, eyeing the stroller all packed up and ready to go by the front door, to the museum. In taking all this in, even Kara could see that she was no longer the bubbling midwestern homemaker sex kitten she used to be.

The next morning, not knowing what else to do, Kara cut Penelope's last Klonopin in half and took it. And indeed, the afternoon passed with ease. She still kept an eye on the Harris building, but instead of an oppressive and unmanageable responsibility, it seemed more like a hobby. For the first time in a while, Kara played one of Oscar's silly games with him—something to do with squirrels and their nuts. She cleaned the apartment as the baby napped and Oscar molded Play-Doh, and this itself was rewarding. The purpose of her time was to accomplish tasks such as these, to give her family the clean and organized home they deserved. She did not need a greater calling than that.

Kara carefully bathed not only her children but herself, taking time to exfoliate and shave and condition and moisturize. She got out the hair dryer and the big round brush and the makeup bags all in their little caddy underneath the sink for the first time in weeks. She applied the carefully chosen foundation, the drugstore mascara. Kara switched on the ring light she had found at Goodwill and stuck to her tiny bathroom mirror. What a pleasure it was just to put on makeup again. How strange she had taken such a long hiatus from this regular activity.

That night, Kara was ready for Isaac to come home. Music played softly on the single Bluetooth speaker, and the kids were asleep. She lit a candle and had a plate ready to go wrapped in foil on the counter: chicken parmesan, Isaac's favorite. More than for him, Kara found comfort in returning to herself, in reminding herself that she could, in fact, still be the clean, well-presented, calm mother and wife she had always been.

Isaac's key in the door brought Kara to her feet. She stood at the small counter, their two wineglasses waiting next to an open bottle of red. "What's all this?" he said, shrugging off his coat.

"Just a wife, happy to see her husband." She sidled up to him and tried for a real kiss, but he just gave her a peck. She poured the wine and lifted a glass.

"Cheers," she said. Isaac clinked, but he did not smile. In fact, he looked downright suspicious. Her simple husband usually wanted nothing more than a drink, hot meal, and quick screw after a day at the gym. The Harris family would move away soon, and that would solve everything.

"Can we talk?" he said.

They sat on the couch together, knees touching. "I don't know what you're doing or who you've been messaging or what you're so anxious about." Isaac took Kara's hand with the scabbed cuticle and showed it to her like he was shoving a dog's face in a mess it made on the carpet.

"No one, I . . ."

"Never mind. Kara, I want you to see someone. Like, a specialist. A therapist. A shrink. Whatever."

At first, this wounded her. Kara was hurting, and Isaac had given up comforting her himself. Even worse, he had concluded something was wrong with her, and she needed treatment. Maybe even medication. And then it dawned on Kara that Isaac was exactly right.

SIXTEEN

VIC

"I think you should know I almost didn't come tonight," Vic said, deadpan into Scott's face before anything else. She had watched him watch her cross the room, the sexual tension crackling from twenty feet away. Her hair, blown into a shiny curtain, spilled over her shoulders. Black spaghetti straps, slim jeans, and black heels, red lips, gold hoops. Classic. It was something she might have worn in high school. With him, she felt like she had recaptured that youthful, Kent, anything-is-possible feeling.

Which was such a goddamn relief from the overwhelming realities of her actual existence. The money would soon run out. The Kent deposit was due in only a few weeks. She had not been able to write a word since just after the playdate. This thing with Scott was the only good thing she had going, other than Jetta. So she had to force herself to at least try and deal with it as the ethical person she believed herself to be.

"Hello to you, too," he said, kissing her on the cheek and gesturing for her to take a seat. "How about a drink?" While he looked for the bartender, Vic studied his perfectly fitted casual jersey shirt, his carefully shaped eyebrows, his moisturized fingernails. Lili's handiwork for sure.

Which was exactly the problem. Vic had never dated anyone with a girlfriend before, and she didn't like it. She had seen with horror the post of Lili and Scott on his parents' sailboat. They had pressed together on the deck, in the golden hour. She was great with light. Also hair. How she got hers to flow like a mermaid's in the natural sea breeze astounded Vic. She had her thin arm around Scott's shoulders, their tan cheeks pressed together even as he planned to meet Vic the following evening. It had to stop.

"I think you know what I'm going to say," Vic started, after they got their drinks.

"You had no idea how much you missed me?"

"Not exactly."

Scott took a swig, and when he placed the glass back on the bar, only ice remained. "Look, Vic, I can imagine how this looks to you, but it's complicated."

"Actually, Scott, I'm pretty smart, so why don't you try to explain it to me?" An edge crept into her voice. But how could it not. Did he seriously think he was going to get away with saying nothing?

"Lili and I, we just go together, you know what I mean?" Scott said. Vic's face fell, and her brows arched. What a mistake to come here. "You and I, though . . ." Scott looked at Vic. "I can't stop thinking about you," he said.

"I'm not going to have an affair with you," Vic said, and Scott started nodding before she even finished her sentence.

"I get it," Scott said. "We're just two buddies having a drink downtown."

"Is that what you told Lili?"

"She has some stupid IG thing."

"Don't you feel wrong," Vic asked, "appearing in front of tens of thousands of people as her adoring boyfriend?"

Scott looked away, embarrassed, then looked her right in the eye and said, "Vic, would I be here with you now if I was happy with Lili?"

"Maybe." Vic shrugged, unconvinced.

"Since we ran into each other at Union Square, I've thought of you every single hour. Sometimes I think of you when we're 'shooting.'" He made air quotes. "Maybe that's why it looks believable?" Scott shot Vic a sideways vulnerable glance that melted her heart. That was the problem: in her core she was drawn to this person. Had been since she was fifteen years old. He was like the archetype of a man to her. The heat radiating off his body felt like a tractor beam drawing her in. The scotch had loosened her defenses.

"Scott, I just can't . . ." The words died on her lips. He looked at her, ice rattling around his empty glass. She just couldn't *what* exactly?

"The truth is," Scott said, putting his arm on the back of her chair and leaning in so she could feel his breath on the outer arc of her ear, "I've been thinking of you, Vic, every day since you broke my heart."

Vic looked straight ahead. She knew to turn toward him would mean giving in, and all would be lost. This was her only chance to decide. Think clearly! Maybe she didn't have to know everything, didn't have to play out every possible outcome but rather do something just because she wanted to for once.

Vic turned her face toward him ever so slightly, and their lips locked together. Of course, Scott already had a room, a beautiful suite, and he took her out onto the veranda and made slow love to her under an awning where no one could see them, but they could peek out at all of sparkling SoHo, and it was glorious, and it made her feel young and sexy and fabulous as long as she didn't think too hard about anything.

Afterward, they held each other under a cashmere throw on the outdoor daybed, counting the stars, and after that Scott ordered a lavish feast from room service that covered the entire cocktail table with delectables.

"How's your book?" Scott asked as he spooned caviar onto a blin.

"Actually," Vic said, "coming along, thank you." Which wasn't, strictly speaking, true. Just that afternoon, as penance for meeting Scott, she had handed in a nearly blank résumé at the local French restaurant. The owner gave it a skeptical look down his long nose before dismissing her. Just thinking about it made her jaw clench with anxiety. Never mind how she would actually survive on a waitress's salary.

"Oh, I know," she said, eager to change the subject. "What's the behind-the-scenes gossip about Kent?" Scott chewed his caviar while Vic helped herself to a piece of bruschetta.

"He's out," Scott said.

"Who?"

"Your old English teacher, Glenn Goodyear."

This was not entirely a surprise, after the letter to the *Times*, but still.

"Because of the letter?" she said.

"Sort of. Obviously, that was no good." Scott piled lobster macaroni and cheese onto his plate.

"And?" Vic prodded, waiting. She felt like she was following bread crumbs, but where they led who could say? She had the strangest feeling that the conversation was about to take a turn.

"Oh, you know, just all that anti-racist bullshit."

"I'm sorry?" Vic said, sure she had misheard him.

"He told the wrong people that, you know, all that woke stuff is just a necessary show," he said, waving a clump of lobster meat around with his fork.

Whatever Vic had anticipated, it wasn't this. First, she tried to convince herself she had heard him incorrectly—to erase it from her mind—but she couldn't. Worse was the realization that this was not really a surprise. Age and money had done their work on him. He finally looked up from his plate and noticed her mild disgust.

"Look, I know we can't have an all-white student body. That's just, in New York, a nonstarter. It's ridiculous. But I don't know about an anti-racism curriculum. I mean, we're not racists," he said, gesturing back and forth between them.

"How can you be so sure?" she asked, and Scott laughed it off. Vic realized that it didn't matter because the question was the answer. Time for her to go home.

Vic got dressed while Scott showered. When he came out of the bathroom with a towel wrapped around his waist, he seemed completely unsurprised that she was leaving. Vic gave him one long last look.

"Are you just, lifting weights or . . . ," she asked.

"Lili's trainer. He's the best. I'll text you his number."

"Cool," Vic said. "Well, I guess this is goodbye?"

"Goodbye?!" Scott said in mock horror. "I'll be seeing you at all sorts of Kent events now that you're a parent, right?" He embraced her, which felt weirdly platonic given that they had just had sex twice, and he was basically naked. It felt like he might chuck her on the chin if she didn't get the hell out of there. If she hadn't already decided he was not who she thought, Vic would have been destroyed by the chasteness of their farewell.

In the cab uptown, Vic's phone buzzed—Scott texting his trainer's information. Which gave Vic a reason to look at the "IG thing" going on with @lilikopelman. What had she been busy with that evening that had left Scott at liberty? She clicked on Lili's stories and was not surprised to find her wearing yet another gem-colored frock in a well-lit room, her hair in high gloss, full glam, and a perfect pink manicure. Only this time, those oval disks were like a crown for an enormous diamond engagement ring. *That motherfucker.*

Vic swiped through images and short videos of Lili greeting everyone inside the carpeted vestibule of what revealed itself to be a boutique hotel in the Adirondacks redone to feel like the Rockefeller who had built the place still lived there. Or his grandkids still lived there and spared no expense renovating and redecorating. There was Lili with her sister, seated on the stone hearth in a room with ceilings so high all she could fit in the frame were the thick wooden beams. Lili and her gorgeous friends gathered on a red plaid couch, antlers and flags and fur throws artfully arranged. The fucking Hope Diamond winked from Lili's finger in every single shot. It was a goddamn engagement-celebration girls' weekend "IG thing," as Scott had called it. And Vic was an asshole. Also, possibly a moron. She had unwittingly facilitated Scott's last hurrah. Vic felt like a piece of garbage. Like she had prostituted herself for a private school admission she could honestly never even afford.

She obviously did not know or understand Scott in any meaningful sense. Susan had withered internally and died practically in front of Vic's eyes without her noticing anything even vaguely off. And here she was, almost forty, stuck in the same rent-stabilized apartment with no career. She had once thought of herself as a substantial, insightful visionary when in fact she was stumbling around half-blind. The thing that was missing wasn't Sean after all. It was Vic! Self-loathing so painful and previously unknown filled Vic's body. It was a feeling she could not tolerate.

Vic didn't think much about pressing the penthouse button on the elevator in her building. From there, she took the stairs to the roof, wedging a shoe in the door, which would otherwise lock behind her. It was all soft blackness around her up there, the velvety twinkling of lights in the windows of all the homes with normal people—not useless, destructive, selfish people like Vic.

The soft putty they used on the roof gave a little under her steps. Vic had not been up here in decades. At the edge, Vic peered over the side down onto East Eighty-Sixth Street. Only seventeen stories and still very far. She pressed her palms into the rough concrete lip of the roof, which barely reached her hips—definitely not up to any sort of code. Easily surmounted. And in less than ten seconds, all the shame of what she had done could be erased. Jetta was happy with Sean and his new family, excited to be a big sister. And if Vic could summon the courage to do this, Jetta's Kent tuition would be paid forever. Her college tuition even. Would Jetta simply be better off without her? The tears refused to come to her red eyes, circled with the dredges of the evening's mascara. It was as if she no longer deserved even to cry. For a moment, she was calm, considering her options. How much Vic would like to stop worrying, and finally, resoundingly, lose consciousness.

But just for a moment. Because if she could just push herself, not off the roof but instead into a new novel, there was hope for redemption.

There was still a chance Vic could figure out how to get back to the way things used to be. All she had to do was act as if none of the bad things, none of her idiocy with Scott or her silly writer's block, had ever actually happened.

Vic went inside to her computer with a renewed sense of purpose, knowing she only had one more chance at this. Thankfully, her fingers began to move over the keys.

Vic called upon all the fragments, those clues she had missed in the fleeting moments she and Susan had spent together. That time, just before Susan died, when they had met at the American Museum of Natural History with the girls. Susan, usually so put together with all that hair rolled or curled or blown or whatever she did to make it look so "grammable," showed up with a greasy bun teetering on top of her head. She wore a boxy, ugly T-shirt and tatty leggings. Without thinking too much about it, Vic had blurted out the conclusion that seemed most obvious. "Did you just work out?" she asked.

And sitting there, in the darkness, at her computer, Vic remembered Susan's reaction so clearly—more so than when she was there in the moment. It was like Vic had reached back in her brain and played the video on slow motion. The sudden jerk of Susan's head, her surprise and dismay. Her jaw slack before the word came. "No!" was all she said, trying but failing to put a lilting spin on it. It sounded like she might burst into tears. Vic felt awkward about her gaffe hitting Susan hard. They were moms; it was OK to be unkempt. And yet, when Susan had shown on her face that there was more to it, Vic hadn't followed the thread. Hadn't taken in how her remark had struck her friend.

As Vic typed, tears slipped from her eyes and fell to the tops of her hands. She was sorry. She was so, so sorry.

SEVENTEEN

BHAVNA

In the three weeks since Dev's aunt died, Bhavna had counted the moments until the independent schools were officially allowed to notify families if they had been accepted. Now that they had, suddenly, plenty of cash, she could not wait to give some of it to Kent, securing Harry's spot among their ranks. This was the next step up, then the move to Manhattan, followed, naturally, by professional and personal advancement for Dev and herself. The good life.

While she waited for the call, Bhavna combed the listings for three-bedroom apartments within five blocks of Kent. Although she knew some might consider it bad luck to have already made appointments with real estate agents, Bhavna went ahead and did it because she wasn't worried about Harry and Kent. It was more like a formality, really, especially after that scathing letter to the *Times*. Obviously, the school would have to bend over backward to assure families of color that they were as welcome as the white families. Bhavna had sighed with relief when she read it. The call now felt, more than anything had before, like the next scene in an already written play. As if *the reason* Dev had inherited so much money was *so that* Harry (and someday his sister!) could have it all. It was, in other words, destiny, and the day it began had finally arrived! Notification day.

At her desk midmorning, Bhavna studied pictures of a Carnegie Hill duplex in a converted brownstone two and a half blocks from Kent. She had heard small co-op boards were the most fastidious in terms of references, even for an all-cash purchase. They would have to renovate the bathrooms, she thought, zooming in to study the dirty grouting and uneven tile. *Gross.* Bhavna sighed, thrilled that these were now her concerns. Money did not free her from all worries but rather released her from the messy problems she was so tired of and gave her much tidier, more glamorous knots to untangle.

Most importantly, the windfall meant she would never reflect on or speak of the grotesque and demeaning event at Susan Harris's apartment. To anyone. Ever. She would package that up and bury it unreachably deep inside herself.

Nor did she obsess about her job. Returning to the office after the strike ended had not increased her productivity. No longer was Bhavna spending every free moment firing off texts and emails. These days, Bhavna mostly gazed at the balance in their family bank account, soaking up the sense of security that it filled her with. Also, she did quite a bit of shopping. Her anger and anxiety about quite possibly losing her first major campaign slipped away. She would find another gig, another way, soon enough. She had been at Bowery forever. Bhavna had practically invented the brand, and she knew there was no need for her to ever worry about her job.

All of which made Bhavna feel powerful. She showed up to work in her favorite suits, some purchased retail even, and no longer worried about staining them or saving them for a "major" meeting. Every day was important! She piled up her substandard clothes one by one to give to Goodwill and ordered upgraded new items with the frequency she used to send follow-up texts.

Bhavna exchanged her used Cartier watch for a brand-new one, and this was like her secret weapon. She felt like a virago walking through the office now; they couldn't hurt her any longer. The CMO would make his choice, and they would all lick their wounds and move on. *Whatever.*

She was studying the Carnegie Hill kitchen, which would definitely need to be gutted, when Marie appeared at her office door. Bhavna quickly closed the real estate listings on her screen.

"Ready for the meeting?" Marie asked, a bit tersely to Bhavna's ear. She looked rather dressed up today—a dark blue jacket over a shift dress, her hair blown out and pinned back. Her dewy face was clearly the result of much time spent with the Bowery Fresh Face palette. All in advance of whatever was happening next.

"What meeting?" Bhavna clicked open her calendar and studied its purposeful emptiness. Today Bhavna planned to sit by the phone.

"Oh, shoot," Marie said. "I think I forgot to put it in your calendar."

Bhavna tilted her head at this new person in her doorway. Where was her cheery, competent, collegial assistant? "So, what's the meeting?"

"The CMO is announcing his decision."

"Now?" Bhavna said, looking longingly at her phone.

Marie nodded and scuttled off to the conference room. Bhavna leaned back in her chair, from which vantage point she could see that the entire marketing team was already assembled. The time was 11:03 a.m. She was obviously already late.

Bhavna hadn't had a moment to check her reflection or gather her thoughts, but right away the room felt off. She wasn't sure if it was because she was the only person who had been blindsided or because she was picking up on something in the air. It didn't help that thanks to Marie, Bhavna was the last to arrive, and it took two long seconds for one of the junior associates to give up his seat for her. She sat at the far end, the CMO at the head with James to his right. The CMO gave Bhavna a patronizing wave coupled with a faux smile, just the muscles of his cheeks lifting the corners of his mouth for a split second. The expression reminded Bhavna of when Harry had a sour stomach as a baby.

"Thanks everyone for coming today," he said, for some reason pointing this statement at Bhavna. Because she was three minutes late? Not a great sign. "And I want to thank you, James," he said as he turned and nodded at him with a genuine smile on his face that went all the way up to his eyes, "and you, Bhavna"—there it was, that flash of indigestion again—"for two terrific campaigns. But I think what Bowery needs now is something particularly twenty-first century. You know, cutting edge." At this point Bhavna felt like everything he was saying described her presentation—with its global array of beauty—over a Super Bowl ad. She felt her hopes lift, as if on a slight breeze, for just a moment. "And for that reason, I've gotta go with James."

Bhavna had seen this coming since she saw the two of them at Yama, so it barely stung at all. Her life had changed, and none of them knew it yet. Everyone at the table looked around uncertainly until one minion started clapping. The CMO nodded. "Go ahead. He deserves it." Everyone but Bhavna gave James a tepid round of applause.

"James is going to run lead on this, and he's going to need all your help," the CMO continued, speaking again directly to Bhavna. Which brought her up short. *Hold up, what?* she thought, a red alarm light starting to flash in her brain. "So, if he asks you for something, please do your best to help him out." That sounded like James had suddenly become . . . her boss?

"And Marie," the CMO addressed Bhavna's assistant, standing in the corner. "We're going to put you on James's team for the time being." Bhavna almost broke her neck jerking it around to get a look at Marie, who was smiling from ear to ear, nodding at James. She almost had goddamn tears of joy in her eyes. Bhavna quickly turned back around, her stunned gaze finding only the dark table in front of her. James was to have two assistants to her zero, and she was now reporting to him. Bhavna had just been demoted in front of the entire company. The CMO was still talking about outreach and assets, and Bhavna's whole world melted down. The campaign was one thing, but that's just it. It was *one* thing. How could *this* have happened?

246

Bhavna's body stayed seated, her eyes on the CMO, her face serene because she herself had left the room and retreated into the inner sanctum of her mind to quietly calculate her options. Dev had a few interviews lined up, and, now that the pressure was off, he'd surely find work soon. They had enough money to be unemployed and fine for a few years. Her best reference was the previous CMO anyway; she had loved Bhavna and her work. Would be filled with empathy and want to help her when she heard this horror story.

The bottom line coming through to her in bold red font was that she could not stay at Bowery one second longer. The meeting continued on all around her as if nothing had happened, her junior colleagues (or were they now just her colleagues, plain and simple?) asking empty questions to display their eagerness, James basking in their attention. Her stomach churned.

At Kent, there would be endless networking opportunities. She had never struggled to find work. There was no way for her to be successful here, and she didn't have to put up with this any longer.

The CMO was in the middle of a sentence when Bhavna stood and said a very quiet, "Excuse me." She left, walking decisively past the stares of the IT department, who sat right by the conference room, and went to her office. She checked her phone, but there were no calls. She looked out the window at the view—a Midtown corridor alive with industry. She had worked so hard to earn this perch. The shelves behind her desk overflowed with Bowery collateral, none of which she needed now. Her desk was completely clear, save one family photo framed in silver, which she took and put in her Goyard tote.

The urge to get out before Marie, James, or the CMO emerged from the conference room seized Bhavna. After twelve years, she would leave this job unceremoniously, practically fleeing.

As the elevator doors closed on Bhavna's Bowery existence, her phone rang. She couldn't believe it: KENT SCHOOL. "This is Bhavna!" she said breathlessly, so happy to know that her luck was about to change. It would be just like when—she wouldn't let herself think of it explicitly—but when that horrible thing happened, and then Dev heard about the inheritance, and all the bad things were washed away forever.

"Hi there, Bhavna, this is . . ." Her name was garbled as the elevator descended. It sounded like "Jenny." ". . . calling from the . . ."

Jenny? Who was Jenny? "Hi, Jenny, I'm sorry, I'm in an elevator, so I might lose you." Bhavna cursed her timing, as Jenny continued breaking up in her ear. Bhavna plucked a handful of words out of Jenny's several sentences.

". . . sorry . . . Harry . . . not . . . luck."

"Whoa, Jenny hold on, what?" Bhavna said, her panicky eyes on the illuminated floors. Three, two, one . . .

". . . not accepted," Jenny said quite crisply.

Bhavna shot from the elevator and ran to the glass wall in the lobby where the reception was best. "Jenny? Jenny, are you still there?"

"Yes, I'm here."

Bhavna took some deep breaths to calm herself and tried to correct what was wrong. "I'm sorry. It sounded like you said Harry was not accepted."

"That's correct."

"It can't be!" Bhavna said, truly for a moment believing it. Every domino had already been arranged in her mind. There was no reason for him to not get in. He belonged there. One of them.

"I'm sorry, but it is," Jenny said.

The memory of grinning Glenn Goodyear looking Bhavna in the eye, shaking her hand. What *bullshit*! "Thank you," Bhavna said automatically, and Jenny hung up first. The nerve.

Robotically, Bhavna walked to the subway as she always had, rode the gondola to Roosevelt Island, having boarded with the masses, and as they hovered together over the river, in a daze, Bhavna thought not of Manhattan and all its glories splayed behind them. Not of the three-bedroom duplex in the converted brownstone with two tiny bathrooms and a forty-square-foot "backyard." Bhavna's view expanded.

Instead of searching for apartments in Carnegie Hill, Bhavna pulled out her phone and looked at what the same money could get them in, say, Saddle River. Or Port Washington. Or Larchmont. How about a stone manor house with a pool and seven bathrooms on five acres? She clicked on the pictures: an expansive island with two sinks, six barstools, a refrigerator the size of Bhavna's entire kitchen right now. The primary bathroom had a whirlpool bathtub for two with bay windows looking out onto the wildlife preserve that abutted the property. Or, for the same money, she could have a five-bedroom house right on the Long Island Sound, a private pebbly beach just steps away from her deck with a hot tub and outdoor shower.

And the kids would go to public school for free. Dev would commute, and Bhavna would open her own business of some kind. In the suburbs, they could live without jobs almost indefinitely. A happy life, mostly free of rejection. No more racing around or constant anxiety. What had once seemed anathema was now the most comforting conclusion of all. Bhavna would leave the city.

EIGHTEEN

PENELOPE

Penelope's job at the meeting, according to her lawyer, was to stay quiet and let things play out. The groundwork was laid, the meeting a necessary formality. "He may try to rattle you," she warned, "but don't take the bait."

Penelope felt prepared for her assignment. Well slept. Serene. A silk crepe suit in a muted teal with sensible but fashionable shoes. She sipped a cappuccino in her blissfully quiet kitchen. The nannies had the kids at the natural history museum, Graham was at work, and she could just breathe and think. Or not think. Meditate.

The rest of Penelope's life became a blurry tunnel, just swirls of color surrounding fantasies of besting her brother Andrew. First, they would have to accept the deal with Amy, which would entitle Penelope to vote. It would take a while to work on Boris—years of carefully interlacing their children in Aspen and St. Barts, sincere listening, and gentle manipulation—but Penelope would win him over. After all, hers was the right side, simply because Andrew was so demonstrably terrible. She could not wait to show him up in that meeting and found herself playing out future scenes in which she developed quality investment opportunities, seized control of the board, and became a benevolent, if firm, ruler.

But first, she'd get to call Amy and give her the good news. Finally.

So absorbed was Penelope in these sorts of daydreams, she'd hardly noticed anything over the previous six weeks since their last family board meeting. Penelope had the nannies take care of the kids more and more while she avoided Graham, who was understandably annoyed when Penelope hardly listened to a word he said. She blew off therapy, not wanting to revisit all that old territory with Andrew and how she wasn't supposed to be getting caught up in old sibling rivalries as a grown-up and a mother.

She didn't want to hear that! Penelope was on the hunt for something. Her life had a purpose, finally, and she didn't want to be dissuaded from it or knocked off course in any way.

Besides, Penelope told herself, this was all temporary. Soon the meeting would happen, and she could return to her normal state. She was allowed a month (or so!) long obsession, keeping Andrew in her mind's eye at every spin class, massage, and blowout. Penelope regularly checked in with her lawyer, who assured her that they had nothing to worry about. Amy's company was on unassailable financial ground, and everything about the deal had checked out.

Penelope had maybe been leaning more and more heavily on her medication through this stress. Nothing helped the time pass like a Klonopin, and all Penelope had wanted these past few weeks was to get to the part where she got to say "Fuck you" to Andrew for keeping her down her whole life. That era was over.

Since there were no birthdays or anniversaries to pretend to celebrate, they were meeting at Andrew's office. Penelope's mother picked her up in a town car, and, as they traveled down Park Avenue, Evelyn tucked the fur trim of her cashmere vest down around her chin with one manicured hand. Her slow turn to Penelope, the leather sighing as she shifted her weight, announced that Evelyn was going to say something cruel. "When you were a little girl, I used to chase you all around the playground. You were always pushing the boundaries of what I thought you could do." Penelope had heard this before; it was a defining shape of their relationship and one she had been over many times in therapy. Her parents had expected basically nothing from her beyond nonprofit board membership.

"So you know what I did?" Evelyn asked. This was a new wrinkle. Penelope could not remember ever hearing this chapter of the story before.

"Made me stop?"

"I let you fall," Evelyn said, "and that's how you learned your limits."

"Mother, I'm an adult. You're no longer letting me do anything," Penelope said, telling herself she would take a cab home rather than share another half hour with this woman. Since Penelope's father had died, Evelyn had sharpened her tongue and her attitude. No wonder she seemed to have more free time lately.

Penelope returned her attention out the window.

The conference room in Andrew's office downtown was a large glass box with a view of the Statue of Liberty. All the family lawyers were already present. Penelope took a seat next to hers, who nodded meaningfully. There was nothing else to say between them. Evelyn remained standing with her coat on so she could scurry off to Andrew's office the moment things started. As Evelyn passed the time by making ceaseless small talk with the lawyers, who all bandied back and forth with her like old tennis pros, Penelope could feel the dread and anxiety beneath the medication. She took some deep breaths. Andrew charged into the room like a bull, knowing just how hard to push the door to get everyone to stop talking and look at him.

"You didn't write that stupid letter, did you?" he said to Penelope without any other sort of greeting. It took her a minute to even remember what letter he was talking about. It hadn't struck Penelope as that big a deal. Some disgruntled applicant airing their weird grievances publicly. And it had been weeks ago.

"Why would I write the letter?" she asked genuinely, already feeling heat rising in her face. Her only job was to stay calm, she reminded herself.

"To get back at me, obviously." Although she had had an entire life to comprehend how self-involved her brother was, Penelope could still be taken by surprise. Kent was his and only his, apparently.

"My kids are going to go there, too," Penelope said, baffled. She involuntarily looked to her mother for the reassurance that was never there and hated herself for it. Evelyn kept her eyes steadily, adoringly, on her son.

"If they all get in," Andrew said coolly, unbuttoning his jacket and taking his seat at the head of the table. *Don't take the bait.* Penelope's lawyer's voice was in her head. She could see his tactics and would not succumb to them. Half a Klon was exactly the right amount.

"Notification day was last week." Penelope loved how clear and unbothered she sounded. "Glenn called me himself well before that."

"Oh did he? I hope you wished him well," Andrew said cryptically, deflecting what she had said. God, she hated him. They weren't even in the official meeting yet. Where the hell was Boris? That guy was always late, always coming up with some dippy idea, and no one ever tried to shut him out.

"What do you mean? What about Glenn?" Penelope asked.

Evelyn and Andrew exchanged a pointed glance that, of course, clarified nothing. Why were they always purposely leaving her out? She wanted to stay calm, but surely Penelope was allowed to insist on . . . something! Information! To be included! To be loved! She felt herself losing her grip on the calmness she had latched on to just the moment before. Screaming was starting to seem like a good idea.

Just then, Boris breezed in, all beard and scarf and balmy energy. Evelyn kissed him on both cheeks before leaving the room. It was painful for Penelope to wait as he shook everyone's hand, then came all the way over to give her a hug. It seemed to take Boris a half hour to make it around the room so everyone could sit again. Penelope's heart hammered the inside of her rib cage, but her mind was placid. Andrew called the meeting to order.

"We did a little digging into your mommy friend's Taipei partners," Andrew's lawyer started, looking directly at Penelope.

"Pretty solid business," Penelope's lawyer said.

"Financially? Rock solid. The deal checked out with legal on their side, and the money is right. They could probably fund ten deals like this one. So, good job, Penelope!" The lawyer's nervous half-hearted thumbs-up brought a stone to the back of Penelope's throat. She was on the precipice of something big.

"Great, so when do we move forward?" Penelope's lawyer asked.

Andrew's lawyer inhaled sharply. "So . . ."

"You know," Andrew jumped right in, which made Penelope very, very nervous. No way would he want to personally deliver any sort of good news. He put his elbows on the table, hands clasped, one thumb stroking the other. "They *are* solid. They have so much damn money, and it all seems liquid and just sort of as if it materialized out of thin air." He said this with false enthusiasm. "Which doesn't happen," he said.

Andrew locked eyes with Penelope. He waited for her to say something. Penelope could not help her jaw from jutting forward in disgust: she hated her brother so much. She emitted a big heaving sigh and said, "Go on already."

He smiled at her. A big, enraging, pitying smile. She remembered this exact expression from his debating days. When he knew he had the other team beat, out came this megawatt grin. "Do you know where Amy's money comes from, Penny?" he asked.

"Taiwan," Penelope's lawyer said confidently.

"Do you know where Amy comes from, Penny?" Andrew said, a giant cat waiting to pounce on his prey.

"Taiwan?" Penelope's lawyer said, with less confidence.

"China, Pen. Your friend Amy and her boatloads of money are all from fucking China." Collectively, no one in the room seemed to know what exactly Andrew was getting at except his lawyer.

"So?" Penelope's lawyer finally said.

"Aha!" Andrew exclaimed. This might be the highlight of his whole year. He was like a kid at Disneyland for the first time, practically jumping out of his seat in enthusiasm. "The thing is, and maybe, Penelope, you remember this about dear Dad, but he hated the Chinese! He wrote into the board bylaw addendum that we could never under any circumstances do business with Chinese money, companies, or nationals."

"What board bylaw addendum?" Penelope's lawyer asked, ready to get heated after being made to look a fool. Penelope thought about firing her immediately after the meeting or sooner.

"The chairman of the board retains the only copy," Andrew said, nodding at his lawyer, who held aloft a worn leather portfolio. This was right up their father's alley in terms of being both old school and nasty.

"Surely, my client has legal right to access the bylaws?" Penelope's lawyer asked.

"Not until she can vote," Andrew's lawyer countered.

Penelope turned her eyes to Boris, but he cast them down, past the edge of his voluminous merino scarf, into his lap.

"Don't you think I didn't try this before? When he was still alive?" Andrew's tone was now a fake fraternal one, as if they were in this together, which was so unfair. Here he had benefited all this time from his position, from the confidence invested in him, from the attention not just from their father but from both parents, and now he was going to rub her nose in it.

"Andrew, why do you hate me so much?" Penelope said, proud that she could get these words out steadily and without any tears.

"I don't, Penelope," he said, softening ever so slightly. "You just don't belong here." He stood up and put on his coat, making it perhaps the shortest family meeting of all time. "Look, go back to Kent and sit on that board. That's much more your speed. Enjoy the fruits of my labor." And with that he was out the door.

Left alone with just their attorneys, Penelope studied Boris. He seemed so goddamn unruffled. He looked at her with his gray-blue puppy-dog eyes that said, *Don't be mad.* It was as if his whole life this expression of his, this way of hungering just to be beta to Andrew's alpha, had greased all the wheels for him.

"Boris, how come you never stand up for me?" Penelope asked.

"Oh, Penelope," he said. "I could never go against Andrew."

Almost every scene Penelope could recall of the two brothers interacting, the younger always showed deference bordering on adulation toward the elder. She was expecting too much from him. "Dad knew what he was doing. If he made Andrew all-powerful, then we'd never get caught up in family squabbles and nonsense," Boris continued.

"So Andrew gets to be Dad now."

"That's how they always wanted it. Besides, Penelope, he's good at it."

After Boris left, Penelope went to the bathroom, where she opened her jeweled pill case and took one pill and then, feeling very blue indeed, another half, making it two total for the morning and one cappuccino. All the things she thought would change had solidified into permanence. There would be no incorporation of herself into the whole.

She had to wonder: Was Andrew right that she didn't belong there? Or had she been made that way by design? And did it matter any longer? All the ways forward had been cut off for the time being.

It would be quite a while before she would marshal the courage to speak to Amy. She'd have to numb herself completely to the day's many embarrassments.

Back in her mother's town car, it felt exactly the same and like everything had changed since the morning. Instead of the adult she had insisted she was, Penelope now felt like a child again, around Felix's age, on some rare outing. They traveled up Park Avenue, unchanged, of course; the only marking of time was the state of the tulip beds, now only a handful of tiny green stalks promising the profusion of petals to come. Penelope tried to remember the last time she and her mother had gone anywhere alone together.

Her mother reached across the back seat and took one of Penelope's hands in her own. "Not everyone is suited to do everything, Penny."

Her mother's drawl, generally as soothing as a chainsaw, sounded like it was transmitted through several layers of cotton. Penelope felt completely anesthetized and infantilized. Here she was, getting a life lesson from her mother, who had never been proud of her.

But all Penelope felt was blessed numbness. It was as if the words were another passenger in the car with them. She gazed vaguely at Evelyn and then back out the window.

"Look, I know it's a consolation prize, but remember what Andrew said? Before the meeting?" Evelyn prodded.

"Hmm," Penelope thought, casting her mind back and finding nothing past the shocking existence of an actual, physical book that would stand in the way of her birthright. How could she be expected to remember anything after that?

"Remember the letter to the *Times*, Penny? About Kent?" But Penelope's eyes were on the corner by Lenox Hill Hospital, where a woman in scrubs and a lab coat stood smoking, her head hung like that of a guilty dog. A doctor. A woman with places to be, stealing an illicit smoke. There was something dreadfully romantic about it, but Penelope couldn't quite put her finger on what.

Meanwhile, Penelope enjoyed not caring how Evelyn tilted her head this way and that like a bird, frustrated with being ignored. Exasperated, Evelyn said, "Penelope! If you listen, you'll enjoy this."

"Oh, all right," Penelope sighed deeply and slid over a bit on the leather seat, pulling her hand away but leaning in to hear better. "Do go on, Mother."

"Thank you," Evelyn said coldly. "Look, Glenn sent this email meant for the trustees out to all the major donors instead." She held her phone out to Penelope, who took it, but could not seem to get it at the right distance from her face to actually read the words. The letters changed shape as the tires vibrated on the pavement. Disgusted, Evelyn took the phone back. She was always so judgy, Penelope rued internally. She could drink two bottles of wine herself over dinner, but one Klonopin (or two, occasionally), and it was like Penelope was a drug addict.

"I'll read the highlights," Evelyn sniffed. "Dear Trustees, Obviously we are all much taken aback by the recent letter to the *New York Times*. I can assure you that . . . blah, blah, blah . . . this anti-racism trend, like all others we have weathered, will come and go." Like all the others? What were the other trends that came and went, Penelope wondered.

"Here's the best part," Evelyn said, licking her lips. "It's simply necessary sometimes to do what's right just because it *looks* right." She jabbed her finger in the air in parody. "What a moron!" Evelyn said. Penelope weighed the sentiment. Glenn had an arguable point but only to be made in quiet spoken words and never in writing.

"Wow" was all Penelope could muster, and Evelyn clucked in disapproval, for Penelope or Glenn, it wasn't clear. "*Who* did he send that to?"

"All *major* donors, past and present," Evelyn said.

"Why didn't I . . . ," Penelope said, not needing to finish the sentence. She hadn't gotten the email because at $10,000, she was not a major donor. "I can't believe he would write that down."

"Oh, he put things in writing like this all the time. It's just the first time he's sent it to the wrong people," Evelyn said dismissively. Penelope's eyes were like thin slits on her mother, trying to understand. Was she saying the tone of this email was no surprise? That, of course, Kent as an institution aimed to look a certain way as much, if not more, than to actually embody those principles?

"Look, darling, I know you don't want to hear this, but for now, why don't you just amuse yourself with getting involved with this sort of thing and leave the family money out of it? What do you say?" Andrew put her up to this, Penelope knew. She could hear him writing this line for her, suggesting it casually.

"I'll think about it" was all she could muster.

"Want to stop for lunch at Bergdorfs?" Evelyn asked, an unusual invitation from a woman who had been too busy her entire job-free life to spend time with her only daughter. But Penelope understood, suddenly, that her mother was older now and a widow. She could see in her mind's eye Evelyn's regal embossed alligator desk calendar, its pages full of careful script marking her appointments. But it must be empty that day, the calls and invitations drying up, and Penelope knew, in that moment, that her mother was lonely. And that Penelope's job was to be her playmate and entertain her. So Evelyn would always be in cahoots with Andrew to disenfranchise Penelope. She'd need to find a different way out from under them.

Penelope shrugged. In the meantime, why not get a new handbag? She had nothing better to do.

NINETEEN

CHANDICE

Chandice had suspected for a while, maybe since that disappointing day with Belinda, that she was not going to get better. She felt terrible almost all the time now, like her body was rejecting her spirit. The islands of wellness in between treatments were flooding with malaise, and soon she would drown.

She kept her fears close. Didn't let them surface around her son or her siblings. Didn't share them with Joseph, who was now twice as busy on this new trial. "Gotta pay that tuition bill!" he quipped happily as he ran to his office, a dinner, the airport. He didn't care about the anonymous letter one bit and acted as if Daniel attending Kent was a done deal, though they had not ever really agreed.

Maybe he was just too distracted to argue. Chandice had seen him like this before, all charged up with the thrill of a fight. He seemed to thrive on the work, the stress, the discovery. And then, of course, the performance. The jury's eyes on him. He was born to do this.

There was a time when that was the beginning and end of Chandice's thoughts about her husband's work. She had admired him for his naturalness as an attorney. But there was a new, darker feeling creeping in at the perimeter, and it took Chandice weeks of introspection to finally name it. Suspicion. Who could be truly comfortable and fulfilled as a corporate lawyer? There must be something, she realized, wrong with him.

Chandice remembered she had been the one to announce, flat out, that he would not need to come to treatments with her, right away putting him ahead of herself. "No need to inconvenience both of us," she said. She was being the strong one, taking it on herself to get well for the family. But something between then and now had changed. Maybe it was Chandice.

For a moment, she considered asking Amy to come with her— Amy, who had become an accidental confidante. Outside Joseph, Amy was the only one who knew how sick Chandice was. But their relationship consisted of occasional quiet exchanges at pickup and thoughtful texts, not middle-of-the-week chemotherapy sessions.

Chandice used to enjoy watching Joseph prepare for work. That morning, she stood in the bathroom doorway while Joseph knotted his tie in the mirror and smoothed it with his manicured hand. The two-handed way he brushed his hair had always tickled her before. But as Chandice beheld the little sparkle of self-love in her husband's eye as he assessed his gorgeous self, she did not feel joy. The motherfucker seemed downright delighted, and Chandice didn't understand why she was so angry about it. That wasn't fair. She wanted her husband to be happy, didn't she?

"Baby, how about today you come with me?" she said out of the blue.

He looked like a kid who had been caught doing something bad and would now be punished. "Huh?" he said, his eyes ponging from Chandice back to the mirror back to his wife again.

"I just . . . it's not that I feel so terrible today, but it's a chemo day . . ." She waited for him to cotton on and say, "Of course, sweetheart! If you want me there, I'll be there." But instead, he just blinked at her. "And . . . I just . . ." Her voice got smaller and smaller as she watched his face. She knew him so well. He was concocting his response. Making up his excuse. It was like she could see the words coming together right behind his eyes.

"Oh, no, baby. I would, but today is court."

She understood. Of course, she did. But also. There was something happening, and Chandice wasn't even sure if it was external or internal. Why had she suddenly felt this burst of neediness? A paramedic once told her that before people die, they experience a profound sense of dread. The body knows when a fatal process begins, and the mind can't help but generate the appropriate emotions.

So when Chandice stepped off the hospital elevator that day and saw her head oncologist waiting for her just beyond the glass doors of the chemotherapy clinic, it was no surprise. She had, on some level, known what was ahead, and she had wanted Joseph with her when the doctor said, "Nothing's working." Had known she would need someone to help her move forward from the spot where she had suddenly become stuck to the carpet. These were the last moments before her doctor informed Chandice that she would soon be gone from this earth.

"No, thank you!" Chandice wanted to shout, turn, and run. As if that was how she would beat cancer. It felt like quite some time that she stared at her oncologist, in her lab coat and the pink of health, a student doctor at each elbow. It felt appropriate that it would take all three of them to give her this terrible news. "Sometimes, it is enough just to move forward," she told herself, words from that damn show *Serenity, Maybe?* Chandice forced herself to face what came next. She put one foot in front of the other and got through the doors. She felt sick, light headed.

"Chandice, it's good news," the doctor said immediately, and Chandice started breathing again. The doctor actually smiled. A big, broad, satisfied face that Chandice had never seen on her before. All three of them were grinning like kids on Christmas morning. Chandice could not quite believe what was happening. The doctors ushered her into a small featureless consultation room she had never been in before. There were two seats on the patient's side. Joseph's would remain empty.

He should be here! a voice in Chandice's head screamed. The doctor sat on the other side of the desk, and her two minions stood, hands clasped for this momentous day.

"So, when we joined the trial, we hoped for a fifty percent reduction in tumor growth."

Chandice could only nod. Her throat constricted, and it made her feel like she could throw up at any moment.

"We got ninety-eight percent." Chandice replayed that number in her head on endless repeat. *Ninety-eight percent . . . ninety-eight percent . . . ninety-eight percent.* It was astonishing. Amazing. Unbelievable.

"Are you sure?" Chandice asked.

"We ran all the scans three times. Chandice, you're not having any treatment today. We're going to scan you again in two weeks."

"But . . . I don't understand," Chandice said simply. This is why they advise patients to bring a loved one to doctor's visits. Because when big news comes down, your brain goes blank. "Let me . . ." She held up her phone and tapped Joseph on speakerphone. The whole room listened to his voice mail answer. Chandice hung up.

The oncologist came around the desk and sat in the other chair. She took Chandice's hands in her own. "Chandice," she said, "if your body continues to respond on the same trajectory, you could be cancer-free in two months' time."

Chandice breathed this information in and out. Cancer-free. Two months. Cancer-free. Two months. She thanked the doctor. It felt surreal to leave the chemotherapy clinic without so much as a pinprick. She walked past the two receptionists, whose knowing nods and beaming smiles made her feel like a celebrity.

It was all surreal, and surely at any moment Chandice would jerk awake from this ridiculous dream. "Life isn't always unfair," the woman said on *Serenity, Maybe?* When she had heard this, Chandice hadn't believed that at all. Now it seemed like an immutable Platonic truth. Like she should get it tattooed on her wrist to remind herself that faith could be restored.

She found herself with several hours of free time and realized she felt much better than she had in weeks. In fact, it was as if she had her entire life in front of her again when, just that morning, she had been prepared to accept its end. She went into a flower shop and treated herself to an armful of seasonal blooms: daffodils, tulips, pansies. As she carried them, in all their untidy beauty swathed in brown paper, she felt like a character in a movie with a happy ending.

She heard a thud somewhere upstairs just as the front door of her townhome shut behind her. "Hello?" Chandice said, instantly charged with alarm. She thought for a moment of just leaving. Wouldn't that be the safest thing to do? Walk right back out and not return alone? There was clearly someone inside her home. But she was propelled forward. Something was amiss. Chandice was an adult; shouldn't she try to handle it? Investigate, at least?

Chandice gently placed the flowers on the floor and proceeded down the hallway with caution. She heard three quick footsteps above her head. Adrenaline flooded Chandice's body, and her hand automatically found her keys, which she threaded through her fingers as she had been taught in self-defense class at college. The jagged metal stuck out from in between her knuckles. She stood for a moment in the living room, her son's latest Lego project splayed on the carpet bathed in that beautiful midday light. She and Joseph had stood in that very window and agreed that this would be home.

And no one was going to mess with that. Chandice felt powerful. There had been a simmering anger in her for months—fury about her illness, of course, but also something else. Something she couldn't quite describe, but in the darkest part of her mind she wanted to find an intruder inside, whom she could pummel with all this painful and unfathomable rage.

Chandice slipped out of her shoes and grabbed a large knife from the kitchen before stalking upstairs. She had never been in touch with this part of herself before, but it somehow felt right. On the second floor, Chandice soundlessly toed open the door to her son's room—empty.

Which left only the primary suite. Her steps became lighter. The refinished wooden planks gave up no creaks. She held the knife down, at her thigh, and pushed the door to her bedroom open with the tip of a key clasped in her other fist.

The bed, which she had made herself that morning, was now disheveled. The door to the bathroom ajar. Inside, the shower was running. Every single possibility flooded Chandice's brain at the same time, rendering them all indiscernible. A mishmash of sensory input. Joseph's clothes on the floor, the smell of his shampoo, but underneath it, some other scent. Was that him? Humming? In the shower? She wasn't ready to drop her weapons.

It still felt like Chandice was in a movie, just a very, very different genre. She peeked in the bathroom door, knife held down and out of sight. In between the fogged glass and the tiles, she caught a sliver of her husband in the shower, all steamed up.

"Joseph?" she said.

"Yeah, hon!" he responded, like everything was totally normal. "What are you doing here? I thought you had treatment?"

"And you had trial!" Chandice could only find the shortest, simplest words. The adrenaline in her body was chilling into something else, something more potent and lasting.

"You won't believe this!" he said glibly, poking his head out to look her in the eye. "I got sick at the office. Had to come home. Took a power nap and a shower." He held her gaze, watching for her response. Chandice could see his thoughts written on his face. To anyone else, her husband might appear calm, but she could see through this mask to the inner panic. All he wanted to know was whether she would choose to believe this half-baked ridiculous story. How many times had he taken her in before? Her lip curled in disgust.

But this version of herself—the badass with the rage and the weapons—was ready to play this game with him. "Oh, OK!" Chandice said lightly. She closed the bathroom door and turned back to the bedroom. Her husband's closet seemed like the right place to start. It was built into the brick walls and only a touch smaller than her own. Chandice slowly opened the door, expecting to find someone or something untoward inside. But there were only Joseph's gorgeous clothes, his expensive custom-made shoes, his grid of silk ties. Nothing amiss. She was almost disappointed.

Then she went to her own closet on the other side of the room. Also built in but larger for her full-length dresses—frocks it felt like she had worn in another lifetime, when she and her husband went to black-tie benefits and danced together. Chandice opened the tall, white door, and there, crouching inside under her blouses, was Joseph's assistant, Jen, naked, her straight brown hair the only thing covering her pale skin. She hugged her knees to her chest and kept her head down, like an animal not making eye contact to avoid being seen.

"Look at me," Chandice said, and this girl, who could not have been more than twenty-four years old, slowly lifted her chin. Tears streamed from the outside corners of her eyes. She shook with fear, which was when Chandice remembered the knife in her hand. Fighting the urge to reassure her, put the knife down, comfort this girl, Chandice resolved just to roll with it. Let her tremble a little.

"I'm sorry," the girl whispered, her terrified eyes flying from Chandice's calm face to the knife and back again. But Chandice knew the anger she had within herself was not toward Jen. This girl was not to blame. Chandice understood fully, finally, what had been just out of her mind's reach. This was not the first time Joseph had slept around, and it would not be the last. All that enthusiasm about trials and travel, about being away and "working so hard"—each case had involved its own other woman.

"Too good to be true," her sister had said about Joseph, and never had more insightful words been spoken. Chandice hated her husband; deep down, she had for some time. She turned on her heels and left them there, in her home, tossing the knife in the sink on her way out and stepping over the bouquet by the front door.

TWENTY

AMY

"I just don't understand how this could have happened," Amy said to Ming, her phone in her hand. Next week had come and gone and then the entire month of May. Penelope's family board meeting was long over and done and still . . . no call, no email, no text. And then, even worse, when Amy had finally broken down and tried to reach Penelope, she received no response. Instead of going herself, Penelope sent nannies to pickup and drop-off at Woodmont. Amy was, for the first time in her professional life, getting blown off, proving Ming right again; Penelope was a fraud, and it was all for naught. Ming had seen it coming, whereas Amy had been blind. Amy hated Penelope almost as much as she hated herself—with the heat and precision of a laser.

Instead of the quiet hum of work, punctuated only by the clink of teacup on saucer, their office had become tense and immobile. Ming, in her dark-gray suit, rubbed her hands together at her desk, her computer asleep. Amy gripped her phone in her hand, stood up as if to do something. Ming swiveled her chair, tore off her glasses, and leaned back at the ready for Amy's instructions. But she just stared down at her associate, her lover and friend, paralyzed.

"We should let the investors know before they start inquiring," Ming said, always ready to pick up the slack when Amy faltered. But

Amy loathed the idea of broadcasting her failure without closure from Penelope. She needed to hear it definitively, and she needed to know why. Her numbers were spot-on. After a lifetime of perfect performance, Amy was desperate not to disappoint her investors or, worse, her father. He seemed especially focused on this deal. She couldn't tell if he was just getting older or if there was more to it.

Amy held the phone like a weapon, passing it from hand to hand. She had never been iced out like this, had always had too much money and influence to be ignored, even at Andover and especially at Yale! But this Kent crowd was a different sort.

Penelope did not seem to care about losing face. If she wouldn't be privately compelled to act honorably, she could be shamed in public. Ming watched Amy anxiously, with naked concern not just for the business. Amy could not let her down any more than she would disappoint her father. Without thinking too much about it or discussing it with Ming, Amy typed Penelope – please don't make me confront you at our children's preschool graduation and hit Send.

The ceremony was the following day, and it was the only place where Amy knew Penelope would have to cross her path. Doubtless, all the moms would be there. Except that stupid cow Susan, of course. Amy still could not get over the selfish pointlessness of her suicide. If Susan had thought first of her children instead of herself, Amy would have made it to that meeting on time and never would have had to get involved with this shamster, Penelope. Perhaps the only person she hated more than Penelope and herself was Susan.

As this played out in Amy's mind, Ming's eyes did not leave her face. So often it seemed as if she could read Amy's thoughts, and, of course, Amy had sent the message without consultation—rashly, impulsively. A creeping sense of dread started up Amy's wrists toward her chest.

"You should call your father. Now. Don't wait," Ming said.

"Give me until tomorrow," Amy replied.

"You're not going to . . ." Ming would disapprove of any public con-frontation that might reflect badly on Pearl, and Amy loved her for it. But if Pearl had to pay a little for her mother to vanquish a foe, so be it.

"What choice do I have?" Amy said, her voice uncharacteristically sharp. "I can't just disappoint everyone without confirming."

Ming clucked at Amy, her highest form of condemnation. "Then I'm going with you," she said.

Generally, they only attended work events together, a ground rule that had been tacitly established by Amy and followed wordless by Ming. The Kent interview had been the first exception, so this would be establishing a trend. Though she sensed that this was in some way ceding ground to Ming, which grated, Amy also felt a relief that she would not have to face this alone, as she had every other challenge. In fact, Amy suddenly realized, she had not truly done anything alone since her father had introduced her to Ming, her first associate, whom he had already hired for her.

It took years for Amy to see past Ming's crisp professional demeanor to the beautiful, warm woman she really was. And although Amy loved Ming, and Pearl loved Ming, too, and they were in almost every way already a committed romantic couple, Amy would never make their relationship public out of respect for her father, and Ming would never question this decision. But where, exactly, the boundaries were between them shifted like the sands of a desert, sometimes still for months at a time only to change dramatically overnight. For years, Ming had her own apartment. Slowly, things built up, and, one day, they lived together.

So it was no surprise to see Ming dress in something ever so slightly less professional: a light peachy silk. Amy watched in their shared bath-room mirror, gently circling La Mer into her cheeks, as Ming put in contact lenses and removed from some previously unnoticed drawer one of those magical hair dryers and a boar-bristle hairbrush. She expertly styled her helmet of hair into a wavy bob, tousled just so to match the ruffles of her dress. Ming lined her lips before applying something pink. Amy had no idea she knew how to do all these things.

Amy looked at her own outfit, the usual silk blouse from her tailor in Hong Kong. The Celine pants she had in over a dozen colors and four different fabrics. Her black alligator Birkin seemed so staid. Ming looked like a flower in bloom, and Amy felt something loosening inside herself, like a new concept of the two of them.

"Now," Ming said, brushing Amy's air-dried, simple hair back behind her ear. "Let's remember, this is Pearl's day."

Penelope had never responded to Amy's text, and the thought of her face made the hate lasers fire up again. But Amy forced herself to agree with Ming, who wasn't wrong, after all. She was never wrong. On their short walk to the elevator, Ming threaded her arm through Amy's and leaned almost imperceptibly into her. As soon as the elevator arrived, she let go, and they did not touch again, even in the car.

Parents in their spring best crowded the courtyard outside the preschool, which was shared with a church next door and bursting with flowers. Seats arranged in the grass faced a temporary stage in front of the building. Waiters in crisp white shirts greeted everyone at the iron gates with trays of sparkling water or champagne. This was the launch-pad for their little darlings to head out into the larger world with all the trappings of their good fortune.

"Smile," Ming whisper-hissed, and Amy changed her expression from furiously seeking out a mortal enemy to a mother's shining pride. Ming elbowed her in the ribs. "A little less." Amy sighed, relaxing her cheeks ever so slightly. They moved along the corridor of people toward the congregation point at the center of everything.

As they inched through the masses, an occasional familiar face would pop up, and Amy would smile a little more broadly or bow her head in acknowledgment, all the while slowly, purposefully stalking. In the medium distance, Vic had her back against a wall with a glass of champagne, her eyes watching the crowd like she was an observer, apart from it all.

"Amy, hi!" Bhavna popped up directly in Amy and Ming's path. "I'm Bhavna," she said to Ming, although they had met a half-dozen times.

"Ming," she said coolly.

"Congratulations!" Bhavna gushed.

"On?" Amy said.

"Graduation! And, of course, on wherever you decided to send Pearl. Did you guys get into Kent after all?"

Amy could not remember ever having shared anything about Pearl's future with Bhavna previously, and she was hardly about to now. "Pearl is still wait-listed," Ming responded when Amy decided to just remain silent.

"Well, we decided," Bhavna said and tilted her head much too close for Amy's liking to faux whisper, "screw it! We're moving to the suburbs."

Though Bhavna said this as if she were sharing a choice tip that might catch on, Amy could not completely stifle the flash of disdain. The only thing worse than the city was a suburb of the city. "Saddle River!" Bhavna gushed.

Read the room, Amy thought, finally choking out, "Good. For you."

Before Bhavna could say more, something at the entrance stopped her in her tracks. Bhavna looked almost terrified, and Amy and Ming automatically turned to see who or what it was that had caught her eye. Michael Harris, pasty, bloated, and about as miserable as could be expected, stood a foot taller than those crowded around the champagne by the gate. He was flanked by Susan's parents. How terrible for them to have raised such a selfish daughter, Amy thought nastily. When she and Ming turned back to Bhavna, she was gone.

Then, finally, Amy laid eyes on Penelope, talking to Nina. From afar, she looked picture perfect in a high-necked avocado dress, flat silver gladiator sandals, and a tiny Gucci bag that Amy wanted to grab out of her hands and smack her with in front of that know-nothing Nina.

There was no way another moment was going to pass with her evading Amy, who barreled toward her. The crowd melted into meaningless sounds and colors. Penelope broke away from her conversation to field Amy like an incoming fly ball.

Before Amy could get a word out, Penelope said, "I'm so sorry, Amy. I know I've been just awful. I apologize."

Awful? The word echoed in Amy's mind. Penelope talked as if she were forever at a ladies' luncheon where the worst thing that could happen is the wrong wine gets poured.

"What's the problem? With the deal?" Amy asked pointedly.

"Apparently," Penelope drawled, "there's a set of secret bylaws." She sighed deeply and just stopped talking.

"Secret bylaws!" Ming gasped, having appeared at Amy's side.

Penelope seemed more than a little drugged to Amy. Had she always been this way? Had Ming seen something Amy had missed but had actually been there all along? She watched the lazy way Penelope's fingers moved, the carelessness of her demeanor. The way each word seemed to spend too long in Penelope's mouth. Ming pasted a placid smile on her face to conceal the nature of their conversation while Amy fought the urge to demand Penelope explain herself further. Amy was ready to hear any feedback—that the percentage was too high, the cash too low, or the timeline too fast. She had answers to each of these business questions, had obliterated questions just like them hundreds of times. She felt limber, like a fighter in the ring.

"And?" she jabbed, after Penelope seemed disinclined to explain further. "Was it about the equity?"

Another sigh. Amy grew even angrier. "Amy, I'm afraid to say our family office is prohibited from doing business with Chinese nationals." Which was like a match to the gas that had accumulated around Amy. She felt like there was a mushroom cloud over her head, which was also on fire. She had been ready for real financial issues not this old saw.

"That's quite a surprise." Amy heard these even words come out of Ming's mouth as if they were in separate realities. How could Ming stay so calm?

"I know, it's disgusting. My father was a real jerk," Penelope said. "And so's my brother." Penelope practically chugged her champagne.

Amy thought, with a lurch, of her own father and everything he had riding on this deal. He had seemed so personally invested in it, as if infrastructure would somehow obliterate all the skepticism of their ambitions for North American expansion. But they had run into the predicted problems after all. After two weeks of preparing for this conversation in her head, Amy lost all her words.

"What about Kent?" Ming said. Amy jerked her head to look at her. At first, she was angry because this had not been her plan, and they had not discussed it ahead of time. But before she impulsively blew it, Amy saw the wisdom in Ming's maneuvers and cleared her throat to cover her outburst.

Penelope blew into her cheek, inflating it in a show of being ever so slightly put out. "I suppose I could call in a chit there," she said breezily, offering up her hand like a limp napkin to be taken or not. Amy shook it. "No hard feelings?" she asked impishly.

"No hard feelings," Ming said, practically removing Penelope's hand from Amy's and then taking Amy by the elbow to a pair of front-row seats.

As Pearl walked across the stage to shake hands with Nina and receive her diploma, Ming stood at the back of the audience, typing away on her phone. It was the middle of the night in Taiwan, so they had at least five hours to get the word out. Ming drafted the official notice for limited partners, then a text to Amy's father. Amy looked back at Ming, noticing that Chandice and her husband were seated as far apart from one another as possible. As the children sang together one last time, Ming slipped into her seat beside Amy and gave her the phone to read the text.

Baba, I'm sorry but the deal fell through. There was nothing I could do. I'll fix it. Love, Amy

"He'll understand," Ming whispered in her ear, although they both knew that was a bald-faced lie. She hit Send just as all the parents rose to their feet applauding. Pearl seemed to not have noticed Amy and Ming so distracted with their phones, or, more likely, she had already learned at this young age that it was most expedient to ignore the things she didn't want to see in the first place.

As soon as Pearl was off the stage, Amy started ushering them toward the exit. She only wanted to escape this crush of nightmarish small talk. She could never seem to find the perfect nonconfrontational, appropriate thing to say to these people. In her haste, Amy bumped into a mother in front of her, jostling the baby in her arms.

"Excuse me!" Amy said reflexively. When the woman turned, she was surprised to see it was Kara, who looked rather haunted. Her eyes were both shadowed and vacant. "Kara!" Amy said.

"Hi, Amy," she said, holding the back of her baby's head protectively. Kara curled her body around the infant, as if into herself. Her hair, generally a perfect espresso, was salt and pepper at the roots, and her dress looked incomplete. The hem hung unfinished midcalf.

"Are you OK?" Amy asked, and Kara's eyes flew to hers.

"Yeah," she said unconvincingly.

"Hi, I'm Isaac," a hulking man added over her shoulder, obviously annoyed not to be introduced. "Kara's husband," he added. Kara eyed him mutely, as if unsure what he might do next. "So, you're in finance?" he said to Amy. "I like to do a little day-trading myself."

Kara winced, and Amy felt for her. "I don't know anything about that," Amy said crisply.

"Nice to meet you," Ming added, gently guiding Pearl toward the door with her hands on her shoulders. Then they were out of Woodmont's gates and on to, where exactly? Ming assured Amy that Penelope could be trusted for a Kent-related errand, and though Amy disagreed, she felt they had nothing to lose. They had already paid the enrollment at another school, and Amy had resigned herself to transferring later.

In the middle of the night, Ming's and Amy's phones both chimed with a text message at the same time. Neither of them had been sleeping anyway, and they simultaneously reached for their nightstands. When Amy saw the sender was Chia-Jung, her father's longtime now ex-girlfriend, she felt a fleeting sense of well-being. *They must be back together,* she presumed.

But there was just a link to a short article in Taipei's *Liberty Times* published minutes before: "Finance Titan Leaps to His Death." Ming sobbed quietly next to her. Amy could not read further. The details hardly mattered. Ming would tell her what she needed to know, and Ming would make all the decisions from now on. Wordlessly, Amy went to wake the staff to get the family prepared to depart. If they hurried, they could make the 9:00 a.m. to Taipei.

TWENTY-ONE

KARA

Everything was reaching its inevitable conclusion, Kara could tell. Home from his graduation, Oscar, with his loosened tie, looked like a tiny junior banker on break from brokering deals and not a child playing with Magna-Tiles on the floor. Kara winced again, remembering Isaac's ham-handed interaction with Amy, who looked like a queen in the presence of some protocol-ignorant idiot. Amy, always unflappably perfect, in her uniform of silk shirts and pants so carefully crafted and stitched that each piece would take Kara weeks to make, and they'd never be right.

Isaac came out of the bedroom, where he had put the baby down to sleep. He retrieved a bottle of Miller Lite from the fridge without offering Kara anything, and she felt like marrying him had been the biggest mistake of her life. Isaac sat on the couch and sipped his beer, enjoying his reprieve from the grind at the gym. The afternoon sun came through their window only for about ninety minutes each day. The rays bathed Isaac in natural light. To the objective eye, her fit husband was very attractive. But as she looked at him, the thing Kara felt more than anything was drained. Every single task, item, and person in her life had become either hopelessly dull or just plain painful, everything merely a distraction.

"God, I hate those people," Isaac suddenly erupted. "What a bunch of pretentious fucks!"

"Isaac!" Kara said, genuinely surprised at his outburst. She pointed at Oscar, whose head jerked up at his father's unusually heated tone.

"I want to get out of the city," Isaac said, not for the first time. Kara had mostly accepted this creeping inevitability, beat it back as hard as she could. But now, when Isaac made this suggestion for the twentieth or thirtieth time, Kara found herself warming to it. A relief! It would be so nice to live among normal, regular people like herself.

"But what about . . . ," she heard herself say, gesturing again at their son's back.

"What do you mean?"

"Wouldn't he be better off . . ." She trailed off, thinking of Kent. They were still technically waiting to hear. When notification day came, Libby had given Kara neither a yes nor a no but rather a "bear with us," whatever that meant. Even though an astonishing two months had passed, wouldn't it be a shame to walk away from that?

"Please, Kara, people move to the country for their kids, not the city." She hated when Isaac took this pedantic tone with her, particularly when he was in the wrong, but Kara was too tired to argue. Besides, Oscar probably wouldn't get in and, if he did, they'd never be able to afford it. Isaac had family in White Plains. He had his eye on the two-bedroom rental over his cousin's garage. Kara might even be special there.

"Did you make that appointment?" Isaac asked, jarring Kara from her contemplation of an unexceptional White Plains existence. In fact, the one thing Kara had forced herself to do since their last blowup was to find someone, anyone, who could prescribe her medication and accepted the insurance his stupid health club offered. The mental health clinic uptown had given her an appointment eight months from the day she called. When Kara cried on the phone, said it was an emergency, and begged for the love of her children, they squeezed her in eight weeks later. Her consultation was finally the very next day. But she only lifted her chin up and down three times to indicate her response to Isaac.

Kara had made it through, mostly unscathed. Her life reduced itself to necessities. She looked back and barely recognized her former self, who had played the role of Wealthy New York Woman. The one who made beautiful clothing and gave herself manicures and dyed her own hair as frequently as most women got pedicures, which she also gave herself regularly. Her former self who played on the floor with her children and sought out free classes for them all over New York and ferried them there on public transportation—never, ever a taxi!—in all sorts of weather. That self had been replaced by someone who managed just the bare minimum. Her son got to school, mostly on time, and was picked up, mostly on time, every day. Her baby was fed, wore clean diapers, and played outside on nice days. The rest of the time, Kara looked for a therapist and fought her Susan Harris obsession.

Every day, she wanted to reach out to the brother. She had all his contact details saved in her phone after calling his real estate agency and pretending to be an enthusiastic prospective buyer of an unsellable, hideous four-bedroom (one bathroom!) made out of coral stucco next to an energy plant. They happily gave her his mobile and home numbers. She had punched them all into her phone and saved them under DO NOT CALL, which was possibly the worst way to avoid suspicion should Isaac ever see it, but also the only thing Kara could think of. She DID NOT call. She had held herself to that.

But it was taking a toll on her, one that she knew was as obvious as the visible gray roots on her head. What did she care now, though, if they noticed anything about her? The more Kara let it all hang out, the more she perceived the depths of city people's disinterest in one another. No one cared. She attended Oscar's graduation in that damnably unfinishable dress she had started months ago. Not only was it incomplete, it no longer suited her skinny but newly soft physique. A few of the other moms and a gay dad definitely clocked the hemline on her skirt, a frayed chiffon that looked chewed on, but what could they say? And why? No one knew her well enough to ask.

Kara had resigned herself to disappearing completely, as soon as possible. But she needed the Klonopin to do it. She planned out the necessary manipulations and exaggerations she could employ to secure the prescription. Kara would start with the truth and branch out if required. The pills were the only thing that dulled the irresistible, destructive urges to seek out answers to critical, impossible questions.

Because even though she knew no one else would ever understand, Kara had come to believe that Susan's death was the final clue to her sister's death, a mirrored twinning over time just for Kara to figure out. She had run from the biggest question of her life for years and years, and here she was, in its clutches fully.

"I'm going to go for a walk," she said, leaping to her feet. She rarely had Isaac at home midweek. The baby was napping. Why shouldn't she go out? "I need to pick up some things for dinner anyway," she added, annoyed with herself for divulging this unnecessary but true piece of information. Did she need a reason to go for a walk?

"Oh, OK," Isaac said after a moment's hesitation.

Outside, Kara went quickly to the nearest collection of benches in a carved-out concrete square, which qualified as public "outdoor space" in this toilet bowl of a city. They hadn't even bothered to install a planter, just bricks and metal. Kara detested the hardness of every single thing in New York and how quickly it all got covered in filth. But it would do for her purposes.

She sat down and dialed Susan Harris's brother on his mobile phone. It was midafternoon on a Thursday. As the woman said on *Serenity, Maybe?*, "Sometimes you just have to do the thing you can't stop thinking about." Kara had written this calm exchange in her head and knew exactly what she wanted to say.

"Timothy Chaney of Chaney Real Estate." He was outside somewhere. Kara pictured him standing next to the closed door of his white

Mercedes, one elbow in the air holding the phone pressed to his ear as the Florida sun beat down on him.

"Hi, Timothy, this is Kara Richards. I was a friend of Susan's." She waited for this to sink in.

"Hello," he said, giving nothing away.

Kara continued with her prepared words. She had been waiting weeks for this moment, and she would not squander it. "I'm reaching out to you as a sibling survivor. My sister also killed herself."

"Yeah?" he said, a discordant note of annoyance creeping into his previously neutral tone. "I'm sorry to hear that," he said insincerely.

"I just . . ." His instant frustration unnerved Kara. Her script fluttered away like pages in the wind. "When things don't go the way you expect, just be in the moment and stay with your truth," the woman said on *Serenity, Maybe?* "I just want to know, if you had any idea"—Kara's voice dwindled, and she worried he wouldn't hear the most important part, which she choked out—"why she did it?"

"What?" he roared.

She thought of her sister. The confusing stories they told themselves in her family after she jumped off the bridge. Was she pushed? Was she on drugs? Was she always sad or just that day? Her sister had been impulsive, but was she *that* impulsive?

"Why she did it?" Kara repeated.

"There's nothing to know!" he exclaimed. She had angered him with her question. "Susan was depressed. She couldn't deal anymore. End of story!"

"But her family . . ."

"Get help," he said and hung up on her.

The therapist's office was in a Midtown clinic. Women in tightly fitting clothes clutching plastic bags crammed the waiting room. *Were they all on lunch breaks?* Kara wondered, her empty hands feeling around for a phantom sandwich sack. She had not had time to eat before thrusting the baby at the sitter and rushing to this appointment, where there would clearly be a long wait.

By the time she was taken in to see the doctor (harried, middle aged, disengaged, projecting bitterness from the top of his comb-over), Kara's stomach grumbled, and she felt like she might reveal more than she intended. But the doctor did not pick his head up from her chart, which said basically nothing but that she was anxious. When he finally looked at her, his saggy face reminiscent of a pug, Kara said, "A friend committed suicide, and it's made me think obsessively about my sister's suicide. I had a few Klonopin left over from a previous prescription. They are the only thing that helps to stop the negative thought cycles so I can care for my children."

Kara hoped that the doctor would hear beyond the rational structure of her statement and see instead, in a way that no one else had, her very real and dangerous pain, and speak to it with words of concern rather than science and data. Kara realized she hungered for human empathy as much as medication. If he saw the tears in her eyes, he said nothing about them.

The doctor merely nodded and got out his pad. He handed her a prescription with five refills. Kara could not believe it was so easy.

"See you in six months" was all he said.

She went straight to the drugstore by her apartment and filled the prescription, taking half a pill before even leaving the store. Instead of going straight home, she went to the park. It was a lovely June day, a preview of the summer's heat, and she sat by the river in the sun and waited for the drug to take effect. She felt the void where her love for the city had been. The space it had occupied in her heart was being replaced by . . . nothing much. Just the lack of longing for something that you can never really have. It would be better for her and her family to be somewhere less expensive and competitive, where Kara would have family, and it didn't matter if she liked them or they liked her. Everyone and everything would be plain average. Suddenly, she couldn't wait to get out.

Her phone rang, and for once, Kara didn't recoil in horror at the thought of answering an unknown 212 number. "Hi, Kara! It's Libby from the Kent School."

"Oh, hi, Libby," Kara said, expecting the inevitable letdown. Here it was, the end of this story line, just as she'd envisioned it: rejection.

"Kara, I have great news!" Libby exclaimed unexpectedly. "I'm sorry it took so long to make it official, but we want to offer Oscar a full scholarship."

Kara doubted she had heard this correctly. "Really?"

"Yes, Oscar has earned a full scholarship to Kent kindergarten. Can I put his name down to join the class?"

Kara's mind spun, mostly with thoughts of endless outfits for Oscar and herself and Isaac. All those times she would have to show up, in costume and character, again and again endlessly. She'd have to face Penelope forever. Just these thoughts neutralized the Klonopin in her system. Kara's chest seized up with anxiety.

"I'll have to call you back" was all Kara could manage. Surely, Libby had never heard that before being hung up on.

When Isaac got home that night, Kara had dyed her hair a fresh shade of auburn, taking comfort in the automatic way her hands knew the packets and the bowls and the brushes. Feeling all right letting the kids watch television while she turned her attention to self-care. Not thinking at all about Susan Harris. Her eyes instead turned to the unexceptional, totally manageable future.

But first she had to tell Isaac about Kent. He deserved to know and was entitled to have his preferences counted. It was good news after all, she reminded herself, trying to set aside the huge amount of unpleasantness their city life would entail versus moving to White Plains, where she could buy some cheap leggings and start calling frozen pizza bagels "dinner." But she would stay and enroll him, if that's what Isaac wanted. Which Kara knew he almost definitely did not. *Almost* definitely.

"How was therapy?" he asked as soon as the boys were asleep.

"Pretty good," she said, although it had been the furthest thing from therapy one could imagine.

"It's such a relief, babe. I knew something wasn't right when you wore that janky dress yesterday. Jesus, everyone was staring," Isaac said, chuckling to himself as Kara threw up in her mouth a little bit. She knew in that moment she was done with the outfits, done with the spectacle of it all, done with the upkeep and posturing. Oscar didn't deserve anything more special than any other kid, and Isaac would never know what he didn't know. Kara called Kent the next morning and did the unthinkable: she declined.

TWENTY-TWO

PENELOPE

Penelope smoothed her grape Bottega Veneta dress over her derriere. She leaned into the wall of mirrors, over the expanse of marble, and applied a final layer of matching lipstick. This color would speak for the evening. It said, *Fun! Welcome! You have arrived! Never mind about anonymous letters and high profile terminations. Kent will endure.*

This was what Penelope had been bred for—hosting private school cocktail parties. It may sound simple, but these sorts of school events required careful planning and execution to make guests from various backgrounds and experiences feel equally uncomfortable. They were, all of them together, Kent parents, and they would be for at least thirteen more years. Except for the unlucky kids who got counseled out.

She took a Klonopin and stuck another one in her pocket—her security object. No need for a bag. She had sent the kids to Water Mill with the nannies so she could focus entirely on making the Incoming Kent Parent Cocktail Party a smashing success. In the living room, the black-vested cater waiters busied themselves with last-minute preparations, tucking cocktail napkins under bowls of nuts, filling glasses with lemon ice water to go out on silver trays, arraying toothpicks and endive spears and pigs in blankets—something Graham always insisted on and Penelope indulged because, truth be told, the poor guy simply loathed entertaining. When would he realize throwing parties was Penelope's main occupation?

The bartender wasn't so handsome this time. Penelope should have gotten the last one's name. "Bombay martini, please, up with a twist," she asked, reminding herself to always request the last guy (or someone equally tall and handsome). See, these were the sort of details an inexperienced hostess might overlook. "Lots of ice shards," she added, when this one only gave the shaker three sluggish jerks. "Keep them coming, OK?" she said, lifting the glass in the air. He merely blinked his dull brown eyes at her. *So hard,* she joked silently to herself, *to find good help.*

Where was Graham anyway? The party was starting, and her husband was nowhere to be found. The elevator dinged, and so it began, strangers stepping into her foyer with the hand-painted Korean silk wallpaper for the discerning among them to admire. As they lifted their water-beaded glasses off proffered trays, Penelope thought fancifully that it was like birds taking flight into the room. She lifted her own hands to catch them.

"Greetings! Hello! I'm Penelope!" she said, her practiced walk in heels carrying her swiftly toward them. She smiled into every unknown, nervous face, drawing them into the living room, where the food and bar were located. She introduced people she didn't know to others she had never met, reeling off names she had just heard only to instantly forget them and return to the front door to do it all again. It was like hauling fish in with giant nets.

As the party grew crowded, Penelope would catch sight of people she recognized. There was Amy, looking dour across the room, with that assistant of hers. She should be happier to be here, Penelope thought to herself, after fighting so hard for it. There was Graham, finally, drinking scotch in the corner, talking to Vic, who had gotten so caught up in Susan's death but now seemed back to her old easy-breezy self. Maybe even better. She always wore jeans and an unusually fashionable jacket that was half a size too small on her. But she was pretty enough not to care and young enough to get away with it. *For now,* Penelope mused on her way back to greet whoever stepped off the elevator.

She drew up short when it turned out to be her brother Andrew. "Hi, sis." In his suit and tie, impeccably groomed, he looked like he belonged at the party, which annoyed Penelope even more. She realized that the unattractive bartender had forgotten to bring her a second martini.

"What are you doing here?" she asked sharply, her eyes indicating it was hardly a good time for a confrontation.

"I came to personally give you this," he said, handing over an envelope. He tilted his head at her in his odd way that had befuddled Penelope their entire lives. She could never tell if it meant war or peace. "It's the official rejection letter to Taipei Partners. I thought you'd like to see that I threw myself under the bus."

"Why would you do that?" Penelope asked.

"It's just business, Pen," he said, sounding almost sorry. "And Dad wasn't always right," Andrew added, clearing his throat as if it physically pained him to make this obvious observation. He had never said anything remotely negative about their father before. As far as Penelope knew, Andrew believed their father was a god. Penelope felt like if she just stayed perfectly still, perhaps he'd go on. Say more. Perhaps even . . . apologize? Open the door for her to do more on the family board? She clutched the envelope, fingers curved against her palm midway between them.

The elevator dinged again, and when Chandice stepped out, Penelope wanted to stuff her back in and continue the conversation with Andrew. She thought for one wild moment about the ramifications of doing just that, before accepting that Chandice had arrived and that she had to be greeted like everyone else. As Penelope gave her a kiss on the cheek, she could not help but observe that Chandice appeared to have been to a spa or on retreat or had some really great work done. Penelope peered at her face a second longer than usual, took in the carefully chosen gold link necklace, the long thin braids that crowded the back of her raw silk saffron frock.

As she stepped back to introduce him, Penelope saw that Chandice was having some sort of effect on her brother. Andrew's whole demeanor changed. He had both hands out, as if he might hug her.

"Andrew, this is—" Penelope started, but Andrew cut her off right away.

"Chandice, my goodness it's been a while," he said, grasping Chandice's hand with both of his. Penelope had never seen him do that before.

"I didn't know you were a Kent parent," Chandice said, also looking quite pleased with this chance encounter.

"I'm not. No kids. Penny is my sister," he said, annoyingly employing her family nickname in this setting. Chandice stifled a little knowing smirk; she had heard Penelope insist on her full name more than once. "And Chandice was one of my stars," Andrew said, filling Penelope in. For some reason that Penelope did not contemplate, this surprised and dismayed her. Andrew and Chandice? Worked together?

Chandice laughed. "I'm guessing Belinda never mentioned that I'm rejoining the workforce."

"Why no, she did not! I'll have to have a talk with her about sharing critical information. But tell me . . ." Andrew crossed an arm over his chest and used it as a table on which to rest his other arm, assuming his inquisitive posture. He wanted Chandice to know how interested he was in everything she said. An irrational spark of jealousy ignited in Penelope, and she wanted nothing more than to leave this conversation. "Why now?" he asked.

"Getting a divorce," Chandice said, the corners of her mouth turning up a bit to indicate that this was sad but not *too* sad.

"Oh, Chandice, I hadn't heard," Penelope interjected, thinking that had something to do with the way her skin was glowing. They both turned to look at her like they had already forgotten she was there. "Oh, excuse me!" Penelope said urgently, pretending to have heard someone calling. She couldn't stand watching her brother and Chandice work flirt or whatever they were doing. In breaking off, though, without a trajectory, she bumped right into Amy, who had been on her way to greet Chandice.

Though all the usual trappings were in place—the perfectly ironed shirt, eye-popping handbag, tailored slacks—Amy herself looked ghostly and insubstantial. That assistant of hers who did all the talking kept one wary eye on Penelope and one on her boss. It was starting to dawn on Penelope that maybe there was more to their relationship. Penelope plastered a smile on her face. She had learned long ago to run toward inevitable unpleasantness rather than hide from it. Better to be the first to talk and control the dialogue—one piece of advice her father had deigned to share with his only daughter.

"Amy, hello! I heard the good news," Penelope gushed.

"Ming," the assistant said, sticking out her hand.

"Thank you for what you did for Pearl," Amy intoned, as if reading her lines.

"Of course! She's a wonderful girl, and I'm sure she'll do well at Kent," Penelope said. She knew nothing about Pearl, but this sounded like the right thing to say as a semiofficial representative of the institution. It was the least she could do for these people after that embarrassing gaffe. She suddenly remembered the letter, still pressed to her palm.

"I just got my copy of the rejection. I think you'll see it was out of my hands."

"Yes, that was very clear," Ming said. Amy stayed quiet. She was so stiff—not Penelope's sort of person at all. Penelope made her hostess excuses and zipped off to join two men eating canapés off their cocktail napkins. Two minutes later, as Penelope pretended to listen to radiologists compare their résumés, she watched Amy embrace Chandice. And not just a show hug. It looked like real feeling between them. Maybe they were actual friends. Amy left with Ming, and Chandice melted into the party.

The physicians went on to compare the various machines they had bought recently for their offices, and Penelope turned her attention to the conversation behind her, like tuning into a radio station, which happened to involve Vic. She chatted with two other alumni whose kids would be attending Kent. How cozy. They had all had a few drinks and were chuckling along with whatever Vic was talking about.

"Aren't you worried?" one of them asked. "About, you know, people knowing?"

"I hope people know! I just sold the TV rights!" Vic exclaimed. They all laughed uproariously together—three Kent kids all grown up. Penelope bristled once more with envy. To feel so at home in a crowd that made everyone else feel like an outsider. To have affirmation from the real world in the form of compensation. Whatever Vic would make from her book was an insignificant amount of money to Penelope, but still, Vic had earned it herself.

"I mean, your mommy friends!" the dad persisted. "Won't they mind being used for creative fodder?" Penelope found herself leaning backward into them as much as possible without drawing attention to herself.

"Well the mom who jumped won't mind," said the other father so callously Penelope swiveled around to see Vic's reaction. Vic glared at him, her cheeks sucked in. She would say something, remind them that Susan was an actual person. It was a goddamn real-life tragedy, and they should show some respect. But, of course, Vic could never claim the moral high ground again. Not since she had decided to write about Susan. Apparently, she was going to write about them all.

Impulsively, Penelope popped the second Klon and washed it down with a watery martini. No one would ever know the difference.

TWENTY-THREE

AMY

Amy's shoulders slumped as they waited for the elevator, the dregs of the party behind them. Ming had insisted they attend to scout out some prospects, but Amy could only go through the motions. She smiled and nodded at all the right times. The only person she was genuinely happy to see was Chandice, who had her health even if she had lost her marriage. Amy tried to find comfort for herself in this sort of thinking, but there was none.

Ming sidled closer and rubbed the upper part of her arm, but for once, Amy didn't instantly withdraw. Her father's death had crushed her. She hardly had the will to turn down any small easing of grief. His funeral was attended by hundreds of associates who kindly did not speak of the way he died, which would hang over her head forever like a cloud that rained shame and guilt in equal measure. She could feel Ming's concern and care for her through the fingers placed gently on her triceps.

Once they were on the elevator with the doors closed, Amy said sincerely, "I guess we should be happy this worked out for Pearl. Solid strategy, Ming."

"The letter didn't hurt either," Ming replied, a devious grin lighting up her face. She looked sideways at Amy.

"What letter?" Amy said, realization dawning slowly. "Wait, you didn't . . ."

"I had to shake them up a bit. Reset the deck," Ming said without remorse. For the first time since her father died, Amy thought entirely of something else for five seconds. She was pleased her partner was such a skilled, wily adversary.

"Ming, you're a wonder," Amy said and meant it.

For the first time, Ming kissed Amy outside their home, the two of them together as part of the world at large. It felt transgressive, to Amy, just to be fully herself in public. She imagined a porter in Penelope's building watching the security camera, the first witness to Amy and Ming's romance, and it thrilled her to know this stranger might exist. They were alone on an elevator, but it was a start.

EPILOGUE

SUSAN

Knowing that later everyone would assume she had been in a hysterical frenzy, running around her house like a lunatic, Susan couldn't help but notice how calmly she moved through her apartment. In fact, Susan had not felt at peace like this in a long time. Maybe her whole life. Which was how she knew this was the right decision.

Susan wanted the kids to have a happy morning with her so that if they did try and remember her at all, it would be a blurry but positive reel they could run in the back of their minds, where they ate sugar cereal while Mommy sang in the kitchen. She had on pink flannel pajamas with the laughing giraffes on them that Michael had given her that year for Christmas. She made pancakes in the shape of Mickey Mouse and let the kids have as much butter and syrup as they wanted. She kissed them both quite a bit. More than usual.

Then she sat at the table with them and held each of their hands and said, "Guess what? Today's a special day." Both kids locked their attention on their mother, eyes rapt. "I want you to know that I love you both very, very much." Oh, no, her eyes were filling with tears. She blinked them away, but Claude had cottoned on to something amiss. Susan swallowed. "Today, you guys get to watch cartoons."

Claude momentarily forgot all about whatever had bothered her and ran to the fluffy blue rug in front of the living room television. Susan placed the baby next to his sister on the floor—he wasn't really a baby anymore at two years old and practically running everywhere, but he was now happily absorbed completely in the television. Susan went to find the toolbox.

Everyone in New York was so *busy* all the time, running to avoid looking too closely at their inner selves and all their irreparableness. This was *all* Susan could see—tatters where there should be whole cloth. She understood, rationally, that as a mother, she herself would never be able to operate for her children in a way that would allow them to develop into normal humans. Nor could she suffer to watch them struggle as she had. This choice she was making was for them. As a mother, she knew the best gift she could give them was her absence.

The television had sucked her kids safely away. They sat slack jawed, the animation reflected in their hypnotized eyes. Behind them, the apartment's single appealing feature was the focus of Susan's attention. The large window overlooking Third Avenue was her favorite thing about this place when they toured this apartment. Recently, it had seemed like destiny and would be a romantic ending.

But what she thought were screws were actually bolts. And those bolts turned out to be unmovable. Susan gave it a shot with a needle-head wrench but got nowhere. Frustrated, she sat on the radiator by the window and looked down on the little buildings across the street. What's her name lived in one of them. Susan thought of the other windows in her apartment.

She was still formulating her plan B when Isa arrived. The way the children leaped to their feet, even the small one, struggling first to steady himself before launching at his caregiver, took Susan's breath away. Irrationally, watching her children flock to this woman, who had already loved them better than Susan herself could, shook her resolve just a very little.

"Good morning," she said stiffly to Isa, her first words to another adult. Susan cleared her throat, wondering if she looked at all strange. She lifted a hand to the back of her head and felt the rat's nest there just beneath the bun.

"Morning, Mrs. Harris," Isa said, rising from where she sat on the floor tickling Claude. Isa could see something was wrong; of course, she could.

"I'm not feeling well." Susan walked past her and into the bedroom.

"Of course," Isa said, her concerned eyes following Susan.

Susan made the mistake of looking back at Isa, her nanny of four years, with her son in her arms and her daughter clinging to her hip in a way that struck Susan as wholly unfamiliar. Had this little girl ever held on to her like that? Which was a dangerous question, because it led to the next feeling, which was wanting Claude's touch. To always be near her daughter. Her one true love.

She swallowed and closed her bedroom door. She had to climb over her unmade bed to get to the windows that overlooked the back alley. They had steel child guards bolted to the outside, but her notoriously incompetent building handyman had installed them. How hard could it be to remove them? She spent fifteen minutes trying, but it was no use. They called for a special screwdriver. Susan turned around suddenly and saw Claude standing in the doorway; her eyes seemed double size.

"What are you doing, Mommy?" her daughter asked, and Susan flinched. This memory could leave a mark. She had to get the kids out of there!

"Isa!" Susan called, feeling a sudden sense of urgency. She rushed past her daughter in the small passage, and the side of her hand brushed the top of Claude's downy-soft arm, and she thought she might burst into a thousand different pieces right there. Isa was in the kitchen slicing up apples. "Could you please take the kids to the park right away!"

Isa said nothing, but surely she noticed Susan's harried expression. Susan had to hide.

"Oh, and don't let Michael know that I'm home, OK?" Susan said, turning her head to look Isa in the eye. Michael knew her history. The hospitalizations. The self-harm. He had signed up for this, and Susan didn't feel bad about what was going to happen to him because he, too, would be better off without her. It was as clear as arithmetic in her mind.

"OK, Mrs. Harris."

"Mommy?" Claude said, standing in the hall by the bathroom door. It was as if there were two choices, a fork in the road. For a second, Susan thought she might rush to her daughter, crush her in an embrace, weep tears of resolution and apology, and resolve to stay on this earth with her, through the good and the bad and whatever might come. Claude lifted her chin, almost intuitively reading what was happening. Any second, she would run to her.

Which would take the solution out of Susan's hands. She couldn't have that. Already, the serenity of just minutes before was giving way to the anxieties of living. Could she really be this perfect girl's mother forever? Was it the best thing for Claude?

Susan ducked into the bathroom as if she was about to vomit. Maybe she was. She pressed her back against the closed door, consciously slowing her panicked, desperate breathing, eyes shut, listening for the sounds of them getting ready to go to the park. Isa got Susan's son in his snowsuit, murmuring gentle encouragements to him. She heard the squeak of the tiny rubber boots Susan had so carefully selected. His hand-knit hat from her cousin in Ohio, made from local llama hair. She could picture it all. Claude pulling on her parka and gloves all by herself, because she was the big sister, of course.

Susan heard Isa's blessed words, "Ready to go?" She held her breath. This was the final test. She just had to hold on to her gumption and get through this, and then there would be blessed relief, finally.

"I want to hug mommy before we go," Claude said defiantly. Susan knew that tone. She had used it herself to great effect as a little girl. She hated the sound of it now.

"Mommy doesn't feel well, Claude!" Isa said.

Susan slumped into the fetal position on the floor, her back against the closed bathroom door. It felt like her whole body was being ripped apart. Claude was growing more and more upset, demanding one last hug. The baby started to cry. She couldn't bear it any longer, this constant struggle.

And she *had* struggled. She hadn't just succumbed to the first wave of sadness to come her way. In high school, when she first could not get out of bed to go to class, it was the boarding school psychologist who explained it to her parents. What had they felt when they heard this news? Perhaps nothing, as they were both made of stone. They had thought she was just lazy. It was that psychologist who had suggested her first psychiatrist, who had put her on lifesaving Zoloft and then later added Effexor and after that toyed with various other cocktails, from lithium to Adderall, to get her to believe living was a viable idea. And it had felt feasible ten years ago when she met Michael, eight years ago when they got married, five years ago when she got pregnant . . .

After Claude's birth, things got murky. She was sinking; she knew it the day after delivery. Their son came along as almost a matter of course—she was already on autopilot, backing away from the controls to turn her attention inward. She had responsibilities. Even as she collapsed internally, Susan remained keenly aware of all her responsibilities! That's why she had tried everything. Everything!

As a psychologist, she subjected herself to every kind of therapy from talk to shock to hallucinogenic. If she wasn't so frightened of surgery and professionally skeptical of the procedure, she might have considered a lobotomy. She tried every applicable medication in the *Diagnostic and Statistical Manual of Mental Disorders*. All the combinations. She spent four years in deep consultation with her psychopharmacologist working out rarefied, controlled, complicated prescriptions and then waiting in line to fill them at the stupid pharmacy downstairs.

She remembered, one night, arguing with Michael about her new medication, some sort of steroid that was meant to activate the latent parts of her brain where most people experience satisfaction. But instead, it was making her so angry. Susan screamed at him outside the drugstore one night because he had eaten all the butter-pecan ice cream at home, and the store didn't have any more. She went off that medication afterward, but there were no others left to try.

She exercised. Spin classes and yoga. A trainer at the park followed by long brisk walks. Jogs, even. Meditation. She tried working. She wrote a whole book, grinding it out in the late hours of the night and the predawn chill of the morning. Even when she finished it, she knew it was a one-time thing. Something to leave the world to remember her by.

She threw herself into parenting, but she felt like a fraud. Claude could always tell, she felt, that something wasn't quite right with her. It was always too much like acting. "Tonight, Susan Harris will be performing the role of doting mother." So she shifted to volunteering, taking on the thankless job of class parent. When that wasn't enough, she became a goddamn crusader, adopting children's nutrition as her raison d'être, if only to blow off steam arguing with practical strangers. An astonished Michael said to her, after that shameful public spat with Nina, "I didn't know you cared so much about corn syrup," and the truth was, Susan realized, she didn't. It was all just another attempt to avoid the unavoidable.

She tried making friends. Penelope was a total waste and all Klon'd up most of the time. Vic was fun to hang out with, but their friendship was hemmed in on all sides by the constant observing eyes of their two daughters. Even when they had one or two opportunities, Vic was clearly not interested in or able to take the relationship any deeper. Susan didn't blame Vic too much when she had worked so hard to conceal the truth.

She tried sex, starting with her husband. Their sex life had always been perfectly satisfactory to Susan before kids. But lately, even as she could feel her body wanting to respond to her husband's touch, she just couldn't stay present. Even that last time, when Michael came for her in the steamy shower. He took the soap from her hand, whispered, "Let me do this," and washed her so gently and thoroughly. Even then! She had left her body for a time, watching her husband making love to her on the bathroom floor until she faked an orgasm, which he knew she did, but they never talked about.

She tried sleeping with other people's husbands, starting with Chandice's. It was just that one time, after the cocktail party, when Michael was on his fraternity golf trip, and Chandice was somewhere— home? resting?—and Susan was so desperate by then to feel something, anything other than constant dread and self-loathing. But it was the same thing, really. Nothing much new to see or experience. Nothing death changing, she joked to herself.

When she first started posting things online, she thought it was making her feel the slightest bit better to receive all that positive atten- tion. It was a charge, a momentary respite from her internal self-abuse. But like any addiction, the plateau did not last forever. Her hunger for it just grew until the response to every post became a disappointment because it wasn't always better or more than the last. It had left her feeling even more hollow.

There just wasn't anything left to try. She had to get out. And Susan did feel sick now, unsure of whether she needed to sit on the toilet or vomit up the emptiness in her guts. Claude was hysterical, flat on the floor directly on the other side of the bathroom door, crying ceaselessly, "Mommy, mommy, mommy . . ."

There was only one way to get this to end, Susan realized. She went from fetal to all fours to standing at the sink, swaying unsteadily. She splashed cold water on her puffy face. She would not miss this feeling of disappointment every time she looked in the mirror. Susan told herself she was already dead.

She slowly opened the bathroom door. Her daughter lay there, heaving with sobs. Susan crouched down and put her hand on Claude's back, and Claude crawled toward her until Susan could hook her hands under her armpits and lift her up and into her arms. The smell of her child rushed directly into her brain, and there it would have done its magic work. But Susan was dead already.

"Mommy doesn't feel well, Claude," Susan said calmly, taking her daughter's hands off her. She looked Claude right in the eye. "So you're going to go to the park with Isa."

Claude shook her head no and threw herself around her mother again like an octopus. But her mother was no longer present in her body, so she was embracing a shell, a former person. She stood up, Claude still clinging to her, the hot tears falling on her neck. She walked to Isa and leaned over a little bit.

"Here, take her," she said. Isa reached in between mother and daughter and peeled Claude away. Limp, defeated, Claude turned to her nanny instead. Susan opened the door for them so Isa could get the stroller out with Claude in her arms.

"Bye, Mommy," Claude said over Isa's shoulder just before the apartment door closed.

And then there was nothing standing in her way. Not really. Susan stayed by the closed door of her apartment, breathing. Waiting patiently, tactically, to be sure Isa did not rush back, having forgotten something. Did not discover Susan was no longer there. When she was sure they had left the building, Susan reached for the door. An unavoidable reflex to grab her bag struck her, but what did she need her keys for now?

On the roof, forty-four stories above Manhattan's streets, the wind whipped against Susan Harris's flannel pink pajamas with the giraffes on them. The giraffes had swimming sprinkled donuts at the bases of their necks and wore insane smiles full of oversize teeth. The metal roof door slammed shut decisively behind her, locking her out.

Susan appreciated these steps. That it was, in fact, incremental. The opportunities for reversal closed permanently one by one behind her. Susan's situation grew more and more difficult to extract herself from until there would be no self left to extract.

The roof was lined by a four-foot-high brick wall, easily surmountable in any direction.

Susan wanted to be sure to avoid the streets where people who loved their lives walked hand in hand with their innocent beloveds. Her building, as big as a city block, had a courtyard at its center. This wasn't perfect, but it was her best bet. She walked to the edge and put her hands on the bricks. Amazingly, she felt nothing.

The rest was automatic and familiar, and it all felt predestined to Susan. This time, this place, this end to her. It was perfect. Everyone she knew would be better off. Not immediately, but soon enough. She would give them this ultimate gift. She climbed onto the ledge and looked down, surprised to realize her feet were bare and yet she felt nothing beneath them. It was over already.

If you or someone you know is in crisis and considering self-harm,

CALL **988**

from anywhere in the United States.

For more resources on how to prevent suicide, go to bethe1to.com.

ACKNOWLEDGMENTS

There are many different ways in which this book would not exist without the inspiration, guidance, and support of my keen editor, Carmen Johnson. The second time around was more fun than the first! Thank you.

Thanks also to my agents Kim Witherspoon and Maria Whelan. You gave me the right notes at the right time, and it made all the difference. Thank you.

Faith Black Ross, what a help! I learned some new tricks working with you. Thank you for making the book make sense.

Sean Berard and Shiv Doraiswami, thanks for saying, "We love your work." I love that about you guys. Let's make some television.

Thanks to Emma Reh for shepherding this manuscript along the editorial process, and our copy editor, Megan Westberg, for her sharp eye and attention to continuity. Thanks, Alicia Lea, for making sure even this sentence appears flawless. Thanks to Kristen W. for reminding me to be more thoughtful about mental illness. I have never understood how evocative, appealing, illustrative book covers materialize, but I'm so thankful, Zoe Norvell, that you created one for me.

Thanks to my friend Alice Lee for helping me make any reference to Taiwan as authentic as possible. Thank you also to my dear friend Kate Granger, who had the worst year and still listened to me talk about this book all the time.

Thank you to my parents, who spent a fortune on my education. I loved (almost) every minute of it. Thank you to my partner, Matthew, who always helps me make the time for this to happen and who understands how much time itself signifies to me. Thanks to my Anna: your support means everything. Being your mom is the best thing I've ever been.

Thank *you*, whoever you are, for reading every single word and (hopefully) all that came before this one. You have no idea how much I appreciate you.

ABOUT THE AUTHOR

Photo © 2022 Rick Guidotti

Elizabeth Topp's debut novel, *Perfectly Impossible*, was downloaded over 80,000 times in its first two weeks of the Amazon First Reads program and went on to become a number one Amazon bestseller in literary fiction. Topp penned her first short story as a second grader at the Dalton School and continued studying creative writing at Harvard College and Columbia's School of the Arts, where she earned a master of fine arts in nonfiction writing. Topp coauthored her first book, *Vaginas: An Owner's Manual*, with her gynecologist mother while she worked as a private assistant, a job she still holds. Topp lives in the same Manhattan apartment where she grew up with her partner, Matthew; daughter, Anna; and their cat, Stripes. *City People* is her second novel.